THE FIDDLE

For Edward, for holding my hand in Glin

Dedicated to my grandson:
Joseph Morgan Ward Minogue

Acknowledgements:
Thank you Elizabeth for your continued encouragement
and for freely giving of your time in order that I had the time to do this.

First Published in Great Britain in 2016 by DB Publishing,
an imprint of JMD Media Ltd

ISBN 978-1-78091-547-0

Printed and bound in the UK

THE FIDDLE

JOSEPH PATRICK WARD

THE FIDDLE: AUTHOR'S NOTES

This, in the main, is a work of fiction. It's just a story, though I have drawn upon characters within and outside my family and friends to flesh out the people who inhabit this story. If they recognise themselves, I hope they will forgive any negative characteristics I have endowed them with.

I introduced Robert Frost's poem 'The Road Not Taken' by chance. Once introduced it just kept on recurring.

This is a tear-jerker – never intended as such but sometimes this is how novels turn out – they develop a life of their own. As I edited and re-edited I was continually brought to tears (was the writing that bad?).

The Fiddle is a story about a clever thief, about his background and his development through episodes which occur in his life.

Chapter 1

AN INSPECTOR CALLS

"Eh up my friends, please don't stand!" says Brendan, jokingly, as he makes his way through the queue.

"I thought we'd left the headmaster's cane behind? Oops 'behind' is the wrong word. I hope you've all got thick fat arses." Then, addressing the group, "Do you mind if I go in next? I've got stuff to do today."

There were no objections to his request. He quotes from a poem,

"Into the valley of death rode the one!"

Brendan, slightly nervous, knocks on the door of the interview room and pushes it open.

"Come in, yes, please come in. Do take a seat."

Brendan enters and takes a seat opposite an inspector and a police constable. To one side, on another desk, is a second constable operating a recording device. The desk is untidy with six or seven half-filled plastic cartons of tea and a couple of plates of half-eaten Rich Tea biscuits, overflowing ashtrays and a packet of cigarettes. The inspector and Brendan eye each other up. In the short staring game the inspector concedes first. He smiles.

"I don't often get beat in the staring game. Hello. I'm Superintendent George Givens. On my left is Constable Jameson and taking notes is Constable Fairview. Just ignore them, it's really me and thee. First things first – cup of tea? And if you can just state your name."

"Hello. Em, no thanks, and yes I'm Brendan Ryan. I'm studying mathematics – sounds like *University Challenge*!"

Brendan starts to twiddle his eyebrow, a nervous tic recently acquired.

"Now, Brendan, you're not under caution, this is purely an informal chat so that we can get a more detailed picture of the situation at the college." He offers Brendan a cigarette. Brendan shakes his head and declines.

"Thanks but, em no, I never touch them and if I did you can bet that Capstan Full Strength would be bottom of the list – they're deadly!"

"Now I don't want you to feel nervous."

"I'm not nervous, I'm happy to help," says Brendan, calming down. He releases his eyebrow.

"This is but a small part of the ongoing investigation into the kidnapping. You'll have heard lots of stuff – most of it is just hearsay and conjecture. We have to speak to all of those that might, and I stress might, be involved."

"This is a bit scary," Brendan remarks. Then Brendan, trying to introduce a touch of humour, asks, in a Deep South American drawl,

"Should I have my lawyer present here boy?"

"Certainly, if you would like to have a solicitor represent you then I can call for one, but take it from me, we really don't need to go down that path. I am sure this will be a friendly conversation. I should say that, of course, you can leave at any time, absolutely. You will understand, more formal conversations may have to take place at a later date."

"No, no just joking. I've seen this situation in so many films – finding myself in one, well it's a tad surreal."

The inspector looks at his file.

"Oh, that Ryan." He murmurs to himself.

"First name Brendan. Age twenty-two, 'old' for a student?"

"Yeah, I was a late developer."

He looks at his notes again, and putting on his glasses ponders over them for a minute or two.

The gap in the conversation gives Brendan time to observe the inspector more closely. Surely on the wrong side of fifty, a greying, full head of hair with circular indent around his head where his cap would fit. Wearing a wedding ring and two further rings on his right hand. He fails to hide a deeply wrinkled face suggesting much laughter in his life. He wears a plain suit. His tie partially open in relaxed form with his top shirt button undone. Though not manicured, his fingernails are clean and neatly presented. He presents a slightly bulbous nose concocted from two halves as if glued together. This leaves a distinct line down the middle from the tip to the bridge. This is a man who feels comfortable in his own skin.

He removes his glasses.

"I see you're Irish. Which bit?"

"All of me," jokes Brendan. "Southern. I came here a long time ago – lost the accent. Am now a Yorkshire lad."

"Unusual – your education?"

"Yeah. Started off in an orphanage, well an Industrial school – bloody awful bugger of a place, like a prison – no lie. I was there for two and a half years. Progressed through the English school system up to a girls' grammar school, yes a girls' grammar. Well, on reflection, that was worse than the orphanage. Girls can be vicious at that age. Then a comprehensive for a year, then, eventually, after some time in a job, university."

The inspector returns his glasses and looks at his notes again.

"Oh, you're the genius are you? I've been looking forward to meeting you. I've been told to be wary of you," says the inspector.

"I'm not a genius, though it may appear so amongst the students here but, you've talked to some of them, mostly thick as planks, from public schools, failed to get into Oxbridge and so ended up here. They are the only ones who can afford London prices. Okay, that's a tad unkind. They're not that thick, but they just don't care. I despise them, they've had opportunity after opportunity but wasted them."

"A hobby horse is it?"

"What?"

"Your dislike of the upper classes."

"Look, let's knock this genius thing on the head. I'm not a genius, far from it, but I guess I have a certain facility with maths. I can multiply quicker than most, that's about it – very popular darts player – just for the scoring! I can think deeper than most but I'm slow, really quite slow. See, I'm over-picky. Things have to be right, I hate to guess. I usually get things right in the end but mostly after a good period of time.

"People seem to think that if you pass an exam in maths then that's it for ever more, you're a genius. I passed two A levels, good grades mind you, got a summer job at the University then my Ma thinks I'm a professor! I'm pretty poor at other stuff, like English, I couldn't tell you how to punctuate properly. Mind you, who the hell out there knows the difference between a colon and a semi-colon – and if they say they do then they're talking out of their arses! Joke, couldn't help it!"

"What joke?"

"Colon – arses. Get it?"

"Oh God," moans the Inspector.

Brendan continues.

"I shouldn't be here, I should have gone to Oxford but I made a mistake on my application form. Can you believe that? It's gonna affect my whole life. That shows how thick I am. Really – if I'm a genius then—"

The inspector interrupts.

"This is a ploy, isn't it? Are you playing a game? I remember this from my training in psychology. You've taken over this conversation. I'm the one supposed to talk, to ask the questions, you're supposed to be the one to answer them and to listen. You're trying to put me off my stride."

The inspector stands up to exercise his shoulders, putting his hands behind his neck and stretching with a loud yawn.

"Excuse me. Been sat down all morning." He picks up a plastic box from the corner of the table. He walks around the table and sits on the desk immediately in front of Brendan. He removes the lid. Inside the box is what appears to be a severed finger.

"Are you responsible for this?"

"What do you mean responsible? No." Then, after a few seconds,

"What is it?"

"What do you think it is?"

"Well, it looks like a girl's finger, with that varnished nail, a finger anyway, possibly belonging to a child. It stinks. Actually it doesn't look real. Oh, that's the finger from the kidnapping. Is it?"

"It's the preserving fluid. That's what's smelling. Sure you have nothing to do with it?"

"Positive. You're observing my reaction, aren't you? I have nothing to do with it, absolutely nothing. That's disgusting."

The inspector replaces the lid and returns to his seat.

"You're doing maths here. You must be pretty bright? Why are you reluctant to admit that you're a bit out of the ordinary? A number of your tutors think you're a genius. Shouldn't they ought to know?"

"Well, I guess I have my moments. But I'm not a bloody genius, for God's sake – how many times do I have to say it? However, I do have one claim to fame that I'm sort of proud of. Only happened last week!"

"And that is?"

"Wait for it, wait for it. It's a humdinger, hold on to your horses."

"Go on then, surprise me," said the Inspector, impatiently.

"Drum roll please…

"I have taken Stephen Hawking to the toilet. That is, *the* Professor Stephen Hawking, to the toilet." The inspector turns to look at Constable Jameson, puckers his lips and nods.

"Well I'll be, there's a thing, Jameson." The constable presented a smile that knows it is going to develop into a snigger. It doesn't, as Jameson controls himself.

"Glad you shared that with us. Now that is something to tell your grandchildren."

"Yes it certainly is," says Brendan.

"And who's this Stephen Hawking when he's at home?" asks the inspector, deflating Brendan.

"Oh dear, dearie, dearie me. You can't be serious? I'd better start at the beginning. This might take some time. I think I'll change my mind about that cup of tea!"

"Before you get started, what was it?" asks Inspector Givens.

"What was what?"

"Was it number ones or number twos?"

Chapter 2

THE LIONISED, THE WISHT AND THE WARDROBE

The day started as normal, lovely warmth coming in waves through the fluid, slowly, slowly swimming up and down, around and around, kicking off whenever he got to the edge. Then suddenly it changed. Everything sloshing around. Turmoil and chaos. What was Ma doing? He could hardly see through the bloodied water and hadn't a clue as to what was happening. Voices all around, shouting, screaming in the near distance. He felt himself running through water, so hard and difficult. He was in pain, unable to hang on to anything except the cord. The pain increased in intensity, now very sharp.

"Where's Ma, help me Ma, it really hurts."

Ma winces in pain but she keeps going, running now. He heard it again, somewhere out there, louder, heard the noise of a horse, galloping, and the screams of a child and a mother, desperate for help. Voices all around. The wheels rattled away on the pitch and stone road getting closer and closer. Ma ran hard and shouted:"Whoa, whoa. Help me Jasas. Oh Jasas Christ will ye not help?"

Could she get there in time?

Relentlessly they came on, on and on, seemingly nothing could stop them. He felt her arms go up and her muscles tighten. She caught the reins and pulled hard. Then, a deep unpleasant thud as the horse and cart exploded into her. She stopped running and fell backwards, but still she held on. Her body bounced on the road. Still she held on. Then it stopped. He could hear the horse snorting, gasping for air. Ma became still and then, inevitably, he became still too.

A voice shouted out: "She's done it. Will you look at that? For Jasas sake she's saved them for sure. Had they got to the bend, by Christ, that would have been it, the devil would have had them then, horse, mother and child, gone from this world. The banshees would have been on their way."

Then, another voice.

"Jesus, she's got a child. Hold that fecking horse, let's get her off the road. Get her inside," they said.

"She's bleeding bad. She'll not live past that, no way. Gee didn't I see the hoof go in and the wheel go over her. I can't see what can be done. What'll happen to the baby? Jasas what'll happen? Why did she do it? Jasas Christ why in the name of Jasas would you do a thing like that? Why would you throw yourself at the horse and fetch it down? And her having a baby an all. She saved them, that's for sure. Jesus get the doctor, get the doctor will 'ye. The new doctor, the English one? They say he's okay. Get her inside. Call the priest – he's over at Clooney's. Get him here before it's too late. Who was riding the bloody horse and trap anyway?"

Then a woman spoke.

"A fox came out, after a rabbit, the horse bolted, me and Mary, she's only three you know, she's over there, couldn't do anything. The egit horse just went mad, we could have been kilt, she saved us, no doubt about that, she saved us for sure. The bastard horse just went mad. Nutting we could do. Thanks be to God for saving little Mary."

"Twasn't God that saved her. Twas that woman there, chur she's a saint and that's no lie!"

Ma was taken inside. A blanket was put on the floor and Ma was laid down. She was asleep. He could feel her asleep. Then she was breathing fine and after about twenty-five minutes she came round, somewhat dazed and bruised but apparently little the worse for wear. She put her hand on me and I felt good again.

The hoof had made a nasty bruise across her midriff. The damage done by the wheel was surprisingly minor, though the effect on the baby within had yet to be discovered. The first unwanted effect occurred almost immediately.

"Who are you?" Ma said.

"I'm due in six weeks, look at me young man, I may need help now, I think my baby's on the way. I think my waters have broken – out on the lane there. Is the little girl okay? She looked so scared. Is she okay?"

"The little girl is fine, the horse is fine and the mother is fine, even the godforsaken trap is fine. But what about you? Are you fine?" asked the doctor who had now arrived.

"Hello Mrs. I'm the doctor here to look at you. I'm Dr Molyneux. I'm here to help you as best I can. I know you're in pain but try and keep still. You'll have to wait for a tablet or two to ease the pain. Can't risk the baby getting stuff that's too strong. I need to assess the damage." He proceeded to examine her.

"Can you feel this? And this? And this?" She nodded "yes" to each of his questions. She was in pain everywhere.

The doctor tried to listen to the baby's heartbeat but couldn't hear for the clamour outside. He stood up and marched to the door. He beckoned with his hands to quieten down and mouthed the words "shush, shush". Very little effect. Then with a strong intake of breath he let rip, in sergeant major style with a command so loud that the vibration frightened children back to their parents and woke a nearby flock of crows from their nests squawking and squealing.

"Wisht will ye, for God's sake wisht," he roared.

"I need to listen, for the baby's sake, for the baby!" The crows continued to circle and squawk but, as for the humans, there was absolute silence for a good few minutes, enough for the doctor to do his work. The baby sounded in good condition considering the trauma that Ma experienced.

"I don't mean to hurt you but I have to check for internal damage. I want to be entirely truthful to you, it's not the outside damage I'm worried about, it's the internal picture I want to get to grips with. Your major nerve systems seem okay. We've stopped most of the bleeding. I can't say anything about your blood pressure levels. You've got a good colour. I'm just going to assume you're okay on that front."

He looked deep into her eyes. She couldn't focus.

"That's okay, the ordeal has affected your eyes a bit, nothing serious to worry about. You'll have to deal with concussion for the next few days. I'd guess you're a tough old bird. I'm going to assume you're okay and that your internal organs are intact. That seems fine. You'll need a bit of stitching here and there. You're a very lucky woman, and from what I've heard a very brave one."

Dr Molyneux was a tall man, tall enough for it to be inconvenient when attending patients in their homes, involving, as it did, much stooping. An Englishman with short cropped hair and an even sprinkling of grey. Clean shaven, wearing spectacles. Cool, in control, he exuded confidence. Luckily he was nearby when the accident occurred. He was attending one of the workers at the "big house" who was seven months pregnant. He rushed to the scene after being told what had happened.

"Now Mrs. Ryan, I don't want you to worry about your own health. In my opinion you'll be fine. Obviously there are a few cuts and bruises we'll have to deal with and we will, but first we need to address your baby."

"I feel right in myself. My elbow hurts, my elbow's scraped bad. The back of my neck hurts like hell. Forgive me if you will, excuse me sir. I need to swear, the buggering thing really hurts. But forget that, I think the baby's on the way. I feel a bit sore down there and I'm scared for my baby." Ma started to cry.

"In her desperation to save the child on the trap she may have damaged her own, a very brave woman, tough decision," the doctor whispered out of hearing, or so they thought. She held the doctor by the arm and slowly, painfully slow, she raised her head.

"Don't you fret about me, I'll do my bit. I want you to do your best. Please help me, please help the baby. You do your bit doctor, don't worry about me, I'll cope, I'll be right with you, I'll play my part – I've played it before."

"Now don't you worry Mrs. Ryan. I'm not in the habit of losing babies. We'll do our best here. After what you've done you deserve the best."

The doctor now took command of the situation. He spoke with authority, he would be the director in what goes on here.

"Okay, I want all of you out, give this woman some privacy. I need someone to fetch and carry, some more blankets and pillows. Need a good sized bowl of water and plenty of water to come. Can someone go to the hospital and fetch a nurse. Tell them Dr Molyneux sent you. It's urgent, tell them it's urgent, now go, now, now for God's sake."

The hospital was a good twelve miles away. There was only one bus a day to get into Limerick. Two men ran back to the big house to get horses. Another took the trap. The more sensible headed for the tractor. The tractor, behind for much of the time, would win this race. The horses didn't have the stamina at the speed they were going.

Meanwhile, the women outside rushed around bringing what they could to help. Mrs. Ryan's husband was called for.

"He's not here. He's in England for God's sake with his brother looking for work."

"Looking for booze more like!" a woman shouted.

"Well that's as maybe, but he'd best be told, drunk or sober."

"Are your children here? Do you have children?"

"Like all of us, aren't we rich in children?" someone shouted.

"The young ones are in the house, they're being looked after, the others are working in farms around here. They've been called."

"How many children?"

"One girl and seven boys." Ma was quiet for a moment.

"One died with an illness, his name was Frank, my second eldest, two days short of seven months. Little Frank was a lovely child. We couldn't do anything. We had no doctor then. You just had to do what you could. The mudder was there to help but chur we couldn't do anything. He was a lovely looking child. He had a bushy head of jet black hair. He was like a Viking, but he lost that battle, always gasping for breath, chur 'twas a great relief when the poor little crater left us. It might sound awful but I was glad. He would have had a lifetime of misery."

"Gosh eight kids eh, you've done this before then! You'll be showing me how to do it."

"Have I, you can be sure of that! Yes, when I'm not cooking and cleaning I seem to be having babies. It's Ireland's biggest export you know." She forced a smile.

"You're right, the baby's on its way, it's in the right position and, from what I can gather, it's pointed in the right direction. All systems go. Scream as much as you want now. Please remember Mrs. Ryan, I'm a doctor. You don't need to be embarrassed."

"Have no fear young lad, we don't live in the dark ages round here. Doctor, I can't pay you. I may be able to do something when the father gets back."

"Don't you worry yourself about that, I'm sure something can be sorted when you're better. Anyway, just in case, you can have this on the house – it's good experience for me!"

"Don't give me that doctor, you need to live like the rest of us."

"Look, let's not think about this now. We need to focus on the matter in hand."

"Don't you worry doctor, I won't forget it!"

The nurse arrived within the hour. The tractor driver, having got on to the main Tipperary–Limerick road hailed down a car and got to the hospital within thirty minutes. The same driver very generously drove the nurse back. There was much for her to do, dressing and re-dressing all her cuts, many of which had to be stitched. Throughout this, labour continued. It was long and painful. Outside, the crowd increased hoping for news. Within two and a half hours the baby was delivered and gave a hearty cry on his arrival. The doctor didn't clean the blood from the baby. He ensured the baby was fed as soon as possible. He put the child straight on to the nipple. A feed of breast milk comforted the child; there would be no lasting problems here.

Ma, despite her precarious situation, smiled and smiled and smiled.

"Ah jeeze another Viking I see," addressing her remarks at the doctor.

"There's nothing wrong with that child – strong as a bull. Looks to be a little underweight though, I haven't got all my gear with me so I can't weigh him, but if he is underweight, he'll soon catch up. I'll send the nurse around again tomorrow to check up on you and little Thor. She'll be with you for the week, possibly beyond. He's got a good colour, his lungs are strong, his heart is beating strongly and evenly. Are you sure it's premature?" said the doctor with genuine surprise.

The news was relayed to the milling crowd outside. Great joy and a heartfelt cheer to the news that mother and baby were doing well.

"Boy or a girl for God's sake?" they asked.

"Oh, sorry, a healthy boy, with loads of black hair, he's learning the fiddle as we speak – I think it's an Irish boy!" the doctor joked, followed by another cheer from the crowd. Some began to sing the Irish national anthem but, after a few bars, thought better of it. Somehow they had all claimed ownership of the child!

"And the name?" the multitude of fathers asked. Dr Molyneux relayed the message.

"They want to know his name. Have you decided on anything? They're very insistent out there," said the doctor.

"The father and me can't agree. We talked about it before he left," said Ma. Ma looked at the doctor and asked him his name.

"Like you he's got the eyebrows, the triangle eyebrows. I'll call him after you, it's a good omen even though you are English. I hope you have some Viking in you!"

"And the name, what's the name," they shouted again.

The doctor came out to address the crowd which had now stabilised to around thirty adults and a playground of children.

"The mother is fine and the baby is in excellent form. The name of this boy is to be Brendan." He shouted the word "Brendan". The doctor threw a fist into the air in celebration.

"Oh God, and I thought you were English!" said Ma.

"No, my father's Irish. They wanted a strong Irish name. Hence the name

Brendan. Good job you didn't choose my middle name – Frederick!"

Brendan Ryan was born in a little hamlet called Caherelly about twelve miles from Limerick City and eight miles from Tipperary. He was born at four thirty-three in the afternoon and the birth was witnessed by the whole village. Many of those there forced their way in just to look at the child, 'twas like the birth of Christ Himself. The boy was named at five fifteen. At five seventeen the music and the dancing took over. Out came a wooden square made up at the cross just down from Ma's house. Far enough away as not to disturb, but close enough to hear the reels and the jigs and the polkas and the rhythmic stamping of the sets, just audible to Ma. She needed quiet and rest. She loved the music and she was desperate to be out there with them.

Out came the dancers, the clogs and the fiddles and the tin whistles and the accordions. Out came the drink and the tea and the bread and slabs of butter, out came the potatoes to boil and to peel, salted and ate in great mouthfuls to burnt lips. The music wafted far and wide and little gatherings of music and dance sprung up all over. About two hours into the festivities it went quiet. A young boy took his whistle and started to play.

"Shush, shush will ye. Let him play, let him play."

The haunting sound of a lone tin whistle filled the evening with the slow air "Roisin Dubh", known to be Ma's favourite. Like most Irish music it was played straight, without embellishment. Ma woke from a light sleep. "Ah Jeez, if only my man was here. He'd love this." But she knew, and the others knew, their "love" was near the end. She shed a tear or two and wished it wasn't true. The whistler played it all through once and then another boy, probably no more than fourteen years old, walked on to the "stage". His arms tight to his body, he proceeded to sing the song in the Gaelic. A truly beautiful rendition. There was to be no more dancing after that. They'd danced themselves out anyway.

A day never to be forgotten. Brendan the Viking certainly stole the limelight that day.

Three weeks after the horse and trap debacle Ma had recovered pretty well. The father would be back soon, or so he said. He had the offer of a job for next week, or so he said. He wanted to come back to see the child, or so he said. Good times are round the corner for him and the brother, or so they said. He'd write another letter soon, or so he said.

Ma waits in hope for all these things.

The Ryans had visitors. An excited Anna rushed into the house.

"Ma, Ma, it's outside, come on, outside, they're from the big house." She pulled at Ma's pinnie.

"What's the rush for God's sake," said Ma as she put Brendan, asleep, back into the drawer on the sideboard and had a quick look at the mirror.

Five foot six, straight, deep brown hair with more than a few grey hairs. She'd long stopped worrying about those. Watery, brown–green eyes set beneath jet black eyebrows, a straight nose, full lips over poor teeth. Happy to smile at life's stupidities. Mostly shy with a soft Irish accent that shone with intelligence. Rough, spade-size calloused hands. Weight on the plump side from eating too much bacon and potatoes, and butter, butter on or in everything. A world weary woman struggling day by day to rear her children. She had a good word for everybody. She hardly ever blasphemed. A churchgoing non-believer. Ghosts and goblins, banshees and leprechauns were more real to her than the Holy Spirit or the 'trinity'. That is, till she was in trouble. Then there would be Hail Marys and Lord's prayers in droves, and candles lit to her favourite saints. Out would come images of the blue and white draped Virgin Mary and of the lovely Jesus with the burning hearts and the outstretched arms in welcome. She had little but her children to comfort her. Poorly dressed. Destined to continue her life of drudgery. Wishing that her wishes would come true.

That was Ma in the mirror.

Her hair could have been neater. It'll have to do. She could hear a lot of babbling, the noise of carriages and shuffling of horses. Warily, she walked outside holding the back of her hand to her eyes as a shield from the bright sunshine. Outside was a gathering of visitors including the priest and the doctor and the Walshes from the big house. Ma was confused and surprised at the crowd that had formed a neat queue at her fence. Ma was still bandaged in various places and walked gingerly through the door and out to her gate. Anna, who'd never seen such a gathering, held on to her pinnie. The pinnie was removed in quick time and a hair clip or two repositioned. Ma was overwhelmed with the size of the crowd. Her initial thought was that Mick had returned from England with great riches and somehow this crowd was here as welcome. She couldn't see Mick. She grabbed on to Anna. They grabbed on to each other for support.

"Well, this is a great surprise you're bringing me. Is there anything I can help you with?" She smiled at one or two she knew as neighbours. She nodded at the doctor.

"Hello doctor, I thought you'd forgotten me!"

"How could I forget the Viking mother?" he joked.

She bowed her head slightly at the Priest.

"Hello father. Is it more Hail Marys you're to give me? These three Sundays I haven't been able to attend Church. You see my bandages – I feel like Lazarus," smiles all round.

Mr. Walsh addressed her:

"Good afternoon to you Mrs. Ryan, this is my wife Ailish and little Mary there. She's a shy one, you'll hardly get a smile out of her now. You won't have seen them since the accident. Little Mary's got something for you." The young child was urged forward by her mother, head bowed.

"Go on now, Mary go on." The little girl had to be encouraged all the way with a helping hand at her back from her mother. Mary thrust a small bunch of flowers into Ma's knee then shuffled back to her mother with the same bunch of flowers! Mary is encouraged to make another attempt. This time with her mother's help she succeeds in landing the flowers in their rightful place, in Ma's hands. Ma looked carefully at the small bunch of flowers, daisies, primroses and a few floribunda roses kept together with a red ribbon.

"What a sweet child. Thank you. I'm not sure what I've done to deserve this." Ma blushed.

"Come here, give us a hug." Ailish lifted Mary up and walked forward again. They hugged each other. The crowd applauded and cheered. Mr. Walsh quietened things down and addressed the gathering.

"Mrs. Ryan, I hope you'll forgive us for not coming sooner and for turning up like this – unannounced. We had a few things to do. I see you must still be in pain."

"Aah 'tis more of a discomfort than pain, you know, it's hard to wash or to do a bit of shopping though my neighbours, God bless them, are like angels, angels from heaven. They see to help if they can. They take Anna, and little Brendan regular like, to help me. He's so popular though I hardly see him myself!"

Normally a confident speaker, Mr. Walsh struggled for clarity, twisting his hat in his hands.

"I've not properly thanked you for saving my little girl and also," with a broad smile addressed to the crowd, "my wife. This is for you and for little Brendan. You saved Mary's life. Sure we're grateful beyond words. We thought this might come in useful with the shopping and the travelling and such."

For the moment Ma thought he was referring to his hat. She couldn't see anything. *What were they on about?* she thought. Mrs. Walsh could see the confusion.

"Sorry Mrs. Ryan, the husband's not clear with his words. It's the trap Mrs. Ryan, the trap." Mr. Ryan took over again.

"We know you haven't one. We've painted it up and tidied it, all the repairs are done, 'tis like new. We painted VIKING on it, I hope that's okay. The pony is yours too, she's placid and a good worker. We've called her THOR. It's for the little boy, well it's for the whole family really. We just want to thank you, what you did, a miracle sent to save my child."

"There are these too, clothes for the baby, little Brendan, and a small cupboard to put them in, you know, like a proper wardrobe. Most of the people in the village have made something or given something. There are cheeses there and bacon and the like. My brother has given this calf."

"It's the best of the lot this year. I'll keep it till it's on the grass and then bring it down, if that's okay missus?"

"Mary's his favourite, see!" said Mrs. Walsh.

Through tearful eyes he pointed to the other things people had brought. He unfurled a piece of paper and began to read.

"I'm not used to this kind of thing but I suppose it's a great deal easier to do this than it was to do what you did." He took a deep breath to deliver his few words.

"Dear Mrs. Ryan, we're gathered here today to do you honour, to recognise what you have done for me and my family, but not just for the Walshes in the 'big house' but to many others in this little hamlet of ours. People have said great things about you, not just the accident but other things, other kindnesses – you asked them not to tell about those things but you did a great thing that day, a truly great thing. I'm not sure I could have done what you did on that day, even for my own child if 'tis truthful I am. To do that you need the heart of a lion. Mrs. Ryan, what you did wasn't a small matter, it was a once in a lifetime event. To me it has great importance." He took a breath and continued.

"We find it easy to lionise politicians and members of the church and stars on the television and on the wireless – we give them more importance than they deserve. But when it comes to the people we know around us, our neighbours, our kith and kin, we fail to recognise them properly. We fail to recognise the contribution they make to our lives. From now on I hope, I'm sure, that's how you'll be treated, as an important person in this village. I think you were a lion to bring that horse down. It's humbling to know that there are people in this village like you. However, many of us, me included, are ashamed to realise what little contribution we have made to our neighbours and to village life. That needs to change. But that's for a different day. I'll finish by saying thank you so much. I'm truly proud to be your neighbour."

He started to clap and was quickly joined by everyone there.

Ma backed off to the fence and turned away from the crowd and, holding her hands up to her face, started to cry at the enormity of the gift and for what Mr. Walsh had said.

"Mammy, mammy, what's up mammy," Anna cried, not understanding what was going on.

"Nothing little Anna, everything's just fine." The doctor held her from falling. All she could say to this outpouring of gratitude was:

"Thanks." She held the flowers up to the crowd. "Thanks."

Everybody roared in approval. Many came over and shook her hands or patted her on the back or gave her a hug. "Good luck missus. Good luck to you and the Viking, good luck to him too." They shared a sense of pride that one amongst them could have done what she did, and also a sense of pride in the way the people of the village responded.

Chapter 3

DITCH THE EXCUSES

Mick returned from England, shamed into returning, following the gifts given to Ma by the Walshes at the big house. They had even found him some labouring work on their farm, repairing roofs and walls and some milking.

Brendan's father returned to complete the family once more. He would be out in the fields or up at the big house earning what he could. The father played the fiddle in the evening and Ma and Anna would jig and dance and sing till bedtime. Out from dawn till dusk. Having a fill of warm soda bread and butter before bed. Life couldn't get better than this.

For his first three and a half years as a Viking, Brendan grew strong and sturdy. He remained on the short side. Cormac, his older brother still living at home, and Anna were his guides as they wandered the lanes and fields around Caherelly, barefoot he explored everything. He met the cows and the chickens, he saw them frozen solid in the frost. In spring he saw apple tree blossom and eel-filled streams, he saw wild plums and haystacks and great dollops of cow muck that, when dry, would be collected for the fire.

The lads were out playing and Brendan was well asleep.

A rare event – Ma was on her own, her work for the day was mostly done – the bacon was on the boil, the potatoes, turnips and cabbage were ready "to go". Within the hour the lads and Mick would pile in to be fed.

She put another peat brick on the fire to keep the oven ablaze and the temperature high enough to boil water. Peat fires would never "roar" like a coal or a coke fire. Coal and coke were expensive so peat it was. Dried cow dung brought in from the fields semi-dried then kept in the dry store to dry completely, was worse even than peat. It was for background warmth only. From time to time the whole family would go scavenging for sticks, particularly following a storm, trees or great boughs might have fallen. The bonanza would be dealt with on a first come, first served basis.

Ma made herself a pot of tea. She stood next to the oven to keep warm and looked out on to the lane and the fields beyond. In the field they owned was a single cow and, courtesy of the Walshes, a pony for the trap. She would milk the cow each morning and early evening. But for now she had some time to herself. She was in a contemplative mood.

Ma was bright but ignorant. Sure she knew that herself. She was married to Mick and to the lads – that was it – she never had time for herself. Her life hadn't turned out the way she'd hoped. At a young age she fell in love with Kevin Doyle, the son of a teacher and well-to-do farmer who, everyone agreed, was "going places". His card was marked for success. Unfortunately, though she loved him he didn't love her. Unkindly he strung her on for a while then, under some pressure from his parents, dropped her like a stone. She didn't quite fit the profile that Doyle's parents were hoping for. There was nowhere in her family that exuded "class", she was pure working class, left school at fourteen, no qualifications but a hard worker. Her interest, and by far her major gift, was for singing.

Heartbroken and confused, she attached herself to Michael Ryan (Mick). He wasn't a bad catch – far from it – as a gifted musician he too would likely "go places". He already earned an income playing for the local dances at weekends. Ma would sing and dance, they made a good team.

Mick was the youngest of five children, two boys and three girls. He was spoilt somewhat as there was a seven-year gap between him and the next eldest. Mick was, after a fashion, a good looking boy, certainly no Romeo, thinning hair with gappy teeth and a heavy upper lip more than dominating his face. Farm work led to sausage-like fingers and hands like spades – hardly suitable for a fiddle player. However, to his credit, he coped. He liked a drink but was intelligent to realise its dangers if taken to excess. He smoked roll-ups or woodbines – they were all he could afford.

She courted him for over a year till one warm summer evening nature took its course, she was well and truly "caught". A quick marriage was arranged, though the shame of having a child out of wedlock was difficult to bear, not just for her and Mick but also for their parents. The marriage got off on the wrong foot and never fully recovered.

The bad luck continued. Their first child, Sean, was born with a fused left hand – three fingers stuck together. He would never play a musical instrument. Mick couldn't fail to show his disappointment. Eventually the baby was sent away, to be reared by her grandparents, rarely returning to his mother. Sean was always Ma's favourite.

As with any good Catholic family, children occurred regularly, mostly eighteen months apart. Bridget and Mick lived with his mother, a widow for some seven years.

As well as an income from playing music, Mick was a jack of all trades – he could farm, repair roofs and walls and a myriad of other things. He even made a violin. It made a noise, though not one that could be classed as musical. Even his talent for the fiddle couldn't scrape a proper note from its strings. His earnings, though reasonable for a farm worker, wouldn't extend to the purchase of a decent violin. His aunt, his rich Boston aunt on his father's side, had a local music shop send him a first-rate violin. It had to be sent by sea as a flight would put it under too much stress. It was his only treasure and he treated it with the greatest respect.

Their life together, though not ideal, was working to a degree and the likelihood was that it would continue in this way; that is, until one fateful day that Mick made a wager with a neighbour.

All the fields around had, at the extremities, a ditch to drain away the excessive water that, driven from the Atlantic, would fall in bucket loads in this part of

Ireland. Even still the ground was, seemingly, always sodden. This wasn't called the green isle for nothing.

Mick claimed he could jump over the ditch outside his house. The neighbour disagreed.

The wager wasn't for money, it was for five bottles of Guinness. John Arkness laid the bet, he'd buy Mick five pints of the black stuff if Mick could make the jump and vice versa. As Mick was smartly dressed he wouldn't be doing any jumping that day; the wager was arranged for Saturday morning at 11 o'clock. It was a fair bet and worthy of note – it wasn't going to be a simple jump. Both protagonists had a good chance of success. As Saturday came round a small crowd gathered – all drinking men. Ma refused to go, thinking it was a stupid thing for a grown man to be involved with. She chastised all those who turned up, with little effect, their blood was on the rise and they were "sporting men".

"For Christ's sake Mick, you'll be in the ditch, and if you're thinking I'm going to be washing those clothes then you're sadly mistaken! For God's sake, grown men should have better things to do," said Ma.

"Ah c'mon Ma, it'll be a laff chur. I'll do this – easy."

Mick and Arkness had a closer look at the ditch. It was wider and deeper than either of them remembered even though they passed it every day. Wagers made in the heat of a *drinking session* were normally avoided by Mick but he was very confident of his skill as a long-jumper. What's the worst that could happen? He couldn't hardly kill himself?

"You'll have your work cut out there," said Arkness in a friendly way.

"Are you sure you want to go through with this?"

"You're not getting off that easy Johnny boy. As far as I'm concerned the bet stands. Five pints coming my way."

"Okay, okay, you have it, the bet stands. Only one jump mind you, no jumping twice or anything like that, you only have one go at it. If you're in the water then you lose! By the way, can you swim?" he smiled the smile of a man feeling very confident.

Mick prepared as best he could. Sleeves rolled up, belt and bootlaces well tied and tight. He was ready to go. Ma had a sly look out the window, with a secret hope that he'd win. She saw him take position.

"Okay Mick, whenever you're ready."

Mick had another look at the spot he would launch his jump from. The small crowd became silent. He was confident he could do it. He paced out the number of steps he was to take. He stepped back about twenty yards, each representing a stride, and another yard back to account for bigger strides when running.

He got to the "ready" position. He rocked his upper body to give him momentum, then like a hare he was off. He reached his fastest speed within two seconds. He ran between two rows of onlookers. As he reached the ditch he lifted his right leg as if to jump and with his left leg placed solidly on the edge for thrust. Disaster – his left foot began to slip – still he got a good push-off but failed to make the top of the ditch on the other side. His right knee banged on to the side of the ditch. Unbeknownst to Mick, or indeed to anybody else, Mick's knee banged directly into a moss-covered rock. Mick let out a cry. There was an audible crunch which most heard. Something snapped. He couldn't help but fall into the ditch. He was up to his neck in water splashing for help. An initial cheer from bystanders, win or lose, soon subsided into concern. It took four strong men to pull him out. He was reasonably well warmed up and, to begin with, didn't feel much pain.

"You okay Mick?" He shrugged off their concern with a false reaction.

"Well, the hip is a bit sore but I'll survive. Bit unlucky with my left foot, it gave way at the wrong time!"

Not wishing to lose too much face he walked away into his house with a clear limp and in great pain. Ma smiled.

"Oh for Christ's sake. Look if you're going to indulge in this kind stupidity then at least have the dacency to win!" As the door shut, he collapsed. Over the next few weeks the pain subsided but the movement in his right hip slowed and slowed until there was no movement at all. He wouldn't go to a doctor, unable to afford any treatment till it was too late. He had somehow partially displaced his hip from his socket which, without treatment, then fused in position.

He was crippled for life, destined always to use a stick for support.

The outlook for him and his family was now grim indeed – unable to work normally – his income was now what he could make from music and a little labouring work. Even at the music he found the accordion difficult to play, restricting him to the fiddle alone. Without the volume naturally arising from the accordion even the income from his musical work slowed tremendously.

Ma took in washing but this didn't help much as she had a large family of her own to look after. From time to time Ma would take herself off to Limerick to appeal for help from charities based in the city. She felt ashamed, but for her children's sake it had to be done.

In desperation, Mick took to going back to Birmingham, where his brother now lived, hoping to find work for a one-legged musician. Some work was forthcoming and some money was sent home. But nowhere near enough. Mick's predicament brought on a depression which led to a drink problem. Homesick, he, of course, travelled back to see his family. As time went by he found it less painful to stay longer in Birmingham. He argued that he would be less of a burden to his family if he stayed away.

The next couple of years saw the Ryans struggle with life – a struggle they would likely lose, it was just too hard to cope with a large family and a crippled husband who'd keep rattling on about greener grass over the water in England.

So, a rare event, she had a little time on her hands. The memories of where and when it all went wrong rattled through her brain.

As Ma sat there thinking of what had become of her life she began to cry, she sobbed uncontrollably. She sobbed alone with no one to comfort her. As quickly as she had started she stopped. It wasn't her habit to feel sorry for herself. She dried her eyes with her pinnie and got back to her work. Ma was unhappy, close to breaking.

On Mick's return there were two bosses in the house now, Ma was the boss sorting out all the problems whilst Mick was the dominant male, the father. This was an unstable situation, disaster would surely follow – and it did.

What happened? Life happened. Economics happened. No work, no wages, no food. The father was back and forth from England trying to get work but no luck. Tensions grew. Ma was left on her own for month after month, another child on the way, that wasn't going to make it any easier. The letters dried up. What was love turned from frustration to indifference to hate. They stopped being a family. That was the end of it. Mick returned from time to time to arguments and to violence. Dealing with a sodding global downturn was hardly his forte, he, and thousands like him, was out of his depth.

A final straw.

Mick could only manage to get work intermittently – continually short of money. They were out scavenging for sticks for the fire. They were down to their last couple of sacks of potatoes. Other vegetables, cabbage, carrots and parsnips, were plentiful, still in the ground. The flour was quickly running out – the situation was becoming desperate. Mick wouldn't sanction the borrowing of money, even from his parents, he had too much pride for that. Unbeknownst to Ma, Mick sold the pony to a neighbour – this was the horse that had been given to them by the Walshes at the big house. That night, when Mick told her what he had done, a blazing row took hold – this was the worst argument that the lads had ever witnessed as they sat on the stairs. It was an argument that would be fuelled by memories of previous battles. Out of frustration, Mick pushed her violently on to the stairs. She responded with any stick she could find. She saw the lads crying on the stairs. That was the final straw, Ma had had enough – she walked out that night never to return. She made her way, in almost pitch black, to her mother's house, over four miles away in Ward's Cross. She stayed there for two days wondering what to do with her life. She was distraught having to leave her children behind. They collected some of her clothes and gave her some money for a ticket to England where her second eldest son Morgan was living.

"Tell her to come back will you. I'm sorry, I'm sorry."

And he was sorry too. But sometimes "sorry" isn't enough.

On a soft, misty morning Ma set out from Limerick Junction, on a ticket to take her all the way on train, on ferry and then on two more trains. Ma was wary of the journey, she had hardly moved outside the Limerick area in the whole of her life.

Unannounced she turned up at Morgan's one-room apartment and slept on an old couch for the first week. There was plenty of work, for a woman, and within a day she got a job in a woollen mill, sweeping up. Within three days the over-looker could see she was capable of more than just sweeping up and, after a morning's training, she was in charge of one of the big spinning machines. Within two weeks she was in charge of three spinning machines and she had arranged lodgings at 27 Bengal Street, Keighley, West Yorkshire. She would arrange for her younger children to come to live in England as soon as she could get the money together for the fares.

Mick couldn't look after the children on his own. Within three days of Ma leaving, Mick went to the priest to ask for help. This "help" was double-edged. Whilst a burden was lifted from Mick's shoulders, the burden was now placed on the "lads" – off to orphanages separated and amongst strangers.

Ma's calculations were in error. The Church argued that Ma had abandoned her children and the father couldn't cope. They would stay where they were till they reached sixteen years.

Despite all her protestations, the Church would not release them to either parent. She would bear the pain of separation for over two and a half years. The family would never recover from this trauma.

Chapter 4

THE BROTHERS GRIMM

Glin is a small seaside town about twenty miles south-west of Limerick. It is home to Glin Industrial School. It comes with a bad reputation. Everybody knew Glin as Grimm – that's the place that bad boys were sent. It was the frightener that some parents would use: "If you don't behave I'll send you off to Glin – they'll sort you out! Those Christian Brothers won't take any nonsense from you my lad."

The school is situated above the town at the end of a long lane. It was run by the Christian Brothers, as unpleasant a bunch of Christians as you were likely to find. Their task, or so it seemed, was to instil a touch of religion (the Roman Catholic variety) into those boys unlucky to end up there. However, in concluding a stay there – and any boy who had spent more than a couple of months there would tell you – the effect was more "turn off" than "turn on".

The school itself is an imposing Victorian building, on three floors, encased all round by six-foot-high iron railings painted a mucky green. As you entered through the main gates on the right was the yard and on the left were the dormitories, the offices and accommodation for the Brothers. Here also was the main hall. On one end of the hall was a raised platform – where the brothers ate. The rest of the hall housed the kitchens and tables and benches for the "boys".

When Brendan was nearly four, Ma ran away to England, leaving the father Mick and her children behind. Mick was unable to cope with the four youngest children: Cormac, Brendan, Anna and six-month-old Roisin. There was nothing to be done. No relative, except one, offered to help. The children would have to be taken into care. Anna was found a place at St Joseph's orphanage situated in the middle of Limerick. It was run by an order of nuns and was well respected. They were high quality lace makers and within days Anna was set to work learning the trade. She was treated well and, in return, she worked hard, eager to learn.

Roisin was still tiny; a place with an aunt was found for her. Within two days Cormac and Brendan were taken away, off to the school at Glin.

To the outside world this was the equivalent of an English public school, but without Matron to get you ready for breakfast, without the uniform to engender camaraderie, without the "tuck" shop, where their weekly allowance would buy sweets, without cucumber sandwiches, or veal, ham and egg pie, without kedgeree and kippers for breakfast, and without the lashings of sweet tea or trips home to Mater and Pater at the end of term. Also absent was the automatic entrance to Trinity College, Dublin and then on to the "City" to make mega-bucks. Glin was nothing like an English public school, unless you were mistakenly thinking of Wormwood Scrubs instead of Eton.

Brendan cannot remember going there. He knew he was going somewhere with his father and had Cormac under tow. He could only remember that suddenly he was there. He remembers, that first night, sleeping in a cold unfamiliar bed and waking up in a dormitory with around twenty other boys. They surrounded him looking at the new boy. Cormac was there but his father had gone. In a second his whole life was turned upside down. His mother had disappeared, the house was in turmoil, he couldn't see his brothers or sisters or his father. He had been with these "animals", for that's what he used to call them, all of his life and suddenly they were gone. These furry, warm creatures kept him safe, kept him happy. Now they were nowhere to be found, with no explanation given. He and Cormac found themselves in the middle of what could only be described as a jail. This institution was unfriendly, unpleasant and unforgivingly harsh. From that day on he could no longer expect to have a normal life. Everything was changed. He was robbed of his childhood. How could his parents and his brothers and sisters allow this to happen? Did they not love him anymore? He was deeply hurt. He would never fully recover from this trauma. It seemed that nobody could understand his pain.

But all kids, at least all of those that have a life, experience pain, of course they do. This was nothing like the pain you get when you fall off your bike or the pain you get when you cut your thumb on a blade of grass. This wasn't the kind of pain that would be cured by a kiss before bedtime, this wasn't a "kiss it better" pain. It was deep, this was pain all the way down to the bone. This was the kind of pain that would erupt into nightmares over and over again. He would be lucky to escape this pain.

At Glin the main yard was surrounded by ten-foot-high walls. It was more of a prison than a school. Outside the walls were three large outdoor pools set close together into the ground. These would be filled with water. Their use was not for recreation. You wouldn't find holidaymakers shuffling around looking for the best spot, worrying about the quality of suntan lotions or sipping cocktails or ordering a second round of canapés.

No, these pools, each about ten feet in diameter, were far more sinister. Here, if the boys wet or soiled their sheets they would be expected to wash the sheets in these large basins. These were used at all times of the year.

Due to the stress of being away from his family Brendan had to wash his sheets very often and, worse, in winter, had to break through the ice to get to the water. If they broke the rules the boys would be given a glass of sour milk to drink, either that or three strokes of the cane. Brendan could only sip the sour yoghurt tinged with green – he rarely made any progress with this unpleasant, unsweetened posset. So, for him, each time he soiled his bed, he faced three strokes of the cane. Presumably the aim was to deter bed-wetters. To a degree the deterrent strategy worked – for Brendan anyway. After a month or so he learned to control his bladder. At the first hint of warm pee trickling down his thigh he would wake and rush to the piss-bucket near the dormitory door and relieve himself.

At the base of the "school" walls was a strip of concrete one and a half feet high by one and a half feet deep. During the day this was where you'd find most of the "inmates", sat there, hungry all of the time, doing very little, thinking, wishing, crying, sobbing, fighting, angry, invariably angry.

After an initial few weeks of sorrow and of upset they hardened up. The tears dried away as they came to terms with this cruel reality they now found themselves in. They complied with the regime and did what they were told and kept their noses clean. These two boys weren't stupid. They wandered the yard together, they looked out for each other. They protected each other as best they could. Cormac, four years older, took most of the blows, physical and mental. As best he could he looked out for Brendan. The young brothers would always be seen together, holding hands.

The lucky ones waited weeks, months, possibly years for their parents to return and take them out. They would get the odd letter from back home. A rare visit might also be arranged. The unlucky ones, without parents, waited till they were sixteen and out they would be booted to exist in a world they were hardly ready for.

Brendan was one of the youngest there. There was no special schooling for him, no time for constructive "play".

Brother Gerrard was head honcho. The whole hierarchy was male dominated except for the domestic staff who were discouraged from fraternising with the children lest they become surrogate mothers. At dinner time and at evening meal some of the women did their best to lighten the highly structured regime, if only by the odd wink or by a friendly phrase:

"Hello boys! And how are we this evening?"

Many children, especially the younger ones, were very sensitive and would cry at the least provocation.

"C'mon now boys – you'll have to toughen up. 'Twill be better for you in the long run."

Some of the "ladies" thought the regime too harsh and, under normal circumstances, would complain, but in a highly religious society those kinds of complaints fell on stony ground.

Senior boys, often within sight of the Brothers, would regularly steal food from younger boys. Though rations were poor no one complained – nothing at the level of Oliver Twist's, "Please, may I have some more?"

This was the accepted routine at some of the Industrial Schools in Ireland around 1950. Cormac and Brendan reacted differently. Brendan spent a lifetime trying to forget Glin whilst Cormac spent a lifetime in memory of the place, it was to be the excuse for everything that went wrong with his life. In that place Cormac was Brendan's protector. They were always together, though they slept in different dormitories.

In over two years as a resident, Brendan could only remember one act of kindness. A kitchen worker gave him a sliver of turkey near Christmas time. He smiled at her and that was good. He rarely smiled in there. That was it, nothing else in over two years. There was no "hello Brendan", "how are you today?" Nobody to ruffle his hair and joke with him. Nobody knew him, nobody cared about him. Even though Cormac was there, without Ma, Brendan felt alone, unloved, forgotten.

The father, Mick, and an elder brother made just one visit to Brendan and Cormac in all the time they were there.

When Brendan left that place he put it, and all its memories, good and bad, into a box that he would rarely open. Brendan wasn't going to let the shadows of the past cloud his future.

Day after day, week after week, month after month the hurt continued. Then, a glorious day in the history of these two boys came completely out of the blue.

On an ordinary day in spring, Brendan and Cormac were called to the office. What had they done? Being called to the office inevitably meant the "cane". Brendan's heart was racing. Through the frosted glass panel of Gerrard's door he saw the outline of a figure. He seemed to recognise it. The door opened and in he went. The figure turned round. He couldn't believe his eyes. It was Ma! They had not seen nor heard from her in over thirty months. They hardly recognised her. Brendan was more sure. He ran straight to her and held her as tight as he could. Cormac stayed back, wary of disappointment.

"Mammy, Mammy. Have you come for us?" said an overjoyed Brendan.

"Well we'll go for a little ride shall we?" said Ma, holding both her children. It was her liberation too. She too had suffered in the last two years. She started to cry.

"Jeez it's good to see you. Thank God. Thank God."

At first they only had eyes for Ma then two other figures came into focus. It was Mick and one of his brothers, Thomas. Their belongings were collected.

"We'll be getting him some other clothes and then we'll get him back." Ma spoke to the Brother in charge, and then they left.

This was the magical time when Brendan said goodbye to the Brothers Grimm. In Brendan's eyes the brothers had stolen them. On her only parental visit Ma stole them back.

After spending thirty months in Glin he was suddenly transported back to Caherely. Then, early next morning, by bikes, on handlebars and butcher's baskets to Limerick Junction, by train from Limerick Junction on to Dun Laogharie and by ferry and a glorious full English breakfast from Dun Laogharie to Holyhead then on to Keighley in West Yorkshire. They arrived with only the clothes they stood up in.

Mick stayed behind. Brendan was sure he'd come on later. No. Mick would stay. After getting them to Dun Laogharie and, after saying his goodbyes, he returned back to Caherelly. The marriage was at an end but those precious objects, the children, were saved. At this time Brendan hardly cared about Mick, he just wanted his Ma and would rarely leave her side. For days and weeks after, Brendan was sure he'd be taken back to Glin. Every raised voice, every knock on the door brought back the fear that he would be recalled to that place.

Legally, his mother had no right to remove them from Glin. But she saved them. In all her life it was the finest thing she did.

Brendan was still too young to verbalise his thoughts properly. However, as best he could, he made a vow, or what he thought was a vow. One day, he would destroy Glin.

He had no idea, at this stage, what form the retribution would take, but from time to time he would remember this vow and from time to time he would refresh and repeat it.

Chapter 5

FIGHT OR FLIGHT

Brendan woke from a terror-filled sleep. He suffered from night terrors in which his dreams appear to be real. Chased by lions or tigers, snakes slithering in the bed, his mother running away, he would wake in terror that they were real. He thought he was still in Glin, the hellhole of an orphanage. He couldn't seem to shake the memories of that place, it would be years for that to occur.

Brendan was small for his age and still somewhat underweight. He suffered from a kind of stress that required infrared and UV light treatments to his scalp as his hair was falling out in handfuls. His hair recovered. His toenails were contorted with having to wear shoes that were too small for him. If you'd ask him he felt fine, he wasn't the kind to complain. His present situation was cramped but, on the whole, fine. Certainly, compared to Glin, he was living the life of luxury. He was recovering quickly in his new country.

He and his brother had been in England just two months and in school, St Joseph's infants, for a month. With each month that passed his Glin-induced shyness evaporated and he morphed into a normal child. Brendan had quickly made friends at school and at home, even though he was Irish (in those days, the late fifties, the Irish were treated by many on a par with dogs, and so-called "blacks"). Despite the hardships Brendan had suffered in the last two and a half years, he was a happy lad always looking on the bright side of things. He had an infectious gappy-toothed smile and a healthy smattering of freckles, unkempt hair and continually grubby knees. He was glad to be back with his Ma and his two sisters, Anna and Roisin. Back in a family.

He was growing fast, faster than Ma could keep up with in providing clothes and shoes that would fit. He didn't need fancy this and fancy that. He was content with second-hand or with hand-me-downs, he understood completely that his family wasn't in the higher echelon of society. No jimjams for him. Mother Nature sent him to bed "au naturel". He was happy to be in a bed of any kind. Even at that age he knew what life's struggles were about. He was undemanding both in terms of attention and in terms of material goods.

On the other hand, Cormac, four years Brendan's senior, who had suffered a great deal at the hands of the "brothers" at Glin, was bitter. He wanted to be back in Ireland with his "daddy" not in England, in digs, with his "Ma" and the landlord, Chipry.

Chiprijans Olekss (Chipry) was an émigré from Latvia, more specifically from Riga its capital city. Towards the end of World War Two Latvia had come under the "sphere of influence" of the Soviet Union. He left his wife and child in fear of his life which, as a policeman, was well founded, if not from the Russians then from many who wanted retribution, who knows what for, in a chaotic post-war

Europe. He escaped and probably brought some money with him. Once left he never returned to his home, the Soviets wouldn't allow free travel between countries. The best he could do was to send letters from time to time to his wife and young son.

Despite poor knowledge of English, he worked more like a Trojan than a Latvian and accumulated substantial savings – enough to put down a deposit to buy a house which he duly did.

Despite his clear academic leaning he worked, of necessity, a forty-five-hour week in one of the cotton mills in Keighley, West Yorkshire. No one knows how he ended up there, though there was a small Latvian community in Bradford some six miles away. He rarely brought home friends or acquaintances, certainly never any female guests. The Latvian community seemed to be entirely male. But when he did organise a get together there would be lots of drinking. In those days all drinks were in bottles: Guinness, Mackeson and Tetley's pale ale. Great news for Brendan and the others. The empties would be returned the next day for at least threepence each – a goldmine! Chipry's idea of hors d'oeuvres would be to pass round plates of salted and oiled fish and German-style bread and rollmops. There was no chance that the lads would be eating any of that.

To help with finances, Chipry would take in lodgers.

And so it was that the boy Brendan, six years and four months old, came to reside at number 27 Bengal Street. It would be his and his family's home for nearly five years. These were Brendan's most formative years, he was desperate to learn, to find out things, to know how things worked, how people worked, how they interacted with each other. He watched, he observed, he looked on. He kept quiet and he learned. Chipry wasn't his dad but Chipry and Brendan struck up a friendly relationship like grandfather and grandson.

The night terror subsided. The light was on in the bedroom and through squint eyes he watched his brother running back into the room as the toilet, in the yard below, roared into a heavy flush. Cormac was still wearing his filthy underwear. For some reason which Brendan wasn't aware of, Cormac had neglected changing his underwear for a few days and, either out of embarrassment or out of devilment, had continued with this neglect for many weeks. By now they were a uniformly dirty grey.

Cormac had other habits which were not to Brendan's liking. Taking salt with porridge was one habit Brendan could never adopt. Neither could he understand how anyone, even Cormac, could eat bread with porridge. Cormac ate bread with almost everything. Cormac even ate bread by itself, no butter or jam, no dripping, nothing. When Brendan had tried this he'd hardly got through a single slice without puking. He couldn't swallow it – out it shot in one gooey ball. In Glin, Cormac was always hungry; this no doubt accounted for his distinctly odd palate. In this sense Cormac was very cultured, he would try anything you'd put in front of him. On the other hand, Brendan was distinctly "picky".

Brendan couldn't work out why Cormac needed to go to the toilet at all. If Cormac ever needed to pee in the night he would normally do it directly out of the window. Without any apparent worry about being seen or being found out he would try and force his jet of pee as far away from the house as possible. Their bedroom was in the attic two stories up and there was many a cat that was rudely woken and drenched by Cormac's pee. On some occasions even Brendan resorted to this "convenience in the sky", though he was always very careful to make sure his pee dribbled down the wall so as to minimise the noise. It was either this or descend two floors to get to the outside lavatory. On very cold nights a potty was left by the kitchen door to be emptied in the morning. As Cormac turned the light out and got back into bed Brendan pushed away and turned towards the wall. He didn't want any part of his body to touch that dirty underwear! The next time he woke it was to the sound of pigeons clambering on the roof. He was warm and snug and happy to lie there. He could hear movement downstairs and the frequent clink of milk bottles as the milkman made his rounds. He continued his daily practice of the last few weeks of slowly excavating a hole in his bedroom wall, gently scratching away, particle by particle. The wooden laths of the plaster were now visible and a neat mound of dust had collected on the floor directly under the hole. He would often do this as he whiled away those delicious moments between waking and getting up. Luckily, the level of the hole was just below the level of the bed and could not be seen from the door. He knew there would be hell to pay if the landlord, or even his mother, discovered the damage; yet he continued. It was like scratching an itch.

After a while he heard the front door shut, which signalled that the landlord had left for work. He jumped out of bed, picked up the clothes he'd neatly thrown on the floor the night before and dressed. He rushed down the two flights of stairs to take him into the kitchen. There he looked at the soap, decided against its use, splashed water in the general direction of his face and moved his hair to one side with the flat of his hand. He polished his shoes to a deep shine, which wasn't difficult as they were still less than a week old. His toilet was completed by a cursory glance at the mirror. Now Brendan was ready to face the world. He came down to a roaring coke fire which his Mother had lit half an hour earlier. By this time it had really "caught" and radiated tremendous waves of heat, preventing anyone getting too close. His Mother's shins were mottled red and white from the heat as she sat supping a very wet sweet porridge. Brendan joined her and enjoyed a mug of "goodey" (a mug of sweet tea into which was dunked pieces of white bread and topped with more sugar). They sat there together, not speaking, listening to the radio. Their relationship wasn't made of hugs and kisses, it wasn't made of gifts at Christmas or cards on birthdays. It was formed from mutual respect of each other's role as mother and son. Each could rely on the other. This "distance" between them occurred during his time in Glin and neither could resurrect what they used to be like. The closeness would return but slowly.

As always, as radio's "thought for the day" began his mother rose and got ready for work. Just before Ma left she brought the guard up to the fire and piled wet clothes over it, almost completely blocking the heat. The sudden loss of warmth brought Brendan back from the daydream into which he had drifted. He watched as Ma collected her black plastic shopping bag and left for work. Brendan rose and continued to watch her, through the window, as she walked out of sight. Within ten minutes she would be hard at work in the mill two streets away amidst the grease and wool, the heat, the rattling, roaring noise of the machines and the mouthing of orders from over-looker to worker.

By now, Anna and Roisin, Brendan's sisters, had made an appearance. Anna had been rescued from the girls' orphanage in Limerick City six months before Brendan and Cormac had made their escape. Roisin was returned from her aunt to complete this young family.

Anna spent much of her morning combing and re-combing her hair. Roisin would sit, fascinated by this continual preening. There was much toing and froing to their bedroom as she altered and changed her wardrobe (slim though it was) with monotonous regularity. Brendan sat, aloof, enjoying the spectacle.

Although Anna found the attentions of Roisin a distraction she always made sure, after her own preening was complete, that Roisin's hair was properly combed and her ribbon properly set.

"I'she gone?" asked Anna. Brendan nodded. Anna got four slices of bread on a plate and, moving the fireguard, proceeded to dangle them one by one on a fork until they were toasted. Roisin waited for the toast and covered them heavily with thick wedges of butter. She and Anna then scavenged the insides, discarding the crusts like squirrels discarding acorn husks. Brendan put on a small pan of water to boil and made himself some porridge. Brendan was a confident cook. He learnt how to make decent chips by frying them twice – a discovery that delighted him for years.

"When ya having this fight then?" Anna asked Brendan.

"What fight?" replied Brendan, feigning ignorance.

"Margaret Fox told me," she said in a smarmy way.

"After school, if you want to know."

"What's it about?"

"Nothing."

"Don't know why you go round with him anyway. He's a bloody sod."

Cormac arrogantly entered the room, bare chested, strutting around looking for something. Cormac's hair was heavily greased with Brylcreem and combed into a quiff at the front, Elvis style. He was apprenticed to a joiner. Today was his college release day so he didn't have to leave till late. He'd overheard the conversation.

"Make sure you deck him. Knee him in the cods. Try this," Cormac made a fist and raised the knuckle of his middle finger slightly above the bunch and hit Brendan hard in the ribs.

"Hey! That hurt" said Brendan backing away, frightened. Brendan was frightened of Cormac because he was unpredictable. Brendan might be happily talking to him and suddenly he would take exception to something Brendan would say, or even the way he said it, and immediately resort to violence. His favourite response was to slap Brendan across the face. He would claim some insult, some affront to his person. There was never any pity, never any sorrow or apology. People avoided him. His own family avoided him. He loved trouble. Brendan always seemed to be the butt of much of his anger. He rarely did this to Anna, with good reason. When Anna got upset she went really barmy – lost control completely; arms everywhere, scratching, biting, screaming, she would throw anything that came to hand irrespective of its cost or the damage it might do. This over-the-top reaction deterred any attack, certainly by Cormac. Anna, Brendan and Roisin instinctively felt it was wise to leave whilst Cormac was in this confrontational mood. Despite their strained relationship Brendan would say nothing against Cormac, who had been his protector in Glin, making sure he wasn't bullied or picked on. However, on leaving the hellhole poor Cormac turned cruel. In the rest of his life he was never happy.

Brendan, Roisin and Anna collected their things together and left for school. They took their usual route, up Bengal Street, on to Holycroft Road, keeping to the far side away from Holycroft School which had a bad reputation for its treatment of Catholics, though they had never experienced any problems themselves.

They separated as they approached Lund Park. Anna ran off to join her friends and Brendan and Roisin detoured across the park into the allotments. The bright sunshine, glowing warm through still air, had enticed the gardeners out, weeding and hoeing. At this time of the year, early summer, the vegetables and fruit were growing at their strongest and something new could be seen almost every day. Brendan had, for a boy of his age, a surprising interest in cultivation. It was an interest that had been aroused just a few weeks past when, for a few pennies, he had helped Martin O'Brien, a friend of his Mother's, harvest new potatoes. As Martin dug, Brendan would collect, first into a bucket and then into three large sacks. Brendan did most of the work and, backbreaking though it was, he enjoyed the experience. He loved the dry smell of the potatoes as they were unearthed. Even though the O'Briens had given up the allotment, Brendan continued to visit. He felt he knew something about growing things and, in some small way, he felt a part of the adult world which he was desperate to enter. Brendan hated being a child.

Roisin's interest lay elsewhere. Today, while Brendan meandered slowly from one allotment to another inspecting the vegetables and giving approving nods to those he felt deserved one, she collected dandelion leaves and old cabbage leaves from the compost heap to feed the goats which were kept at the end of the allotments. Whilst Roisin busied herself, Brendan ended his tour of inspection prematurely to investigate the commotion coming from the piglets, in the adjacent sty. They were annoying the sow. She seemed particularly distressed today. It was too dry. She was unsettled, too hot, continually changing her position on the ground. Suddenly the sow grunted in anger and furiously ran to escape the attentions of the piglets. As they followed, falling over each other in the scramble, she turned on them, head down, and charged. Brendan was amazed at their resilience. He would see them go soaring four or five feet into the air, propelled there by the sow's powerful snout, only to crash down to earth with a squeal. Even Brendan grimaced in pain as they fell, amid rising clouds of dust. Undaunted, they would immediately dive back in to try and suckle once more. No matter how cruel the sow seemed to be they nearly always returned, eager to be back with her. He'd observed this on a number of occasions and didn't quite understand it. Was it pure hunger that drove them back time and time again? *Who'd be a piglet* he thought.

The morning was idyllic; still air, bright sunshine with the promise of much warmth to come. Brendan and Roisin reluctantly left the allotments and made their way into school. As Brendan made his way through the main gate he felt a developing tightness in his chest, accompanied by general unpleasantness in his lower stomach area. The main source of his malaise, as always, was primarily concerned with the tensions that would arise in his first lesson. This always began with a question in the form of a brain teaser. Though the class didn't have to get involved, Brendan always did even though he experienced much difficulty with thinking hard, particularly in competition with others – like being in a race. It was agreed that Brendan was a very bright child, but he wasn't quick like some. He preferred to take his time with problems.

Today there was a further worry – his fight with Foxy which had been fixed to take place after school. This was Brendan's first real fight. Of course, Brendan had had lots of "scraps" before. Those encounters had been immediate responses to some aggressive act. If somebody pushed him he would certainly not hesitate to push back. There was no time to worry or fester over the possibility of losing. In this rite of passage, due to take place later, as with most fights, there was always the definite possibility of losing. The consequential shame and embarrassment would be difficult to cope with.

The brain teaser was not as difficult as he imagined it might be (they never were). He answered correctly (though he was by no means the first to do so) the question put by Mr. Wild on how many gaps there would be between twenty fence posts. The correct answer (nineteen) merited an extra bottle of milk. Although he was glad to get the answer right he didn't want the extra bottle of milk, which by this time was warm. Showing genuine interest, Brendan asked Mr. Wild what the answer would be if the fence was circular. Mr. Wild quickly moved on. This was the first time that Brendan showed real intelligence, it showed that he was thinking outside the "box".

The school day started uneventfully. In geography, Brendan spent much of his time colouring round the shape of Africa with a blue crayon. He couldn't believe that anywhere could be called Addis Ababa, let alone be the capital city of a country. It amused him to repeat the words over and over again – Addis Ababa, Addis Ababa; saying it with what he thought was an African accent "Adeece a baaaba". He failed to understand how colouring round Africa or India or England could be of any use to anybody. He complained to the teacher that Madagascar had been left out of the Africa page.

"Oh, just get on!" said the teacher, not wishing to get into a discussion. Teachers were becoming wary of Brendan. He had a habit of engaging in unusual ways of thinking of the world. They didn't like to display their ignorance, neither did they like to accept a challenge.

Break time was spent alone as he wandered up and down the yard fence. He would have happily spent the time with either of his sisters but during break time at St. Joseph's the girls and boys were segregated by an invisible force field operating down the middle of the school yard. Cross the line and some squirt was sure to tell the nuns, or worse, one of the brothers. An appropriate punishment would follow. He did spot Foxy at dinner time but carefully avoided direct eye contact. He also managed to get a game of football though this wasn't particularly special as there appeared to be about thirty boys on each side. There was much excitement, though little actual football; hordes of boys chasing the ball from one goal area to the other. To actually see the football, let alone kick it, was an achievement. There were no goals scored though Brendan did impress with his speed. To play, he changed from his new shoes into black and white baseball pumps he had to have for PE. It was somewhat of a novelty having two pairs of shoes, back in Ireland he managed without any at all! He loved to run on the smooth asphalt surface of the playground. Although it was smooth there was sufficient friction to allow for sudden changes of direction. He delighted in frightening other boys by running directly at them and then veering off at the last second. The afternoon session promised to be as dull as the morning session. His class were rehearsing *HMS Pinafore* in which Brendan was given a minor walk-on part. This involved him walking round the stage with a paper plate full of papier mâché strawberries and, from time to time, giving "knowing looks" to the audience.

Much to Brendan's (and the rest of the cast's) annoyance, the "star" had half a real strawberry tart to eat, which he did with great delight and much lip-licking and arrogant head-shaking.

Brendan's worries about his impending encounter with Foxy became more and more intense as the afternoon dragged on. He tried to concentrate on delivering the best "knowing look" he could but, with his thoughts being elsewhere, gave the look of a frightened cat. A cat that had just been peed upon by Cormac. A cat that had just eaten salted porridge with bread and had been peed on by Cormac.

"That's it Brendan. Excellent. Excellent," shouted Mr. Wild to Brendan's surprise. In fact, Brendan was so surprised that he made the mistake of reacting to Mr. Wild with a slight turn of his head, attempting to acknowledge the rare praise directed toward him. Mr. Wild knew a little about Brendan's background and had a bucket of sympathy for him.

Oh dear, Newton's laws, as yet unknown to Brendan, continued to hold. As his head turned, Brendan's body continued to move in one direction whilst his head was pointing in another direction. Disaster ensued. Brendan clipped the edge of HMS Pinafore's wheel, pulling it and most of the other scenery to the floor. He, now trying to compensate for the loss of balance, and continuing to try and keep his papier mâché pile of strawberries on the plate, increased in speed. As his paper plate inevitably moved further and further away from his body he crashed into the crowd of sailors, each with their own plate of papier mâché strawberries, who were stood transfixed by Brendan's antics. The result was bodies everywhere and papier mâché strawberry jam all over the stage. Brendan's acting career seemed to be ending just as it was beginning.

"Well that's just excellent isn't it Brendan," said Mr. Wild with the shake of his head. Brendan felt that this "excellent" didn't have quite the same cache as the previous "excellent" and blushed profusely. By the time the mess had been cleared up it was nearing home time. Brendan changed into his pumps just as the 4 o'clock bell began to ring. Tying his laces, he hung his shoes around his neck as he made his way out of school. However nervous he was (and now his hands were shaking) he certainly wasn't going to be late – he thought that would signify weakness – that would be worse than losing. Brendan got there in good time and put his shoes down by the wall. Clenching his fists, tensing his whole body, he attempted to control his shaking, without success. Waiting for what seemed like ages, though it was in fact only a few minutes, he hoped and hoped and hoped that Foxy might just have conceded by default. No such luck; in the distance, at the top of the alley he saw three figures walking toward him. There was no doubt that Foxy was one of them, distinguished by a head of flaming red hair that was strongly highlighted by the back-lit sunshine. Brendan's heart beat faster. He wished he was anywhere but here. There was nothing he could do now. He'd got into this situation and would have to suffer any consequences that followed. Foxy arrived with two of his friends. To be fair, Foxy looked nervous too as he took off his jumper and handed it to his "seconds". The fight started almost immediately and with some formality. Brendan and Foxy took a stance some four feet apart (just over two arms' length) in the centre of the alley. Brendan took guard. He held his left hand across his chest, like a shield, and used his right arm to strike. Brendan adopted Cormac's suggestion, forming a fist with middle knuckle raised. He had, painfully, experienced its effectiveness at breakfast time and indeed his lower ribcage on his left side was still tender. Foxy, a chubby boy, was less capable but took guard as best he could. He had a considerable weight advantage and a two-inch height advantage but Brendan had the advantage of speed. Brendan had a good deal of experience in the fight game. There were regular fights in Glin. Brendan lost a few but he'd also won a few.

These two casual friends were there at the appointed time, at the appointed place. As many young boys do, the two had vied, like rutting deer, for supremacy over the last few weeks ever since they had met. Brendan was a fiercely proud young man but still needed to be pushed into a fight. He had been goaded and chided once too often. Foxy made fun of his "oirish" accent. He had rather sheepishly accepted Foxy's domination for a while and then reacted, in retrospect over-reacted, rather like a jack-in-the-box.

The appointed place was the alley running along the boundary edge of Lund Park. On one side was a small stone-built wall, densely bushed. On the other, the back gardens of a long row of Victorian terraced houses, also stone built.

The fight was to be opposite the white-painted gate, which was about halfway down from the school side. At the appointed time, just after quarter past four, it was deserted. Anyone spotted entering the alley could be seen a long way off and the fight stopped. Fighting was frowned upon by the nuns at St Joseph's. In level of seriousness it was grouped together with missing confession or with swearing in the yard. Unusually for early summer in Yorkshire it had been warm and dry for over a week. Yet the alley was still damp with much moss on the light shingle surface. Although Foxy had provoked the fight, when it actually came to put fist on to nose, his enthusiasm was somewhat lacking.

Still, however reluctantly, he threw the first swing towards Brendan's shoulder.

Quick as a flash out came Brendan's left guard with tremendous speed to parry the thrust. Brendan responded with a straight right-arm jab into Foxy's ribs, extracting a not very well disguised wince of pain. Foxy rushed forward both arms flailing ungainly in front of him. Brendan retreated, taking blows on both arms. Brendan's urgent backtracking took him, embarrassingly, into the bushes. Foxy forced a smile.

Brendan's back was tingling with tension. His whole body was tense. He could feel every nerve. After the initial flourish and exchange of blows the fight settled down and became more ordered. The sparring continued for some time.

Brendan was doing much better than he had feared and warmed to his task. There were long periods of inaction in which the young pugilists circled each other, waiting for an opportunity to strike with little risk of retaliation. The anger between the two came in waves; yet somehow it was always constrained to a level that both could control. If there is such a thing, it was a civilised fight. There was no scratching, no biting or kicking. To the honour of both neither aimed a blow at the head. There was no intention, on either part, to hurt the other, or to draw blood, at least not seriously. The intention of both was to win and to be able to leave the fight with some dignity.

As the fight continued it was clear that Brendan had the beating of Foxy. He had the stronger will and he was just too fast for the overweight Fox. Foxy had hardly landed a punch of any weight and those that did seem intent on doing damage were deflected away by Brendan's left arm. On this day Brendan would never have given up. Somehow Brendan's determination was transmitted through his stance but especially through his eyes which coldly fixed upon Foxy throughout. This, more than the physical exertions, drained Foxy's confidence. He quickly realised that he wouldn't win this encounter but wasn't blessed with the intelligence to understand that a stand-up fight was to Brendan's advantage – he would have been better advised to change it into a wrestling match – then at least he would have had a chance of some success. He began to look for an excuse to stop. During a lull in the fight Foxy saw an opportunity to escape the inevitable. He thought he detected some weakness in Brendan's determination to continue.

"Wanna stop?" he said, hoping for a draw. Brendan didn't bother to answer. No longer angry, Brendan did, however, now have the self-confidence of one who knew he was certain to win. Brendan arrogantly increased the pace. Foxy was in danger of being overwhelmed by Brendan's speed. Foxy was sweating heavily now. Twice he slipped on the mossy surface, crashing down on to his backside trying to avoid one of Brendan's right-arm thrusts. Before long Brendan asked his own carefully worded question.

"Give in?" Brendan wasn't going to settle for a draw. No honourable shake of the hands would follow this fight. He wanted to win and to be sure that everyone knew. Short of breath, with aching arms and drained of spirit, Foxy had no alternative.

"Yeah, okay," said Foxy, dropping his arms in defeat.

"Do you give in – say it," repeated Brendan. As soon as Brendan uttered these words he knew he was being arrogant and regretted it. It wasn't him speaking, it was the adrenalin doing its rounds. It nearly devalued his victory. (Later he would always blush in embarrassment when he remembered what he had said.) Somehow Foxy knew this demand was just "talk". He didn't respond.

Brendan and Foxy stood there for a few seconds and then Foxy left the "ring".

Quite intentionally, to emphasize his victory, Brendan stayed put until Foxy withdrew. Without speaking, Foxy's two friends, who had been silent throughout the fight, handed him his jumper and waited for him until he led them away. One of them offered his hand to Brendan.

"Good luck to you. 'Twas a fair fight and you won. See ya round."

Chapter 6

LOST SOLES

It was almost two weeks before Brendan and Foxy would speak again; and then it would be a "nod" hello. Their rather tenuous friendship was broken. Even though, in the future, they would often do things together, they would never be proper friends. Brendan walked down the alley, elated and without doubt the happiest boy that ever lived. The knuckles on his right hand were bleeding. He must have caught Foxy's belt. In a strange way he was glad to be able to show some damage from the fight. This somehow made it more significant and, since he had emerged the victor, he wanted as much significance as he could muster. His left arm was sore, partly from absorbing most of Foxy's attack there, but also from the self-induced stress of keeping those muscles completely rigid throughout the whole fight. He celebrated by buying two giant "Nice" biscuits from the shop at the Ring which he passed on the way home. They were filling and all he could buy with his few coppers. He went home and had his fill of sweet tea and cider bread (the end crusts) thickly spread with butter. Nothing tasted so sweet as the tea and bread he had that day. He made more tea and bread; he was ravenously hungry. He'd won!

All the worry he'd gone through had been worth it. His elder sister came home from school. He didn't tell her about the fight. He was proud of his victory and, uncharacteristically, strutted about the kitchen hoping Anna might have asked how the fight went. He was desperate to tell someone.

"Ma'll be back soon. Table, come on, table," said Anna excitedly. Brendan had forgotten. They always laid the table for Ma before she got back from work. Brendan always did the butter. He would get the slab and make delicate curls of butter for the glass dish. Today it was difficult. They didn't have a fridge and the butter was too warm. His fingers were hot and sore from the fight and he could hardly grip the knife. Anna would arrange the slices of bread into a nice pattern on a plate. Brendan poured the sugar back into the packet and then back into the bowl so that it would be a perfect mound. Then he swept the floor. Anna arranged cup, saucer and spoon as directed by Brendan – spoon handle pointing along the cup handle, the butter knife parallel to the dish. Brendan opened the back door to let in some air and to settle his sweepings. Anna cleaned the teapot and put the kettle on to boil just as the clock struck five. They heard the faint low note of the factory whistle. Ma got home a little early – the kettle hadn't even come to the boil.

"Hah, ah," she said with a beaming smile as she inspected the table, set to perfection.

Brendan was unable to give Ma a hug, though he desperately wanted to. He wanted to show how much he loved her, how much he wanted to say thanks for saving him from a lifetime in Glin. His failure to show affection was the legacy bestowed on him by the experiences he suffered in that place at the hands of the Brothers Grimm. This table setting would suffice – this was his hug to her. As usual she then moved into the small sitting room and, still with her work pinnie on, flopped into the sofa. She smelled heavily of work, of wool and of oil. It was a smell they liked. Today, as on every other day, she was tired, really tired. Her fingers swollen from pulling threads of wool all day long. She kicked off her shoes to reveal blackened toenails and heavily calloused feet. Anna brought her a cup of tea and buttered bread which she quickly consumed. Meanwhile Brendan heated a large pan of water to which he added two large handfuls of salt. This was transferred to their large tin bowl and brought in to his Mother.

"Ahhh," she spurted as she gently slipped her feet into the bowl.

"Oooh that's good." She laid back, closed her eyes, and drifted into a brief sleep.

"I'm off to the field," said Brendan quietly as he donned his red football shirt. Brendan raced out through the front door (just in case his mother might call him back) and down Bengal Street. The street was lined with fresh washing strung out over the cobbles. On a hot day like today most of the women could manage a second wash. Ma would sleep a while before starting her own washing.

Brendan flew down the street, passed the witch's house on the left-hand side, through the snicket, down further in and out of Lower Cambridge Street, and on to the main road. He quickened; even faster now down the hill until he reached the fence above the field. He stopped there and watched, for a moment, at the kids playing below. He was there for a game of football. He didn't know most of the kids, and they didn't know him, at least not by name. There was always a group of kids there about this time, especially if it was dry. You just joined in. Someone would always have a ball. Brendan had a bit of a reputation for being very fast, so each of the teams called for him to join their side. But if the game had already started then Brendan would have to wait for someone else to turn up so as to even the numbers. As he watched, a ripple of tension moved through his body. He couldn't understand why but he felt very uneasy about something. It was the kind of feeling he got when he missed church on Sunday. There was a difference however; whereas missing church pricked his conscience, it was a temporary problem which only lasted a matter of seconds following each reminder. This unease lasted all through the two-hour kick-around. It returned strongly as he took his turn in goal, just as the sun began to set. Try as he might, he couldn't focus his conscious mind on the source of his worry. The game ended in the dark; their games always ended in the dark – the score was 14–11 to Brendan's side. After football they all went to the building site. Someone had got matches and they would make fires. They made one large one. Paul Marshall, who lived at 17 Bengal Street, went home and returned with three gigantic potatoes. These were thrown on to the fire and left till they were burned black. Brendan would have liked to wait to try the potatoes but he had to go. His mother had only to call once, the whooping cry

"Brendannnnnn", for the order to be acted on. He retraced his steps through deserted streets. His street was dimly illuminated by two gas lights, one at the corner of Cambridge Street and the other halfway up Bengal Street near his house. He slowed as he passed the witch's house. (She was the witch because she shouted at children if they played in the street and she was old and never smiled.) He made his way through the back yard and into the kitchen. Ma was busy making sandwiches for the next day. Ciprijans, the landlord, was reading his pink newspaper (a Latvian paper which he had to order specially). Brendan sat down quietly, not wanting to engage in conversation. He asked if he could turn on the radio. Ciprijans nodded yes and kindly switched it on for him. However, before it had a chance to warm up his mother came into the room. She pointed at Brendan with a friendly finger and a smile.

"Shoes," she mouthed.

"After this programme. Then I'll do them. It's Dick Barton. I'll do them after that."

"Make sure you do," she said as she squeezed his shoulder. Suddenly it dawned on him. The reason for his unease flooded back unpleasantly into his conscience. Shoes! He'd left them in the alley at the fight.

"Oh God," he shouted to himself under his breath. At his present stage of his development this blasphemy was the worst swear word he knew. As he grew older he would learn a more appropriate response to his discomfort. His heart sank.

He began to shiver and the hair at the back of his neck stiffened. Brendan ran from the room and out of the house. He ran up Bengal Street making sure he kept to the middle of the street so as to avoid the shadows and the ghosts. He raced back to the alley. It was very dark and very frightening. Brendan slowed to a walk and nervously edged into the alley. His eyes quickly adjusted to the deeper, purple darkness of the alley. Finally, he got to the spot where he'd left his shoes; opposite the white gate. He could find nothing.

"Shit, bollocks, shit." He tried to use every swear word he heard his brother use. He became distraught. He looked and looked and looked. He looked till his eyes hurt from looking. He looked into the bushes. He climbed over the gates and searched through the back gardens. He searched and searched. Every few yards he would burst into prayer.

"Dear Jesus, please let me find them, please, please, please." He said Hail Mary after Hail Mary and the whole of the Lord's Prayer. But the shoes were not to be found. He was scared enough to knock on a few doors asking if they'd seen a pair of shoes. No luck. No amount of praying could help him now. He knew this was serious. He'd always been so careful before. A pair of shoes in his family was rarely bought and they were meant to be looked after. He was angry with himself for being so stupid. How could he forget his shoes, his new shoes, not his second-hand shoes, not his hand me down shoes but his new shoes? What pleasure he'd experienced in his victory over Foxy quickly dissipated. It was now a hollow victory. He would have quite happily lost the fight if it meant not losing his shoes. He couldn't even cry properly, he was so scared about what Ma would say. He returned dejected and slinked quietly into his bedroom. Cormac was already in bed. As Brendan undressed in the dark Cormac shouted:

"Forty-three days." This referred to the number of days he'd gone without changing his underwear. On most nights Brendan might have found this amusing; not tonight. He got into bed and squeezed tight against the wall.

"What's up with you, eh?" Brendan didn't respond.

"What's up with you?" Cormac repeated.

"Nothing," Brendan whispered. Cormac kicked him.

"Bugger off then. Twat."

"You bugger off," whispered Brendan. Brendan hardly slept. He woke avoiding his mother. He spent the whole of that morning back in the alley looking again for his shoes. For all his courage and bravado on this day it would take him two days before he admitted to his mother that his shoes had gone. Even then he lied, claiming that they had been stolen. He told her on Saturday morning as he was sat at the kitchen table with Roisin and Cormac. He felt safer with others around.

She didn't believe him. He knew what would happen, and it did. She started to beat him. Roisin left, frightened for Brendan. Cormac watched. Ma held Brendan with one hand and beat him with the other. As his mother's blows rained down on him his left arm was his shield again. This time there were no retaliatory thrusts with his right. There was no circling, no tactics. There was no defiance on Brendan's part, no threatening stare. He was compliant. She beat him until her hand hurt. She changed hands and continued relentlessly on his legs and on his shoulder. Strangely, as he was beaten, Brendan thought, his mind in a trance-like state. He saw Cormac watching and he thought. He'd been beaten like this in Glin. Only now did that experience return. He saw the chairs and the cupboards in the kitchen as they seemed to spin round him and he thought. He wasn't angry with Ma. Brendan thought of the piglets. *Who'd be a piglet?* he thought. He could have run away, but he didn't. He knew he had this coming and it was best to get it over with. He was thrown around the room, crashing into the table into chairs and on to walls. Ma, now tiring of hitting Brendan on his back and head and legs, picked up the sweeping brush and started to whack him with that. As suddenly as she had started she stopped. She began to cry.

"I'm sorry Ma," Brendan said, beginning to cry also.

"Jasas won't you all leave me alone – just go away. I wisht you'd all go away," she shouted. This rejection hurt him more than the beating he'd just received. Brendan slumped to the floor, and, like a frightened animal, stayed very still, and sobbed quietly, gasping for air every two or three seconds like a wet hiccup. Cormac delighted in his younger brother's beating. Ma saw Cormac smirking.

"I don't know what you're smiling at. Take that brush and go and clean your room."

"Bugger off," Cormac replied defiantly. Ma, still incensed, went to strike Cormac, aiming for his head, she struck him a glancing blow on the shoulder as he ducked out of the way. Cormac stood up and pushed Ma away. Ma, now frightened, picked up the brush and waved it at Cormac.

"Just keep off," she warned. He pulled it from her and again pushed her away against the corner of the table. Ma crashed heavily to the stone floor, clutching her side in pain. Brendan, who had been watching, now leapt from the floor to defend her and pushed violently at Cormac. Cormac, momentarily surprised, lost his balance and staggered back against the wall, banging his head on the row of mugs which hung there.

"Leave her alone, you bastard!" swore Brendan, trying to give himself courage. That was all the excuse Cormac needed. Brendan thought he was quick but Cormac was faster. Unfortunately for Brendan, Cormac was also bigger, and heavier. In every dimension a boxer might think relevant, Cormac was ahead. Cormac regained his balance and threw a ferociously heavy punch at Brendan, catching him squarely in the mouth. Brendan's head rocked back violently in pain, his body crumpled into unconsciousness. He fell, a dead weight, straight back on to Ma, his body rigid in shock. Had it not been for the fact that Brendan's fall was cushioned by his mother, Brendan would have been seriously hurt. As it was, it took many minutes before Brendan came round. His mother cradled his head in her arms and gently wiped the blood from his face. His upper lip was sore, bulbous, seeping a mixture of blood and plasma and a front tooth was loose.

"It's okay. He's gone. That bugger has gone. He's a bad one, Jasas he's a bad one," said Ma. Cormac was away all that day.

On Monday, Cormac abandoned his dirty underwear, and his apprenticeship, left home and moved in with his Uncle John in Birmingham. No one was sorry to see him leave. No one wrote to him or wished he would come back. Brendan, however, always remembered him. Every time he looked in a mirror and examined his greying front tooth, Brendan would remember Cormac. But he also remembered Cormac from Glin. He was the one to hold Brendan's hand during two hard years. Cormac was damaged, they thought beyond repair.

That's when Brendan remembered his vow to destroy Glin. Mentally, he renewed that vow.

Two weeks later his Mother had recovered her composure and took Brendan to town to buy new shoes.

She was sorry for what she had done but wasn't in the habit of apologising to her children. Instead she took Brendan, Anna and Roisin into a café in the market and bought them (though she could hardly afford it) a beef dinner to share. Brendan knew things were back to normal.

He had new shoes, Cormac was gone; he was a happy piglet once more.

Brendan's family struggled on, seemingly always on the edge of disaster, close to breaking up completely.

Chapter 7

'BOMBS AWAY!'

Brendan was a thief. No doubt about it. It was his forte. Amongst the inhabitants of Glin there were numerous "Artful Dodgers" and many aspired to being Fagin. He learned a lot from the boys in Glin. His skills were, primarily, related to relieving staff of their cigarettes (not so many as would be missed) and removing food from the locked pantry and from other boys. As Brendan didn't smoke he would swap his cigarettes for food and, though rarely available, sweets. He knew how to utilise his personality to get round the domestic staff to get an extra spoon of mash or a little extra mutton.

"Chur can't you give me anudder spoon of spuds here – I'm only a small one."

"I remember you 'cos you're the pretty one!"

"Do you think I'll get a letter from my Ma today? I think she's forgotten me!"

From dawn till dusk there was a continual desire to get more food. The boys weren't starving but food was used as an "encouragement" for them to comply with the rules.

He was only in the country five months, having spent the previous thirty months in the infamous boys' home that was Glin known locally as Grim, situated on the south-west coast of County Limerick in Ireland. He had been reclaimed, unlawfully as it turned out, by his mother.

His mother, Bridget, had abandoned the family home and her eight children in a rare show of independence following, late one night, a cruel fight between husband and wife. The youngest children, all crying for their mother, sat on the stairs witnessing the awful spectacle. To see your parents cry is a hard sight to endure but to see them fight is heart-wrenching. It was a fight like many others, born out of frustration with their lot, seemingly on a downhill spiral as a family. Mick would always have the upper hand. It would have ended like all the others except this time, instead of going to bed battered and bruised, Ma left the house. For the first time in her married life she abandoned her children. Her pride dictated that she wouldn't come back, not this time. She fled to England and had arranged rented rooms with the eldest son Morgan who had made his escape from the drudgery and the desperation of rural life in Ireland in the early 1950s.

In their wisdom the Catholic mafia judged that Mick, the father, probably correctly on this occasion, wouldn't be able to cope and so removed those children under twelve to area orphanages. His sister, Roisin, just fifteen months old, was found a place with an aunt whilst Anna, six years old, went to St Patrick's in Limerick City. Brendan aged four and Cormac aged eight were carted off to Glin. In those thirty months in Glin, Brendan and Cormac survived, as best they could, a harsh unloving regime. Throughout that time their father only managed one visit. Parents and visitors weren't allowed into the home lest they see the horror their poor children had to endure. Instead they all met in Limerick City for a few hours. Socially inept, they only managed their time together by holding hands and sitting on the street kerb or at the park. Neither Brendan nor Cormac spoke of their mother. They hung on to their father and smelled him, that scent had not filled their senses for over a year. No Christmases, no birthdays, no playing in the beck catching eels. None of that any more. They said nothing of the cruel "Brothers", they said nothing of regular bed-wetting or soiled sheets, they said nothing of the soiled sheets that would have to be cleaned in large outdoor pools through shine, rain or even ice. They said nothing of bloodied fingers having to weed the grounds all day long. They said nothing, forgetting how to speak to their father. They could see his pain and didn't want to add to it. They knew he was their father but they didn't know what a father was any more. That's partly what Glin stole from them. On that day Brendan grew up. On that day Brendan became an all-knowing man in a child's body. They said nothing of those things.

As the time for separation drew near, each child would have an enormous bar of plain toffee thrust into their hands, presumably to ease the pain of separation. Cormac was clearly upset. The two boys would have to stay in Glin for a while longer. Brendan didn't cry as the bus began the return journey back to the home. Cormac sobbed, inconsolable. As the bus gathered speed, Brendan was sure he saw his father turn to wipe away a tear. That night in the privacy of his own bed Brendan shouted for his Ma and his Da. He woke the place up and was beaten black and blue until he was quiet. He too, on that night, was inconsolable in grief. He was sure he would spend the rest of his life there.

Brendan began to steal, in England, exactly one week before his seventh birthday. He stole a banana from a place he had only seen from the outside, a fruit and vegetable store. He had never seen such a wondrous place. At first he only properly recognised three things, potatoes, apples and oranges, everything else was new.

Being Irish of course he recognised potatoes, and their family was not so poor that he had never had an apple or a plum or an orange at Christmas. Apple cakes or rhubarb cakes were high on his list of "treats". As he stared and stared he recognised more and more: onions, carrots, parsnips, green cabbage, plums. Apart from what he half-read on the labels he didn't know anything about cauliflowers or green beans or pea pods or grapefruits, which were all there on show. His eyes were all over the shop till they began to focus on a green-yellow banana.

What's that? he thought.

"Ma, Ma, look at that," he shouted to his blushing mother. She blushed because she was shy. She didn't want to look anybody in the eye. She blushed because she was poor and she didn't want her child drawing attention to her predicament. She hoped he would not point to her torn jacket and then shout at the top of his voice "THAT JACKET IS TORN MAMMY!" The quicker she got out of the shop the better.

"Shush," came the response from Ma as they waited in the queue. She squeezed his hand hard in an attempt to keep his excitement and her embarrassment under control.

"Would you boil that Mammy?"

A smile cracked on the face of the assistant. Poor Brendan couldn't possibly know.

How could he possibly know what a fruit and vegetable shop was? He would know what a porridge shop was. He'd know what a boiled cabbage shop was. He'd know what a shitty trouser shop was or a "slap round the earhole" shop was. A tidy, neatly presented fruit and vegetable shop in one of the "wool" towns of West Yorkshire was a world away from what he recognised.

However, his time in Glin wasn't entirely a waste of time. Young Brendan was an intelligent boy and certainly intelligent enough not to show too much of it. He learned from the other boys how to steal and not get caught. In Glin they were constantly hungry and such lessons in thieving that he attended helped keep some of the hunger pangs at bay. Brendan was as tough as old boots. He was a match for most lads in the home. His brother Cormac was a match for everyone else. The two together ruled the roost. 'Course, they couldn't care about ruling any roost. They just wanted to be home.

The corner shop was only a short walk away from their lodgings. Ma was still protective of Brendan and held tightly on to his hand as they picked their way past the lines of washing hung across the street. Brendan too was protective of the banana he'd stolen. However, shortly before they got to their front door Ma spotted the yellow appendage to Brendan's other hand.

"Argh Jasas Brendan, will you be the end of me? You can't do that in this country. You'll have me in the jail chur," she said as she delivered a strong clip to the head.

Brendan had many lessons in life, all of which he learned from. Today would be a day full of lessons. This was the day Brendan first saw a banana. As it happens, it also coincided with the day that Brendan learned to "run-jump-drag" whilst being dragged by one arm. He would run whilst being dragged by his mother, trip, then to be catapulted into the air, run again, trip again, drag again and so on down the street. They walked back to the shop at a quick pace. There was some relief as they both made it back to the shop, Ma the whirlwind and Brendan the "run-jump" boy whose left arm was about to snap back into its socket. A left clip round the "earhole" and an order to return the banana to its rightful owner took the gloss off the relief he felt at regaining some feeling in his arm.

"Well, what do you have to say for yourself?" Ironically she was no longer shy. No matter how poor she was she couldn't abide thieves. She may not be able to afford much but she could afford scruples by the bucketful.

"Sorry mister," said Brendan.

Another clip round the ear after the banana was returned reaffirmed in Brendan, even then, the strongly held belief of the first three rules of thieving:

1. *Don't get caught.*
2. *If you do get caught, have a good excuse lined up.*
3. *If you do get caught and don't have a good excuse, then eat the evidence.*

Brendan broke all three rules. Firstly, he got caught. Secondly, the excuse "I didn't have one of those" didn't cut the mustard; and lastly, the banana was still intact and so it had to be returned. Had he eaten it, even his mother would have refrained from frog-marching him back to the shop.

At this time in Brendan's life "stealing" only applied to food. The concept of stealing anything else just didn't cross his horizon of things to do. Stealing the banana was just a continuation of the life he led in Glin. There, you stole food because you were hungry or because you knew you'd be hungry. In this case Brendan wasn't hungry, a new sensation to him, so nicking the banana came under the heading "for future use!" It took months of not feeling hungry for him to stop the habit of stealing food for later consumption.

The next time Brendan was accused of stealing he was nine or thereabouts. This time he had no idea what he'd stolen because it wasn't he. He was mister innocent. He made the mistake of being in the general area in which something had been stolen and he looked guilty when questioned. It was in fact the two boys he'd entered Woolworths with that carried out the deed, stealing a small penknife.

Their lack of skill in stealing led to their demise and Brendan was found guilty by association. No amount of protestation, on his part, would convince the attendant of his innocence. There was only one thing for it. They "legged" it out of there pronto. His compatriots in crime might have been inept on the stealing front but they exhibited skill of Olympic proportions on the "getting out of Woolworths" front.

Eric Bell was pretty fast for a chubby boy and Paul Marshall could get his skates on when the need arose and Brendan, the quickest of the three by far, just couldn't be caught. He could run and dodge at speed, all his senses were on "sharp alert" when in escape mode. It was like a cheetah being chased by an elephant, no contest. There was nobody to catch him. And they didn't. The other two escaped the elephants too. In future, if there was any thieving to be done he would work alone.

Exactly three weeks later Brendan's long career in stealing began in earnest. It was Saturday morning, a nice, warm, sunny day with more heat to come. He tidied himself up, put on a clean shirt and, a rare event, polished his shoes.

"Ma, can I come wid ya today?" he enquired.

Thinking he was angling for money his mother was somewhat discouraging. "You've had your spending money this week."

"Ah gowan Ma, gowan, can I? You'll need help with the spuds."

His mother looked at him and pursed her lips. He felt she was close to conceding. A further, "Gowan, Ma, gowan," did the trick.

"Well comb your hair and wash behind your ears, but you're only having a thrupence and remember to keep your hands in your pockets."

Brendan carried out his instructions, got the large spud bag from the cellar top and off they went.

Ma was like a fish out of water. In Ireland there was a set routine she was familiar with, every day fetching water from the well and washing in the tin bath, every day making soda bread, every day boiling a great pan of potatoes for Mick and the lads back from the fields, or back from mending roofs, or fixing wheels or repairing walls. There would be work to do every day up at the big house. Saturday morning they'd hitch up the cart and ride into Tipperary to stock up on a few provisions and to talk, in the pubs for the men, and in the shops, for the women and children. Saturday evening, if the weather was fine, would be dancing and music, at the cross, where everybody would gather. Ma led the dancing and Mick played the fiddle and accordion. That's how they met and for many enjoyable years that's how they lived. Every Sunday morning and evening she'd get the lads dressed tidy ready for church (Roisin and Anna were always called the lads, despite the fact that they were girls). Like clockwork was their lives, tick, tock, tick, tock, tick, tock. Until one day the clock stopped, and they stopped with it. At the end they had nine children and a bucket full of memories and a great regret, a truly great regret that they couldn't keep the clock ticking. They weren't aware of the dreadful consequences this would have on their younger children. Domestic violence forced Ma to escape to England.

She knew nothing of England, of smog, cobbled streets, cars, buses, the mills, the coldness of people, especially to the Irish, the coldness generally. She knew nothing of gas cookers or twin tubs or how to make a cake or how to write a letter. She had no friends.

In Ireland, Ma was a bright button in a dark suit. In England, she flapped like a bird trapped in a room. She had to learn quickly, but her learning days were over. She did what she could. She was alone, in a foreign country. She wouldn't see her younger children for over two and a half years. She needed help. Painfully slow she got her children back, the two girls first, then a few months later she got Brendan and Cormac. They learned about their new country far quicker than Ma. Within a few months, apart from their Irish accent, they were comfortable calling themselves English.

Keighley town centre was a fifteen-minute walk away from their rooms. The shops were still interesting for Brendan as they contained almost everything he, or his family, couldn't afford. They went to the market for vegetables, the butcher's for a little meat and fatty bacon, the Co-op for cheese, bread and butter, and occasionally the charity shops for clothes and shoes. The first part of the "shop" would be window shopping, nothing would be bought. The buying of "stuff" would be left to their return journey.

The standard of living of his family was slowly improving and they felt confident enough to visit some of the stores dealing in "luxury" goods. Woolworths' store was on the cheap end of the luxury market and, on Saturdays, was heaving. On this Saturday it felt as if the whole town had decided to visit. In those days, gardens were a rarity. Any excuse for "getting out", especially on a warm day, especially a warm Saturday, was grabbed at. Sunday wasn't Sunday but "dull-day". The best thing you could do on a warm Sunday was to visit the park – exciting or what? On those days Brendan and his pals would traipse the three miles to Bingley, through farms and farmers and farmers' dogs and cows with frighteningly long horns. They would be out all day seeing what they could find. They would get back about five, ravenous with hunger and desperate for cold water to drink.

A Saturday into town shopping, even with your Ma, was a good second best of things to do.

He and his mother squeezed through crowds and excitedly entered Woolworths. If truth be told, Brendan was on edge. This was the very store he'd escaped from just three weeks previously and he wasn't confident that he wouldn't be recognised.

Brendan had a plan.

As well as a plan, Brendan was the proud owner of two stink bombs, tiny glass phials containing hydrogen sulphide which, when smashed open, exuded a horribly unpleasant odour. He'd acquired these from Paul Marshall who'd got them from his dad – a chemistry teacher – for just sixpence.

"What ya want em for?"

"Oh, I'll think of something to do with them," replied Brendan.

"They're an investment."

"What's an investment?" said Paul.

"It's like a bet. You put some money down and hope it wins. You know, like on the horses."

Of course he had visited Woolworths many times before and knew exactly where everything was. The hardware counter was two rows down from the front doors and he and his mother were sure to walk past it. Just before they reached the counter, with its enticing display of cigarette lighters and penknives, he released his hand from his mother's supposedly to tie his shoelace. As he bent down he quickly removed one of the smelly bombs, which he had hidden in his stocking, and placed it softly on the floor. His lace tied, they walked on.

The plan worked better than he had hoped. Just as he was passing the hardware counter Mr. Clodhopper walked on the glass bulb, releasing its ugly vapour to all and sundry. The effect he was hoping for took a little time to materialise, but when it did, oh boy! The panic that followed was hilarious and spectacular. Men, women, children, even dogs stampeded away from the smell. Store staff, at first repelled by the odour, went towards it to try and find the source of what they perceived to be the worst thing to befall the world since Hitler's rise to power. Unprofessionally, many left their counters.

It is a rare event for people to own up to a break-wind "event" and simply apologise. It is in the nature of people to deny their responsibility for such an event and to exaggerate a break-wind smell, particularly if it's accompanied with a noise; presumably, that by openly referring to it, it would add credence to the idea that the smell wasn't due to them. "How could they be responsible for such a smell?" The stink-bomb smell was far beyond that due to a breaking wind odour. It was tear-inducing. In this case their reaction was merited.

Brendan held his position while customers hurried past. He quickly bent down and released the second bomb on to the floor. A second clodhopper, eager to get up speed and run out, stood on top of the second bomb. Further madness ensued as he trailed the odour through the shop on his shoe. In the general chaos Brendan deftly removed one of the nicer penknives from the display counter and away he ran along with the others of the stampeding herd. He quickly found his mother outside.

"What was that Ma?" he said innocently.

"I don't know. Something smells funny." She looked at him accusingly.

"You're telling me. Do you think someone's had a second helping of cabbage?"

"I think that was well more than two helpings." Ma joined in the jovial reaction.

His mother couldn't help but smile, the smile turned into a laugh. Ma was happy for her son to make a joke. It told her that this was a boy brighter than most. They hadn't laughed together like that for a long time. It was a turning moment for her. With that single remark she thought her family would survive. At least one of her children would succeed.

Brendan was desperate to tell Eric and Paul of his derring-do deed but chose not to. He didn't trust them not to snitch on him. The knife he swiped wasn't much use to him so later he swapped it for an Airfix kit of a Spitfire. A boy brought up in Ireland would normally have little knowledge of the war and their fighting machines, but a few weeks in England reading the *News of the World* soon brought him up to speed. It wasn't long before he knew all about Churchill, Dunkirk, El Alamein and Britain's fighting spirit. They were his heroes now! He also learned of Auschwitz and Bergen-Belsen. Whenever he got into a "Glin" mood he would think of those poor people suffering under the Nazis – compared to them he was in heaven, or, at least, on the outskirts of heaven!

He learnt from a young age that stealing was exciting and a great buzz, particularly if you shared the escapade with fellow conspirators, but sharing hugely increased the possibility of getting caught. If he was to steal it would have to be a private endeavour. No one was ever to know. Neither could he steal things which couldn't possibly belong to him. How could he steal a camera or a gold watch or a briefcase or a make-up bag? He couldn't possibly be able to afford these items so it would be "obvious" that he must have stolen them. Brendan would steal from time to time but only when he was absolutely sure that he wouldn't be caught or that suspicion would not fall on him.

Brendan's brain was, in age, only nine years old. However, in experience, he was at least sixteen. He was particularly adept at analysing situations and in forward planning. Within a couple of years of leaving Glin for the civilised world he had worked out, within his family and his peer group, who were the movers and shakers, who he needed to take note of and who to ignore. All of his siblings were opportunist thieves. If they could steal it and they thought they could get away with it then they would have it. Unfortunately, many of them could not avoid getting caught. They seemed not to have Brendan's powers of analysis. Mostly, they gave up thieving, they were caught too often. Though Brendan knew nothing of probability, that would come later, he had an innate concept of risk and could judge very accurately the value of the stolen item against the "charge" to be paid if caught.

Apart from the bananas, Brendan was never caught stealing though, to be fair, he rarely attempted to steal between the ages of ten and sixteen. Brendan would often contemplate stealing, going through in his mind what needed to be done, how he might break into offices and cupboards, when to steal was just as important as what to steal.

Quite often he would leave his house in the early morning just before daybreak, quietly, unheard, unseen and simply walk the neighbourhood and sometimes the town centre. He would know who was awake, who was delivering, what the police were doing, especially what the police were doing.

The police had regular patrols which were rarely changed. They were becoming more and more dependent on cars. If they could help it, they would rather stay in the warm car than run after Burglar Bill. On a few occasions Brendan would dial 999 and call for police help. In the hills above Keighley, the reaction to the 999 call could be observed. They were painfully slow. If he wanted to be crude he could, with ease, break into 70% of the premises in Keighley without fear of being caught. His interest, he hoped, was at a higher level. For the time being he would not use his knowledge to thieve unless it could be carried out elegantly and if he could be 99% sure of not being caught.

Brendan thought he was out on his own as a thief, but he was wrong. On one of his early morning jaunts he was sitting on a hill near to the train station warming up like a lizard before the day's work. He could see below in one of the many "yards" in that area a truck driven by what looked like a small man. It was driven round and round in circles raising volumes of dust. *Distinctly odd,* thought Brendan. He got closer, thinking that there might be something wrong with the driver. Perhaps he needed help. As Brendan walked through the open gate to the yard the truck was brought to a halt and out jumped the little people. The "little man" was a young boy. Both little men were clearly unwashed with stiff, dirty hair. The elder of the two was hardly four feet six inches tall. He could only just reach the gas and brake pedals in the truck. Beside him was an even smaller younger brother, full of scabs around his nose and ears. They didn't ask for help, but Brendan could see they were in a desperate state. Brendan knew them by sight, he'd seen them from time to time around town, always together, but didn't know their names. The younger "small man" said nothing and shyly clung on to the elder. They were poorly dressed, not that Brendan was any kind of judge in this area, he was often poorly dressed himself. But it was the kind of poorly dressed description that suggested that they were on their own, orphans perhaps, sleeping rough, possibly travellers. Brendan engaged in conversation.

"How'd you get that?" said Brendan, pointing to the truck.

"You can drive?"

"I'm only eight, Tommy there has just gone five. They leave the keys in. My dad taught me to drive, how to get it started anyway, but he's gone now, the mother will come back soon. Do you want some chewing gum?"

"Okay, thanks."

The leprechaun opened the truck door to reveal four large boxes of Wrigley's chewing gum, one of which was broken into. They were sitting on boxes of Mars bars and other chocolate goodies.

"You stole it. You stole all that?"

He responded in a matter-of-fact manner.

"Yeah, there's loads of it over there, loads of stuff. Have a look." He pointed to a small warehouse, the door was swinging open. Brendan went across to see. Sure enough, it was a sweets warehouse – there was enough "sugar" in there to last a lifetime!

Brendan returned to the gang of two and climbed into the cab to get a better look. By the passenger seat he could see a fiddle, broken near the bottom.

"Where didje get that?" said Brendan.

"Me Dad's. He gave it us."

"Who broke it?" asked Brendan, picking it up.

"Tommy stood on it, accident like, broke the fecker. He won't let it out of his sight. He won't let go of it. I've told him a hundred times to chuck it away. It's useless. He won't let go. Careful now, he'll fight you for it. I tell you he's like a dog. He's keeping it till the father's back. The strings and stuff are long gone."

Tommy shouted up at Brendan.

"That's mine. It's mine. Make him give it me."

"Sorry Tom, I was only looking."

Tommy snatched the fiddle back, holding it to his chest.

Brendan began to feel uneasy, if he were caught here he would be accused of breaking and entering and of stealing a truck! For his age this was way outside his league. His rational brain started to tick over. There was only one exit, the yard was surrounded by a large wire fence topped with barbed wire. If the police came at that time he would be caught, no doubt, and caught in the act at that. It was time to scarper.

"Want a go? It's easy to drive – just keep in first gear."

Brendan didn't have a clue what first gear was.

"No, I've got to go. If you're smart you'll get out of here, if you're caught they'll hammer you. Think of your brother. If they catch you they'll split you up, they'll put you in a home for sure. I'm off."

"The mother will come back, you'll see. She's gone off with some bloke to Blackpool. She said she'd be back by Saturday."

Brendan thought he could hear a faint *ne nah, ne nah* in the distance. Brendan hurried away, still hardly believing what he'd observed. He moved back to the hill. From there he could easily disappear if needs be. He decided to disappear in any case, he was frightened of being caught for something he didn't do. Perhaps they'd send him back to Glin? Brendan emptied his pockets of Mars bars and of chewing gum. If he was found with all this "stuff" they'd clobber him. Brendan wouldn't adopt this kind of stealing, this couldn't-care-less approach was too risky.

The tiny pair got back into the truck and re-started the engine, and off they went round and round in circles.

Brendan never saw the brothers again except for one occasion. He caught sight of them, in the distance walking away, holding hands, holding a fiddle.

His worst fear, perhaps they had gone into a home?

The episode got close to convincing Brendan that thieving was not the career move he thought it to be. But, there were other things he could do to occupy his developing criminal mind.

Chapter 8

THE GETTING OF WISDOM
(OR YELLOW SHITE, OLEKSS AND THE GOLDEN
HAIR)

Brendan's family, Anna, Cormac, Roisin and Ma, occupied two rooms and use of kitchen and cellar at 27 Bengal Street, Keighley. Ma, who had now been there for over two and a half years, paid a reasonable rent made more reasonable by a landlord sympathetic to Ma's predicament, effectively a single mother with four children. The other members of Ma's large family were old enough to stay in Ireland and look after themselves or emigrate to Birmingham, which many of them did. The husband, Mick, had escaped responsibility. Eventually their separation was recognised more formally. They divorced. They divorced on the grounds of cruelty. Brendan was a witness at the proceedings in Bradford Council Offices. Brendan was there to describe how his father had abused his wife. Mostly nonsense of course but a necessary "story" to obtain the divorce. They had fights like most couples under stress, and this family was definitely under stress.

At the pivotal moment in the proceedings the judge asked:

"Mrs. Ryan – in your own words how were you treated in this marriage? What violence was used against you?"

Ma was hardly a confident speaker, certainly unused to formal "speak". She responded:"He hit me in the lughole sir," she replied.

"Sorry, Mrs. Ryan, I don't understand. Your husband struck you in the lughole? What is a lughole?" One of the court aides, trying to prevent a laugh through clenched teeth, explained it was part of the ear.

"Which part? What does the Oxford say?" The aide flipped through the *Shorter Oxford English Dictionary*.

"It simply describes a lughole as a person's ear."

"Oh, I see," said the judge.

"I do apologise, I should have known. It must be old English." Even Brendan laughed at the use of this word, which he had heard many times but not in a formal context. Ma blushed, realising that her command of English was somewhat lacking.

There was a short delay as the judge completed his note.

"Was that the right lughole or the left lughole?" said the judge.

Neither would marry again. Throughout the remainder of their lives they would remain friendly. By this time Mick too had sold his smallholding and his two-bedroom cottage and defected from Ireland to England. Mick went to Birmingham and Ma stayed in Keighley.

After a year in each other's company a liaison between two lonely people, Ma and the landlord, was bound to occur. Let us just say that the liaison occurred and the sleeping arrangements simplified from four in a bed to two in a bed. The landlord was Chiprijans Olekss (Chipry). Ma was Bridget Ryan. She decided to keep her married name. They had similar stories to tell, both were in a foreign land amongst strangers, amongst people that would rather they weren't there. Both had left families behind. Chipry had left a wife and son behind, Ma had left four grown-up sons and a crippled husband.

Chipry's terraced house – quite untypical of the area, three storeys, stone built – was a significant step up for an immigrant and something which he was rightly proud of. It was in fact the biggest house in the street, blessed with an outside toilet and a small yard. In winter the outside pipes leading to the lavatory were heavily insulated wrapped round with torn cloths. As a further guarantee from burst pipes he would hang a small paraffin heater. Still very cold, this, at least, prevented their arses sticking to the ceramic bowl. Toilet paper consisted of cut up newspapers. This didn't help Brendan or the others with their understanding of English as more often than not the neat little squares of paper were in Latvian!

As well as a toilet, the house had three bedrooms, a kitchen with a door leading to the yard. Then there was a front room accessed directly from the street and a dry cellar where previous Italian lodgers dried chilli pods and hung long sausages from the rafters. They had left leaving substantial rental arrears.

Despite his poor command of English, Chipry was clearly talented. He could make enormous fruit cakes (more cake than fruit) in tins used for roasting turkeys. He could take the meat from pigs' trotters having first boiled them out of existence to make a jellied brawn. On some occasions he would eat a good-sized bowl of tripe. He would smile and laugh as we all left the kitchen in a hurry not wanting to endure the noises made in the consumption of such an awful meal. Worse still he would, on occasions, consume boiled cow heels – a gut-wrenching torture to those within hearing distance, certainly a step down from tripe.

This wasn't the end of his culinary delights. He could suck eggs without feeling at all ill. He knew how to make shoes, but mostly he would repair them keeping them "alive" for a good six or seven years. Chipry elevated shoes to a culinary delight as he often told us how he had seen starving people eat them.

He made his own beer – the yellow stuff now generally recognised in Ma's family as being "yellow shite". Impatient, he would always partake of the filthy stuff well before it was properly brewed. This would be offered, in very small glasses, to all and sundry – including Brendan – to taste, thus ensuring that Brendan would rarely touch alcohol again!

He was one of the few men who could smoke Capstan Full Strength; he would divide each one into three pieces – no filters in those days – and push one of the pieces into a cigarette holder before lighting and inhaling the thick yellow smoke into asthmatic lungs. To be fair, he hardly coughed at all.

On the day that Brendan tried the "yellow shite" he was offered a puff of full strength – thus ensuring that Brendan would never smoke again! He couldn't understand why anybody smoked at all, the first puff would make you cough and splutter and go a light shade of green. Why would anyone want a second puff?

On rare visits to the countryside he would first of all warn the kids about, in order of danger, holly, roses, nettles, brambles and the deadly thistle. He showed them what a damson was and how its tartness would make their mouths shrink back like a horse baring its teeth. He tried to convince them that it was good.

"Is gud, yah, gud, gud," pointing his fingers to his mouth. Even though it was clearly sour Chipry would gnaw away at the flesh to show them the stone hidden inside.

"Is gud," he shouted as they grimaced in pain.

Every nettle clump they passed he would shout

"Nu, Nu, dangr, dangr", which Brendan was sure meant danger. Yet, reduced to sign language, he showed them how to pick nettles without having to endure the sting. He would pick many, many stalks without any apparent ill effects so they all had a go. He tried, in vain, to show what the trick of it was but they all failed, Ma, Brendan and Anna (Roisin was far too young) ended up with blistered fingers and they were still smarting the next day. They wouldn't be picking nettles in a hurry ever again. Even more remarkable; he took a bunch home and proceeded to make a soup which he heartily supped! Needless to say the Irish contingent didn't try, and never would try, the green concoction or the tripe, or the hoof, or the trotters, or the yellow shite or the yellowed smoke. The very mention of just one of these so-called delicacies was enough to induce puking and a screwing-up of the face and an ejection of the tongue. The faces wouldn't look out of place in a gurning competition. A noise that always accompanies these contortions of the face cannot be described.

Chipry's personal habits were worthy of note. When shaving, which he would do every day of the week including Sundays, he would always use a cut-throat and leather. To do his hair he would first wet it all over then partially dry it. Then a parting would be added. The final touch would be to use the back of the comb to make wave-like depressions on the parting side. On special occasions he would add gold paint to brilliantine before combing it through his hair, giving a shiny gold appearance instead of a distinguished grey. Luckily, not many people seemed to notice the golden-haired Latvian. He would always wear a tie. Braces were the order of the day. Black, highly polished shoes completed the ensemble. His dimpled chin suggested an early attack of smallpox. Many thought him the Latvian version of Gary Cooper. No Stetson for him though, if he ever wore a hat, which he would on cold winter's days it would always be a flat cap. He had assimilated well into the Yorkshire psyche.

To remind him of his home and simply to just show it could be done, Chipry would plant, from pips, apple trees – in small pots, – there was no garden – just the back yard. When they had reached a sufficient size, about six inches, about a year of growth Chipry would take us on planting expeditions in scrub areas of ground in and around Keighley. Digging a hole with a hammer he would leave the saplings to sink or swim, mostly they swam. Years later a good number of his apples trees, now in fruit, still adorn the local scrubland areas of Keighley even though the house and the street have long since gone. He repeated the exercise with plums.

Chipry taught Brendan how to catch pigeons – not a simple task – but great fun.

First, take a long piece of string, about eight feet long. One end is formed into a noose, about six inches in diameter. The idea then is to lay the noose on the ground, put breadcrumbs or some other delicacy into the loop and wait for the pigeons to arrive. Brendan quickly realised that pigeons are particularly stupid birds, forever on the lookout for food – have you ever seen a pigeon that sits down for a rest? They would home in on the food even though they were still wary of the string contraption. One pigeon eating will attract many more, soon there is a flock gobbling what bread they can. When one or more pigeons are well within the loop the other end would be pulled sharply, forcing the noose into a smaller and smaller circle, hopefully capturing a pigeon foot. With a little luck one pigeon is caught, the remainder escaping with great commotion to nearby roofs. The caught bird was quickly calmed down by removing the lasso from its leg and placing the bird in a darkened box.

As well as lacking in grey matter, a brain, pigeons have a memory span about as short as a goldfish. It would take five or six minutes for the roof pigeons to revisit the reset lasso, replenished with fresh bread. Within an hour or so, six or seven pigeons were caught – by Chipry. Brendan, having been given a similar contraption, only managed one, though, with a little practice he could see how he might perfect his technique.

"Will we let them go now?" said Brendan innocently.

"Nu, nu," said Chipry firmly, fearing the box would be opened and the grey birds escape. His English was far too poor to give any kind of explanation. A demonstration would suffice. He removed one pigeon at a time from the box and simply pulled its neck away from its body, killing it almost instantly in one short motion. Chipry offered one to Brendan. He declined, shaking his head. Though Chipry had caught pigeons with ease he was disappointed with his haul. He was more used to the Latvian-speaking plump wood pigeons than the scrawny house pigeons that frequented the streets of any large town or city.

The dead birds were conveyed to the kitchen where Chipry removed all the feathers with a sharp pulling motion – he had clearly done this many times before. The heads, wings, feet and entrails were quickly dispatched with a very sharp penknife and thrown to the crows and to the odd magpie. The dead birds, many still warm, were presented to Ma for cooking. Ma shook her head in determined fashion.

"No way – I can't do that. You dirty dog."

A hen would have presented no problem for Ma, she'd often removed the feathers and was happy to do so, but there was no way she was going to cook the dark meat of a pigeon let alone eat one. Chipry smiled at her inadequacy and cooked the birds himself, roasted brown in the turkey dish and then braised for an hour and a half. When cooked the meat was removed as best he could and proceeded to make a jellied pigeon brawn. Slices of this would fill his sandwiches for the following week. It would seem that Chipry, like Cormac, could eat any kind of food, no doubt a useful survival strategy learned over many years of hardship and hunger.

At this stage in his life Chipry was the main influence on Brendan. Chipry was sometimes in a black mood and Brendan recognised the signs, when to leave him be. Brendan never saw him cry, though he was often close to tears, particularly as he read letters from home or when reading his Latvian paper. He kept his emotions to himself, he didn't want pity. From the snippets of things he let out he was lucky to be alive. Brendan knew, he'd been landed in a difficult position, he lost his wife and his son. Like the rest of them he was making the best of it.

Chapter 9

WINIFRED THE POO

Once a week, unless an excuse could be found, Brendan had to visit the slipper baths for a cleaning dip. He and Chipry usually went together. As man and boy they were getting closer, Chipry could trust Brendan and Brendan was happy to help when he could. A weekly wash at the slipper baths was a good deal. For a moderate amount they were handed a wedge of rough green soap, hacked from a much larger block, and a large bath towel. Each bather would be assigned to a cubicle with an enamel bath (a slipper bath). The attendant would, surprisingly quickly, fill the bath with hot water up to regulation level. The user added as much or as little cold water as they required.

Brendan's first task, and a pleasant one at that, would be the ritual removing of black muck from between his toes and behind his ears. The next task would be to convert the soap into a lather to wash away his weekly dust from his hair. This would need to be done two or three times in order to soften his hair and get a reasonable lather. Sometimes Ma would give him a sachet of shampoo to make the whole exercise considerably easier. Opening a sachet wasn't easy. His fingers were slippy with soap – he had to resort to using his teeth to nick a hole in one corner. This often led to a gob full of liquid soap followed by the noise a machine gun would make if filled with bullets of spit!

Once his extremities – ears, toes, fingers, head and hair – had been dealt with, he could ease down and drift away in the lovely warm water. This idyllic situation lasted till a loud bang on the cubicle doors reminded all that there was five minutes, out of thirty, left. There would follow a rush to get out of the water, get dried, get dressed and get out. The slipper baths were for men (and boys) only, all except for the attendant.

The door-banger and attendant in charge was Miss Winifred Brakes.

Winifred Brakes was straight out of a Dickens novel. She had the name. She was certainly ugly on a Dickensian level, she was a grump and an irritant. She had short-cropped, mousey hair. She spent very little time in a hairdresser's salon. She wore trousers, and if she ever was lucky enough to find a partner she would still wear the trousers. Ugly people can often be redeemed by having a pleasant personality, no such salvation was available for Miss Brakes. She even had an ugly dog, the Bill Sykes type. She certainly wasn't a people person and was, politically, to the right of Attila the Hun. Apart from the usual dislike of the Irish, she held an illogical dislike for those recent immigrants who couldn't speak English. She held a particular dislike for Chipry who was a homeowner and she wasn't. The two were on nodding acquaintance, except that when Chipry nodded Miss Brakes would invariably ignore him. She also lived in Bengal Street, in a one-room flat at number 52 further down towards town.

She shared an outdoor toilet. When using the toilet, she would bring her own toilet seat – she was more than happy to share this fact with all and sundry. According to her she was destined for greater things. The one room she lodged in was simply a stepping stone. She had found out about Chipry from the paper shop at the end of the street. Technically a newsagent's, but in reality it was a place where gossip reigned. Everyone and everything on Bengal Street and Coronation Street, and the streets up as far as Holycroft Street and, towards town, the streets down to the cotton mill was fair game, up for discussion and gossip. Who was in, who was out, who was "with child", who was in work, who was on the dole, the state of mothers pushing prams, who had a TV, anything and everything was within the gossip compass. Chipry would often bump into Miss Brakes when, every Saturday, he collected his Latvian newspaper. Brendan would go with him to help with the language problem but primarily in the hope that Chipry would get him a "lucky dip", a small bag of small sweets. You were "lucky" to get any real sweets in this bag. Miss Brakes was not reluctant to voice her opinion on all matters political. Chipry was oblivious to these rantings but was aware of the tension in the shop on body language alone. Brendan's English was excellent however and he could certainly appreciate the hurtful remarks directed primarily towards Chipry.

Brendan's accent put him clearly in the Irish domain and he had one or two unpleasant comments directed at him. Brendan was far too young to engage in any kind of conversation with Brakes, but there was a growing feeling in him that something should be done. She needed the equivalent of a good slapping and Brendan was the one to exact some kind of retribution in response to her rudeness.

As well as working in the slipper baths, Miss Brakes was also in charge of the town's swimming pool. The slipper baths and the pool were connected by a small passageway and swing doors, primarily used by staff. Many older bathers would buy a double ticket – a bath and a swim. They would use the connecting door to get to the swimming pool without having to dress and undress needlessly. Here Miss Brakes kept her dog, which was restrained by a simple leash. Keeping dogs on site was not allowed – everybody knew that.

It was a truly ugly dog – an English Bull Terrier – a dog that would frighten a herd of elephants. It didn't bark much, it didn't need to; all it needed was a "stare", an item which it had in spades. It is often said that dogs and their owners grow alike as the years pass by. In this case this was so true. Unfortunately, the dog got the worse part of the deal. It grew more to be like its owner.

A plan of retribution, codenamed "Pooday", was growing in Brendan's brain. It would need some preparation. Brendan thought he could put things in place in three weeks. Brendan knew that on that day Chipry would not be able to attend his usual slipper bath session. That day was the day each month he visited the Latvian Centre in Bradford. He never missed his monthly visit. He could speak his own language there and reminisce.

For the next two weeks, on a daily basis, Brendan "borrowed" some money from Ma's purse. This way the loss wouldn't be easily noticed. When he had sufficient funds he took himself to the magic shop on the outskirts of town with the intention of stealing three particular items, each one a super-realistic false dog poo, all shiny and wet-looking with an effective and realistic curl. It was truly disgusting. The disgust, of course, was all in the brain, it was nothing but a simple copy, in plastic. Brendan had seen their effect on many occasions. They were particularly effective on ladies with children, on ladies above a certain age (about thirty-five) and to anyone aspiring to be middle class and above. It is surely well known that those people using the word "poo" to describe excrement were of a higher class to those using the word "shit". The word "shite" was one level above "shit" and easier on the ear. Those who referred to it as "number two" displayed a certain ignorance of language, those referring to it as faeces had a medical background. The word "crap" was common, generally used by young people. Many use the terminology "spend a penny" for a pee or "spend a sixpence" for a poo. "Bottom silage" might be used if humour was involved. Of course, if you're a farmer then you might use the work "muck", which is quite a friendly term. You're far more likely to say "that's mucky" rather than "that's shitty". It's always a quandary as to what word to use when consulting a doctor. Humankind have achieved great things but failed, and failed miserably, to answer the question,

"What do you call shit?"

He waited outside the shop looking at what was for sale. He would wait till the shop was quite busy. After about twenty minutes there were six people in the small shop which was manned by just one attendant. Brendan entered and, unseen, quickly piled two of the items into his trousers. (He thought it would be funny if he was caught now with two false poos down his trousers – a visit to a psychiatrist might be warranted!) An over-large jumper (courtesy of Auntie, an unrelated good deed neighbour) kept the items well hidden. They wouldn't be paid for. The third poo was taken to the counter and purchased legitimately. A short conversation with the attendant about the poo's effectiveness gave Brendan's purchase greater legitimacy. From the attendant's perspective he was clearly an ordinary customer prepared to pay for his goods. Brendan learned this lesson very early in his career, stealing from a crowded shop was far easier than stealing from a poorly attended shop. Also, the strategy of stealing whilst a purchase is made, preferably an expensive purchase, is to be recommended. Attendants are flattered by customers who engage in conversation and who are prepared to spend. Seven days later, on Pooday day, Brendan initiated the second part of his plan. Early on Pooday day, Brendan scoured the neighbourhood for a cardboard box with a tight lid. His second task was to begin to trap as many pigeons as he could. An hour and a half's work and, using a much improved technique, Brendan managed to catch seven pigeons. Brendan used his amended technique of using a "whippy" long slender branch, with string attached, to ensnare the birds.

All the items, together with the false poos, were stored inside Ma's large shopping bag, the one with the zip along its upper edge. He stored the poos in the bag's side pockets. In the darkness the pigeons, now transferred from the cardboard box to the bag, hardly made a noise. Brendan added a couple of well wrapped uncooked sausages to his stash.

At about 3.00 p.m. Brendan made his way to the slipper baths and paid his usual entrance fee. Miss Brakes paid no attention to the extra-large bag that accompanied Brendan. One or two of those in the queue thought they heard a soft cooing noise but couldn't properly locate where it was coming from. The birds in the bag were a little drowsy with the lack of air. As usual, Brakes was there collecting the entrance fee and dishing out soap and towel combos. Brendan undressed and put on his swimming trunks. After about ten minutes, when all the bathers were well into their routine and Brakes had moved into the swimming pool section, Brendan made his move. He crawled under the cubicle door dragging the bag behind him; the gap was too small for an adult to get through but just right for an Artful Dodger. He crawled the twenty yards to the swimming pool passageway. Now he stood up and approached the swing door between the pool and the slipper baths. Judging by the noise the pool was pretty full, mainly of mothers and their young children. He came face to face with England's scariest animal. The dog moved forward menacingly and poised his body up and hind legs pushed back ready to strike! The dog let out a single bark, more of a growl, thinking one bark would be enough to frighten anyone. The dog was right, Brendan was petrified. In the swimming pool Brakes's ears pricked up.

Was that her dog? she thought. Brendan removed the sausages from the side pocket of the bag. The dog began to salivate and pull on his leash. Brendan threw the sausages in the dog's direction. Would the dog eat or would the dog bark? A crucial question, especially for postmen and paper boys. Not surprisingly the dog decided in favour of the sausage and kept shtum. Brendan and the dog were now buddies. Brendan, stroking the dog, removed the leash. The dog stayed chomping on sausage. It was now or never. He took the three poos and fitted them in his trunks.

Crawling again he partly moved into the swimming pool. He could see Brakes at the far end, settled down again. Thankfully she was chatting to someone and had her back to Brendan. Brendan, normally cool as a cucumber in these situations, was nervous as to the outcome. If he was spotted now the game would be up. He quickly unzipped the bag and, still in the shadow of the tunnel, forcefully threw its contents out towards the pool. The pigeons sucked up fresh lungs of air, full of oxygen. Quick as a flash the dog left the remnants of the sausages and decided to go for fresh game. He didn't know which way to turn as pigeon after pigeon flew for freedom. The dog's bollocks now began to bark as if he hadn't barked for a month. The pigeons responded wonderfully. One by one they flapped and flew upwards to the light.

Unfortunately, for the pigeons, the light was the Victorian atrium above the swimming pool. The middle classes below erupted into screams and shrieks not knowing where or what was happening. Against the light the pigeons were black; for all they knew they could be bats or owls or pterodactyls. Later, according to those swimming happily below, there were between twenty and thirty of them. The poor birds in their bid for freedom crashed into the atrium, their beaks now making progress into their brains. They had little choice but to fall back down. The poor swimmers thought the roof was falling in. Chaos erupted and the pigeons did what any animal under stress will do – they pooed and pooed and pooed, great big dollops of it, wet white and grey poos. Brendan's plan was going better than he could ever have thought possible. The pigeon poo was a bonus! The blobs of poo hit the water like small bombs and the women below tried to swim to safety as if escaping from a crocodile. In the midst of this chaos Brendan made his second move. He merged with the swimmers, adding to the chaotic shouting and screaming along with those in the pool. Unnoticed, he quickly laid the plastic dog poos near the exits to cause even greater panic and disgust. The barking and the chaos at last awakened Brakes. Now Brakes turned round to see pterodactyls flying and crocodiles swimming in a writhing swimming pool, her swimming pool and her dog. She saw Uglydog make little piles of its own and she saw Uglydog cock a leg on each false poo as if it was made by a rival. This increased the realism many fold. She shouted for the people to come out of the water and make their way to the exits, they obeyed as best they could but were held back by a dog scarier than the hunchback of Notre Dame running backwards and forwards, this way and that, following one pigeon after another.

By this time the poo-infested pool was almost full again, the swimmers corralled together by the three beautifully shaped dog poos, flapping pigeons and Mr. Uglydog. Brendan's plan had gone swimmingly. Chaos in the pool, poo, real or imaginary, everywhere you looked, dog running wild – brilliant!

Brendan now made his escape and withdrew quietly into the slipper baths and back, with Ma's bag, into his cubicle. He had an enormous smile on his face and a terrific feeling of absolute joy in his lower stomach. Brendan slipped into the bath, washed his extremities, and then sank back into the beautifully warm water.

"Take that Bloody Brakes, take that you fat sod," he said to himself.

There was no door banging that day!

The outcome? Winifred Brakes was reprimanded for having her dog on site and for allowing a chaotic situation to arise. Winifred the Poo, as she was often called from then on, wouldn't be quite so cocky in future.

Chipry never found out what happened that day. Miss Brakes remained

Miss Brakes, just as obnoxious, just as unlikeable. There was to be no Road to Damascus moment here. She did move on as she always claimed she would. She moved into the arms of a wool mill worker, they left Bengal Street for a two-roomed flat opposite Holycroft School. Her area now put her close to another corner shop. The gossiping began again. They never had children but they did get another dog – another ugly one!

If he ruled the world, Brendan thought that there should be a law against owning an ugly dog, let alone owing two. He also thought that people like Brakes should be "encouraged" (forced would be a better word) to smile at least three times a day and that all children should be given a free plastic dog poo so as to create havoc from time to time; it's great harmless fun. A final diktat would be to force adults eating hoof and tripe and such to eat within a soundproofed room. They should also be banned from pretending that tripe is pleasant to eat – it's in the name. No matter how much you tart it up it is, and it will always remain, TRIPE!

Other laws and wishes of a less serious nature are (in no particular order):

Lucky bags shouldn't be called "lucky" bags – they should be called "lucky to get a sweet" bags.

Pigeons shouldn't be called "pigeons", they should be called "stupid pigeons".

It appears that neither of these wishes were granted.

It was about this time, around "Pooday", that Brendan noticed a definite swelling in Ma's belly. He knew what this meant – another child (at least one) was on the way. There was no history of multiple births in her family so the baby was very likely to be a singleton.

Time seemed to go very quickly as, the next time he looked, there was a baby suckling from Ma's breast. Mr. Stork brought another child for the Ryan family to deal with – a baby boy to be called Andrejs (Andreish).

Of course the father was Chipry, a delighted Chipry. To Ma, in many respects, it was just another burden to deal with. However, like mothers the world over, her hormones took over. She loved the baby as she loved all the others.

Prams, cots, nappies, lots of nappies, baby's clothes were bought. The baby was welcomed by all the lads.

Brendan was the only one amongst the lads sensible enough to look after the baby so was often to be seen wheeling up and down Bengal Street trying to get him off to sleep. Whilst still less than a year old the lads were given the responsibility of looking after him whilst mother and father were at work. This turned out to be a reckless move. There were many close encounters between the world and the baby that, but for fortune, would have ended disastrously. This practice ended shortly after Andrejs' first birthday. The baby was in Brendan's arms. It had not been ten minutes since Ma and Chipry had left for work. As usual the baby would struggle to escape. Brendan couldn't hold him, he fell from shoulder height directly on to the solid floor. Brendan knew immediately that this was serious. He told Anna to go next door and bring the woman. She hurried over. By this time a huge bump had developed on the side of Andrejs' head. The woman, Anita Taylor, took over.

"Anna, go down to the phone box and call for an ambulance. Dial 999, tell them to come to 27 Bengal Street. Go on now, as quick as you can. Remember, a baby hurt at 27 Bengal Street." Anna rushed away. Then Anita addressed Brendan.

"Go and get yer Ma. Tell her I asked her to come. She should be here when the ambulance gets here."

The ambulance arrived. Ma arrived in tears when she saw Andrejs. The baby didn't stop crying until late in the evening. He was taken to the hospital to check that serious damage had been avoided. Andrejs and Ma were kept in overnight. In the morning Andrejs was back to normal, running around, giggling, mad hungry and continuing to bump into things.

They had to wait for the doctor to make his round.

"He's very lucky. This could have been really serious. Don't hesitate to come back if he becomes lethargic, you know, quiet, doesn't want to do anything, just flops about. I'm 95% sure he's fine. He'll be okay. The bump will take a day or two to go down. You can go home."

Ma was so relieved that there weren't more serious problems with such a fall. However, there were consequences.

Ma gave up work for the next three years to look after the toddler. After that Andrejs would attend the local nursery. It was the lads' responsibility to make sure Andrejs was delivered and collected each day. Andrejs cried and cried each time he was left. He would have to harden up, like the rest of the lads.

Chapter 10

BIG SCHOOL: RACKET OR RACQUET?

In those days, the late fifties, it was every parent's desire that their child would pass the 11-plus and gain entry to a grammar school. Brendan attended a Catholic junior school up to the age of eleven. He failed the 11-plus which could be mainly put down to having spent two and a half years in the industrial school in Glin. The term "school" was an inappropriate tag. Much of the work was mundane and physical, much was based on religion, like having to learn the Catechism or the Stations of the Cross. The Brothers who were responsible for the home cared more for obedience to the Catholic religion than for academic success.

Failure of the 11-plus was, for many, somewhat of a relief, going to a grammar school was well known to be a costly business, having to buy lots of uniforms, shirts, ties, trousers, the full paraphernalia, gear for swimming, gear for gym, football boots and sports equipment and aprons for woodwork and another for metalwork. Waterproofs for excursions around town and so on. You'd also be expected to go on expensive field trips and social functions. You'd also have to write racquet instead of racket but Brendan thought the second version was the more appropriate epithet. Has the country gone mad? Of course, if one set of parents buys all this "stuff" then, not to be outdone, the next set of parents feel they have to do the same. At the end you get a clothes shop, not a school. Brendan's family, which meant just one person, Ma, just couldn't afford that level of support despite generous grants from the state. He'd have to go to a secondary modern school and "lump it" as Ma would say.

Due to his failure he would normally attend a Catholic secondary modern school till he was sixteen. After years of Hail Marys and of being ruled by the Jesuit brothers and the nuns, his mother felt that he would be better off in a Church of England School. A little less religion and a tad more schooling would be the better option. Brendan couldn't believe that Ma would take it upon herself to sort out his schooling. But she did. After much deliberation by the school hierarchy it was decided that Brendan could transfer to Eastwood Secondary Modern School, a school no longer dominated by religion. Brendan, had not canvassed for this but he felt liberated by the move.

Poor Brendan. On his first day at "big" school he had to join the first year pupils in the main hall. He was late. As he entered all the pupils were sat on the floor listening to the headmaster. They heard the heavy doors at the back squeak open and, as one, they turned round. Even the head stopped for a moment and looked over his glasses to see who'd entered. What did they see? A young lad with a poorly kept blue suit, black and white baseball shoes, and short trousers. He quickly realised that everyone else was in school uniform with long trousers and freshly polished black shoes. He was the proverbial fish out of water. A number of kids began to giggle. Bravely he walked through the seated masses and finally sat down. The grant for the basic school uniform was late. It was always late and it always came after term started. He blushed all morning. Everyone looked grown up, he looked like a baby, a baby with blue short trousers and a blue jacket that screamed, "look at me, look at me why don't you look at me, look at how stupid I am". That was his welcome to Eastwood Secondary Modern School. He was allocated a place in the top set, class 1S. This was the class that just missed out on a grammar school place. Even at this late stage some parents were going through an appeals process to overturn the exam result. Despite his embarrassment with the short trousers, which would last three weeks until his grant, for blazer, badge, shirt and (hurrah, hurrah) long grey trousers came through. He felt "he was on his way, back on track to adulthood". Strangely, the layout of Eastwood School was not too dissimilar from the layout at Glin. During the summer holidays he had come down from North Dene Avenue, Braithwaite (over a mile away) to recce the place.

On two adjacent sides to the front, the school was bordered by iron railings and two entry gates. Facing the school was row after row of terraced houses. On one part of the area bounded by the railing was a working allotment.

On one of the other sides was a large enamelling business employing hundreds. The remaining side was a high wall, about six feet tall with an open exit to Victoria Park. At the end of the Victoria Park wall were the outdoor toilets and along the opposite side was a covered area where the kids would congregate when the weather was poor. In West Yorkshire the weather was often poor, or was it that our memories are poor? No it was definitely the weather.

Immediately opposite the main gate was a shop, mainly there to entice the children to buy sweets, crisps, cigarettes (woodbines in packets of five or in singles if necessary) and drinks, in fact anything.

The main two-storey building of the school housed many classrooms. On the ground floor was all the paraphernalia connected with schools: cloakrooms, indoor toilets, administration offices. Adjacent to the school at the front was a large building, formerly a church, but now requisitioned by the school to be used as a gym and badminton court. The main hall, on the ground floor, doubled up as a meeting place for the whole school and as a dining hall. Nearby outbuildings were home to woodwork and metalwork areas. In break times and at dinner time the children would not be allowed access to the main buildings. At Eastwood children could leave the premises should they wish, and many did leave, especially at lunch time where they could access the pleasures of Victoria Park.

Keighley boasted four large parks. Victoria Park was the worst of the bunch, mainly set to grass and used to locate the yearly fair (or fayre if you went to grammar school), for Keighley this was the highlight of the year. At one end of the park was the town's slaughterhouse and, if you got too close, an unpleasant smell. Later, in an attempt to improve its image, it was called an abattoir.

Most of the main yard was the football pitch or the cricket pitch. Another game played, in pairs, throughout his time at Eastwood used a tennis ball. The enamelling business had numerous large windows protected from the school by large mesh guards. The game was like tennis, you'd throw the ball so as to hit the bricked area between the windows (you were "out" if you hit the mesh). The ball was allowed to bounce at most once before the other player caught it. The catcher would then throw the ball on to the bricked area. The idea was to arrange matters so that your opponent let the ball bounce twice before it was collected. Simple game, great fun. Playing "doubles" with two on each team was even better.

There was no leaving Glin unless you were supervised. Still, the Eastwood experience was two or three levels above the comfort available at the orphanage in Glin.

Despite the short trouser incident, Brendan quickly formed new friendships, something he always found easy to do, and established himself as one of their brightest sparks. His peripatetic teachers followed him to make sure his maths was up to the mark. Actually, his maths was well up to and beyond the mark. Concerned with such a dramatic change, the school directed one of its staff, Mr. Sangster, to take an overview as to how Brendan was adjusting. Mr. Sangster and the school needn't have worried, young Brendan adjusted quickly to the new regime. Mr. Sangster found him in the school library on one occasion.

"Hi Brendan, what's the book?"

Brendan closed it hurriedly, slightly embarrassed.

"Oh it's a book I've been reading for the last few months. Nothing really."

"Don't be shy, let's have a look."

Brendan pushed the book towards Mr. Sangster.

"Good grief, that's a bit advanced for this school. Not sure I could read this myself."

"Oh it's not hard, quite interesting actually," said Brendan.

"What are you on, I mean, what page?"

"I'm near the end now. I'm struggling with the last part. I could do with taking it home actually. We've no books at home – this would keep me away from the telly."

Mr. Sangster handed back the book.

"You take that home whenever you wish, take any of these books. They're only gathering dust here. Nobody else reads this stuff. Who read this to you?"

"No one, picked it up myself. Don't tell the staff that come to visit me, will you? They're a bit behind me and I don't like to embarrass them."

"No worries. Your secret is safe with me."

"Can I take this other book as well? It's a book on algebra – never seen anything like it. I wish they'd teach it here. I get most of it, it's like a secret language."

"Yeah, yeah. Any book, any book at all."

Mr. Sangster went immediately to see the headmaster, Frank Newby.

"Frank, you'll never believe this."

"Surprise me."

"I've just spent twenty minutes with Brendan. Guess what I caught him reading?"

"*Playboy*? No? Go on, tell me then."

"Only Euclid's *Elements*."

"My degree was in History. You'll have to illuminate me."

"Well it's a basic book on mathematics, on geometry actually. It shows he's gifted at least. He should be at the grammar school. He's way ahead of anybody here, and I include the staff in that assessment. But he's shy, he doesn't want anybody to know. He's got a book on advanced algebra as well – that is way beyond me. I'm telling you, this lad's unusual. I've taught a lot and I've only encountered this kind of thing just once before, but he was an autistic boy, well he was in the autistic spectrum. I don't think, in fact I'm pretty sure that Brendan isn't autistic; we ought to test him though."

"He's got rights too. If he'd prefer to stay here, if he's more comfortable here then it's our duty to see that he thrives. Perhaps he prefers to be a big fish in a small pond than a small fish in a big pond? We can apply for a more qualified teacher to visit, perhaps someone at the university, at Bradford, could be assigned the task. You look into it and keep me informed."

Brendan was tested for autism. It turned out that Brendan was on the autism spectrum, but only just. The examiners thought that this was due to his poor background. Eventually, this mild form of autism would disappear into the normality spectrum. At the same time his intelligence was tested. Here he hovered around the one hundred and forty mark, which is well above normality but not particularly unusual. Mr. Sangster thought that Brendan fiddled the results so that his score would not be too high. He didn't want to appear to be "special".

Within three months of joining Eastwood School he had his regulation fight – like his previous fight it started over nothing – simply bumped into Danny McBride, a lad a year younger than himself. They both said a few words they wish they hadn't said and another after-school get together saw Brendan emerging victorious – don't they know he'd never give in. Brendan won his fights not because of some innate skill he possessed but because he simply wore down his opponents. However, despite his prowess he decided not to have any more fights. From that day on he would simply say "sorry" and move on. Fighting was a child's game and he'd been a child too long.

All schools used a form of corporal punishment. At Eastwood there were three forms – the cane, the slipper and (a speciality, this one) the severe pulling of hair on a boy's sideburns. This latter form was more akin to sergeant punishment than to corporal punishment – it always brought tears to your eyes. It was the favourite choice of torture practised by Mr. Wilkinson the deputy head. His previous job was in a borstal, he was used to dealing with so-called tough guys. He was the friendly type. If you played by the rules then he'd laugh and joke with you. But step out of line then he'd be down on you like a ton of bricks.

The cane, to either hand, was used primarily on girls. It was not used on girls wearing skirts as the billowing material absorbed the "whack" very effectively. Brendan wondered where all these canes came from. Every teacher seemed to have an endless supply. He never saw an advert for a cane – perhaps they came when the teacher was appointed – supply of chalk, duster, ink, pens for those kids who couldn't afford a pen, pencils, rubber, protractors and, right at the end of the list, a large supply of canes!

He imagined possible adverts.

"Get a cane – keep your class under control."

"Get a cane giving you whip like control with the fewest whack number – a real tear-jerker!"

Some of the teachers gave them names like "the red devil" or "Mr. Whippy" or "the book beater". Some distinguished between males and females. Not surprisingly the two canes would be called "his" and "hers".

The slipper was used for misdemeanours at a lower level – on the hand for girls, on the backside for boys. From a teacher's point of view the nice thing about a slipper is that you could get a really good grip giving you greater "purchase", providing a deeper whack and a more deeply unpleasant sound. It really proved to be an effective deterrent. It wasn't as severe as a cane, the force was dissipated over a larger area with a commensurate reduction in pain.

The headmaster obviously had his own supply of upmarket canes – he never used anything else. He referred to his cane as the Newby special. He wasn't going to barter about which implement to use, for him it was the Newby special every time. If you went to the head you got the cane, usually six of the best, three on each hand. Boys and girls were treated equally. It was almost a rite of passage. Walking back to the classroom after the regulation six, red-faced, false smile you knew you'd been caned and everyone else in the class knew as well despite the effort to mask its effect. You wouldn't want to be caned too often that's for sure. Habitually the head would fail to aim properly, resulting in a whack to the wrist part of the hand or to the tips of the fingers – very painful! Worse than that he would sometimes fail to count properly – unpleasant! The severest case would be six of the best from the head followed by a letter to your house.

By this time, unbeknownst to Brendan, he had lost his Irish accent, and also unbeknownst to Brendan he was busy acquiring a Yorkshire accent. It wasn't clear he'd made a good swap. He'd replaced the thick Irishman voice, the butt of much humour at that time, with the even thicker Yorkshireman voice, also the butt of much humour of all those "up north". It wasn't till the arrival of the Beatles that the accent from those "up north" had some cache.

So Brendan had changed religions, of a sort. He was no longer an incense-swinging Irish Catholic, more a Church of England non-believer. Instead of churchgoing two days a week, he would only have to attend at Easter and at Christmas.

Funnily enough, despite the fact that Brendan had changed allegiance he continued attending Catholic Church on most Sundays, but this died away after a few months. Perhaps he had overdosed on incense?

In the Catholic Church there were Hail Marys ad infinitum and the Stations of the Cross. Every church was adorned on either side with the various stages taken by Jesus from the Betrayal of Thomas in the Garden of Gethsemane, the hand washing of Pontius Pilate to the carrying of the cross, the crucifixion and the ascension into heaven. Other attractions were the palms and the donkey on Palm Sunday.

Missing church on Sunday was a sin and attracted a large number of Hail Marys to be recited in penance. Continual absence would incur a visit from the priest himself. On these occasions Ma would hide, and Brendan would have to fend off the wrath of the entire Catholic Church on his own.

It was always surprising to Brendan that the cross was the main symbol in the Catholic Church yet it was a symbol of torture used against Jesus.

Then there was the confessional. Admitting to your sins and accepting the consequences. Brendan found that to be the trickiest of arrangements as a "believer".

On the other hand, there was the Church of England. All you needed there was a knowledge of a few hymns, especially 'Onward Christian Soldiers' and 'Jerusalem' – far less hands-on, much more efficient.

In terms of weight, Brendan thought the Catholic Church was the heavyweight, the English Church came down as a lightweight with aspirations for the top spot.

Chapter 11

THE GREAT TRAIN ROBBERY
(OR MUCH ADO ABOUT NOTHING!)

The school year started in early September. This was his second year at Eastwood. This school had a more "serious" atmosphere which Brendan thrived on. He was assigned to Mr. Sangster's class and towards the end of the first term was made class rep, responsible directly to him. The teacher and pupil hit it off immediately. For the time being Brendan was completely trustworthy and would often remind the teacher what he was supposed to be doing. In this place, Brendan was content not to thieve. His family's income was just about adequate. In any case there was little opportunity for stealing – small items yes, but nothing substantial. It is almost more shameful being caught stealing small items like a few coins from a pocket of a coat than it is stealing a relatively expensive item like a watch. However, he liked to keep his hand in if at all possible. At this time his thieving was almost risk free, for example he wasn't averse to changing the cost labels on goods, from expensive goods such as cork floor tiles to much cheaper items such as plastic floor tiles. This would be particularly true if the attendant was young, who perhaps just worked on Saturdays; they would be unlikely to have an adequate knowledge of the value of things. In this way large amounts of money could be saved. Brendan carried out this practice until the medium-to-large stores cottoned on to this ploy and changed price labels to be in three parts, making this practice of label swapping very difficult to carry out. Brendan even considered the possibility of buying a price gun of his own, but in the end he decided against it mainly because this practice would only be saving him money, it wasn't a way of making money. Of course, Brendan had long realised that the word "save" only meant that you spend less. You still had to spend something. This family didn't have enough income to "fiddle". Best not to attempt it at all. Fiddling is a middle-class occupation, not a pleasure to be enjoyed by the poor. Middle-class thieving or fiddling was on the level of stealing paper and paper clips or removing staple guns from the office. It might even be extended to taking half an hour off at the end of a shift or falsely claiming expenses, or worse, taking days off work with the deadly back pain!

This second year at Eastwood was largely benign apart from two events, one internal, the other hit the headlines in a big way. The first involved an experienced teacher, a teacher of French. It made the local newspapers. He was charged, and found guilty, of the embezzlement of substantial amounts of money, money that students had paid for an excursion to France to enhance their studies. Brendan would often talk about this to mates and even to some teachers, if they'd listen.

"What was this bloke thinking about?" asked Brendan to himself.

This teacher hardly needed the money, with his salary levels, and even if he did he could surely borrow from the bank. Why risk a career for a paltry amount of around twelve hundred quid? This embezzler had been given responsibility for the money for goodness sake. The police wouldn't have a great deal to do to find a possible culprit. They'd search his house, look at his bank account, bingo, it would stick out like a sore thumb. Brendan would try and think what was going through his mind. Why would he do such a stupid thing? Perhaps all that French teaching made him go soft in the head? What the hell for? He's lost his salary, he'll never be hired again, certainly not as a teacher – *what a berk*, thought Brendan. Such an idiot deserved to get caught. They give a decent embezzler a bad name. Brendan thought that this embezzling business seemed a nice way to make a few bob, clean work, no violence involved. He might try a bit of that when he gets older. Difference is he'd do it "properly".

He had numerous plots in mind but almost all involved an older person to carry through the crime. He'd have to wait a few years to gain a further inch or two in height and to put on a good deal of weight – he was painfully thin. His best feature was his eyes. Mainly brown with green streaks running through, a deep brown, almost black hair and black triangle eyebrows inherited from his father. He had good teeth apart from slight gaps on the top set. He attracted the attentions of one or two girls but he wasn't interested. He was shy and, in his view, too poor to "tango". Euclid was a much greater attraction. Brendan needed to fill out some more. No matter what he wore he still looked like a boy, he was desperate to look like a man.

About that time the national news was full of the great train robbery. Not surprisingly, it had the feel of a Robin Hood character – stealing from the state always seemed to have some merit especially to the average pub goer – the more money they would steal the more popular they seem to become.

Brendan even chastised the Great Train Robbers, which seemed to occupy the newspapers for months and months. From what he could read it was well planned but then at the end they let themselves down by having a safe house (or safe farm in this case) too close to the action and in getting a single individual with a dubious background for carrying out orders, to "clean up" after they divided the loot. Brendan would have torched the place, make sure everything was destroyed. Also the money went to their heads, they were shocked by the amount of money they stole. Poor research, poor forward planning he thought. He would debate these points with his mates over and over again. Why did they need a safe house in any case? Why couldn't they simply drive away? By morning they could have been over a hundred miles away in an even safer house. And also they didn't have decent alibis, none of them. They were known to the police as being robbers. They must surely have thought that sooner or later they would have a visit from the police. It's clear that they, the usual suspects, would be picked up sooner or later. Also, by stealing such a large amount of money the police would work considerably harder to solve the crime. No thought given to the "escape". Brendan would tell all and sundry that the getting of the money isn't the difficult part of thieving – it's the keeping of it and the avoidance of being caught. Best not to steal so much, that way they would have a better chance of keeping it. No point in stealing large wads of money if you're not going to be able to keep it. Had they got away with it they would have been heroic Robin Hood figures. Having been caught they were regarded as chumps, no match for the Flying Squad. It's so frustrating. He wished he'd been on the job. He was sure he'd make a better fist of it. And another thing, most of them had families, with family responsibilities. They couldn't just wander off to Spain and start spending. They'd miss their families, they'd get lonesome, they'd start returning to England in dribs and drabs, the police can play the "long game" and just wait for things to crack. What was Buster Edwards thinking of? Having more than fifteen robbers, 'course that was going to break down, sooner or later. The police led by "Slipper of the Yard" could afford to make many mistakes in the hunt, the robbers couldn't afford to make one mistake. With such a large group of robbers, mistakes would be made then you get the domino effect to take hold. One mistake leads to another. The robbers would break, blaming others in the group. The whole thing would break down. That's exactly what happened. And the great train robber who escaped? Gone to Brazil, sounds romantic but what a miserable life for Ronnie Biggs.

Brendan was daydreaming.

"Brendan, Brendan – are you with us?" asked Mr. Sangster. The whole class laughed as Brendan woke from a daydream, clearly miles away.

At the end of the lesson, Mr. Sangster quietly called Brendan across for a "chat".

"Brendan, you seem to be morbidly interested in crimes. Is there a problem? I know only too well that books on crime are some of the most popular amongst the public. I love reading them myself. All you have to do to see how popular this stuff is in to look at the programs on TV. A good detective story will always attract excellent audience numbers."

"No, no problem. I just like reading all that stuff. It's like doing maths, for me anyway. Any decent crime has to be well researched. I see myself as a lone criminal, only in theory of course. The "problem" is to commit the crime without being caught, but not just not being caught. The perfect criminal has to commit the crime without even a hint of suspicion being laid at their door. Then it's beautiful, just like the solution to a maths problem."

"Well that's as maybe. I tend to think on a lower level on these matters. Anyway, how is your maths coming along?"

"Okay. Pretty good actually. I've started looking at a problem – a serious problem – to do with branch of geometry, polygons, you know pentagons, hexagons and so on. It was suggested by Dr Ferentes from Bradford University. Well he says it's a serious problem. It's not just an exercise. It's a real problem that's been known for some time but no one has yet managed to solve it. Look at this."

Brendan took a piece of chalk and drew four dots on the blackboard.

"You can put these points anywhere, okay. Now join the dots with straight lines."

Brendan got the triangle and drew the straight lines.

"This is a quadrilateral."

"Yes, I know what one of those is. I'm not that much of a dumbo."

"Okay, this is the last bit, and the most remarkable. You find the mid-point of each of the lines and then join these mid-points with four straight lines, use a different colour chalk, it'll be more obvious. What do you see?"

Mr. Sangster took the triangle and drew the four straight lines which joined the mid-points of the quadrilateral.

"So?" said Mr. Sangster.

"Well, what do you see? Can you not see? It's staring you in the face!"

Mr. Sangster looked and looked. Finally he saw "it".

"Oh God, I've just seen it. That thing I've just drawn is a parallelogram. Is that it? Is that what I'm supposed to 'see'?" said Mr. Sangster.

"That's it. Isn't it remarkable? No matter what four points you choose originally you always end up with a parallelogram."

Mr. Sangster didn't quite see how remarkable this result was.

"Can you explain it to me or would I get lost?"

"Well you said it! I have to learn a lot of maths new to me. It's called Matrix Algebra. Dr Ferentes is teaching me. I see him every two weeks. You see" (but Mr. Sangster didn't see) "this is just the simplest case. Now we have to look at five-sided figures, then six-sided figures and so on. "Look, if you take a five-sided figure – an irregular pentagon – and then join the mid-points, as we've just done then it doesn't work you get nothing 'nice', why? Perhaps we just can't see the 'nice', not yet anyway. That's what we're looking at, that's the problem?"

"Matrix what? Never heard of it. But good luck young man. Let me know if you get anywhere with it. Anyway forget the crime stuff. If you continue this interest in crime then believe me, eventually you'll be tempted to 'have a go' – that's a slippery slope. Get on to the polygons – I'll be much more satisfying in the long-term – you get my drift?"

"Okay, will do."

Except it wouldn't do. Brendan was determined to keep his interest in this area. However, he decided not to share his interests in this area, lest he draw attention to himself.

Chapter 12

ROLLING, ROLLING, ROLLING, RAWHIDE

Brendan had his jobs to do before school which, this being a weekday morning, required him to feed his little zoo of animals: a mouse, soon to be released, a cat that came and went of its own accord, with a friend, usually a bird, a bluebottle held in a blue bottle now deceased and a recent addition, two goldfish. They had acquired this shoal two weeks previously at the town fair. To young Andrejs's delight, Brendan had captured two plastic ducks. The reward was a goldfish for each caught duck. They, the goldfish, went home in a plastic bag. Brendan argued that if they could survive in a plastic bag, they would surely survive in a large flower jug. They were not looking too well. Brendan fed them with lumps of bread and potato skin. They didn't seem to like it.

The two were named Rowdy Yates and Gil Favour after the two stars of his favourite programme, *Rawhide*. Brendan, unusually for a boy of his age, was, for the want of a better phrase, a cowboy freak. His love of all things Western probably derived from his older brother Patrick's interest in Western theme music. This too was odd, to say the least, as they hardly saw each other, Brendan living in Keighley and Patrick back in Ireland. Communication between the two was sparse. Their last encounter was over two years ago. Patrick took Brendan to the cinema to see *Shane*. This film had almost zero sexual content apart from the odd "wistful look" from the female lead, Jean Arthur. Brendan had previous knowledge of this style of acting involving a plateful of papier mâché strawberries. For good measure the next day they went to see *Dr No*. Here there were oodles of sexual content which embarrassed Brendan somewhat, to be sat there, next to his elder brother. He didn't know what to say or do. Ursula Andress (or more realistically "undress") was the female lead, inducing much shifting of seats and clearing of throats in the packed cinema. The male lead – Bond, James Bond – was the only person that Brendan knew who had the same first and last names! The film had a rousing ending with much running and shooting and bombs exploding which allowed testosterone levels to come down to normal before the lights came up. Obviously Bond, James Bond got the girl and saved the world. In the years to follow, Bond, James Bond would get the girl and save the world many times over. Ryan, Brendan Ryan thought he would like to try a bit of world-saving when he got older. But for the moment Ryan, Brendan Ryan would have the settle for a bit part in the "saving the world" stakes.

Brendan's interest in the Western genre continued to the television age. He particularly liked *Rawhide* for its rousing theme song which he knew by heart and which, to the annoyance of his mother, he whistled incessantly. It was his greeting to every new day:

"Rolling, Rolling, Rolling; Rawhide, any kind of weather, dum de dum de dum dum."

He had even got his auntie, an excellent singer, to greet him with 'Do Not Forsake Me, Oh My Darling', the theme from *High Noon*, each time they met, which was at least twice a day as they lived next door.

Auntie Joan would smother Brendan in gifts especially in knitted items. Joan wasn't a real auntie but that didn't matter. Joan's heart was in the right place, like her politics, left of centre, but her prowess in the world of knitting left something to be desired. Often, jumpers would be too short, usually at the back, revealing, for Brendan's taste, far too much "bum". Far too much wind in that area he thought. Out of politeness he rarely said anything hoping his mother might drop a hint or two. When she did finally manage to master the problem of dimensions her choice of colours – pinks, yellows and whites – made Brendan far too conspicuous – more suitable for a Brenda than a Brendan. It was fine for his sisters Anna and Roisin and his year-old brother Andrejs, whose critical faculties were very much still in the formative stage.

The Ryan family was struggling, they were always struggling. They couldn't seem to get ahead, when they did there was always something to knock them back. They were doing the best they could. Generally speaking, despite the hardships, they were a happy bunch, forever optimistic, the "bottle half full" was their approach.

His gang of friends was known as the Rawhide gang. When the gang was first formed, Brendan was known as the Marshall, his next in command was the Sheriff (his closest friend, Eric Bell, who for many years, lived three doors down from him, but now had moved to another part of the town); the others were mere deputies.

They quickly grew out of this close-knit structure. A Marshall wearing 'Auntie Joan' yellow jumpers edged with pink gave somewhat a softer ambience to the gang than they desired. It was hardly cutting edge. However, most of the original members stayed friends and could usually be seen together either playing football during school breaks or, on Saturday mornings, messing around in the town centre. The formal addressing of the gang members with the Western terminology had only lasted a couple of weeks though, from time to time, remnants of the original hierarchy erupted.

Brendan would usually take the lead. On seeing something unusual he would halt the gang, assuming an imaginary position as if seated on a horse, by raising his arm and shouting

"Woah there boy," and then, in a very acceptable Red Indian accent he would say,

"White man speak with forked tongue."

No one quite knew why, having started out as Gil Favour, the boss of the cattle drive, he would immediately take on the persona of the Indian chief Sitting Bull. This cameo routine could be loosely interpreted as "Hey, look at that!" After the matter had been investigated, and if he remembered, he would conclude by saying

"Head em up," and then following a short deliberate silence, which the whole gang respected,

"Move em out."

After that, all sang the words "Rolling, Rolling, Rolling" and then they would revert to some kind of normality. This apparently childish behaviour was surprisingly accepted by this bright group, probably because it was accepted by its brightest member, Brendan, who, they all agreed, was a gifted child.

"Have you done the fish?" his Mother enquired.

"No, but I have fed them," he replied cheekily.

"Do they have a short life? I can't see these two lasting the weekend. Perhaps we can take them back."

"The fair's long gone son. It might be better that we put them down the toilet – at least they'll have their freedom?"

"Yeah, but if we do that they won't be goldfish any more, they'll be more like brownfish, if you catch my drift!"

"Mmm."

The relationship between Brendan and his Ma was generally what one would recognise as holding between old friends, though when the need arose his Ma would take the normal dominant role. There was no hugging and kissing in this family except when directed to Andrejs. (Andreish to his family but "Andrew" to friends). He was of a new generation and, for this boy, new rules and habits would be adopted. Perhaps inevitably though, relations between Ma and Chipry grew cold. Chipry and Ma's relationship was nearing its end. Brendan had seen the signs before. Short-tempered with each other. Disagreements over how the family income should be spent. Disagreements on how Andrejs should be brought up. If that relationship was to fail, then another avenue of support for the Ryans would be effectively closed off. To Brendan, it was inevitable, simply a matter of time.

> When love is young and love is fine,
> it's like a gem when first tis new.
> But love grows old and waxes cold,
> and fades away like the like the morning dew.

There were just too many cultural differences between the two.

Chipry, now responsible for a child of his own, not surprisingly wanted to spend the household income directed more towards his child rather than Ma's children. On a Friday (payday) Chipry would always bring goodies and chocolate bars and an odd bunch of bananas and other fruit, not for general consumption but for Andrejs's, to be rationed throughout the weekend. There was very little jealously between the rest and Andrejs, they long knew how these "rations" would be dished out. Apart from those gifts from a loving father there was no unfairness within this family group. At least Brendan had Chipry as a surrogate dad, a dad, of sorts. Brendan's real dad had long since gone, unable to support his family, he left to inhabit the pubs and bars of Birmingham where he played his fiddle and reminisced about Ireland, the craic and the good old days of long ago. Of necessity Mick used a walking stick to aid a long-injured hip, ignorantly left to fuse rigid. As a younger man he could deal with the affliction but as he got older he became unemployable.

Mick, in all the years of being a father, acknowledged Brendan on just one occasion with two ten-pound notes stuck inside a birthday card. Despite the scarcity of meetings and communications, Brendan loved and respected his father and wouldn't have a word said against him. He never bad-mouthed him. Brendan was mature enough to realise how difficult life was and that sometimes the "cards" that were dealt were unplayable. He thought his father's hand of cards fell into that category. Brendan did have a dad, well in his own mind he had a dad, it was just that he was far away.

In the home, without a male role model at hand, and despite his age, Brendan took the lead in many ways. His mother had had a lifetime of stress and was happy to see Brendan take over. Quite simply, she was tired. Brendan was a perceptive child more than aware of his mother's trials and tribulations. Brendan wasn't an angel, far from it, but from time to time he would try to lessen his mother's great burden of raising four children, on her own, in a foreign land amongst a people that still treated the "oirish" as dogs. What would George Bernard Shaw or James Joyce or Oscar Wilde or William Hamilton (the Irish Newton) or a hundred other poets, writers and scientists have thought?

However, though the "big" decisions would be a matter of discussion between Ma and Brendan, when it came to a matter of personal hygiene Ma was still "top dog".

"Oh look," she said in pretence of puzzlement.

"I wonder what this could be for?" she said, throwing a comb in his direction.

"It's a comb mother. It's for combing the hair," he replied even more cheekily, putting great emphasis on the words "comb" and "combing".

"Oh well! You can show me how it's used then can't you?"

"Well of course I'll show you. It's not a difficult tool to use and, with some practice, even someone of your age and disability will eventually get the hang of it. Now pay attention and watch me very, very carefully. As you will no doubt know I'm an expert in the matter of hair cuisine. You could learn a lot from me!"

He followed her around the room using a deliberately slow combing action mouthing the word "comb" each time he did so. She was struggling not to laugh out loud. Eventually she conceded his prowess in this wordplay with a forced,

"Ha, ha, ha. You've got a tongue on you that could clip a hedge. Enough joking now time's getting on!"

Throughout this little cameo he would adopt a thick rural Irish accent keeping Ma in stitches.

The general good feeling between the two continued through breakfast. To call it breakfast is not really the appropriate term unless you call a cup of sweet tea, dunked with bread, breakfast. No full English, no poached kipper, no kedgeree.

The other three would be presented with porridge, they'd eat it if they were hungry.

Eventually it was time for Brendan to go. She pressed half a crown into his hand and brushed his hair back from his forehead.

"That's your dinner money. Work hard – it's important."

After the umpteenth time of being told "It's important" he knew what that meant. He ruffled his hair back into "ruff" and got his school bags together.

Although the meagre income into Brendan's household justified a claim for free school meals, his mother would not make him endure that stigma. She had suffered many indignities in her own schooldays and was determined, despite the difficulties, that her own child would not be subjected to similar treatment.

"By the way, this thing I'm doing with Bradford University, you've not to let anyone know. It's embarrassing when you tell people and it might lead nowhere. You know I don't like to count my chickens before they're hatched. I haven't told you but Dr Ferentes is trying to get some money for me – a grant of some sort, he doesn't know when it'll come through, if it comes through at all. Apparently he knows a couple of people who like to support students from a poor background, you know, kids who are good at maths but can't afford things. I think if I get a grant it'll be money to be spent on books, pens and paper. I don't think it can be used to get clothes or money for the gas or electric. I have to sit a couple of exams, well not exams but apparently, they give me a few topics, maths stuff and I'm to talk about them, just talk about them. I've done one of these so far. It was on Euclid's book that Mr. Sangster let me have. I think I did okay, but you can never tell. They can give you stuff to talk about that you haven't heard anything about before and you only have a week to prepare – that'll be difficult, but what can you do. I'll try my best, but don't get your hopes up, my best mightn't be good enough. I'm good at maths but I don't think I'm that good. Anyway, I might be good this year but I might be poor next year, I don't know how it works. Anyway we'll see. But don't tell people, please don't tell anyone. Let's see how it goes – agreed?"

"Agreed, you're the one that's doing it. I think you're doing brilliantly, however it turns out."

"Now don't forget what I've taught you about combing! See ya Ma," he shouted as he pulled the door closed behind him.

Chapter 13

THE DRAUGHTSMAN'S APPRENTICE

When Brendan was fourteen, Ma and Chipry separated. Ma and the kids moved out to occupy an almost new council house with front, back and side gardens – a semi- at 64 North Dene Avenue. For the first time in her life she and the rest of the family enjoyed a bathroom and, joy of joys, an indoor lavatory. No more frozen arses, no more Latvian squares as reading material.

There was heartache of course, centred round their son Andrejs. Clearly, he would live with Ma, there was no way Chipry could look after a young child. To begin with Andrejs made regular visits to Chipry, usually on a Sunday morning. Brendan generally accompanied Andrejs. After all, Brendan got on well with Chipry and Brendan would never forget the support he received over the years of living at Bengal Street. It was a relationship rather like grandfather to grandson.

They would have a mug of sweet tea and Andrejs would be inundated with chocolate and sweets. Brendan was rarely jealous; he understood the psychology of what was going on. Plain and simple, Andrejs was seeing Chipry less and less, he was "leaving", perhaps not immediately, but dragged out over a number of months, perhaps years. Chipry knew this as well as Brendan, the gifts were there to try and stave off the inevitable. Brendan was particularly sorry for Chipry – he had a son in Latvia and he had a son in England and would soon be estranged to both of them. How cruel life can be.

Brendan loved the new house. It was warm and modern. In that summer every day seemed idyllic – the weather was fine day after day. On this particular day it was one of those very warm July days. The warmth was there, even early in the morning, as Brendan made his way downstairs rubbing the sleep from his eyes. He would doze for another hour in front of Breakfast TV before he would wake properly.

Four miles away, over the dual-carriageway which split the town in two, in the single-bedroomed flat at 28 Derwent Drive, Mr. Sangster was also getting ready for school. This was his fourth day on his own having left his wife, on the previous Saturday, after six difficult years of marriage. He was twenty-seven years old and was temporarily depressed, realising he would have to start all over again. Well not quite all over again – he did at least have his matching bookcases (antique pine, pleasantly edged and suitably "stressed"); his classical music collection (almost all on tape); his virtuoso violin (an excellent machine-made French instrument in the style of Guaneri); and all their pictures (two very fine drawings, five moderate paintings and numerous prints). Unfortunately, he had failed to come away from the marriage with any books of note; didn't manage to take the tape player, nor his chromatic tuner and failed, in his rush to escape, to bring any picture hooks with him.

His flat had only a small two-ringed cooker so, apart from boiling eggs for breakfast, he had for the last four days existed on sandwiches and a takeaway curry. He had by now realised that more than one towel might be useful as he dried his face on kitchen paper. But his salary was due on Friday and he would be able to stock up then. Meantime he would have to bear the slight inconvenience of not being able to wash properly and of spending his evenings looking at four walls and contemplating his future.

His alarm clock reminded him with a *pip, pip; pip, pip* that it was time to go. He threw his bag over his shoulder, locked the door behind him and fetched the bike from the shed at the rear. Yes, his wife had managed to keep the car as well. Still, on a fine day like this, it was going to be a pleasant cycle to school and that cheered him considerably. His drop-handlebar bicycle was old and little used, designed more for speed than for comfort. On this bright summer morning Mr. Sangster enjoyed the ride and was happy to coast much of the way. He arrived ten minutes later than usual and parked his bike outside the already full bike shed, walked rather gingerly and stiffly, surreptitiously adjusting his underwear as he went, through the yard and made his way to his classroom. There he was met, as usual, by his class monitor.

"Good morning Brendan."

"Good morning Sir."

"There's nothing to do today. You can push off if you want."

Brendan didn't need much encouragement and began to leave before Mr. Sangster changed his mind.

"Oh Brendan."

Brendan stopped in his tracks. "Oops. Now what have I done?" he whispered to himself.

"I'm sorry. I forgot about your birthday. I've been a tad busy recently. Here's a little present for you."

Mr. Sangster chucked him a Mars bar from his lunch box.

"Oh thanks a lot," said Brendan with genuine surprise.

He left for the second time somewhat embarrassed. Mr. Sangster quickly consumed his other Mars bar as he moved toward the window.

From his elevated position – his classroom was on the first floor – he watched his colleagues arrive; some on bikes, one or two on foot, but mostly they arrived in cars. His eyes relaxed into the distance and his mind drifted into his recent past. He indulged in self-pity for a few moments and, almost inevitably, tears filled his eyes. However difficult his marriage might have been, the thought of being alone was not one he wanted to contemplate for long. His over-emotional state quickly dissipated and his eyes began to re-focus on the real world. In through the gates his eyes followed, blinking through the tears, the progress of a Caribbean-blue Metro. When it finally parked, out stepped the Head of English, a petite, neatly dressed woman some six years older than he. This was Elizabeth, his estranged wife. His heartbeat quickened considerably as he watched her collect her case and lock the door. It almost stopped as he gasped for air, his attention drawn to the passenger side. Out stepped Frank Sutton, deputy head of English, and well known ladies' man. They giggled and laughed together as they walked into the staff room. Mr. Sangster's palpitations were slow to disappear. However, his concern over his personal problems would, temporarily, be subsumed by the more immediate worry of crowd control. His classroom began to fill.

He took the register first. There was no assembly today. Instead, form teachers would have to focus the kids' attention on a proverb or saying chosen from a selection of 300. Mr. Sangster began to speak with his authoritative voice that all recognised immediately as the signal for them to stop what they were doing and to come to order.

"Okay, okay. Settle down now. We'd better start. Louise – give me a number from one to three hundred."

By now the class all knew the routine. Louise stopped chewing and shouted out the number 73. Mr. Sangster turned to page 4 of his booklet, picked up his chalk and began to write proverb 73 on the board.

Never do anything by halves

he wrote in his rather ornate writing style. He allowed the children a few moments' thought.

"Any ideas as to what this means?" he asked.

After a long embarrassed silence Brendan, as usual, was the first to participate.

Brendan said it was the same as being killed for a sheep as a lamb. This contribution, involving as it did soft furry animals, rather confused the class as many then thought that *halves* had been misspelt and should have read *calves* which, to some degree, were also soft and furry.

Louise, seeing an opportunity to impress, then said, with only the merest hint of a smirk that the proverb should read *Never do anything to calves.* Before Mr. Sangster could intervene Fiona, who had a marked stutter, then rose enthusiastically and explained, eventually, that we shouldn't do anything to harm calves but should wait for them to grow up before they were killed. Mr. Sangster had long been encouraging Fiona to get more involved in class discussions and didn't have the heart to stop her mid-discourse. However, his patience quickly evaporated when Dominic, normally an attentive rather studious boy, mishearing Fiona's contribution, focussing on the word *killed*, extrapolated wildly and said that the proverb meant that war was bad and that the Russians shouldn't invade other countries. Now even Mr. Sangster was confused.

"What?" he said, losing control.

Dominic confidently expanded on his theme.

"All those Slavs being killed in Czechoslovakia by the Russians."

"No, no! No!" Mr. Sangster said exasperatedly. "Never do anything to halves."

Now even Mr. Sangster was making mistakes. He immediately corrected himself.

"No, no, I mean never do anything by halves. This is the proverb. Never do anything by halves," he repeated.

He thought he'd not risk any further misinterpretation and drew the discussion to a close.

"Okay you may as well go to your first class – I'll see you back here after break for geography."

They trooped out and he and Brendan, who, as monitor, was always last to leave, exchanged a knowing nod and smile, as they passed and shared the humour of the failed discussion on the day's proverb.

"Don't forget Brendan – whatever you do always give it one hundred per cent."

"Yes sir – you won't catch me doing anything to calves," laughing as he walked through the door.

"Oh God, I nearly forgot. I need to speak to you. I can't believe I nearly forgot! Forget your first lesson, we have a more important task. Slightly embarrassing. I'm not sure how to approach this. Let's be direct. You do tech drawing don't you?"

"Yes, next to maths it's my best subject, I really look forward to it. Drawing stuff. Drawing solid objects as they intersect with other solid objects. I seem to be the only one who can do it properly. When you finish off a drawing, front elevation, side elevation and plan, it's so satisfying. Everything is important, even the shape of arrowheads used to label dimensions."

"Yes, well it's not about the subject, it's more to do with the administration, you know, how the lessons are organised."

"Oh, I think I know what this is about. It's about the tea, isn't it?"

"Yes, how did you know?"

"Well, it's crazy and embarrassing. It's got to be that that you want to talk about. For the last four weeks Mr. Wood has singled me out. It's a double lesson and towards the end of the first hour he brings me a cup of tea. Tea in a cup with a saucer. I know I'm the best in the class and I am seated next to his desk, but this is funny peculiar! He comes over and takes the 'order'. Do you take milk, sugar? I don't know what to say. I drink them but I feel very uncomfortable, the rest of the class think it's hilarious – he's not done anything – if you get my drift, but where will this end. I don't think it's right, but I don't want to complain too much either. I know what happens in these cases, the bloke gets sacked. And he's a good teacher – that wouldn't be right, would it?"

"Well now that you've told me, it corroborates what we already know. If it's any consolation you're not the only one. There's one other boy who's treated in this way, he's a couple of years older. Look, this is confidential, there's a problem with Mr. Wood. You won't know this but before the Easter break Mr. Wood's son died in a road accident, he was only sixteen. He was riding pillion, the rider lost control, went straight into a tree. He was advised to take time off work but he thought it better to keep busy. The school was happy to accede not realising that there was a 'problem'."

"Oh, I see. I understand. The man is ill."

"Look, Brendan, take the rest of the day off, I'll square it with your teachers. I know you have a double in tech drawing at the end of the day. I need to speak to the head. Come back tomorrow, as usual, will you?"

Brendan, now concerned for Mr. Wood, spoke up.

"Look, what's wrong with a cup of tea once a week? There's no harm. He's a great teacher. I don't mind if you just want to leave things as they are – if it helps?"

"Well that's very generous of you Brendan, but modern life is not like that. There's been a complaint, got to be investigated. There are bits of paper to fill in, there are sensitivities to be dealt with, we've got to make sure our students are 'safe', if you know what I mean. If I'm any judge, he'll be given three months off. He'll get back on an even keel and all will be right with the world. I think all he wants is a big hug, o'course he wants his son back, but he's not stupid, that's not going to happen. I think in some small way he regarded you and the other lad as the son he lost. He'll recover. He'll be fine."

Brendan got his coat and made his way home. After about a hundred yards he turned back, back into school and into the tech drawing room. Mr. Wood was there sat alone in his office. Brendan stood there a while not knowing what to do. He was only a kid. Even so he wanted to do or say something of comfort to the poor man. Brendan knocked on the door and entered.

"Brendan. You'll be getting a new teacher from next week. I'm going off for a while. You're good at tech drawing. Keep it up will you. It'll be a shame to let it go."

He looked at Mr. Wood. He didn't know what to say, but thought he ought to say something. Brendan nodded and smiled. He said nothing.

Brendan couldn't meet him eye to eye. Mr. Wood didn't say anything. He too just nodded. Brendan left for a second time.

Mr. Wood did take three months leave of absence. But shortly after his return to teaching duties he left. He got a job as a draughtsman. He couldn't handle being around youngsters any more. Brendan moved away from "male" endeavours – metalwork, woodwork and tech drawing – and moved to domestic science.

Brendan was now accepted as English. He was now, to a large extent, on a level playing field. The "Glin" effect had almost worn away. He and his family were still poor, very poor, which severely restricted the avenues open to them. Brendan knew that despite all his efforts he and his siblings were looking at low-level careers. The girls were looking at mill work at best, though Roisin might possibly succeed, though in her case success might mean attracting a good husband. She was and would remain for a while under the influence of her elder sister. Though still very young with many hurdles to jump, Andrejs stood the best chance of improvement. He didn't disappoint. From an early age he was showing strong signs of "normality". He had a fair group of friends and interests. He was interested in English and in the "arts" – he was often chosen to play the lead in school plays. He looked a strong candidate as a fine artist. Recently one of his drawings was described by his Art teacher as the finest drawing she had ever seen! Of course these things have to be taken with a pinch of salt. "There was many a slip twixt cup and lip." Still, he had his father to support him, at least financially. From a family point of view that "project" appeared to be going well.

Despite his strong potential, Brendan could look forward to a career as a draughtsman, or a cashier at a bank or clerical work of some kind. Even this would be regarded as success in his family, but not to Brendan. His ambitions were far greater than that. For the moment he would bide his time. Like Chipry before him he also would work like a Trojan. Despite the loss of the Irish accent, which had gone before his eighth birthday, he was still deeply Irish. Brian Boru Irish. Irish to the bone. Ma continued singing the Irish ballads, she'd even encouraged Brendan to learn them too. She would still listen to Radio Eireann, and on many occasions would be found dancing a leg at the music.

At the end of that summer, disappointment followed disappointment. The University of Bradford benefactors recognised Brendan's mathematical skills as being in the "gifted" category, but with many similar applicants appealing for limited funds they felt others were in greater need. They would look at his case once more in a year's time.

Mr. Sangster moved schools. For all the time that Brendan was in Eastwood Mr. Sangster was Brendan's champion, and it was a major blow to Brendan's academic future that he was no longer involved. The relationship with Bradford University lapsed and, for one reason or another, Brendan now found himself directing his own research in mathematics. Without strong direction academic success could hardly be guaranteed, his interest would likely wither and die. Brendan had no idea what was significant, what was not significant. He didn't have access to textbooks or to relevant research journals and he was far too shy to ask. He had one problem, the Polygon Problem, which continued to attract him. Until he knew better he would pursue this until he could solve it. To solve a problem that remained unsolved for many years would make his reputation, at least it would open doors, what he would make with what he found beyond the doors was down to him.

From time to time his family were informed (through school reports, and "parents evening") that Brendan was "bright" or "gifted". "He's got a great future." However, when it came down to it all he had to show for it, as far as his family was concerned, was that he was incredibly fast when dealing with darts scores, which only involved subtraction of whole numbers. This was simple arithmetic but magical to the outside world, as if it was an important talent.

Inside, also, he knew he was still a thief, prepared to practise his art if given half a chance. With money now being scarce again Brendan's thoughts were once more veering off in that direction.

Society abhorred a thief but Brendan took a different view, the moral position wasn't clear cut. Thieving went on all the time, in different guises. Wouldn't a starving man steal food, and who would blame him? Stealing from the rich to give to the poor, is, apparently, acceptable, but somehow stealing from the rich to keep is not acceptable. In Brendan's mind the moral position followed a fine line. He kept his views to himself. Others would feel threatened if they knew that Brendan would happily steal from them. Yet and yet Brendan wouldn't contemplate, for one second, claiming for himself the mathematical results that others had obtained. Academic "thieving" would never be contemplated. The academic world held strict moral positions on properly attributing the work of others. Brendan would always adhere to this position. In fact, anyone breaking this long held rule would be ostracised by the scientific community. Once you lost your reputation in this manner it would never be recovered.

Chapter 14

HEY MISTER POSTMAN, LOOK AND SEE…

The distance between Chipry's house at 27 Bengal Street and Ma's house at 64 North Dene Avenue was over a mile and a half. It was half that distance if you were prepared to go along two snickets, down the side of an allotment and over a small field. You wouldn't go the short way if it was at all wet or damp – you'd get soaked going through the field. In either case it was hardly a short walk between the two.

As the months passed by Andrejs's visits to his father, as predicted, became more and more irregular. Every excuse would be employed for not making the visit. If the weather looked dark and foreboding then the journey wouldn't take place. Sometimes Andrejs would even feign illness to avoid going. At the end, Andrejs stopped visiting altogether. To compensate, Chipry would make the odd unscheduled visit to see his son, roughly once a month. Despite Andrejs's lack of enthusiasm to visit his father, Brendan continued with fortnightly visits over the next few years. Sometimes he would bring a helping of salted herring or herring in oil, if he could afford the extra cost, or a portion of poppy seed cake. Brendan had often, with Chipry, visited the Polish deli where these delicacies could be found. Brendan couldn't stomach the fish but loved the seed cake. As well as the "goodies" (bags of sweets and fruit to be relayed back to Andrejs) Brendan would be offered a small glass of the "yellow shite".

"No way, no thank you, even for old time's sake." They laughed.

Brendan made as best an attempt as he could in keeping the conversation going but it was a struggle. The generation gap and the language barrier were just too large to traverse. The visits were characterised by long silences or discussion of the same topic over and over. Even Brendan's visits were becoming more and more irregular. But it wasn't entirely Brendan's fault. By the time Andrejs stopped going Chipry had slowed considerably, he was less secure on his feet and generally less alert. Senility was burrowing its evil way through his body.

Brendan made the odd unscheduled visit – these were the ones he would have to make to borrow money. Brendan was the go-between. These money transactions would usually occur on Sunday evening when Ma would discover that the Bank of Bingo swallowed too much of the green stuff. She had no money left for the week ahead or for the gas fire, which functioned on a pay-as-you-go meter. These visits were embarrassing affairs on both sides. Chipry would know immediately whether the visit was an "I want to borrow some money" visit. Brendan couldn't come straight out and ask for half a crown or a pound, the niceties had to be observed. There was much conversation first and then after half an hour or so Brendan would ask the question.

"Can Ma borrow a pound or half a crown? She needs it for the gas."

There followed Chipry's head-shaking routine and much moralising before he took his purse from his back pocket. He counted out the appropriate amount and handed it to Brendan. A few more words in reprimand were to be delivered to Ma from Chipry that Ma should get into this predicament. Brendan could do nothing but agree. Brendan knew that without Chipry's help his family would have sunk. At the moment they were hanging by a thread. At each of these occasions Brendan would return home promising, when he was famous, to tell the world what a great man Chipry was. Kids always make these promises, they weren't promises, they were more like prayers. As he walked home with Chipry's money in his pocket, he would say "thank you" on every step back to his house.

The Ryans struggled forward in time from one embarrassing episode to another. To Brendan's annoyance, Ma couldn't seem to deal with organising income and expenditure. In his early teens Ma still held the reins in the family and no amount of wise counsel from Brendan would change that.

About this time Ma received a letter from Ireland.

"Will you look at this!" It was a rare event for Ma to receive a letter – it was usually a bill. This was hand-written and had a small green Irish stamp. Inside, wrapped neatly inside the letter was a ten-pound note, in Irish money.

"Who's it from Ma?" said Brendan excitedly. It was from Cormac.

"Cormac? You mean our Cormac? What's he say?"

"Get my glasses will you?" said Ma, wary, thinking some disaster must have occurred.

> Dear Ma, Just a note to say I'm okay and I hope you are in fine fettle as I am here. Please say hello to the lads. I miss them. I hope you can say sorry to Brendan.

"After all this time. Are you sure it's Cormac? Let me look!"

"It's his signature at the bottom and it's sent to me so wait till I've read it." Ma continued from where she left off.

> Sorry to Brendan. Back then I was stupid wild. I live in our old house as Da has gone off to Birmingham. I'm here with brother Thomas. He's farming with the Browns. He's away in the week but back for Saturday and Sunday. He doesn't like it but it pays for his food and drink and stuff. I have landed on my feet and have a great job at the quarry – you know the one, about a couple of miles up past the big house. I have a pushbike to get me there and back, it's okay, really good. They say there's plenty work for the next twenty years at least. I'm trying to get Tom in here but there's loads wanting jobs.

> I hear I have a little brother. I'd like to see him sometime. They

have trained me up in using dumper trucks and giant excavators. I learnt some of this when I was in Birmingham, ye know, on the buildings. That's how I got the job here. In a couple of months' time I'm to be sent on a course up in Donegal on using dynamite!!! – it might be with those IRA boys – joke!

I might be able to send a bit of money then but you know the Irish – all gob, all show!

Well, I'll say goodbye.

Your loving Son

Cormac.

By the way I hear Brendan is good at the sums – good luck to him, Didn't I know he always had brains to burn.

"Will you look at that. A letter from Cormac, and a nice one too," said Ma. Brendan read it through a couple of times.

"Aye, it's a nice letter all right. Fair play. Good for him. Good for him. He's a tough character you know – tough to know what he's thinking." A feeling of pride came over Ma and Brendan, that, even after all the time since he left, he could say sorry.

"Well, he wrote the letter, and a nice one too. Should I write back Brendan?"

"You can at least thank him for the money. Give him a chance Ma. He sounds as if he's turned a corner. Everybody needs a chance."

"You're right son. He's had it hard. Well you've all had it hard. I know that. Glin an' all. I'll send him a picture of Andrejs, you and the lads."

Brendan thought to himself.

"If I had that dynamite I know what I'd blow up." Visions of Glin raced through his mind. He had to leave the room, he was close to tears. Brendan often thought that he was "finished" with Glin, but no, something would bring it roaring back into his thoughts. He was still vulnerable to its long tentacles.

She wrote back but it was over a year that Cormac wrote again.

Ma continued to gamble. It was too late for Ma to become sensible, the attractions of gambling were just too great. She wanted to win "big" to save the family, to pay back what she put them through. Ma became a Bingo and slot machine slave and continued to be so for the rest of her life.

By the time Brendan was sixteen he had almost caught up, academically, from the disastrous start he had to endure at Glin. There were no books at home so all the information he obtained came from comics, the *News of the World* or listening to *The Archers* on Radio 4. Failing the 11-plus led him to spend a year in a Secondary Modern Catholic school but, after a year there, due to the insistence of Ma, he was transferred to Eastwood School – a Church of England School. These schools had textbooks on woodwork or metalwork but nothing on Shakespeare. There were no art appreciation lessons. The teachers too were poor quality, certainly not inspiring. His best subject was mathematics – he didn't need to be widely read to cope and more than cope with that subject. At his secondary modern school he was already outpacing some of the teachers. Peripatetic support was organised every two weeks. He loved Euclidean geometry and the Calculus. He didn't properly understand the Calculus but he knew how to "do" it and how to use it in different applications. He realised he was "different" from his peers.

His social life was non-existent – in his mind he was too poor to have friends or girlfriends. He would be far too embarrassed to bring a girl home to their poorly furnished house. He "knew" it would be like this till he left home and enjoyed a decent income. He would just have to get his head down and, for the moment, stick with academia – it looked as if it was the best option for the moment. He ploughed on and made progress in many different directions. In class tests he would now regularly come first or second in every subject.

Chapter 15

OPPORTUNITY KNOCKS

Towards the end of the academic year an opportunity occurred, which would make him choose between taking the traditional road to adulthood or to take Robert Frost's advice:

I shall be telling this with a sigh
Somewhere ages and ages hence:
Two roads diverged in a wood, and I,
I took the one less traveled by,
And that has made all the difference.

Brendan was not for reading poetry but Frost's particular observation seemed to come to the fore from time to time in his particular journey through life.

On this fateful day he would have to choose. It would be a hard choice.

It was the second lesson of the day, the teacher, Mrs. Smith and the whole class were engaged in Geography, in particular how the contour curves could be used to work out the steepness of the terrain. A loud knock at the classroom door brought the class to attention.

In came the deputy head Mr. Feather and a visitor holding a violin.

"Oh, gosh, I am sorry…completely forgotten," said Mrs. Smith.

The deputy head introduced the visitor.

"Good morning everyone. I'd like to introduce Mark Gibbons. Mark is the senior luthier at Sharples & Son. Do you know what a luthier is?"

There was no response.

"Well the violin should have given you a clue. A luthier is a maker of instruments and Mark is a specialist in making violins. Mark is here to describe a fantastic opportunity for one of you. He's looking for an apprentice." A buzz of excitement went round the class. Apprenticeships were much sought after, particularly by those in secondary modern schools whose job prospects, compared to students from technical schools or grammar schools, were poor. Mark moved forward and addressed the class.

"Hello. You all know what a violin is? Yes? Violins have been made in this form for at least three hundred years – around 1680." Mark walked round the classroom showing the violin. He played it like a guitar and then he got his bow, wound it taut and played something a good deal faster.

"You will all probably know that violins were made by someone called Stradivarius. Yes? Well he didn't make that many – I think just over one hundred and twenty in his lifetime. In all that time many were destroyed in fires, kept in private collections or severely damaged in one way or another. Our job is to make new violins that sound just as good as a strad. I make violins, but I need help, so today I am looking for just one person who thinks they might be able to help. It's a proper apprenticeship. The money is reasonable – never mind once a week, you'll be able to go to the pictures twice a week!" (Brendan thought with a wry smile: *I can't afford to go once a month, let alone twice a week.*) "Okay I want you to stand up if you're interested in this apprenticeship?"

About three quarters of the class stood up, mostly boys.

"Okay, that's brilliant. Keep standing if you will. Now to make violins you have to be musical. No point making a violin, or any instrument, if you can't tell whether it's in tune or not. If you are not musical, if you can't sing a simple song in tune, like, for example can you sing the national anthem? If you can't you may as well sit back down. I was trained as a musician, but wasn't considered good enough on music alone. That's a tough career. However, I found that I had a talent for craftwork. Making a violin is craftwork of the highest order. Being musical doesn't fall to everybody; it's a very magical gift, once musical, always musical."

About half slumped back in their chairs. Brendan stayed put. He thought he had music "in him". He knew Ma was musical, as was his father, so he too was likely to be musical. He knew the scales, and as a young child he often sung along with his mother, singing in Gaelic, but to him it was just sounds.

"Good, good. Okay now you have to be able to sing a song on your own. For example, if I strummed the notes to 'Frère Jacques' could you sing along?" Over half of the remainder of those standing decided they couldn't sing on their own. They sat down too. There were just six people left standing including Brendan. By this time all the girls had sat down. The remainder, to Brendan's knowledge, were quite well-to-do which, to some extent, he found intimidating. He thought all eyes were on him. They could see his raggedy wool-based school blazer and his off-white nylon shirt threadbare with washing. Could they also see his shiny trousers patched and darned at the knee, his cheap grey socks and the hole in his shoe? It seemed like an age standing there. Could they see his house and his orange boxes they said he sat on? Could they see, surely they could, the greasy cooker, the overgrown grass? Brendan was sure they could see it all, he was sure they could see his whole history unfold; but despite the embarrassment he stood his ground.

"Now, now for the real test. Those of you left standing have to be able to sing the scales perfectly, without accompaniment, you know doh ray me fah so la tee doh and so on. Okay," he pointed to Ray Fields, "can you start? "Ray thought about it for a while but decided that that would be too embarrassing. He sat down as did the next three. It was between Brendan and Jonathan Meers. Both Jonathan and Brendan sang the scales pretty well though Jonathan had not quite the control that Brendan displayed.

"Okay, both of you, pretty good. Fine. To separate you two I'm going to ask you to sing a song without music, this is called a cappella. Can you both come to the front? Let's make a proper competition out of this. "Both lads walked to the front. Pointing at Jonathan, Mark asked,

"Would you mind going first?" Then he thought again.

"No, no, sorry. I think to be fair we ought to toss a coin." Brendan called correctly and beckoned to Jonathan to go first.

"Sorry, I can't think of a song, sorry, my mind's gone blank," said Jonathan.

Mr. Feather intervened.

"Surely you can think of something. What about a Beatles song…say, what is it mmm, 'I Wanna Hold Your Hand'?"

"Okay, okay. I know that one." Jonathan started to sing but paused after a few words, his voice was breaking up. He couldn't breathe. He started again with the same result. A glass of water was offered but it didn't help.

"That, Jonathan, is called stage fright. I've seen this many times. You've done pretty well though, thing is your voice box is affected by stress. Come on, let's give him a hand."

Mr. Feather led a round of applause. The class responded with a weak show of support. Somewhat reluctantly he returned to his seat.

"Okay, representing Ireland, it's Brendan. Your turn lad. What you gonna sing? 'Danny Boy'? 'Galway Bay'?" A few giggles went round the class.

"'Roisin Dubh', it's in the Irish, it means 'The Black Rose'."

"C'mon now. Let's give him some quiet."

"Can you give me a 'C' ?" asked Brendan.

Mark plucked one of the strings and, thinking to trick him, he played a 'D'.

"No, no a 'C' please – a 'D' would be far too high for me!" Brendan said with some authority.

"Good, you saw through that. Very good," said Mark.

Brendan nodded in approval, hummed along with the note until he had it in his mind. He stopped humming, cleared his throat and hung his arms straight down as if to attention and began to sing without any nerves whatsoever. Brendan sang the Gaelic version. None of the class, including Brendan, could understand a word of the song (he had long ago lost the "Irish"). But everyone could hear the beauty and emotion of the song. He sang out loudly, sweetly, with confidence. He sang like a professional. Classes nearby pricked up their ears and listened too. Their teachers came to the door to better hear. As with many Irish ballads the first stanza started quietly, making those who listened just struggle that little bit to hear. Their attention was now focused entirely on the song. The volume rising to a crescendo as Brendan, now fully opening his lungs, started on the chorus. He finished silently, quietly. For two or three seconds no one said a word. No round of applause but a great banging of tables and desks.

"Woah, wow, some song, brilliant Brendan, brilliant. Where the hell did that come from? You never told us about that! What's it about. It was like opera – couldn't understand a word but lovely to listen to, absolutely lovely. What's it about?"

"Dunno. I think it's about freedom sir – the rose stands for Ireland. My Ma taught me it a long time ago. I thought I'd forgotten it but it was easy, it just came flooding back. I don't know what the words stand for." His voice began to tremble. Brendan took a deep breath to control the emotion. He quickly wiped away a single tear.

"My word young man, but you have a voice in you. Yep, nice song, very nice, really very well sung. Now let's get back to the apprenticeship. Can you tell me anything about the violin?" asked Mark.

"My father made violins sir, you know, ordinary sort of violins, they weren't brilliant but they played okay. He once made a metal one, after a fashion, and was a decent player, ya know, in pubs and stuff. It was in his blood, playing traditional stuff, he couldn't read music but he could certainly play by 'ear'. Play a tune a couple of times and he would have it."

Brendan asked Mark for the violin.

"What do I know about fiddles? I know the belly is made of pine, slow growing Swiss pine so you get these very fine growth rings. It's cut from the tree in such a way that you get two identical pieces, I think it's called 'on the quarter'." Brendan showed the class what he meant.

"The same with the back though some backs can be made with a single piece of wood. The back is made of a denser wood, twice the weight of the belly. I've forgotten what the wood for the back is. I know it's made of twenty-seven pieces, separate pieces, glued together with animal glue – there's not a bit of metal in the violin, not a bit, well, apart from the strings. Nowadays the strings are metal."

Mark was genuinely surprised with Brendan's response.

"Where did you get all that knowledge from?"

"There's a book on violin-making in the library of the school. It was left here by a previous member of staff when he retired."

"Impressive. Can you give me your name and address? No promises. I have other schools to visit. I'll let you know in a day or so. I'm very interested though, very interested young man. I don't mind saying you shocked me today. And I'm not often shocked."

Brendan returned to his seat. As the class ended, four of his class, including the class bully, which was a surprise, came to Brendan and patted him on the back. He knew them all. They were all Irish lads acting like English boys. For that twenty minutes they were proud to be Irish again. After that performance Brendan gained an admiring respect throughout the school.

Brendan heard nothing for three weeks. Indeed, Brendan had forgotten about the whole business. That is, until a letter arrived on the doorstep addressed to Master Brendan Ryan. He was invited to go for an interview to Sharples & Son for the position of apprentice to the master violin maker, Mr. Mark Gibbons. Needless to say, Brendan attended the interview. Somehow or another Ma and Brendan managed to borrow a bit of money to buy a better quality blazer, some decent trousers and some shoes, mostly from charity shops. Brendan went to see Chipry himself and asked for a loan of ten pounds. After he explained what the money was for Chipry gave him the money and said, and he was very clear about this, it was a gift not a loan. His English had not improved much in the year or so since they had last met.

"For all fishes you bring me, for give little Andrejs to me so often times." For the first time in their lives they shook hands. Chipry then brought out a half empty bottle of "yellow shite". He poured the fluid into two small glasses, more for holding whisky than for under-matured beer. They clinked glasses, shouted "prosit" and downed the lot in one go. Brendan only coughed once. They shook hands again and then Brendan left.

Chapter 16

POOR FINANCES: A SOLUTION COMES INTERVIEW

For the first time since his confirmation ceremony, Brendan felt smart. He looked the part. Nonetheless, he was still very nervous. He didn't know what the other candidates were like. The interview was short. Mark Gibbons had seen enough. Brendan was offered the job.

"You looked worried. I can tell you now Mr. Ryan, you were the only candidate. Others I'd interviewed at schools just didn't come up to the mark."

"That's quite a responsibility then."

Though he accepted the offer there and then he was in two minds. He couldn't start till after the summer holidays so he did have some time to think about it. Should he take the path less travelled or play safe, stay at school, complete his education, perhaps even try to go to university? Still there was a great deal of pressure to contribute to the family finances now that Ma was on her own again; now with Andrejs – Chipry's son – Roisin and Brendan. Anna had moved away, still in Keighley but now ensconced with the boyfriend's family. To Ma's annoyance Anna was now supporting some other family. Ma's entire income was supplemented through the state in a small way, by what Brendan earned through his Saturday job at the town's delicatessen and by a couple of paper rounds. Roisin couldn't earn for another four years and Andrejs would have to wait at least eight years. Yes, there was some pressure on his decision. On the advice of poet Robert Frost, Brendan decided to take the path less travelled and became an apprentice to Mark Gibbons. For the time being it was way outside his comfort zone.

He did, however, place a range of bets on his future by attending night school to study English. To attend university he would need an English qualification. Luckily the requirement to have Latin was recently dropped by most universities, especially the new ones. He saw a glimmer of hope in that direction.

However, let there be no doubt, Brendan was still interested in stealing but had not done much in the last five years. He simply didn't have the time or the opportunity. Stealing, if you don't want to get caught, is a time consuming operation. Done properly it's like a career, but it's like a career you don't want anybody to know about. It's to do with risk of capture against benefit obtained. The family's finances were in dire shape. In fact, they had been in dire shape for the whole of Brendan's life. Brendan's mind began, once more, to drift in the direction of thieving. At the outset there were no obvious items at Sharples & Son that you might steal. All the violins were accounted for on each three-monthly audit.

Sharples & Son was a smallish concern of ten instrument makers. It was organised as a cooperative business. The makers had their own area to work.

They pooled together to buy expensive equipment and shared storage and energy costs. The owner was Mark Gibbons. He had the final word on matters affecting the business, though he always consulted widely before taking decisions which affected other makers. Mark was the only maker in the group who regularly took on an apprentice. The other makers chipped in in support of the apprentice in any way that they could. This was to their benefit too as the apprentice, as well as learning this most exacting of skills – instrument making – was responsible for much of the paperwork affecting the makers. This excused them from a great deal of drudgery, they were interested in making, not in number-crunching. The apprentice also doubled up as cleaner once a fortnight, cleaning away shavings and generally tidying up. He had access to all parts of the building.

Security at Sharples & Son was very poor. It occupied a detached single-storey Victorian building in Keighley's industrial complex. Well now it is a "complex" but, in reality, it was a clapped-out building situated on the edge of the woollen mill area of Keighley. During the war, buildings either side of Sharples & Son had been damaged or destroyed leaving it isolated for many years. Many new units had been recently commissioned. They had never in eighty-four years been burgled. Surely, previous and present owners argued, they didn't need such a high level of security. However, three nearby premises had been burgled in the last six months and the problem of security might have to be revisited. The police had warned all the businesses in the area to be vigilant as there were a number of gangs operating in this neighbourhood.

The only entry to the building was a steel-faced door operated with two three-lever deadlocks. Mark had recently added a heavy duty padlock. The premises were further protected by iron grilles over the windows. This gave the appearance of high level security but, in reality, the grilles on most of the windows were locked in position by a single padlock. These would be easily broken off and the grille removed. Mark Gibbons didn't want such a high level of security as, should a fire occur, far more likely than a burglary, staff may be trapped inside unable to get through the grilles. This had only happened once in their history as, unbeknownst to "the last one out", a maker had fallen asleep at his desk. He was released the next morning none the worse for wear. That was before a telephone was introduced. However, there was a room, known as the transition room, which was less secure than other areas. The transition room kept instruments that were on the way out to customers and dealers or on the way in; recent purchases, violins for re-varnishing or violins with completed repairs. If you could get through into the transition area then there was relatively easy access to all the other parts. Temptation was rising. There were so many very valuable violins and other instruments in the violin family, violas, cellos and double bass. Surely Brendan could think of a scheme to remove some of these valuable items? One thing he did notice early on is that violins are not stamped in any way. There is no numbering or identification system like you have with gold or silver. Unless you have a knowledgeable "eye" for these things one violin looks much like any other. Only an expert could tell if a violin is man-made or machine-made. Only an expert can tell the difference between an old machine-made violin and an old handmade violin. This was an obvious weakness in the whole system of buying and selling violins. They are hard to trace, once stolen they were usually gone for ever. One violin can be compared to another on the basis of sound quality, on the quality of the varnish, the "patina", and of the feel of the instrument. Only expert makers and expert players can make such a judgement.

At Sharples & Son there were about 60-70 ordinary violins and 150-170 "old" violins, of quality, all hanging up by their scrolls; each one labelled and priced. The quality fiddles were held in the more secure part of the premises.

At any one moment in time it is not clear how many instruments are "in". This is because there are an unknown number in the transition room. Also, the makers may take some instruments home to work on them there, or to study other instruments. Many of the makers found working at home more peaceful and productive. Some members were more talkative than others which could be disruptive. The accurate number of instruments would only be known at the end of each quarter when a detailed audit was held. At this point all instruments would be returned from home and put back in the workshop. A whole morning, usually on a Saturday, would be set aside for this count.

Now Brendan began to think about the possibility of stealing a violin. What if the labels were interchanged on two old violins, one valuable, one not? Brendan would then remove the cheap one (really the expensive one) from the premises, say, simply by buying it at a cheap price. Brendan continues to think; before the three-monthly audit how can an expert be convinced that the expensive violin (really the cheap one) is expensive? Brendan realises this is impossible unless, unless, unless the expensive one (really the cheap one) is destroyed or "appears" to be destroyed before the audit. The company's insurance will surely pick up the bill. Sharples & Son will have its loss covered and Brendan will be the proud owner of an expensive violin worth, possibly, many thousands of pounds. This can be sold and is unlikely to be traced. Brendan argues that he would not be stealing from the company but from the insurance company which, according to Brendan, is a worthy exercise!

This was the germ of an idea that needed further thought. He did realise that if he was to engage again in thieving in the violin domain he would only have one opportunity to carry it through. For what he had in mind, at least in overall terms, he could not repeat the exercise else suspicion fall on him. He would need the upmost care in the planning and in the execution. If he was caught it would mean jail – and disaster for the family. He was coming to the view that the risk might just be worth it. There was a chance he could make many thousands of pounds. His adrenalin began to pump round his body whenever he thought of this scam. On every spare moment he thought how he might steal a violin or two, or three or more. This would be his first major "project", to make some significant amounts of money from stealing. He would give it his full attention. Of course, it was a gamble, if it wasn't a gamble everyone would be doing it. It was Brendan's main concern that the odds of being a success far outweighed the odds of failure. On his side he had the germ of an idea that had a great chance of working. Match that with his ability to analyse situations, his ability for forward thinking and his realisation that if the project became too risky he would simply abandon it and wait for another opportunity. The apprenticeship put him in the right place, amongst highly valuable items. He had (or at least he would have) inside knowledge – always a positive feature. An initial analysis led him to believe that there was money to be made here with a low risk of detection.

Meanwhile, of course, he had an apprenticeship to consider. On his first day he was given a set of specialised tools he would need for the next five years. He would pay for these out of his wages over the next year. In the first six months of the apprenticeship he was handed the task of making a violin neck and scroll. This was a relatively easy introduction to the kind of work that he would be immersed in over the coming years. Of course, he would then have ample opportunity to meet everyone else and to get experience in how the place functioned. For this exercise cheap wood was used. Mark Gibbons would give Brendan the plans – containing all the basic measurements and a small handwritten booklet explaining the procedure to be followed. He also gave him some one-to-one lessons, particularly on the making of the scroll. He would first learn how to keep his tools sharp as a razor, he would learn how to make and use curved chisels and small planes (less than an inch in length) used for smoothing curved surfaces. It was all new to him but he gobbled it all up. He had embarked on a great adventure. Being an instrument maker was something to be proud of. Certainly Ma thought so. She thought now that Brendan had a proper job, one to tell the neighbours and friends about. The initial enthusiasm turned into a degree of frustration. It was harder than he thought it might be, but he wasn't a quitter, no doubts at all, he would stay the course.

His sixth attempt at making the neck looked okay but the measurements were out. Every violin, particularly at the neck, has to have the same dimensions otherwise even gifted players would find them difficult to play. A violinist from the beginning of his or her training would expect, on an adult-sized violin, a neck length of precisely 27 entimeters. As a mathematician he was well aware of approximations, however, he underestimated how accurate the dimensions should be.

Brendan persevered. Some days he worked well and achieved, on other days everything would go wrong. The business of making a consistently quality object was proving to be very, very difficult. Brendan realised that making such a complicated object would take more than a couple of weeks. During all of these failures he was learning to use the tools, his eye and brain coordination were getting better and better. It was not until his twenty-third attempt that he made what he considered to be a professionally acceptable neck and scroll. By this time he would check and re-check all the dimensions before presenting it to Mark Gibbons for inspection. In his own judgement this twenty-third attempt looked "okay", but would it get past the exacting eye of Mark the master? Mark looked carefully at the neck and scroll. As well as looking, Mark would feel the finished article. He would make accurate measurements of various parts. Apart from the odd nod of his head, Mark said very little. Brendan was nervous but confident that he had done it. The other makers looked on, eager to know the result. Finally, Mark Gibbons said a single word.

"Acceptable."

Brendan smiled in relief.

"Thanks, thank you so much. I thought I'd never do it."

The other makers showed their approval across the room, whistling and whooping, some doing little dances, this rather serious bunch took a few minutes to let their hair down.

"Good man, good man, but don't get too cocky. The average number is twenty," said Mark, intentionally deflating Brendan's ego at this apparent success.

"If it's any consolation, you might also want to know that I thought it would take you at least thirty attempts before you mastered it. Your dexterity has certainly improved. I'm particularly impressed with your plane work. All students struggle with that aspect. Your scroll is fine, very nice. Keep that standard up. Your skill level is now excellent. You're at the right standard now."

He would now have to make three acceptable necks in a row before he could move on to the next stage. He duly made the three necks of the right standard and was awarded a certificate marking the occasion. This was a significant step in his training. Being able to make a neck and scroll essentially meant that the other tasks, like making the belly or the back, would soon be within his skill level. The other makers came round to his station. They clapped, he blushed, then they got on with their work.

It was a requirement of the apprenticeship that he learn to play an instrument, preferably the violin. Brendan agreed to this if he was allowed to focus on Irish folk music. Mark agreed to this. Brendan learned very quickly, not surprisingly as he was brought up with this music certainly from the age of four. At St Joseph's infant school he continued to learn, using the school's instrument up to the age of eleven. Then he stopped for a few years. He was happy to take up the instrument one more time. He discovered that he too had his father's ear in that he could play a tune after only hearing it three or four times. Slow tunes gave him no problem, apart from learning vibrato. The faster tunes, double jigs and reels needed a good deal of practice before he "got it". Despite his natural ability he, for a small charge, attended a lesson with a renowned player of traditional music, Bevan Ward.

His training involved all aspects of instrument (especially violin) making, repairs and "fitting"; adjusting sound post, strings, bridge, et cetera to ensure a quality sound. He was also introduced to the business itself: selling, exchange, insurance work, auditing. From time to time he would be expected to take new or repaired violins to customers' homes as a final fitting.

Mr. Gibbons and the other makers had little interest in doing the books, in auditing. Their real interest lay in the making, their aim, always, in making the perfect instrument. Something to rival a Stradivarius or a Guarneri. They would talk for hours on this and that to do with violin making especially on the varnish. However, their bread and butter money came from repairs and from fitting.

Mark was a renowned maker and many well-known players would have him look at their instruments in the afternoon before a concert. They would often be called out to "do" a whole orchestra, usually a children's orchestra, carried out for a bulk price or to set up the instruments at the beginning of term for the numerous private schools in the area. They were happy to delegate bookwork to Brendan. Brendan was excellent at this aspect of the work – possibly for ulterior motives – he wanted to know everything he could on the business side. They thought, and he was happy that they had this impression, that his long-term aim was to open his own shop. Little did they know that he had other plans, but for different kinds of shopping. After about eighteen months Brendan had 90-95% knowledge of the company.

He knew all the violins by sight, he knew their intrinsic value. He was allowed to sell instruments to the general public getting a nod first from one of the more experienced makers. Business was brisk, there was little doubt about that. Sharples & Son was making money, a lot of money, and Brendan wanted some of it. As an apprentice Brendan's income was just above meagre. Normally, he would go all day at work without food to keep costs down, stocking up in the evening with heavily potatoed suppers, courtesy of his mother. He couldn't afford to wear smart shirts or suits to work like some of the makers, for him it was a down-market pair of dungarees.

He was forging ahead on the "making" side as well. It wasn't long, and not much after his eighteenth birthday, that Brendan was able to make a complete violin to a good standard. Of course, he would still only be allowed to work with (from a sound point of view) poor quality pine wood. It would be at least another year before he was allowed to use good quality Swiss pine and two or three years beyond that before he could sell his violins to noted violinists. A maker has to build up a reputation for making quality instruments before they could think of making a living in this area. He would have to content himself with repair work or tuning children's instruments. He was allowed to make half-size violins in good quality wood but he was very keen to move on to the real McCoy.

Chapter 17

MR. TREV, THE WINK, WINK, NOD, NOD MAN

The clientele of Sharples & Son was mostly in the West Yorkshire area, though they had customers from Greater Manchester and a growing interest from London. As part of his training Brendan was taken to other dealers and makers. On some occasions, especially if it was London, Brendan would be sent alone, the makers didn't want to spend a whole day away from their babies. On one of these lone visits he met a dealer who was interested in purchasing any violin on a "wink, wink, nod, nod" basis. The dealer was "Trev", a very well-known high-end stockist of violins, operating out of a small unit in Covent Garden. Trev was very tall, distinguished white hair, heavily jewelled and impeccably dressed. The overall effect was impressive until he spoke. Across came the undeniable sound of a cockney. Not just any cockney but a cockney in the style of Dick Van Dyke from *Mary Poppins*. There was some talk that he was homosexual but Brendan never detected any such leaning. He dominated any room he was in.

"Hi son. They call me Trev but it's Mr. Trev to you. You see I've earned that. Bin around a long time. Ask anyone round here, they'll tell you who Mr. Trev is. Not all good o'course but at least I'm up front about it. At least I know I'm on the bent side of straight. I'm only interested in one thing here, violins. Bring any violin here, preferably old. I'll give you a price you won't find anywhere else. No questions asked. I can get the fiddles off to America or Canada; big, big market – no questions asked, no paperwork. Savvy? See, they don't want machine-made stuff. They don't trust the Chinese makers, just not their thing. They'll eat anything we send them. Also looking at Singapore and Hong Kong – they've gone fiddle mad recently. I put it down to Yehudi and that Kennedy bloke, why can't the young lad dress proper? There's no need for that rubbish he wears. He can play a fiddle yeah, second to none, but when he talks, my God. Then, what he wears, where's that from? And I know I can be a bit 'loud' on the clothes side but that's just having a larf."

Brendan laughed out loud.

"Where was I? Oh yeah, don't think you can set up your own scam. I've got the contacts. Taken me thirty-odd years and more to build my business. Don't get me wrong, I can do legit as well – no problem."

He looked Brendan up and down.

"Why am I telling you this? Looking at you, well, it just looks as if you could do with an injection of cash. I'm perceptive see – can tell you're not quite on the straight and narrow. True or false?"

Brendan made no reply except a giveaway raise of an eyebrow.

"You could certainly do with some decent clobber. What the hell do they pay you up there? When you're ready. When you're all qualified and such, move to London son, you'll make twice the money. And, if you're on the fiddle then

London's your oyster. They won't say it but everybody's on the fiddle down here. Part of the game, that's what it is. You're not earning unless you're fiddling. How do you think I can afford this clobber," as he points to his gold rings. "

I have a different set for each day!"

Brendan was immediately at his ease. Cockney or not, Mr. Trev came across as a diamond "Geezer". Brendan relaxed.

"God, is it that obvious? In the way of violins I've nothing yet but in the future…possibly…It would have to be on a cash only basis, and on an 'I deny everything basis'."

"Don't deal in anything else pal – anything with her Majesty's head on then we're in business."

"How many can you deal with at a time?" said Brendan with a degree of arrogance.

"Oh, we're in that game are we; multiples of said items, well, well, well, that's the game you want to play, multiples is it, multiples of said item. Let me just say this. If you've got em I'll deal with em – guaranteed! If you're really interested I'll give you 70% of their true value, no questions asked. How does that sound?"

"Yeah, sounds good, we can do business."

"I don't do this for everyone, but here's my home phone number. Give me a ring before you come down, I can have cash ready then. You describe said item – or items – to me and I'll know what ball park we're playing in, you get my drift.

"I dunno son, I thought I was in control of this conversation here but you seemed to have taken over. Nice work son, nice work. I think I'm gonna hear more from you!"

Brendan was left in no doubt that "Trev" would relieve him of any old-looking violins he got hold of by fair means or foul, and with Brendan's resources it would have to be foul.

"I dunno what you on son, but a piece of advice – don't get greedy, simple as that, leave Mr. Greedy at home. Mr. Greedy is the father of Mr. Failure. Wouldn't like to see you put away, you get my drift?

"On a more serious note, remember my lad I know the difference between quality and shite. If you do come here don't bring any old tat. Do that and you'll find your arse, together with the end of my boot, on them cobbles out there. Savvy young man?"

"Savvy! I'll see what I can do," said Brendan, not wishing to commit to any kind of deal. Brendan left the shop.

"Mmm. Well, well, well. Fancy that – just what I'm looking for," Brendan said to himself. "

Just when I want one, one turns up – a bent violin dealer. Someone on the fiddle." He smiled to himself. "Someone up there likes me. "He could now see how he could make a good lot of money primarily by foul means. On the train back to Keighley, there was a long delay at Stoke-on-Trent. During the 90-minute holdup (appropriate he thought) he sketched out his "plan". It was just a first draft. Brendan would have to be very careful about this one. He expected to embroil himself in a good level of research and homework. Firstly, he noted down the various aspects of the plan that he had in mind:

1. Single out five, possibly more quality violins. Listen to Trev. DON'T GET GREEDY!
2. Replace the quality violins with five ordinary ones.
3. Remove the five quality violins from the shop.
4. Destroy (preferably burn) the ordinary violins in such a way that it appears that the five quality violins have been destroyed.
5. Sharples & Son can claim damages from their insurers.
6. The quality violins can now be sold, one, possibly more, at a time, via "Diamond Geezer Trev".
7. What can go wrong?

Brendan started to have second thoughts. He had grown to like all his colleagues. He had grown to like the work and the whole business of making beautiful musical instruments. If he carried out his plan it would feel like a betrayal. At the same time, this was an opportunity that doesn't arise often. He would continue, at least through the early planning stage.

Chapter 18

PLANNING APPROVAL: OBTAINED

Now he starts. Do these bullet points stand up to analysis?

The first, on choosing five violins, is straightforward. After two years in the business Brendan knows the true value of almost all of the violins. Those he is unsure of can be found in the audit list to which he has access. So, yes, he can single out five quality violins – not the most expensive though, as that might create problems later on in the plan, but five near the top of the list in terms of value.

The second is also doable and is tied in with the third point. He can simply interchange, on a one-for-one basis, a quality violin with an ordinary one – this is likely to work unless one of the makers wanted to look at a violin in close detail. It would appear to those giving a cursory glance that all the quality violins were in place. As for the third point, the five quality violins singled out could be removed off the premises over a three- or four-day period. These three days would be toward the end of the week. Brendan often had need to take violins home – he might be delivering next day to a customer or he might take it home for study. Security within the group is fairly relaxed and there would be no need to record on any document where each violin was at any particular time. Brendan was trusted implicitly. Also, he often worked late together with a colleague. He could easily slip past him with the two or three of the quality violins without him noticing.

But where would he keep the quality fiddles? If suspicion fell upon him, as it might well do in the early stages, the police would surely make a visit to his home. Indeed, they would surely visit his home in any case. He was intending to steal goods to the value of ten to fifteen thousand pounds. It would not be surprising if one or two coppers came by, that would be expected. The only hiding places were the outside coal shed and the attic. The attic was damp, easy to access and out of the question. The coal shed was a possible candidate as a dry storage area but Brendan would have to build some kind of inner sanctum. He didn't feel he could make such a building to as good a standard as would be required. It would not require an eagle-eyed copper to find the hiding place. Also, it would put Ma under suspicion – if Brendan was caught the police might well charge Ma as an accessory – handling stolen goods. Brendan would never put Ma under such a threat. So, using Ma's house for storage is ruled out from the off.

That left only three feasible possibilities for storage:

- On Brendan's allotment.- In some kind of hired storage unit.- In the attic at Chipry's house.

The allotment might, at first sight, appear to be a good choice. Encouraged by the local council to get youngsters back into growing things, Brendan had an allotment since he was fourteen. The hut which came with each plot was sturdy with a strong padlock. The mice, which came with the hut, would, sooner or later, find any pencil-thin gap and start nibbling away at any bit of varnished wood. A two- to three-hundred-year-old bit of Swiss pine would do nicely. The strong padlock was overkill. There were very few thefts on the allotment to warrant such a high level of security. Indeed, many of the huts were unlocked and left on the latch. The padlocks were taken home and used for other jobs.

Not many self-respecting gang members or burglars would waste their time stealing vegetables or packets of seeds or spades. There was more of a problem with holders damaging other gardeners' prized vegetables or polluting their water – it's a jungle out there. More of a worry to Brendan was the temperature inside the hut in summer, even late summer, it could get very high. He hadn't yet decided when the "hit" was due to take place, if at all; at the moment he favoured September or October and in either of those months the temperature was erratic. Brendan wouldn't want the glue to melt – a disaster worse than a visit from Mr. Mouse. As well as that consideration he wouldn't want anyone simply wandering in to see what they could find. The violins would possibly be stored over a two-month period – it would be difficult to keep them away from prying eyes over that period of time. So storing the varnished bits of wood at the allotment hut was ruled out.

His next thought was renting a unit like a garage space? In theory this was a serious option. He could put his own, high security lock on the premises. However, serious burglars might be tempted to break in, in a strange way, because it had a smart lock indicating that there might be valuables within. All a burglar would require to gain entry was a pair of upmarket cable cutters. A more down to earth reason for rejecting this option is that the deposit required and the ongoing rent was beyond what he could afford. There was no money in the piggy-bank and there wasn't likely to be any for some while. He would have to borrow money – not a realistic possibility on his relatively low wage. He doubted that even Chipry could help. He wasn't going to ask, the less anybody knew what he was embarking on the better. The "heat" would, sooner or later, discover a bank account in his name without a clear reason as to why it was there. He quickly went off that idea.

Storing at Chipry's house seemed like the only possibility. Indeed Brendan would often be asked, by Chipry himself, to put stuff up or get stuff down from the attic – Chipry was too slender and fragile any more to go into the attic. It required good balance together with the use of a rickety pair of stepladders. Chipry could hardly shuffle from one side of the room to the other. His unsteadiness resulted, partly, from drinking too much of the "yellow shite", but partly from the slow onset of Parkinson's disease. Storage at Chipry's would have the added advantage that since Brendan was now, as far as anyone knew, "estranged" from Chipry – very few would now connect the two together. There would be no reason for anyone to ask the question "do you know anyone else who might be used to store stolen goods?" Brendan had a key, obtained in the times when his son Andrejs would visit. Chipry was happy to allow Brendan to come and go. Even before the apprenticeship started Brendan would do a bit of shopping, a bit of washing, some cleaning. He would even scrub the floor from time to time. Brendan was looking after him. He would organise doctors to call, district nurses to attend to deal with bed sores, prescriptions to pick up. Brendan thought he owed Chipry a great deal, least amongst which was a life. Brendan knew that without his help and support over a number of years he and his family might not have survived as a unit. Brendan was returning a favour. Brendan would normally access the house on a Sunday morning to do his "chores". On most Sundays Chipry would be absent, having gone to the Latvian Centre in Bradford. At these times Brendan could get into the attic space and store his violins without fear of discovery.

Assuming that his project to steal would go ahead, Brendan made spaces between the rafters to house six violins. A standard violin is about two feet long and at it deepest no more than four and a half inches and about nine inches wide. They would fit beautifully between the rafters. They would also be difficult to reach if pushed under the roof overhang. As camouflage they would be covered by a thinner layer of insulating material and then dusted to give the appearance of age. Anyone going into the attic (in particular Mr. Clodhopper) would be very wary of stepping between the rafters lest they go through the ceiling. Brendan thought he would be very unlucky if anyone should, first of all, discover that Brendan is still a regular visitor to 27 Bengal Street, and secondly that they should discover his treasure.

Though not ideal, Brendan concluded that storing the violins in Chipry's attic was the best choice.

Bullet point four needs greater thought. This is the tricky one. Firstly, Brendan thinks the best bet is to blame a local gang of teenagers for carrying out the burglary. He doesn't want to invent or encourage the belief in a violin-theft mastermind. The press would have a field day and likely keep the story of the theft alive as the weeks went by. Brendan would rather trivialise the theft, blame it on a gang by making it look as if the gang was uninterested or unknowledgeable about music. A gang prepared to "mark" their territory with the odd unpleasant calling card (thanks to Mr. Poo and to Mr. Dog Turd) would be even more realistic. The police like the challenge of a mastermind to catch. They have little time or interest in banging up a gang of teenage yobbos.

Chapter 19

DIGGING OUT THE GROUNDWORK

In the mock-up of the intended burglary Brendan would play all the parts. To make the crime scene as realistic as possible the imaginary gang would vandalise a good deal, remove some of the goods and look for what cash could be found. Of course the "burglary" would be carried out by Brendan. Authenticity is the name of the game. The police need to have the ingredients of a believable story which they could tell to the staff, in particular the owner of Sharples & Son.

Even though Brendan had worked at S&S for nearly two years, he realised how little he knew about the premises, and its environs. To rectify this, in part, he developed a lunchtime exercise routine. He really needed better information, about the building and about its geography. In recent months Brendan ate his lunchtime apple on the move, whilst taking a stroll round the premises. An innocent enough exercise.

"Just trying to keep fit" or "I'm starting to look like a double bass" would be his excuse. This had more than a grain of truth in it and, mainly because of the potato diet, he was looking a tad plump. Often he would make two or three circuits. He was, of course, sizing up the "job". He confirmed that all the windows were protected by metal grilles, each one held by two hidden hinges to one side and a strong padlock on the other side. He noticed that the grille on the transition room window was guarded by a very flimsy looking padlock. This was a lucky break; it would mean that, with a suitably sturdy crowbar, he judged that it would be an easy task either to remove the hinges or to remove the padlock. It would be straightforward to gain entry there. What's more, only a part of this window could be seen from the main road. He looked at the area around the building and chose a small region, about fifty yards away, almost hidden by overgrown shrubs, where a "gang" might hang out and possibly start a fire. The police, if alerted to a fire he was to start, wouldn't bother to send a car down just for a small fire and more often than not the yobbos would be allowed to "yob" in peace. The police had better things to do than chaperone a gang of young kids.

As the burglar then he would use a crowbar to attempt to gain entrance on four windows to the main building, bending the grilles to make it obvious that someone tried to gain entrance here. Then he would break into the external transition room window removing the metal grille (assuming it is as weak as it looks) and then smashing through the wired glass. Once inside he would break through the door into the general area where most of the valuable instruments were kept. Of course, he could have copied the key to this door but then if he'd used it, it would obviously be an inside job. At all costs he had to avoid this thought. He'd be the first one the police would want to question. His aim was to throw suspicion away from him and on to the imaginary gang. To this end he mentioned to Mark how poor the security was.

"I don't mean to interfere," he said one morning, quite innocently,

"but isn't the security here a bit wishy-washy? The grille on the window there," he pointed to the transition room, "is almost falling off!"

"Well that's a bit of an exaggeration," said Mark, slightly irritated by the comment.

"We've never been broken into, in over seventy-odd years. There's no problem."

"The lad's got a point Mark. We'd be buggered if someone got in here," said Geoff, hearing the conversation.

"I've said for a long time that security is an issue. I've got a lot of very expensive stuff stored here, our rent should cover this."

Now Brendan thought, for his own purposes, that Geoff was labouring the point. He was going too far. He didn't want Geoff to complain too much – that might just be the kick up the backside that Mark needed to actually do something to deal with the security situation.

"Anybody for a cup of tea?" asked Brendan in an attempt to diffuse the situation.

"Okay, okay, point taken, I'll get the hinges sorted. I'll definitely look into it."

But of course he didn't get the hinges sorted. Brendan suspected he wouldn't. However, it would, at least, stick in their memories that Brendan had concerns about security. Hardly the stance taken by a prospective burglar.

Geoff got his cup of tea and Brendan moved the conversation on to football.

Continuing his imaginary tour, Brendan would knock a few instruments down from their hooks and give one or two a hefty kick – yobbo-like. Brendan would try get into the main office and he would open as many cupboards and drawers as he could, piling them in the centre of the room. Paperwork would be thrown around.

Whilst the delayed train shunted out of Stoke-on-Trent, he entertained the thought of burning the whole building down. On reflection Brendan thought that "job" would be too big so early in his career and would attract (literally) too much "heat" from the police. The loss would run into the hundreds of thousands and it would mean the likely loss of eight jobs. He had a great respect for working men and would avoid any plan that led to loss of livelihoods. He discounted arson immediately. However, the ploy of using arson to cover up a crime looked very attractive and Brendan would consider this in future "jobs".

His thoughts returned to his smaller scale plan:

He would remove five ordinary violins, a quality violin, two violas and a trumpet. He couldn't easily carry much more. He would then, if convenient, urinate as much as he could in various places, on the paperwork and in drawers. For the sake of the plan and to keep the authenticity level high he would defecate in places. Apparently this kind of unpleasant behaviour was all the rage amongst burglars, it was the equivalent of marking territory by wild animals. Dog excrement, picked up from the street, would be thrown about and wiped over some of the surfaces. He would throw the goods through the window before exiting himself. He would take all the stolen goods to the hidden area he had seen in his lunchtime walks. A fire would be started with a copy of the *New Musical Express* and all the ordinary violins thrown there. A strong fire would surely result, he'd experienced this in making many a fire on the allotment and the violins were tinder dry. He would arrange two of the violins in such a way that after burning only the neck and scrolls were untouched by fire. One of the expensive violas would be placed so that the bottom of the viola was sticking out. With any luck this would be clearly identified as a very expensive instrument – a criminal waste by this "gang" of uncouth idiots. He would stand on the trumpet before hurling it deep into the bushes. After an hour this smallish fire would turn to ash. All that would be seen was an outline of a viola (a valuable one) and two half-burned violin necks warped with the heat and a few remnants of the newspaper. Near the fire was a viola which Brendan would stamp on. He would collect some cigarette butts and place them around the area. The idea behind all this destruction was that the "gang" might realistically conclude that it would be very suspicious if this teenage group was seen walking round town with some fancy instruments. The only thing to do was to destroy the evidence. Hence the fire. This, more or less, was the crime scene as would be created by Brendan. He thought it was a work of art.

Chipry also had a strong metal pole to be used as a deterrent against any would-be burglar should his house be broken into. The pole was always kept next to the front door. However, Chipry had, long ago, lost the agility to make effective use of this large cosh. Indeed, it was far more likely to be used by the burglar! This, at a push, would be a good candidate for a crowbar.

As for tidying up; the crowbar would be removed from the scene of the crime and thrown into a local beck. Hopefully the police would find it, providing further evidence that this was an amateur gang looking for easy money.

Two old boots were removed from the allotment and kept in his bedroom till required. Due to the lack of value it was unlikely this boot theft would be reported, and if it was it would be logged down and simply ignored.

"What were they expecting? The Flying Squad? Should we have called Scotland Yard?" were the likely comments. The boots would be used to create a "crowd" scene of gang members. He would need a pair of gloves to be worn at all times.

He would wear a balaclava just in case he was spotted.

All that remained was to choose the date that it was to go ahead.

Brendan argued that it was best to do the job on Saturday evening sometime in October, about 8 o'clock. That way it would be unlikely to be discovered till Monday morning. He would have a whole day for his adrenalin-filled body to calm down. In front of police questions he would be more relaxed. As for the time, it would be quite dark by then. At that time of night the industrial site wasn't the place for joggers or dog walkers or lovers. He thought he was unlikely to be disturbed. Most would be inside their homes watching TV. The fire would be partially hidden by overgrown shrubbery and, in the darkness, would not be seen. For such a fire the smoke would be clean, not highly visible, not like burning rubber. After the deed was done he would walk home avoiding speaking to anyone. He would enter his house, quietly go to his bedroom and after a few minutes go downstairs and complain bitterly that he had not been woken for his favourite programme, *Bewitched*.

He would try to make sure that, if questioned, Ma would quite truthfully be able to give him an alibi as to his whereabouts earlier in the evening – he was upstairs in bed.

His plan had some weaknesses, there were parts of the plan susceptible to random events which he had no control over. However, it was time to put up or shut up.

For no particular reason he chose to become what he describes as a professional thief on Saturday, 29 October. This was a proper "job", an adult job, not like nicking bananas or penknives from Woolworths. This was the real McCoy. He knew this was his real forte. It was his destiny. He looked in the mirror in his bedroom.

"I know this is what I'm good at. You've just got to keep cool. I would be a fool to miss this opportunity. I'm not doing this to be rich or for my family. I'm doing this for me. There's no way I'm going to get caught."

Chapter 20

THE POINT OF NO RETURN

On Wednesday, 19 October, the weather is cloudy but dry. Brendan is hoping for dry weather for the next fortnight for his plans to bear fruit. He needs to remove five quality violins before Saturday week which, to him, is D-Day.

During the day Brendan unhooks a quality violin and places it in the transition room. There are no comments from the two colleagues who had seen the transfer, not surprisingly, this was common procedure. Near to closing time he puts it into an old violin case and removes the violin from the premises. He will store it in his bedroom till Sunday morning.

The next day, Thursday, Radio 4 informs him that the weather will be poor. It will be overcast all day and there will be drizzle in the evening. Brendan gets to work with the empty violin case.

During the day he removes a further two of the quality violins, one in the morning (in the violin case, unseen by anyone), taken home at lunchtime, and one in the evening in another old violin case (these cases were littered around the premises and had little value). This was seen but not commented upon. Again, they were transferred to his bedroom.

Friday's weather was very poor. Drizzle on and off all day.

Brendan came to work with a violin case. He made sure he was noticed by Geoff by engaging in conversation – on football – simply wanted to be seen to be carrying on "as normal", not hiding anything, just being open and above board. During the morning another quality violin was placed in the case and transferred to the transition room. He takes it home.

The next day saw a marked improvement in the weather.

Warm and dry all day. The radio weather forecast predicted good to excellent weather for the next week or so due to high atmospherics. With fine weather predicted it was clear now that the "project" would go ahead.

Three of the staff and Brendan were in work in the morning. Howard looks for one of the violins which had been removed by Brendan. This was one of the scenarios that Brendan had dreaded.

"I need it Brendan – it's the 1890 strad copy. You know, the one I was working on last week. The one with the single back. I want to look at the purfling and the bee sting."

"Sorry, sorry Howard. I took it home. I was using it to do some work on my belly. I'd forgotten you were using it. I was going to get it back today but I'd forgotten it till I was on the bus. I'll go and get it. I thought I'd bring it back tomorrow!"

"Could you. I'd really like to look at it today." Within the hour Brendan was back with the violin. Not a comment about why he had taken it home and Brendan didn't volunteer much either. He was nervous but he had his feelings under control, he didn't even blush. This was the routine in S&S. The violins weren't regarded as precious objects – this was reflected in their attitude towards security.

He removed another quality violin and, at the end of that shift, took it home. He now had four quality violins. If Brendan was caught now it would surely mean the sack for him. The police probably wouldn't be involved – it wouldn't look good from a business point of view. But he wasn't going to get caught – unless he was very unlucky.

Later that night, around 8 o'clock, Brendan left the house and walked the whole distance to his works premises just to get a feel of what it will be like in a week's time. He sees no one, everything is quiet. He waits forty-five minutes outside the main entrance, standing in the shadows, to see if anything develops – not a sausage. *This is going to be easy. Easy, peasy, dog bollock easy.* He thinks to himself.

He returned home in confident mood.

"Bring it on!" He couldn't wait for the action to start.

On Sunday the weather remains dry and warm. The forecast suggests improving weather for the foreseeable future.

He had a cardboard box, small enough not to be cumbersome but large enough to house four violins and a little padding. The violins were packed and, whilst everyone was still asleep, transported to Chipry's attic. As usual Chipry had been picked up by the Latvian bus. There were no hiccups. He didn't meet anyone on the way there or on the way back.

The following Thursday the weather was cold in the morning, but remained dry.

There were no incidents out of the ordinary. Brendan removes one of the quality violins towards the end of the shift and takes it home.

The next day the weather is very good. An Indian summer is predicted.

Brendan, making himself busy, converses with most colleagues about the making of the belly. He gives the clear impression that he will be at S&S for the long haul.

Saturday 29th, D-day and the Indian summer arrives. Very warm. Dry.

Brendan gives a repeat performance to the one given on the previous Saturday. He makes tea for those in work and gets on with the violin belly he is working on.

Without anyone noticing he pushes a couple of chairs by the window in the transition room. A burglar would find that useful. Behind the chairs he places a couple of sheets of cardboard. This wouldn't look at all unusual for the transition room. Broken glass would be a severe hazard, a protecting layer of cardboard over the window ledge would alleviate that problem.

If an audit was carried out at this time it would show that five of their most valuable violins were missing. They were, of course, in Brendan's hands, either at Chipry's attic or in his bedroom. So far so good.

At 1.00 p.m. he goes home to prepare for the evening. He familiarises himself with what is on the TV that night. The stress in his body is now at fever pitch. Even he is on edge, unable to keep still for long, drinking mugs of tea one after the other. Even Ma detects unease in Brendan.

"Are you all right son? You're very pale. Are you sickening after something?"

"Nothing, nothing. I'm fine."

A not-so-surprising development occurs. Ma announces she will go to Bingo.

"Are you in?" she asks him, expecting him to get the kids to bed.

An audible

"oh, jeez do I have to?" tells Ma that he will "be in", though reluctantly. Brendan starts to experience high levels of stress. How has he gotten himself into this predicament? Why couldn't he simply accept the situation he is in, always short of money, like millions of others? He is of half a mind to cancel the whole project. He never expected nerves like this.

He didn't really want to cancel at this late stage or make a big thing of it. He has five quality violins stashed away and sooner or later – probably sooner – their absence will be noticed. He wouldn't get away with that. His professional career as a thief would be over before it had hardly begun. In probability terms this was in the "a possibility" category, but in the real world it was in the "bloody hell" category. His stress levels continue on their upward trajectory but still very much under control. His plans will need a slight adjustment.

At 7.30 p.m. Ma goes off to Mrs. Bingo, a bus and a short walk is required, leaving Brendan in charge. Andrejs is in his bed and, thankfully, fast asleep. Roisin is fractious, tired but awake, she's too warm. She wouldn't even be pacified with a bottle. However, she does compromise; Brendan agrees to read three stories. Towards the end of the second story Roisin is fast asleep.

Coldly he now goes about his business. He puts a box of matches in his pocket and a few sheets of toilet paper for Mr. Dog's droppings. He takes the *Musical Express*, purchased some three weeks previously from an out of town shop, with him and puts on an old pair of trousers and an old shirt. Both would be discarded after the job is done. A similar fate would be applied to one of Ma's knitted jumpers. He picks up the metal pole removed some days earlier from Chipry's house. He didn't wear an overcoat – he only had one and didn't want it taken "on site". The nervous energy now flowing through his body would keep the cold at bay. He is more nervous than he had previously thought he would be.

Chapter 21

WE HAVE LIFT OFF

Though reluctant to leave the two kids alone he checks on them one more time, then he turns off the gas fire, planning to be back within the hour.

He looks in the hall mirror.

"You're on," he says quietly.He leaves the front and back doors unlocked just in case the kids have to get out of the house in an emergency. True, he left the road open for potential child molesters, but regarded such an occurrence to have a very small probability of occurring.

He stands in the darkened hallway for a few minutes and checks there is no one about. The police, if they came, would possibly check the neighbours for any information. It was crucial that he was seen by no one, certainly no one living locally.

"Did you see Brendan going out on Saturday evening, about eight o'clock? Was he carrying anything?" the police might ask.

He slides the metal rod up one sleeve and holds it in place with his hand. He puts the allotment boots into a sturdy brown bag and makes his way from the house at a brisk pace. As usual he avoids people as much as possible making use of the balaclava. On his way to S&S he collects a variety of cigarette butts and dog poo.

He gets to his workplace, his heart pounding. Something within him is telling him to stop, not to go through with it, but the stronger voice urges him forward.

"Go on lad. You've got the balls haven't you. Now's yer chance. You're not doing something bad – God it's only the insurance company that'll pick up the bill. Go on lad, get it done. You're the dog's bollocks. You're not hurting anyone, are you? It'll do S&S good if they have to sort out their security. It'll bring them into the twentieth century. They were warned. Everyone in S&S knew there was a problem. This is just a wake-up call. Go on lad. You're the dog's bollocks. This is easy meat for you. You've done the research now claim the rewards." His inner voice pounding away. Slowly all the voices stopped and everything became calm. There was only one clear voice now.

"Yes I have the bollocks to do this and I will do it. I have to stay calm otherwise the whole plan will disintegrate." He says it out loud. His shivering stops. He looks around one more time. The coast is clear. Workman like, he begins.

At the place he had chosen for the fire he makes a "crowd" scene, exchanging boots with his own shoes and just walking around. After days of warm, dry conditions the "crowd scene" holds up well with boot imprints holding their shape. The boots go back into the bag. He throws a few cigarette butts on the ground. Then, standing perfectly still, he backs off the path, into the shadows, for a good ten minutes and observes the neighbourhood. He can see no one and all appears quiet. His eyes become accustomed to the poor illumination away from street lights. He puts the plan into action. "Thunderbirds are 'go'. Fiddle man is 'go'." He could hardly believe he could make smart remarks at such a time.

Putting on his gloves he goes back to the main entrance.

He drops the pole and attempts to prise off the metal grilles on the front of the building. With the first three there was no movement except for a slight bending of the grille itself. It would be clear that they had been tampered with which was Brendan's intention. As for the fourth grille, the pole actually began to cause serious damage. He stopped working on that window – that wasn't part of the plan. He moved to the side, to the window at the transition room, and within minutes the grille was wrestled off. He tore into the glass with the pole. He was well aware that the noise he had to make in gaining entrance seemed terrifically loud; it wouldn't seem so bad to anyone fifty yards and more away. In any case it only lasted no more than twenty seconds. Not enough time for a passer-by to focus in on the source. There would be little further noise. Again, after this segment of the work he halted and paused, intensely listening out for noise or for any unusual movement. All of his senses were now on high alert. Except for two dogs barking out their territory all remained quiet. There was some traffic, a few cars and numerous double-decker buses taking passengers in and out of town. The rush hour was over more than an hour ago. The odd distant police siren would get him to stand to attention. When it was clear that the siren was receding he would get back to his work. It was imperative that he get moving with some urgency. The shorter the time he was "on site", the less likely that he would be discovered.

It was proving more difficult than anticipated. The pole was okay for getting the grille off but not the best implement to remove the wired glass. He looked around and found a large stone – much more useful. Now he made progress – easily removing the bottom part of the window in minutes. Due to the wiring the top half remained attached. The opening was big enough.

With some difficulty he took the cardboard and bent it into a guard for the bottom ledge of the window where many fragments of glass still remained. Lifting one of the chairs that he had placed carefully earlier in the day to the outside he stepped up off the chair, through the gaping hole on to the other chair within. All very easy so far. He proceeds with great care. At this stage he wouldn't want to cut himself – that would be a certain give away to any investigating policeman, even Mr. Plod would manage to put two and two together and apportion blame on to Brendan. Once in, he made immediately for the strong room where most of the quality instruments were housed. It was darker than he thought it would be so he had to tread warily about the room. A stroke of luck – he hardly deserved – found that the padlock to the strong room wasn't engaged properly. He simply removed it and walked in. On further consideration this wasn't the stroke of luck he had initially thought. It might be that the police now deduce this is an inside job. One of the workers must have been assigned responsibility for this task. They would be due and they would get a bollocking on Monday. This saved Brendan a great deal of effort – there was certainly no guarantee that with his slender pole/crowbar he could gain entrance. He had assigned twenty minutes for this task. He followed his plan, selecting out a trumpet, six ordinary violins and a quality viola. As quietly as he could he removed drawers and paperwork to the centre of the room. Some drawers contained small amounts of cash – not more than twenty pounds though. The money was removed and pocketed. He then urinated into mugs and paperwork with as much pish as he could muster. A few cigarette butts were thrown around. Parts of the interior glasswork was smeared with dog poo. When push came to shove, though, he couldn't carry through the plan to defecate despite the fact that he, due to the adrenalin surge, was in "loose stool" condition.

Brendan threw the instruments out of the window into the overgrown shrubbery. He followed, remembering to bring the pole with him. He also brought out the cardboard he used. Finally, he cleaned the chair legs from soil and pushing the chair back inside he threw down the chair he had carefully positioned earlier in the day. He didn't want to give the impression that those two chairs and the cardboard were in any way necessary for a successful break-in.

He made two trips to transport the fiddles, the metal pole, the stood-upon trumpet and the viola to the site he had chosen for the fire. He carefully laid the instruments down, the viola half in, half out. Two violins were positioned near the edge so they would burn completely but leaving the burn shadow. So far it had taken twenty-three minutes from getting to the site to setting fire to the paper and the instruments. He had not cut himself, a major relief. As the fire got hold Brendan left, threw the pole into the beck by the premises. He threw away anything that might look suspicious, balaclava, gloves and boots. These would be chucked into dustbins, into backyards as he walked home. There was one item he'd not accounted for, the cardboard. Quite a bulky item. He didn't want to put it on the fire – the blaze would be too high. He took it with him, throwing it over the wire fence of one of the nearby factories. It would merge in with the detritus already there. Almost done!

He returned home as quickly as he could. Again he made sure that he returned to his house unseen. On entering he checked the kids – thankfully still fast asleep. He washed his hands, especially his nails, cleaned his shoes then took them out back and dirtied them up again but with different soil, the soil of home not the soil of S&S. Brendan turned the gas fire back on to get some heat back into the house which had cooled down considerably. He quickly undressed. He put his old trousers, his old shirt and his knitted jumper in a bag, replacing them with newer items. He took the bag next door and quietly, very quietly, put the bag into their dustbin. That would be removed early Monday morning, courtesy of the Council's regular collections. Indeed, all of his throwaways dotted around the town would be removed on Monday – alleviating a major headache. Nothing left to incriminate him. Finally, his tidying up complete, he sat down, occupying Ma's chair. He was calm. He was confident that he'd done a good job. More or less the "plan" worked so far. He wasn't going to be over-confident, there were a few cards still to play. He wasn't going to underestimate the powers of the police to see through Brendan's alibi, an alibi which was on the "thin" side. It was far from being a cast-iron alibi. He was half looking forward to the encounter.

He sat there thinking – had he forgotten anything?

Chapter 22

MR. PLOD MAKES AN ENTRANCE

Over two hours later, Ma returned.

"Didjeh win?" he asked.

"Na. I was one number away though on two cards. Jeeze would have won £21,000!"

This was a common remark of Ma's. Always the bridesmaid, never the bride. Her obsession with gambling would never diminish. But then again, who was he to judge? His obsession with thieving would never diminish either.

"Want a cup of tea?"

"Ah go on." Said Ma

After that short interaction, Brendan went to bed. Obviously the actions of the last few hours kept him awake all night, but as the night and the next day wore on he became more relaxed, as predicted.

On Sunday 30th, one day after the robbery, Brendan transfers the fifth violin to Chipry's attic, making sure the camouflage is as good as he can get it. He spends the rest of the day tidying his room and making sure there is no incriminating evidence, bits of paper, early drafts, et cetera. The police, when they put their minds to it, can be very, very thorough.

Brendan is desperate to find out what is happening at S&S. He knows, however, that any self-respecting burglar would never return to the crime scene – a dead giveaway of guilt.

On Monday, Geoff is the first to discover the break in. He calls Mark and then the police. The police arrive and declare a crime scene. All that meant was that another two officers arrived and had a good look round, inside and out. Various photographs were taken of the site and of the damage discovered inside the premises. All the staff would be contacted and a time arranged for taking statements. Brendan arrived late, claiming he'd slept in, which he had. The nervousness he was experiencing was balanced by the demeanour he presented following a rush to work. As he talked to colleagues he calmed down. The business of lying is all about controlling one's emotions. Brendan was very good at this but by no means perfect.

"Gordon Bennett, what's happened?" he exclaimed, feigning surprise.

Geoff filled him in with some of the detail.

"When you didn't arrive we thought it was you!"

"What was me. What's gone on?"

"Apparently someone's broken in. Bloody made a mess of the inside. They tried to get in there, at the front – you can see where they've used a crowbar. Then they went round the side; got through the window. I told them. I've said all along we needed greater protection." Mark pretended to listen.

"Can you remember I pointed it out about four months ago. Remember? If they've damaged any of my stuff I'll get bloody angry with somebody here, I'll tell you that now for free. We paid for security; that's why we all grouped together.

"Shit and piss all over the place. They nearly burned it down. All the stuff was in the middle of the floor! They nearly burned it down. Can't believe it, we nearly lost it all; all, can you imagine that? They must have been disturbed and skedaddled. I told em about it," Geoff ranted on and on in "I told you so" mode to anyone who would listen.

"Yes Geoff, you did, but as I remember it right young Brendan there pointed out one or two things too, it wasn't just you. This has been going on for years," said Gerrard, who had served at S&S the longest

All the staff were called to the premises. They would be briefed by the police sometime that afternoon. They remained and stood around waiting for further information and instruction.

A relatively short briefing meeting between the officer in charge, Sergeant Brian McClusky, and Mark Gibbons took place at midday. Following that meeting Mark addressed the workforce.

"Well I don't want to state the obvious but we were burgled over the weekend. Not sure whether it was Saturday or Sunday yet, probably Saturday. The police have been in and I have been in too. The place is quite a mess but luckily the damage is not as great as we had initially feared. We have been asked by the sergeant to give them a list of what was stolen. A cursory glance by myself suggests that only a handful of our most valuable instruments are missing. Unfortunately these appear to have been burned.

"Bad news, looks like an inside job. The main lock to the more valuable instruments wasn't locked. They walked straight in."

"Sorry Mark, that's down to me." Harry Pave spoke up.

"I was last out on Saturday. I couldn't find the key for the main padlock and I didn't want to lock the padlock in case the key had gone missing and we couldn't get in on Monday. When I got home my wife found the key in my inside pocket, it was mixed up with some other stuff. I didn't think it would matter if I brought it in on Monday. We went away for the weekend. I was going to get in early like, but I completely forgot. Sorry!"

"Oh for God's sake Harry, that's bloody criminal. I hope you had a bloody nice holiday," said Mark, visibly irritated.

"Well that sorts that problem out." Mark pulls himself together and continues.

"We need to make an up-to-date audit of what we should have. They also need an estimate of the value of the stolen goods. Looks as if the brass instruments have hardly been touched. About fifty yards away the police found the remnants of a fire. It appears some of the violins have been destroyed there. They just used them to make a fire – can you credit it, just to make a bloody fire. The police wouldn't know whether one or two violins have been burned or whether a larger number was involved.

"Looks like the work of a gang of kids. Bloody kids! We'll have to shut down for a couple of weeks to clean the place and get it habitable again. I don't know how kids are brought up nowadays. They'd got dog muck and smeared it all over the place. Why do that? Why?" Mark was shaking, close to tears.

"Anyway you can still draw your wages whilst we're closed but of course you'll still have your private work to deal with. I'm going to ask Brendan to do the audit – he knows more about this than the rest of us. I'm sure you'll give Brendan your support in this. We need to know what stuff you're working on at home and what you had here. We can't work here so Brendan will likely contact you by telephone at your home address. If your phone numbers need updating or if you haven't a phone then let us know. Geoff, can you go with the sergeant and have a look at the fire. Just see what you can see will you? Can you tell your clients that there will be a delay in dealing with their instruments. Anything really urgent come and see me."

Mark invited the sergeant to continue.

"Now, one of the unpleasant things we have to do in robberies involving a good deal of money is to suspect everyone. I will need to take fingerprints of each of you and to answer a few questions. If each of you could come down to the station sometime tomorrow, at your convenience, we can get this done and out of the way there. If you can't come tomorrow or if you want to come down today, then by all means do so. It won't take more than half an hour each. I should emphasise that the purpose of this exercise is to see if we can match fingerprints that we find that are not yours to any burglars on our books. Basically we want to eliminate you from our investigations. Please bring some identification, preferably involving a photograph with you – we don't want to jail the wrong man!" he said, trying to lighten the atmosphere.

McClusky was a tad on the intimidating side. It was easy to imagine him being the bad cop in a good cop–bad cop scenario. He was the tallest man there, at least six foot three. He owned a light grey head of hair, cropped fairly short. A pallid complexion highlighted jet black eyebrows. He smiled a lot, through yellowing teeth, with a happy gruff voice from many years of smoking. The rule that a copper wasn't allowed to smoke in public seemed not to apply to him. He was the kind of bloke who was immediately your friend, happy to share a pint and a smoke, which came across as being quite shallow. He wasn't to give anything away from his body language. He asked few questions of the group, happy to let them talk. In fact, he would hold on to those long silences, almost forcing the recipient to divulge more than he was initially intending to. When addressing members of the public he would look directly into their eyes, making it difficult for them not to tell the truth and nothing but the truth. He was a copper's copper, married to his job, a man with excellent hunches. On the up side of fifty he was tiring of the whole business, looking forward to retirement.

"Now I should also stress the following – I am only a sergeant but that doesn't imply that we won't be taking this matter very seriously. We are and we will continue to take this very seriously indeed. This is now normal practice. I will assess the robbery and decide if it needs an inspector to head up the investigation. I should tell you that at this moment in time I would classify this robbery as being class B, no persons were injured and arson wasn't involved – at first sight, it would appear to be the work of amateurs, teenagers. There are some parts of what we have found so far that, at first sight, are difficult to fathom. I expect they will come clearer as we proceed. There are some gypos, travellers if you prefer, around but I don't think they would have done a job like this. Just not their style."

Then McClusky raised his index finger and turned his head slightly in headmaster mode.

"Gentlemen," he said, to get their clear attention. He removed his helmet and wiped his brow. The helmet was replaced. A further few seconds of silence with each of the makers getting the "eyeball" treatment.

"Now gentlemen, a word of warning. If one of you is responsible for this musical then I'll have you, little doubt of that. I've been in this game quite a while now, I think I know what I'm doing. If I get a hunch then look out, 'cos I'll be after you, I'll keep going, on and on," he said with a serious and somewhat threatening tone.

This mention of amateurs carrying out the robbery relaxed Brendan a good deal. It was obvious to him that they, the police, had already made up their minds about the nature the robbery. Brendan would like the investigation to be as low-key as possible. He wants the police to jump to the obvious (but incorrect) conclusion – that this was a run-of-the-mill robbery not worthy of expending too much time and effort. A class B robbery deserving nothing more than a class B investigation.

Geoff was escorted to the fire and made his assessment. Of course he recognised the viola; his heart dropped, it was a lovely instrument now destroyed. He picked out the shape of three scrolls and an outline of one violin, all of them reduced to a white ash. He counted twenty-four metal strings each one warped in the heat of the fire, this would account for at least six violins. That's all he could spot. He saw nothing of the paper that Brendan had used to start the fire.

Brendan hoped that the mere appearance of fragments of the *New Musical Express* would further cast blame on a gang of youths. This was a naïve thought on Brendan's part and simple-minded. The copper with Geoff didn't bother to look at the footprints. He walked all over the crime site without a thought for physical evidence. He did discover, however, the squashed trumpet and another viola some sixty yards from the fire. With a little luck it could be repaired. A more extensive search carried out that afternoon uncovered nothing else. The pole, acting as crowbar, lay in the beck, undiscovered.

A further meeting of staff would take place on Wednesday afternoon to discuss progress and to get an update from the police.

Brendan conducted the audit and reported back to Mark and to the police. Brendan had been careful not to damage the previous audit records too much in his setting of the "crime scene". His work was done by Wednesday morning.

At their meeting later that day Brendan, by his calculation, reported they had lost, either burned or severely damaged, six of their most valuable violins, five of their least value violins, two of our most valuable violas and a trumpet of medium value.

Sergeant McClusky continued with the proceedings.

"Thanks for coming again. We thought, Mark and I, that you'd like an update to the investigation. You've just heard that you've lost about fifteen instruments. Could have been worse. I think you've got off lightly here.

"Okay firstly, we now think the offence took place on Saturday; well, at least, a fire was started here or around here on Saturday about nine o'clock – a neighbour came to the station yesterday complaining about kids and a fire somewhere in this area and could we do something about it. As far as the missing items are concerned you have lost, burned or severely damaged, twelve violins and a trumpet."

Brendan intervened, "To be precise, five of the good stuff, five of our ordinary violins, two valuable violas and the trumpet. Geoff tells me that he could only see evidence for the loss of two violas, one trumpet and six violins so four violins appear to be missing. They could have been burned beyond recognition, of course we have some unstringed violins, or they could have been removed from here altogether. I guess it could have been worse."

The sergeant continued.

"Yes it could. It looked as if they might start a fire inside the building. From what I've seen with so much flammable material here, gas burners for your glue, wood chippings all over the place, untidy and such, it's surprising to me that you haven't burned down years ago. Anyway they clearly thought better of it. They just did a bit of damage instead. I guess they realised that if they burned the place down then all hell would be let loose. The 'heat' in the way of police on the ground would most probably lead to arrests – their arrests. Anyway they thought better of it. I will be informing the fire service of this situation. I think they'll want to pay an urgent visit. You really must get this situation in order. You may even be facing legal proceedings. Workers trapped in a fire. You must surely have to replace those metal grilles. You get my drift?

"Now, back to our burglary. We haven't made much progress. We need to know where each of you were on Saturday evening. We have that information from all of you except," he looked at his notes,

"for Mark, Geoff and Brendan. We need this stuff just to complete our records. Mark, Geoff, can you see PC Robbins – yes we know he's got the name for it –

as soon as I've finished here. Brendan, can I come around to your home this evening? Say 7.30 p.m.?" Brendan looked at his colleagues with raised eyebrows.

"What? I can do it now, I've nothing else to do."

"No, if you will, this evening please." There was a short silence and McClusky carried on.

"I'm going to state the obvious and this will probably constitute what I will write in my report. On Saturday, approximately eight to ten o'clock, the premises, your premises, was broken into by removing a grille and padlock to the window in the 'transition room'. Following that it appears that thirteen musical instruments were stolen. Some superficial damage was done to the interior. A small amount of money appears to have been stolen. The instruments that were removed from the premises were either burned or damaged beyond repair. I have been informed, according to your last audit, that the value of the goods stolen or damaged is in the region of fourteen and a half thousand to seventeen thousand pounds (five valuable violins: two to two point five thousand each, five 'ordinary' violins: approx. at a hundred pounds, two violas at two thousand pounds each). That's a sizeable loss – I just hope you were properly insured.

"It appears to be the work of a small gang – about three or four people. Part of the crime scene has been corrupted by, apparently, a family of foxes visiting last night. Mark has given me the rundown as to areas of responsibility. Some fingerprints have been taken.

"We haven't found anything untoward. We will be visiting a number of individuals who might be able to cast light on the goings on over the weekend and some larger groups who have recently entered the area – I think you'll know who I mean. However I don't hold out much hope – unless someone has tried to sell some of the items. Nothing on that account as yet. So that's about it. I have some loose threads to tie up; that shouldn't take too long – couple of days at the most. You will be able to go back into work by Friday. Remember, this is a rare event, burglaries on this scale are few and far between. Shall I tell you why?

"Well I will tell you why! It's because, believe it or not, we usually catch the little buggers.

"My final report will be out by the weekend; by then the proceedings will be complete.

"Thank you for your assistance and your patience."

Chapter 23

A POLICEMAN COMES TO CALL

The group stood around for a while passing pleasantries – it seemed clear that the sergeant thought that Brendan had some involvement. The best that Brendan could do was to shrug his shoulders.

"Not me, not me," said Brendan protesting his innocence with the kind of smile and hand gestures that only an innocent person could muster. Brendan was an excellent actor.

However, this tactic genuinely concerned Brendan. Was it just bluster on McClusky's part? Did he know something? Brendan left for home thinking:

What does he know? Is he just guessing that it was me? Did he know about Chipry's attic? Did he know about Chipry? Had he found something incriminating? Brendan's confidence had been shaken. Nothing he could do but sit it out. Brendan got home about 4.00 p.m. Ma was watching TV with Andrejs. Roisin was out playing or coming back from school.

"Ma. Ma we're getting a visitor – a copper, a sergeant. Can we tidy up a bit?"

"What's it about? You've not been nicking bananas again," she said jokingly

"Ha, ha, ha. No it's to do with the burglary. He wants to speak to me here! I don't know why; he must think I did it. After all I'm the youngest there so naturally he might think I'm the one; all the other workers are mostly married men with a lot to lose if they were caught doing something like this. I don't know why he's coming here."

"You be careful son," she said with genuine concern. "The police can do all sorts of things, you know things they shouldn't be doing just to put somebody away. Remember those poor Irish lads jailed for doing sod-all, you know them Guildford four lads or is it six? All that evidence was planted. Be careful son. I know you're clever but they're coppers, sometimes they can get away with blue murder." Ma thought the worst, she started to cry.

"Oh jeeze be careful son."

"Ma, for God's sake Ma. It won't be like that. He'll ask a few questions and that'll be it. Believe me. They've learnt their lessons since those days. He's just trying to throw me, it's psychological. I can deal with it – no problem."

"Do you want me to say something?" said Ma.

Brendan held her by the arms and looked into her eyes.

"For God's sake Ma, whatever you do just tell the truth. Don't be going inventing stuff. Promise? The truth. I'm depending on you telling the truth."

"I promise son, I promise." It was a rare show of emotion between the two.

"Right, he'll be here about seven thirty. Just let's tidy up a bit. When he comes make a cup of tea will ye. Have we any biscuits?"

"No. I'll go and get some. Watch Andrejs will you. Roisin's out playing. I'll be back soon."

Brendan watched TV, as best he could, without his mind continually returning to the case of the five violins. This visit would the severest test of his nerve.

"Okay, if I'm caught, I'm caught." Caught for a burglary of this kind won't be the end of the world, though his chances of a career in violin making or getting into university would be scuppered for a few years.

Ma returned with a packet of digestives, a packet of garibaldi and some fruit for an empty bowl.

"Garibaldi? God he'll think we're middle-class. I have a reputation to keep up. Put the garibaldi away for God's sake. You can also leave out the bananas, bad memories!"

"I don't know what you get up to son but I want you to know that I'm very proud of the things you've done. You know, all the things you've done. And you stayed with us. You could have gone to your father in Birmingham but you didn't. Just remember that, for what it's worth we're on your side. Your family is always with you. I'm sure even Chipry would support you. He thinks a great deal about you, you know. He told me so."

Oh dear, Brendan thought. Ma has mentioned the "C" word – Chipry. He hoped she would really rather forget about Chipry, just for today anyway. Brendan has to hope that it won't come up in conversation.

All that afternoon the whole crime turned over in his mind.

Why the Christ did he do it? That's what he thought. Why take such a risk? After all he now had a good job, if he just keeps it up then he'll eventually earn a good salary. He went to have a bath to calm down. He felt he was being physically attacked by this policeman. There was nothing that he could do about it. And at this crucial moment in his lifetime all he could think of was:

were there enough biscuits? And that for the man that might put him away for a few years. At that very moment he thought how strange life is, how odd! The human brain is quite remarkable.

Sergeant McClusky was on time, he knocked on the door and Brendan invited him in.

"My mother," he said, pointing to his mother.

"Hello luv. How are you?" said McClusky with a noticeable wink. Brendan thought, what's going on there?

"Fine thanks, Fine. Will ye have a cup of tea, constable?" replied Ma with a face that hinted prior knowledge of the policeman.

"No thanks. We'd better get on. Have you somewhere quiet to go?" said the sergeant. Brendan took him up to his bedroom. "I need to have a quick look round, do you mind?"

"Help yourself. Excuse the mess."

On almost a quarter of the bedroom Brendan had laid a dust sheet. Often he would bring work home. At the moment he was working on a belly, the sheet was full of small wood chips and to one side there was a bookshelf where he kept his tools. He had a small workbench with a craft vice on the other side.

"What's that?" McClusky asked, pointing to one of Brendan's gadgets.

"Oh that's a thicknesser. You'll never guess what it's for?" he joked. Brendan was relaxing.

"The back and the belly have to be carved out to very precise thickness and that's what we use that for. It's different thicknesses over the whole area of the belly and the back. We have to go very carefully lest it gets too thin. Too thin and you might as well throw it away. Of course, if it's too thick then you can have another go at getting it right."

But, even though the dust sheet was almost covered in chippings, it still remained a very tidy room. The mess was non-existent. Brendan was always a tidy lad. McClusky gave the room a thorough once over.

"Who's that?" asked the sergeant, picking up a framed photo.

"That's Ma and a friend. I think they go to the Bingo together."

"This is a small room, I didn't realise these council houses were like this – two doubles and a room that can just accommodate a large suitcase. Oh I see you can get into the attic from here."

"You're not looking for a few fiddles are you?" said Brendan rather cheekily.

"Well it would save us a bit of time."

"I've only got my practice fiddle; I need it for my lessons. I know you think I stole those fiddles but even if I did would I stash them here for God's sake? You can have a look in the attic if you want. Use that chair if you wish. As it happens I had nothing to do with that burglary. The only thing I've ever stolen was a banana when I was about five I think. My mother beat me black and blue which was a lovely contrast with the yellow-brown of the banana. I didn't repeat that I can assure you."

"Don't be so presumptuous young man, you have no idea what's going through my mind. However, putting that to one side I may as well go along with the usual routine. Where were you on Saturday 29th, between the hours of six p.m. and ten p.m.?" The atmosphere in the room was electric. It was like a boxing match.

"For the first hour I was here at home. From seven p.m. I was watching the kids. Roisin was still awake so I spent a bit of time playing with her. Ma had gone off to the Bingo. Andrejs, the young lad was asleep most of the time and Roisin was awake but at about eight thirty p.m. she got off to sleep as well. For the rest of the time I watched a bit of TV. There wasn't much on at that time so I worked on my violin belly a bit. There it is." He showed him the belly.

"Not bad actually. This is my eighth," said Brendan. "The last seven had faults in them. I can't move on till I get em right." He pointed to the part he was working on but McClusky didn't bother to look.

"What was on TV at that time? Quickly now."

"Erm, I don't know. I've no idea. Charlie Drake? Oh no it was *Bewitched*, though I didn't watch much, it wasn't very funny this week. I usually like it, but last Saturday it was off a bit. Soon after I turned it on I turned it off. Ma came back at around ten to ten fifteen – the news was on. Yet again she failed to win us the fortune she says she's gonna win every week. I did a bit of reading, here that's what I'm on at the moment," Brendan passed him a book on the Calculus.

"Oh, the budding genius are we?"

"Well, if you've got it, flaunt it. No, no, I'm not that good. As it happens I'm trying to catch up to the other kids, not the easiest of tasks but I'll get there. See, I get special help, I go off to night school once a week."

Brendan was deliberately changing subject away from the burglary to break McClusky's rhythm. Brendan had a fair alibi, he was confident it was good enough.

"So you live here with who precisely?"

"Ma, the Bingo queen, Roisin, she's about eight, Andrejs is nearly four and me. My dad is back in Ireland. Families aren't his thing. They're divorced now. I write from time to time. I haven't seen him for over three years. If you know anybody, preferably rich, I'm open for adoption!"

"So you're an apprentice. How's it going? Any good?"

"Yeah not too bad. It's a long training though. Don't tell Mark Gibbons but I'm hoping to get to university. Mark thinks I'm going to stay here for the rest of my life. Well, I could just about hack it and in a few years' time I could be earning quite a bit, but we'll see. It's a fifty–fifty thing at the moment."

"Okay Brendan, let's stop beating about the bush. I think you know what I know." McClusky's demeanour changed to a more sombre mood.

"Sit down, sit down lad. I'm going to tell you a story. It's a story that's not to be repeated. If it gets out I'll be blaming you. Diye get me?" Brendan sat on the edge of the bed.

"My lips are sealed," said Brendan as he listened to this softer tone.

"As a young lad I was a bit like you, a thief, not bad either, bit of a villain. You're obviously a bit brighter than I was. I wasn't in your league, I think the maximum I got away with was just over seven hundred quid and I can tell you at the time it came in very useful. This was all before I was a copper. I always worked alone. Every job I did I thought about very carefully. You're the kind of thief I like, you're probably doing it for your family which I applaud. I'm against violence, obviously I'm not really against thieving – depends what the motive is. There are good thieves and bad thieves. I'd happily steal from the Third Reich but I'd think long and hard before removing anything belonging to Winston Churchill. See what I mean? Like you I came from a very poor family so I could easily justify a Robin Hood existence, except when I stole, I stole from the rich and I gave to the poor, the poor just happened to be me!

"I never got caught. Certainly can't afford to get caught now. You think going to jail is bad, I can assure you it is but going to jail as a copper is horrendous, wouldn't wish it on anybody. Some inmates can be evil. Just the thought of it even frightens me.

"I planned very well but I was also very, very lucky. I should have been caught on at least four occasions but luck intervened and saved my skin. The last time I stole it was too close for comfort. I've never stopped stealing and I don't think I ever will but I decided to get a proper job. Did well to get on to a police training course. I'm a sergeant partly because I know how thieves, well some thieves, think. That gives me an edge on my colleagues. Look I don't want to see you get caught. It'll ruin your life and your family. Think of them. I have a sure thought that you're the one, you planned it, carried it out and now you'll wait, for months if necessary, though you might have done it already to get rid of the evidence. I think you did it, not sure why I think that except it's all too clean, almost too well planned. We won't be able to convict in this case until we find some evidence. I think you're lucky, you've got away with it.

"So that's my little story. Now what are we to do? If I was intent on bringing you in I would need the stuff that's missing. That would be tricky see, 'cos I don't know where it is. You probably got it well hidden and you can probably leave it where it is till the heat has died down. We're not going to put a 'tail' on you. The crime is just not that serious. You could have already got rid. Could be years. Well we're not going to wait that long are we?"

Brendan remained silent throughout this diatribe.

"Okay, given what I've just said I'm going to suggest something which may surprise you. I'll drop the search for our 'burglars', that won't be hard to do, we haven't got much evidence anyway. The insurers will pick up the bill so Sharples & Son won't be out of pocket. They're going back on Friday, same wages so the men won't be out of pocket either. The whole matter will quieten down. No doubt they'll improve their security. By this time next week we'll be looking at new burglaries, ones that haven't been so well planned. You'll be back working on your 'belly' no doubt and I'll be back as Sergeant Plod.

"Now, listen carefully 'cos I'm not going to repeat it, in fact I will deny anything I've said here, take my word for it, I'll be believed, you won't. And remember if this 'gets on the street' I'll find out, so be very, very careful in saying anything to anyone, even your mother – get it?

"Right, listen up, in about a year's time you will send me a registered envelope containing five hundred pounds to my address, nothing but used notes please. You don't know my address – I expect you to find it. That'll be your first task. Don't worry, if you don't do as I ask, if I don't get my Christmas bonus there won't be any comeback – I'll just put it down to experience. But if I'm any judge of character, I'll be having a decent holiday in around fifteen months' time – get me? I could make your life very difficult, so think very hard about your next move."

Brendan said nothing, Brendan admitted nothing. He sat there motionless.

"I'm going now, so I'll say goodnight. Remember five hundred quid, fifteen months' time."

Finally, Brendan stirred.

"Well thanks for coming round. I see the position now. Hope you have a good Christmas."

McClusky left. Brendan sat back on the bed.

"Bloody hell!" said Brendan. He wasn't expecting that. "God, good God," he said through clenched teeth as he laughed and laughed. He jumped up and down, not believing his luck.

Hearing the front door close Brendan came downstairs.

"What are you smiling at?" said Ma.

"I can't say. Honestly, I can't say, just can't say. Just had a bit of luck, that's all."

"You know who that was, don't you?" said Ma.

"McClusky? Sergeant McClusky. He's the man in charge of the investigation."

"I know that now, now you've told me, he's at the Bingo though, he takes his mother to the Bingo every Saturday, unless he's on duty, me and her share a table together, just on nodding terms. She never said he was a copper – I guess most people try to keep that kind of thing quiet. He's not in the Bingo himself, he's just the taxi. He's often given me a lift home. Nice man, very polite. Always dresses well. I think he might ask me out for a drink. He's been angling for that in the last few months. He lives with his mother you know. We seem to get on okay. On the shy side."

"What!" Now he understood. Brendan was now relatively safe, he had a copper on his side, clearly prepared to bend the rules and a thief like himself. And not just any old copper, one that's sweet on his mother. For once he delighted at the word "Bingo".

Brendan went back upstairs and had a very restful sleep. His concerns over being caught dissolved into thin air. However, Brendan was disappointed. Despite all his planning the suspicion that he was the burglar fell on him. If there was to be a next time Brendan would make sure his alibi was airtight, beyond reproach.

Over the next seven months one violin after another made its way down to London and Mr. Trev to be exchanged for cash. He was good to his word. Only a relatively small amount would be spent on personal matters or the family, the remainder would go into a savings account. In all he managed to accrue £8,255.

Chapter 24

AND THE WALLS CAME TUMBLING DOWN

Now that he had a bit of money Brendan made a couple of trips back to Ireland, to see his brothers Thomas and Cormac and as many first cousins as still remained there. He also sent Ma and the lads on a couple of two-day breaks to the seaside at Scarborough. Ma never questioned where Brendan got the money to do this. Brendan said it was partly a bonus from work and Chipry made a contribution as well.

Cormac and Brendan were back on brotherly terms but not close, there had been too much bitterness for that. On his second visit back to Ireland he got Cormac alone. They climbed up the hill at Palais Green near to Caherelly. It took thirty minutes to get to the top, from which they could see the lush county for miles and miles around.

"Remember this?" said Brendan. This spot was a favourite of all the family. In the summer, usually on a Sunday after Mass, the whole clan would get a few sandwiches together and a couple of bottles of "pop" and climb the hill. They would have a little picnic. Ma would sing a couple of songs and Mick would play a few tunes on the tin whistle.

"A lot of water under the bridge." Brendan looked him straight in the face. On this occasion he brought up the subject of Glin. This was normally out of bounds, Brendan normally refused to discuss the topic.

"You'll remember Glin. Well, of course you do. But you probably don't appreciate that I have some inkling as to what they did to you. We just chose to treat it in different ways. Just because I don't make a fuss about it doesn't mean I don't care. Actually I care a great deal – more than you'll know. We're different people. We have different ways of dealing with it, 'with that stuff'. I prefer to keep it hidden. I think it would hurt Ma if she knew how they treated you. She already blames herself for what happened."

Brendan looked at Cormac. Brendan began to cry. His voice was breaking up. He took a deep breath to control his emotions.

"I've always wanted to say what I think when we were both grown. Now that we are grown it is still too painful to say." He bowed his head as if in salute. He took another deep breath. He could hardly get a sentence out.

"Thank you for holding my hand in that place. In reality, you held my whole body." Brendan broke down. Cormac had to hold him up lest he fall. They hugged each other, and now both were crying. The deep emotion that both of them felt at this moment made them laugh in embarrassment. After a few minutes they recovered their composure. Brendan took another deep breath.

"Jeez, three deep breaths in a row. Let's try again."

"I want to blow it up," Brendan said with no apparent emotion. Cormac instinctively knew what he was talking about.

"Don't we all," said Cormac.

"Well, one way or another I intend to have it done. I think you can help."

"How?"

"You have access to dynamite. You know how to use it – I don't. This is what we should do – it's quite simple. Get enough dynamite – you won't need a lot. Steal it from your firm over the next few months. Take it bit by bit. I'll bet they won't miss it. We only need it for the walls anyway. Eight to ten sticks is all we will need. The rest of the building can be burned. What do you think?"

"I know how to use it and if you only need ten sticks then, yes, I could get that without causing much fuss. The detonators too. A few cans of petrol should do it for the main rooms."

"We'll need a car or a van, something like that. You go down, size the place up. You know it's shut down now, for over a year – the locals told me, all boarded up. I went down by myself a couple of months ago. From what I could make out it looks easy to get into. We'll need some hefty cutters to get through the front gate. This is good for us as we can get on with our work without anybody disturbing us. We don't want to injure anybody – I'm adamant about this. I just want to obliterate the place so that no one else can be sent there."

"Okay, you know I'm game. Let's do it."

"Here's some money. If you need any more let me know. There's a thousand quid in there, in Irish money. Do everything using only cash. I don't want you to get caught so be careful and hide your tracks. Keep your business to yourself and no one is to be told, no one. No bragging. It's just between us two. Agreed?"

"Agreed."

"We'll need to hire a car – it'll just be easier with a car. I can't drive. If you're not old enough then we'll have to steal one. We'll do it over one weekend. Drive down on a Friday evening, suss out the place; we might have to change our minds, depends what we see when we get there. Get a B&B for the night then early Saturday afternoon we do what we have to do. You'll have to do all the dynamite stuff and I'll do the offices."

It took just over three months to organise. On one Friday night they drove down, recced the place and decided to go ahead. The weather was very poor which suited them down to the ground; this would keep young kids away. They spent most of Saturday morning preparing. Cormac set the dynamite and Brendan set up the accommodation buildings to burn using timing devices supplied by Cormac. They would delay ignition for about two hours, both for the dynamite and for the petrol bombs. They locked the entrance into the yard so that no one would be injured following the explosion. Cormac arranged matters so that the walls would fall inwards when blown up. The windows and doors to the accommodation blocks were prised open so that anyone straying into the place would be able to escape from the inferno.

Cormac and Brendan set the timers and without haste, calmly left the scene of the crime. They would have liked to stay to see it go down but this was second best. It would have to do.

From Glin, Cormac drove Brendan to Limerick Junction to catch a train in time for the midnight ferry and home.

"Thanks Cormac. I've always wanted to do that."

"You and me both." They shook hands and parted.

Two weeks later Ma happened to buy the *Limerick Leader*, which she did from time to time to keep up with the gossip, the news and most importantly the births and deaths section which she examined with a fine-tooth comb. She read the report into the demolition of Glin Industrial School. It was the lead story.

"Have you seen this son? Somebody blew up the school in Glin, yes that's it – the Industrial School at Glin, they've got before and after pictures here. Look! My God, there's nothing left of it. It's like an atomic bomb hit it." She began to read out loud:

> *"The explosion occurred at precisely 7.30 p.m. on Saturday evening. It was followed almost immediately by a fire engulfing the main accommodation blocks and offices. Fire tenders were called to the scene but it was too late to save any significant part of the structure. The building was isolated and of little value so a decision was made on site to let the building burn. It was not worth risking the lives of firemen to engage. The building was still smouldering two days later. A few wall segments which were left standing in the accommodation block and in the yard were regarded as unsafe and so were reduced to rubble.*
>
> *"Initial thoughts are that it was the work of vandals but a more detailed examination strongly suggests that it is more likely that it is the work of professional bombers and arsonists. Though the IRA haven't claimed responsibility the thought is that only they were capable of carrying through such a professional job. The question as to why the act was carried out is, as yet, unclear though the rumour that many children were abused in that place may have stirred the IRA into a kind of reprisal."*

"They're putting it down to the IRA. Here look."

"Not interested." Brendan rejected the paper with a flick of his hand.

"Good for the IRA, they should have bombed that place years ago, years ago – the poor craters who suffered in there. At least on this we can say hooray for the IRA.

"The fire people said that as far as they can work out there were no injuries."

Brendan was unusually quiet. Ma never considered the thought that Brendan might have been involved. The burning of the Industrial School at Glin was not a topic that ever came up in conversation again.

On the first anniversary of the robbery, Brendan tucked five hundred pounds into a registered envelope and posted it off to a Mr. Brian McClusky.

Chapter 25

BRENDAN MAKES A VIOLIN OF NOTE

It was shortly after the first anniversary of the robbery that Brendan completed the task of making a violin to the appropriate professional level. It is a tradition in S&S that the first tune to be played on his first instrument would be chosen by the maker and played by the maker in front of all of the makers – a rite of passage. The wives would bring cakes along with tea and beer. Not being a very good cook, Ma brought a packet of Mr. Kipling's finest and two bottles of Guinness. His family, Ma, Andrejs, Roisin and even Anna turned up and shyly sat at the back as if they had no right to be there, as if they'd come in out of the rain. Brendan invited Chipry but the offer was declined. Mr. Sangster turned up. Brendan shook his hand.

"Hi Sir, how did you know?"

"Oh I have my sources. I contact Mark from time to time to see how you're getting on. He's got nothing but praise for you. How's the maths coming along? I guess it's taken a back seat all these years?"

"Still on the polygons. Remember? Actually I've made a bit of progress. I haven't enough for a paper yet, but it shouldn't be long before I have a chance of getting my name in print."

Brendan stood up. The good-sized crowd came to order.

"Before I play a tune I would like to read a snippet of a poem which, in all this time, has kept me focused on my path ahead. Actually, I don't know the title. As far as I can fathom it's about being adventurous in life about taking the path less travelled. That's how I see it anyway."

Brendan began:

"This is a poem by Robert Frost, written in 1916 I think. I hope you will forgive me if I shed a tear or two – I always do with this poem:

"Two roads diverged in a yellow wood,
And sorry I could not travel both......Yet knowing how way leads on to way,
I doubted if I should ever come back.
"I shall be telling this with a sigh
Somewhere ages and ages hence:
Two roads diverged in a wood, and I —
I took the one less traveled by,
And that has made all the difference."

Brendan halted once or twice, hardly able to finish.

"Thank you to all of you. You have all helped me, not just to carve out a violin but also, and more importantly, to carve out a life. I will forever be in your debt.

"For the tune, I have chosen one both familiar to Mark and myself and to Ma. I may not finish this either without shedding a tear." Mark went to the back and, taking Ma by the arm, brought her up to the front.

Brendan tuned up and played "Roisin Dubh", last sung over four years ago to his classmates and now played to his workmates and his family. As for the violin, it was a good sound – not on the same level as a strad but nevertheless a good sound. Then Brendan looked towards his mother.

"How about it Ma, can you remember it? Will you sing it for me? You should be up here, you deserve this as much as I do."

She nodded. She stood up and stood by Brendan.

"I'll give it a go. Give me a note will ye?"

She cleared her throat, arms down by her side and eyes closed she sang "Roisin Dubh"; faultless.

At the end they all stood and clapped. Gathering round they held his arms and wished him well. Some gave their baby of the workforce a hug. Through damp handkerchiefs they all celebrated with beer, tea and cakes. Mark had a particular word for him.

"Look Brendan, I know you have bigger fish to fry, but I hope you will stay with us for a while longer."

"I'll do my best and thank you so much."

Mr. Sangster congratulated him.

"Brilliant. Very well done indeed. Look – I've gotta shoot off. I'll pop by in another year!" They both laughed. As Brendan stood there away from the crowd he remembered Chipry and the "yellow shite" and the tripe, the trotters and the nettles, and the enormous cakes, he remembered the short trousers, the yellow banana, the lost shoes, the pigeons and poo day, frozen arses and blowing up Glin and mouthed to no one in particular, the word "thanks". He knew his success wasn't just down to him alone. Like Isaac Newton, the only reason he could see what others couldn't was that he was standing on the shoulders of giants.

Ma came up to him and told him some secrets.

"I'd forgot I taught you that. I thought you'd forgotten it. Thanks for remembering. Thanks for staying with me and the lads. I wished that yer Da was here. Life is never right is it? Life is always up and down, it's all cods'td up most of the time. When you were born, you know, we nearly lost you. I caught some horse from going mad, it had a baby on it, a little girl. For an instant I thought it was you, I rushed to save you not the little girl but thanks be to God she was saved too. Then the fine doctor saved you. His name was Brendan too. I can remember the dancing and the singing all that day. I'm sorry about the home, you and poor Cormac having to go in there. I didn't know about them. I didn't know about them kinds of places. Your Da didn't know either. Then we left for Keighley. Your Da stayed behind. That was all cods'td up too. We should have tried harder, but sometimes the hurdles are too big. That's how it was for us. We were stupid, couldn't see the path ahead. Chipry was good. Without him God knows what would have happened. And now you're here son, doing well, doing great chur. I know you won't forget us. You won't forget us will you? Don't forget us," she said in desperation.

They embraced each other, then the whole family came up and all hugged each other.

"Forget you, how could I ever forget you and the lads. You all mean everything to me. I just hope I don't cods it up."

The men were let go early. They said their goodbyes.

"I've saved up," said Brendan.

"We're going to have a treat. It's fish suppers all round, and tea and bread." They all piled into the fish shop. For once the Ryans were "on the up". Proper haddock and chips for everybody, not the cheap scone they normally have. Tea for the grown-ups and lemonade for the rest.

Brendan stayed on at Sharples & Son for another year honing his trade, but, inevitably, as Mark had surmised, the call of mathematics and deeper study became an attraction that could not be denied.

In the two years following the robbery Brendan learnt much. He excelled in mathematics and was now able to direct much of his own study. He knew more than enough to take him to university. He chose to go to Queen Elizabeth College, London University, for two main reasons. He wanted to know London and the research carried out in the mathematics department was General Relativity, under the leadership of Hermann Bondi. Professor Bondi was a name that continually cropped up – he was a popularizing mathematician and was often seen on television. Also, any serious mathematician would study relativity, which was on the border between mathematics and physics and on the border between hard and impossibly hard. It was considered to be a difficult topic and Brendan wanted a challenge. It was a little later, a full year into his course, that he realised that Bondi and his team of researchers were based at Kings College, not Queens. Brendan was still very ignorant of the whole university system!

Despite his academic prowess, certainly in the sciences, he was still under-prepared for life as a student, he was poorly read (not counting the knowledge gleaned from TV, he knew all about scoring in cricket, football, tennis, golf and rugby) and his knowledge of etiquette would, if measured in the range from zero to ten, occupy a prominent position in the negative register.

Brendan was always a lucky boy, always landing on his feet. His luck, as he would appreciate later, in the matter of "digs" was purple. He didn't just land on his feet, he landed on all fours!

As he left Keighley for London he had just two cases; a single large, very large, suitcase into which he crammed everything he owned of value, and the second was his violin case.

A tearful Ma and Anna, Roisin and Andrejs waved goodbye at the bus station in Keighley.

Chapter 26

UNIVERSITY CHALLENGE

Brendan didn't know how to say goodbye. How should he act? A kiss, a shake of the hands. He could have said he was coming back. He could have said, "I'll miss you all." He was a coward, he hurried everything along making out that driver had to get going.

"Bye Ma" were the only real words spoken between the two. Ma, heavy with emotion, had to lean against the pillar lest she fall. After all this time together they were separating. It wasn't those two words that described a life together, a life of hardship and struggle. It was the look. Ma's cheeks filled. She didn't cry. She knew that if she cried then she'd never stop. Brendan had never seen her face like that before. She mostly kept her true feelings hidden from her children. She was heartbroken, that's what that face was. All these years she had hidden that face. Now she couldn't hold it back. She was heartbroken to the bone. She thought he was gone for good.

No hugs, that family wasn't the physical kind, they had seen too many bad things for them to act "normal".

No hugs then, just waves and even then it was more of a salute than a wave. He was reminded of the time he bid goodbye to his father as he left Glin and he stayed behind. What could Brendan do? He had to go on this journey if he was to rescue this family from a meaningless life of drudgery; he wanted to contribute, he wanted his family to contribute. He was at least going to give it a go. He knew that staying behind was the more difficult option. He was a clever lad, he'd be okay. It was sure that those left behind, Ma, Anna, Roisin and Andrejs would have to endure the struggles. Brendan was off to the bright lights.

A long journey in many senses was ahead. He was about to travel on the path less used one more time. It would seem that Robert Frost and his few words would forever pull at him:

Two roads diverged in a wood and I
I took the one less traveled by
And that has made all the difference.

"Go that way, that way, go that way." Would he always have this monkey on his back?

The coach, enjoying a couple of breaks in the six-hour journey from Keighley, turned into Victoria Coach Station just after 3.00 p.m. He then had to carry the enormous case and his violin over two hundred yards from the coach station to the Tube station. There were many porters on the way offering their services to carry bags for a half-crown. He continued with his luggage alone. Once on the Tube, and standing all the while, he changed on to the Central line and from there about twelve stops to Ealing Broadway. He then faced a half-mile, perhaps further, journey with the case and fiddle. He could have got a taxi but that wouldn't be his habit. He could have got a bus but didn't want to go the wrong way. He walked and a half-hour later turned into Sutherland Road. The bell at 23 Sutherland Road didn't work. Brendan's continual loud knocking eventually brought the landlady to the door. She was guarded by a couple of black Scotties, except their "blackness" was more like "greyness". Pushing the dogs back into the house with her foot she managed an off-balance handshake. Of course they had written to each other during that summer, but now he saw Dr Sheleagh O'Hara in the "flesh". She was a striking woman with fine features, black hair with grey streaks surely in her early sixties. Her teeth, not all of which were her own, would move in and out as she smiled and spoke, but it wasn't at all off-putting. A stroke of luck, she was Irish. Not just Irish, but the kind of Irish that felt and acted superior to the English. She was a member of the Irish upper class. Despite his very heavy case she gave Brendan the attic room which turned out to be an act of kindness. He was the first of the students to arrive, three days before the start of term.

The room contained a single bed, a sink, a desk, a chair and a small gas fire, requiring a shilling if in use.

His room pointed along the flight path to Heathrow Airport. Every ten minutes or so he could track the path of the planes as they prepared to land.

Brendan spent the next year there, learning how to cook, how to set a table, how to tell a fish knife from a knife, how to eat, how to signify that you've "stopped eating", how to talk, knowing when to keep quiet and when to be forceful in conversation. Knowing not to use one's greater intellect to the detriment of others and how to acknowledge and to give deference to your elders no matter how stupid they may act. All these things were learned by looking and watching and by just being there. She could see he was desperate to learn about the niceties of cultured living. She was sympathetic to Brendan's cause and helped a great deal to smooth his rough edges, of which there were many. She knew he was on the lower rungs of so-called "society" and she could help him up a step or two. She did. The students who shared those digs affectionately referred to her as Mrs. Woman. She had a very large detached house which could accommodate eight students. In the vernacular, she was coining it in. She had another house near Oxford. Whilst most of the students returned home at weekends, or at least three or four times during term, Brendan would stay the full term until the college broke up for Christmas. Brendan was happy to help with jobs around the house and with dealing with the garden at Sutherland Road and also at the Oxford house. By profession she was a psychologist. No doubt Brendan was an interesting case to analyse. Her style was refreshing. If ever Brendan complained of depression, which he did from time to time and was tearful from time to time, she didn't set up a series of fancy consultations to get to the bottom of his problem, rather, the single cure she would recommend for all these so-called syndromes was to take a hot bath. For Brendan it worked every time, possibly because every time he took a hot bath he couldn't help remembering the slipper bath episode and Winifred the Poo, which always brought him out in laughter. Within hours he was back to normal, annoyed at being sorry for himself. After all, even twenty years after, he was boosted by the thought that he had escaped from Glin. His main problem lay with the opposite sex. Basically he didn't know anybody from the opposite sex. He was determined, over the next few years, to rectify that situation.

Brendan was twenty-two when he enrolled at Queen Elizabeth, which was based between Notting Hill Gate and High Street Kensington. When at college he was within walking distance of London museums, Hyde Park, Kensington Park, Holland Park and Imperial College. It was a thrill to find out that Isaac Newton occupied properties no more than fifty yards away. Brendan's digs at Ealing were forty minutes away, by Tube, from High Street Ken.

At his age he was referred to as a mature student, though it seemed obvious that "mature" was an accurate descriptor for him as, so he found, most other students, the eighteen-year-old ones, were immature!

The government was very generous. He had a full grant to include daily travel and four trips home each year, together with an extra income from a scholarship. He didn't need the money, his venture into the violin business saw to that, but it did mean that he could send money home on a regular basis primarily for Roisin and for Andrejs. The last thing he would want is that those two would suffer the indignities and the shame of being poor and bright at school. Of course it was dependent on Ma spending it wisely, implying that it would mean curtailing her trips to Mrs. Bingo and Mr. Slot Machine which was a new deadly interest representing, as it did, one of the quickest ways of throwing your money away in the western world. He had little faith that that would happen. Ma found it difficult to write or call, she was missing the basic skills in communication. On one occasion whilst he was having supper, with all the other students present, the phone rang. Mrs. Woman, at the head of the table, left the room to take the call. After some time in discussion with the caller, she re-entered the dining room and, quite embarrassingly, told Brendan that there was a strange man on the phone for him – it turned out to be Ma!

On his fourth weekend away, towards the end of October, a letter arrived from Ma. He could tell it was from Ma with her recognisable, but almost unreadable, scrawl and the fact that she had written on the back in biggish letters "from Ma".

It wasn't often that Ma wrote any kind of letter, this worried Brendan and he was quite concerned as he tore it open.

Son, tanks for the money. I'm going to spend it all on the Bingo – no, no, that was just a joke.

Ma rarely made jokes.

I'll get some clothes for the two of them. You know that copper, the sergeant Brian McClusky, he came round for a cup of tea. I thought I might go out for a drink with him if Anna will watch Andrejs. The lads seem to like him. Mind you he brought lots of sweets with him so they might be thinking of the sweets, ye no. What do ye think, shall I go? What are yer digs like? I hope ye have settled in London place. Andrejs and Roisin are missing you!
Ma.

Brendan wrote a fairly long letter in return, part of which read:

The digs are good but I am missing some decent soda bread. The landlady is a bit posh but Irish from the Waterford area. Her two sisters live here with her – it's a huge house about four times the size of Chiprys. She's taught me how to cook spaghetti which is very different from the stuff we have in tins. I have also eaten a curry with rice – not sweet rice pudding – really good. She tried to get me to eat mussels – and pigeon - but I draw the line there! They always boil potatoes after they take off the skin! No white bread only brown!

Brian is an okay bloke. Please yourself but the kids have got to get on with him but in the end you've got to please yourself. Good luck. I've got a few more weeks here but I'll be back for Christmas. This might be a year we can afford a turkey?

Look after yourself and for a change I've included something for yourself – yes you can spend it on Bingo, but if you win we share now! Good luck!

From Brendan.

Chapter 27

THE RYANS, FROM RAGS TO RICHES

The first day as a university student he bought a Queen Elizabeth scarf, only to ingratiate himself into the "student" club and at the social gathering that evening drank cider, medium strength. He wouldn't be drinking much more of that as the similarity between it and Chipry's "yellow shite" was too great. By day two he had relegated the scarf to a drawer, it was far too scratchy on his neck. He thought, *Serves me right for being so bloody pretentious.* He soon settled into university life though always considered as a bit of a loner. He joined football and badminton clubs. He got his head down and worked hard. He found the work easy. He looked forward to getting back at Christmas.

His trip home took longer than expected due to heavy snow from Bradford to Keighley. Brendan didn't think to tell Ma when he was coming back. It was still his home and he still had the front door key. He turned up just after six.

When he opened the door, there was Ma sat by the gas fire watching television. When she saw Brendan her face broke out into a broad smile. She clapped her hands and said "ah ha". The lads flew down from their bedrooms to say hello.

"Put the kettle on," she said, a friendly order after three months away. Brendan went to make a cup of tea and found the walk-in larder pretty low on rations. Brendan gave Roisin a tenner to go up to the Co-op and buy a few cakes and a loaf and a slab of butter. She brought back his favourite, a large shortbread concoction covered in jam, white soft icing and coconut.

The tea was made, the cake consumed. That was it, within minutes of his return they were back to normal, back as a family. There was a deep happiness within each of them that none could explain. Brendan was back. They knew he would go away again but future goings-away would be okay, they knew he would return again and again. He was not abandoning them. In the twelve weeks he was gone, he got soft, used to pleasant temperatures, showers and regular hot baths. Though the fire was on "full" the council house was cold, the bed freezing. He would have to make up a hot water bottle from a large empty glass bottle of lemonade, covered with towels, this needed care – there had been quite a few breakages over the years. Despite the hot bottle he could hardly sleep for the cold.

He had a good deal of money left from the violin caper so he bought a couple of presents, it wasn't what they normally did but Brendan felt he had a responsibility to do "something". His presents were functional, coats and a pair of shoes each for winter. He gave the lads some money so they could buy Ma a present each and buy paper and the like to make simple decorations. Turkey and presents for Christmas, the Ryan family never had it so good.

He didn't bother to tell them how well he was doing, they could hardly care less. They still had struggles of their own. After just twelve weeks as an undergraduate, Ma thought Brendan was now a professor.

Even though he had only left Keighley for a short while it felt like a lifetime. He knew it would never be a permanent return. Keighley was his past, for the time being London was the place to be. He returned to London in early January.

Surprisingly, in semester two he joined RAG - a student-run charitable fundraising organisation. They organise trips out to collect money and generally have a whale of a time, all in the interests of collecting money for various charities. It only involved a few hours a week so Brendan, who was easily coping with the course, forced himself to lighten up and join. He could certainly collect money by wafting a bucket around but his natural shyness prevented him from doing much more. As a further "plus" to joining RAG there was a good proportion of females – interesting! He was aware that he was becoming a lonely bird and this was an attempt to rectify the situation. His apprenticeship at S&S was male dominated, here, at least, he had good opportunities to meet females. After all, now he had a bit of money saved he could wine and dine with the best of them.

However, there was an incident in his month with RAG that spurred on his long-term interest in stealing. His interests in females might, once again, have to be put on hold.

The mathematics department at QE occupied a new (less than eight years old) four-storey-high building. It slotted snugly to the left of a large private dwelling – more of a mansion than just a dwelling. To the right of the mansion, as it was known, was the grounds of a school. On the other side of the school was Holland Park, few flower beds but lots of trees and dense bushes. Housed within the park was the London headquarters of the Youth Hostel Association.

Staff offices were on floors one and two and lectures were usually held on the top two floors. Each floor had windows on each side, south, north, east and west. The top floor offered an excellent view of the west end of London over Hyde Park and Kensington Park to the east and to Holland Park to the west. The building was erected with planning restrictions attached. It could only be built if due consideration be given to the privacy on the east, a private dwelling. The windows were to be opaque and blocked from opening. There was a flaw generally accepted as being down to the builder. The windows on south, west and north were normal windows as planned. However, the windows to the east were the top-opening, opaque type, allowing a four-inch opening gap so, at a stretch, you could see much of the goings-on in the private dwelling, particularly from the toilets on the east side (if you went on tiptoes and if you pulled yourself up a bit). The goings-on were of considerable interest to the peeping toms amongst the students; they could see into the back garden, including a good view of the swimming pool and the enormous Jacuzzi. The then owner of the private residence was unabashed and carried on regular weekend "adult parties" at which there appeared to be a preponderance of females of the "Ursula Andress variety". Unfortunately for the "Toms", the building was closed to students at the weekend.

Some students were invited over; their reports of the goings-on were disappointingly ordinary; plenty of drink, plenty of food, bit of a laugh, but that was about it. If anything, student parties were considerably more liberated. The frisson of excitement at the mention of a party at the "mansion next door" soon died away as semester one rolled into semester two.

The private residence was owned by Chas Earl, the clothing magnate with shops in over fifty towns and cities, mainly in the north. Even Brendan had heard of Chas Earl through TV adverts and the annoyingly memorable ditty:

"Earl, Chas Earl, the window to watch."

Brendan wondered for a second or two if he was related to Bond, James Bond. Indeed, following the violin theft the one luxury Brendan had allowed himself was a handmade suit from Earl's, Beatles-style with the turned-up collar. The light grey suit was made and delivered within three weeks. Brendan was very disappointed, the style wasn't really him and the trousers were an inch too short, bringing back unpleasant memories of his first day at "big school" in which he stuck out like a sore thumb. With this suit he looked like Norman Wisdom from the waist down. Brendan was too shy to complain. After all, what could he complain about? The suit was approved at each stage of its construction. To his embarrassment he wore it on three occasions then dumped it. He was even tempted to shout *Mr. Grimsdale, Mr. Grimsdale* on one or two occasions. His body, his demeanour, didn't really suit high fashion. He would be more careful next time and dress more like "Pitkin" than Paul McCartney.

From the snippets of information that Brendan had gleaned from the grapevine, Earl Chas Earl was a show-off and a braggart and he knew it. He happily accepted that as a descriptor.

Each work day as Brendan walked down from Notting Hill Gate to QE he would see Earl's deep blue Lamborghini parked near his house with the number plate UGE 1 presumably a vital statistic, not referring to the car. Not to be outdone the jovial head of the nutrition group, which was a world famous department at Queen Elizabeth, tried to match the Lamborghini with a more affordable Citroën and a number plate NUT 1. Brendan would always smile at the contrast and, for him, the nutritionist won hands down in the "cool" stakes.

In his defence, Earl Chas Earl was known as a generous giver, always making a substantial gift to RAG and to the college each year. He didn't mind people knowing how wealthy he was, quite the opposite. He had a lot of money and typical of the very rich he didn't seem to know what to do with it. Of course he would spend on this and on that in the way of consumables, all top of the range, all flown in from somewhere exotic, but where was the money to be put in manufacturing and innovation, into new ideas. If he was guilty of having too much money then Brendan was planning to help with that problem.

Chapter 28

EARLS AND VISCOUNTS

Earl was a widower and, since the death of his wife, often arranged parties for his friends.

Two weeks into semester two the yearly invite to members of the RAG committee was received by the Students' Union President. All were instructed to dress as smartly as they could. As was now becoming traditional, the vice chancellor and his inner circle were also invited. It was a friendly get-together amongst neighbours.

Each of the three groups, the RAG committee, the Students' Union committee and members of the "suits" (the VC and his cohort) gathered by the main entrance. They walked next door, all looking forward to this upmarket yearly binge. They were greeted by the domestic, Dorothy, followed by Earl himself. As Earl waited at the entrance to shake hands, a very amiable man ferried them into the ultra-large lounge which spilled into the swimming pool area. There were so many lights illuminating every painting, every piece of furniture, every gadget; Brendan thought the main switch at Battersea Power Station had been resurrected and switched on. He confided to others that he'd wished he'd brought his suntan lotion.

Chas Earl was not a man of great sophistication. His guests were welcomed with a glass of wine or a glass of champagne or a cocktail or hors d'oeuvres. Their coats taken. After the niceties had been dealt with, Earl clapped his hands together to gain their attention.

"Ladies and Gents, thank you so much for coming to my home. I express a particular greeting to those here for the first time. I hope you won't be disappointed. Those of you who were here last year will know I'm a man of few words – I know many of you will say 'thank god for that'!" That brought the first laugh of the evening.

"Don't worry, I'll soon release you to the buffet. If you have any special dietary requirements then please have a word with Dorothy, my personal assistant." Earl, ushered her to the front so that people might see her.

"She's been with us for so long, she's one of the family, and someone I couldn't do without! I've booked a great chef for tonight and he and his team are desperate to get going. This year I'm going to string it out a bit – I've a special announcement. I would like you all to meet my daughter Christine." He looked around to see where she was. Reluctantly, Christine joined her father, somewhat embarrassed by the situation.

"She's going to join King's in October, I'm really sorry, I tried my hardest to get her to come to QEC but she was adamant, stubborn like her dad! I'm really sorry about that but it's what she wanted. She's going to do marketing, it's a two-year course. Is that right love?" She nodded in agreement.

"So I hope you'll say hello and make her feel at home this evening. Oops! I guess she is at home – well you know what I mean!

"Now the second thing I want to announce is that I'm even richer than last year," a statement followed by pleasant laughter, "and I am able to be more generous this year than last. I am, this evening, announcing a gift of fifty thousand, yes I said fifty thousand, to Queens University." Embarrassingly he failed to get the name of the college correct.

"The plans have been discussed between myself and your boss, the vice chancellor, for some weeks now. It is to be used to set up a research post for the study of retail selling and dedicated to the memory of my late wife." Led by the vice chancellor there was a generous and genuine round of applause.

He continued.

"Of course I could tell them a thing or two about retail selling, perhaps I ought to have a degree, hint, hint, nod, nod, Mr. Vice Chancellor," a more than blatant attempt to be considered for an honorary degree. The vice chancellor smiled the kind of smile that suggested that that was a real possibility.

"Come and look at this, come round," he shepherded them toward a large circular picture on the wall. On closer examination the picture was made up of thousands of images of twenty-pound notes of varying sizes arranged to look like "Britannia" on a penny. It looked like a picture that would hide a safe, and so it did.

"Look at this Ladies and Gentlemen, boys and girls," as he proceeded to open the safe. It was hinged on one side. He played the usual trick of twisting the central dial clockwise and anti-clockwise, building up the tension.

"You don't actually need to do this – it's just for show." There was an audible gasp as he opened it wide and took out neat bundles of money made up of twenty-pound notes. He passed some of them around to students and staff for them to hold and for them to wonder.

"You might have seen this in the papers, a couple o' months back – people think it's odd. Well I don't care, they can scoff all they want. I think it's just jealousy – them reporters are so high and mighty. I'll bet they'd do the same if they had my money. As a kid we had no money. Well I've got some now, and I'll show it off at every opportunity – sod the reporters."

The extra staff, employed as waiters for the evening, continued to mingle with alcoholic drinks in various guises, not believing what they were seeing.

"Do you know how much is in there? Any guesses, anybody – well I'll tell you it's over fifty thousand, it's over fifty thousand, that's for sure. Well I'll tell you, there's seventy thousand in there. I always keep at least fifty thousand in cash – it just makes me feel better." One or two laughed.

"Just looking at it gives me an adrenalin surge!" He punched the air with both fists.

"Ladies and Gentlemen, I like to know it's there. I like to take it out and count it and repackage it. I'm not shy about this. I'm proud of it. It's what I've worked hard for. That's what you students should be doing – working your butts off just to get money like this, that's what makes this country great."

And, twirling round, his arms outstretched:"To get stuff like this, my paintings, my furniture – that's a Chippendale you know." A student quickly rose off the chair to his feet.

"Oops sorry, didn't know."

"Don't worry son I won't charge you for any damages," he said as the student sheepishly withdrew to the back.

"Anyone recognise these?" He pointed to two "modern" paintings."They're not Hockneys are they. Surely not?" volunteered a member of staff.

"No they're not Hockney's, they're mine!" A well-travelled joke, resurrected one more time. Smiles all round.

"Yes, Hockneys, both of them – I can't say I like his stuff, but what the hell, he's a northern lad – all right he might swing the wrong way but nobody's perfect – get my drift," embarrassed smiles all round.

"I often bring my managers down here, show them the money, let them feel it. It's quite a boost to them, they leave enthused. I fling them a couple of hundred quid just to keep them interested. They know that if they do well then I'll be generous. They'll benefit directly. Don't tell the tax people though, they'll have it back off them as soon as you can shout bastards!"

The visitors looked at the money, rolled it through their fingers like a pack of cards, becoming intoxicated with it.

"Pass it round – get to know how it feels. Say to yourself: I want some of that. Then you just might succeed."

Brendan turned to a student friend, Robbie.

"Christ, that's what you call money. What I could do with that. That must be close to what we'll ever earn in a lifetime. If he's got this here think how much he must have in the bank!"

"Bank you say," as he overheard Brendan's remark.

"Don't trust them son. Course I've got to have some in there, but not the UK banks. I'm into Switzerland, that's where my money is, not so much 'offshore' more 'up high' – they're bloody discrete too you know, I think Hitler's still got an account there." More laughter.

"Just in case you're wondering son, I've got more than sixty-three million quid. Just think about that for a while. It just rolls off the tongue, doesn't it? Just over sixty-three million smackeroos. Of course it's earning a good interest just sitting there, it's increasing all the time." The guests were speechless at that revelation.

"Anyway, I've said enough. Time to hand 'em back. Pass 'em back please." The wads made their way back to the safe though not before many students pretended to pocket it.

"You can't hide it son, I know, down to fifty quid exactly what I have. No one leaves till it's all accounted for," he said half-joking.

"Oh, nearly forgot. The RAG thing. Christine has asked me to give you some money too – as long as it's for charity." Christine, twenty years old, squirmed with embarrassment.

"How much did you say Christine, what should I give them?"

"Well, we thought five thousand would be about right, I hope that's okay," as she addressed Brendan, thinking, due to his age, that he must be in charge.

"Not me actually but George over there, that handsome bloke. He's the man you need to see."

George was suitably impressed with the gift.

"Do you want to do it in cash or by banker's draft or just an ordinary cheque?" Another round of applause greeted the gift.

There was much fun and joviality throughout the evening. For a few hours Brendan enjoyed the high life. There was food of high quality, cocktails on stream and tours of the house for the staff.

"Aren't you scared of being burgled?" said one of the students.

"No, not a bit. Look I'm surrounded by buildings – there's only one exit apart from the fire escape. You'd need a helicopter to get in here. It's an excellent safe, far better than you'd get in a bank. As I said I always keep at least fifty thousand in cash in there, that's what I like to do. I like to enjoy my money. To see it and to feel it through my fingers. No petty criminal is going to cheat me out of that. Should they by some streak of good luck get into the house and then, by another streak of good luck, get into the safe, then my insurers would pick up the bill. To be honest I'd probably get more back than I'd lost. No, I'm not worried about burglars, in any shape or form. However, I have some knowledge of the criminal fraternity and they have knowledge of me. I've made it clear that if they target me then I'll use my wealth to hunt them down. They won't be in a hurry to burglar after that."

After the initial embarrassment of a father overplaying his cards, Christine settled down and made a genuine attempt to excuse her father's crass behaviour.

He may be filthy rich but it was generally agreed that he ought to spend some of it buying a smidgeon of "style". He had money, money to burn, but he had no class. Even a bucketful of style wouldn't be enough to give him "class".

"He's not been the same since Mum died. But he does have a bloody lot of money which he doesn't know what to do with. Money came to him late, corrupted him a bit, you know like a pools winner."

Within the first hour of the gathering George, with his chiseled good looks and his private school accent, showed distinct signs of being besotted with her. His perfectly white teeth and ruffled, unkempt, boyhood hair ensured that she felt the same.

"Why don't you come round with us on our trips out? Do RAG for us, not King's. You'd have a great time. Far better than at King's," George said to Christine.

"My dad likes to keep tabs on me. He likes to know where I am."

"Oh don't worry about that, we can arrange something. Tell him I'm the son of a viscount – that usually does the trick." Even Christine's eyelashes flickered at that knowledge.

"I know what we might do. In about eight weeks' time, on a Saturday, we've got a trip to Paris organised. There are many teams of two, a boy and a girl, have to get to Paris, quick as we can. You're not allowed to use the telephone, no going into post offices to get injections of money – anything like that. This year we're trying to get on the radio. You've got to get sponsored. Can you manage that? My father won't give me anything. He says I've got to sort myself out. At least think about it. Could be fun!"

Christine rushes off to her father hand in hand with George.

"Daddy, this is George, his daddy's a viscount."

Brendan thought,

Mmm, crassness runs in the family then! "Gee, is that higher than an Earl son?" he joked. "

Very nice to meet you, young man." They shook hands.

"Good grief, you've got baby skin. Have you ever worked?"

"Not if I can help it," he said laughing. Earl joined in the joke.

"Well done you. You're okay, you've got money – somewhere. These poor bastards," pointing to the students, "have to scrape a living."

"Daddy, the RAG committee have invited me to have a short tour of their premises – it's just round the corner. I'll be back in an hour, I promise."

Chas Earl didn't get where he was today without seeing an opportunity when it arises. This could catapult the lowly Earl dynasty, just one generation old, on to an entirely different echelon. His "new money" background is sure to open a door or two. Money speaks a very persuasive language.

"You take as long as you want love, we'll be here for another hour anyway. A viscount's son eh. Well I'll be. Bring him round for lunch sometime. You can use the swimming pool and the Jacuzzi, just let Dorothy know. But not on a Saturday. You know that that's my counting day – not my viscounting day; joke, get it? I do business on Saturday – keep it to yourself now – I catch up with the shops, see how they're doing – it keeps 'em sharp and focused. I'm always here on my own. Well, with Dorothy of course, I need the odd cup of coffee. I need to think see, Saturday is strategic thinking day."

"Oh thank you daddy, thank you." She said giving him a generous hug and a kiss on the cheek.

"But remember young man, viscount or no – back before midnight otherwise I release the hounds," he said with half a smile.

"Certainly sir. I'll look after her. With the vice chancellor looking on I have to behave!"

George and the RAG team, having eaten their fill and drunk like Thor, retired to their "offices" which was the bar, just two minutes away in the Students'

Union common room. True to his word, George released Christine in good time, escorted her back and gave her a respectful kiss on the cheek. Christine responded with a kiss on the lips.

"Goodnight. Thanks, here's my number. Give me a call in the week. It'll come through Dorothy but she's a pal, she knows how tricky it's been for me in the last few years. I'll tell her to expect a call from a dishy young man – oh, and one from you as well! Nite."

Chapter 29

BRENDAN DEVISES A COPPER-BOTTOM PLAN

Brendan had retired to the bar too. He was sat alone, on one of the comfy sofas, cogitating. Thinking about wads of money. Thinking about sixty-three million pounds to be precise.

Robbie came to sit down beside him.

"You okay Brendan? Sat there by yourself. It's not healthy. You should be up at the bar getting me a drink. Why don't you get the fiddle out and give us a few tunes?"

"Yeah, I'm just thinking about a few things," said Brendan

"Did you see all that money?" said Robbie.

"Oh yeah, I saw it all right. Didn't seem fair really, him having all that money and us having none. He didn't know what to do with it for God's sake. There should be a law against it. I tell you, there should be a bloody law against it. Not surprising the number of left wingers in this country; you know, bankers, business and City people they've either got too much money – they don't know what to do with – or they've got the status – given to them umpteen years ago by William the bloody Conqueror. What the hell are we doing accepting that? One day, even in this country, there'll be a bloody revolution and I'll be marching ahead with a flag that says 'bollocks to all you twats, bollocks, bollocks, and a further bollocks for good measure!'" Brendan calmed down.

"I didn't know George was the bloody son of a bloody viscount, did you? I must remember to bow in future," said a slightly irate Brendan.

"Well I knew he was some sort of earl or lord or something like that. Anyway he's George, that's how I treat him. He shits just like the rest of us you know."

"I'll have you know young man that my shit isn't just any old shit, it has breeding with a rather cultured aroma. I purchase only the finest, softest paper and treat it with the utmost respect. It is shit of a very high quality and not to be sniffed at!" Robbie laughed out loud. "Anyway, as a member of the middle classes, it's not shit – it's poo," said Brendan.

A plan to extract money from that safe full of the green stuff was, even now, brewing in Brendan's brain. Within a couple of hours he had formulated an entire plan. He was really pleased with the overall structure. It was to be a simplistic crime, without a break-in, without violence. His body was tingling with pleasure at the thought – he would arrange matters such that Chas Earl would simply give him the money! It would be a diversion to his course. He would get a great deal of pleasure from working out the detail. Mr. "I don't know what to do with it all" needs to be taught a lesson in humility. Brendan was looking forward to the contest.

For the moment he would need to speak to someone back home. He committed the plan to paper and prepared what he could for his return back home. On the following Friday, the second Friday of semester two, he travelled back to Keighley on the coach from Victoria. Ma and the lads would be glad to see him again so soon after Christmas. It reminded him of the travel back from London and getting delayed at Stoke-on-Trent a few years previously. This journey too gave him the time to think through his plans for Chas Earl, or, as he would often refer to him, Earl Chas Earl the dumbo to watch.

The day after Brendan arrived in Keighley he knocked on Brian McClusky's door. In his hand was a small brown paper bag, the kind you get when you order a small bag of sweets.

"Hello. Remember me? Brendan. How are you? Still with the police I see."

They shook hands.

"Well I'll be. Long time no see. You're the one who coughed up the goods at Christmas a few years ago. It was a pleasant surprise. I thought you'd forgotten. I would have contacted you sooner, you know, a get together about me and yer Ma. We get on well you know. Stops us both getting lonely. I'd like your approval, not that I need it, but I'd like it all the same. There's no way I want to upset your family. It's still early doors, I can still walk away."

"There'll be none of that talk. I'm okay if Ma's happy and she seems to be. But you've got to be nice to those kids, please, the kids are the ones that always get it in the teeth in matters like this, I know only too well."

"Yes I heard all about your past. You have my word on that. I'll help them grow up, give them a bit of stability. You needn't worry on that account. I have a good salary and an excellent pension. I'm reasonably well balanced. You're away a lot of the time. They could do with a bit of a figurehead, someone to guide them, day by day, you know, keep them on the straight and narrow."

"Look, can we talk about that some other time? Let's forget that now. I need your advice on another matter if you know what I mean. No beating about the bush. Can we talk?" said Brendan, lowering his voice.

"I have a mutually beneficial plan, a violin type plan. You'll have a minimum amount to do, I'll be organising stuff, taking the risks. If you agree to it then there's £10,000 in cash for you and £40,000 for me. If you don't want in then say so now, I'll use someone else. If it's yes, then we'll go out for a drink and I'll tell you more. But before you make your decision look at this." Brendan passed him the bag.

"What do you want me to do with it?"

"I worked on that for the last three hours solid. Open the bag, look inside."

"Oh dear, what's that smell, what the Christ is that?" said Brian, reacting to a particularly nasty smell.

"Now I don't want you to jump up and down till I explain, just calm down and don't be squeamish. It's a girl's finger. I chopped it off earlier today, the blood's dried a bit. What do you think? The nail is still intact." Brian dropped it in horror and physically pushed Brendan away.

"Oh for God's sake, Jesus Christ. What the good God are you up to?"

To Brian's horror Brendan picked up the bag, removed the "finger" and made to eat it.

"Oh for Christ's sake Brendan, that's disgusting."

"Calm down. Don't worry, I'm not going to eat it, it's not real Brian, well it's not a finger but I suppose you could eat it. It's false, I made it, but you were convinced it wasn't false, weren't you? That's my third attempt. I'm pretty pleased with it. It's mostly made out of chicken."

A voice interrupts the conversation.

"Who's that son, who are you talking to?" said Brian's mother from inside the house.

"Okay Mom, I have to go out for a while. Just having a small drink. Don't worry, I'll lock the door behind me."

In short Brian was "in", at least at this level. He was keen to know more. The phrase "your lot will be £10,000" helped a great deal.

They found a quiet spot in the Fox and Hounds, a pub on the outskirts of Keighley.

Brendan started with the story of the man who had so much money he didn't know what to do with it.

"I'm not going to tell you everything – it would take ages. I'm going to tell you what I'm going to tell you four or five times, what I know, and the gist of what I intend to do. It's partly down to you to pick holes in it, okay? At any stage you can walk out, no comeback! I'll just get somebody else."

"Okay, there's a guy in London who's filthy rich and I mean rich. You'll have heard of him for sure, Chas Earl, the guy who sells suits in most towns in England, up north anyway. He's a recent widower, well, two or three years ago with a young daughter, Christine, she's nineteen, I think, or thereabouts. He lives in a fancy house, runs a Lamborghini. His house is next to my college. It's more of a mansion than a house, in a really plush area – very upmarket. He thinks his house is impregnable. Well I guess it is for ordinary burglars. I've seen his safe – quite legitimately – can't be touched by an ordinary burglar, unless you've got weeks to spare with fancy drilling equipment to burrow into it. You'd need to be in heavy engineering to get in! Out of the question. Nobody's going to get any money that way. Then I thought, how can we get him to cough up some money? All I could think of is kidnap."

"Whoa there, that's getting a bit deep for me, sorry Brendan I couldn't get involved in that. I'm still a bloody policeman for God's sake. I have a pension to think of," said Brian.

"Keep your voice down for God's sake, people will hear!" said Brendan. He continued:"That's exactly the reaction you'd expect from any civilised person. Kidnap is almost as bad as murder, not to be lightly entered into, depriving someone of their liberty – not good. But that's the kind of reaction I'm banking on," said Brendan.

"Not bloody surprised."

"But I intend to carry out a civilised kidnapping."

"And what precisely is that when it's at home?"

"It's kidnapping without the victim being kidnapped! In American jargon, the kidnapper has to convince the father of the kidnappee that this is a genuine kidnapping. The kidnapper has to pile fact after fact on to the father's mind to make him think the kidnapping is genuine and that the kidnapper is ruthless."

"Yes? I'm just about listening. 'Kidnapping without the victim being kidnapped.' That's a new one on me," said a bemused Brian.

"Okay, I can understand your scepticism, but listen. This guy, Earl, and his daughter, Christine, are very close. He's very protective. What you need to do is to – sorry – what we would need to do, is to convince Earl that Christine is kidnapped or will be kidnapped unless he pays us fifty thousand quid. Look, let's say this Christine is your daughter. If you were told that if you don't pay up your daughter would be kidnapped and possibly her fiddle-playing finger chopped off – would that make you think – if I was him, the Earl bloke, then I'm going to do everything to free my daughter 'intact'. I wouldn't want her hurt physically or mentally. Sod the police.

"Now wait for it, the *pièce de résistance*, if as well as that we deliver an actual chopped off finger or something that looks very much like as if it's a chopped off finger, to focus his attention then 'bingo' he's going to pay up immediately. Particularly as he is filthy rich and fifty thou to him is less than five per cent of his yearly salary for God's sake! I'd pay up, you'd pay up, ninety-nine out of a hundred would pay up, no questions asked. With the scenario I'm going to present to him he's going to pay up, no doubt about it. Earl wouldn't go through the television scenario of demanding to see his daughter is still alive before he'd pay up. In real life that wouldn't happen, particularly as this bloke's got more money than soft mick, as my Ma would say."

"Look, Brendan, I'm not chopping any fiddle fingers off – out of the question. I'm not having anything to do with violence or anything near to violence."

"Quite right too. You and me are the same. We're in it for the craic. What I'll do is to make a finger, for me, an easy task. It'll be in a plastic bag covered in beef blood – easily obtained. I can make it out of chicken. It'll look the bee's knees, so real. You saw it, you had a good look. I'll put a false nail on it – you can buy them for god's sake. There's no way he's gonna examine it closely. He's gonna be appalled by it. You saw how realistic it is, and that was just my third attempt! He'll accept it immediately. He'll think it's a real finger, he'll think it's his daughter's finger, he'll cough up. What do you think?"

"Nope, not satisfied. I need to know how you make a finger. If I'm to go into a thing I need as much info as I can get."

Chapter 30

PLAN A

"Okay, I'll describe the process to you, you'll have to trust me that I can do this for real. Look I am not bad on making and modelling stuff. I can make a violin for Christ sake. Look at your own index finger. Think how you might make something like that, one cut off at the second knuckle.

"Look, what you do is get a small raw chicken, you know, from a raw chicken shop," said Brendan with a tad of frustration.

"Then you get a very sharp knife, like a craft knife. Then on the breast bone towards the parson's nose you cut out an area that looks like the outline of a butterfly – but without the head, so just the butterfly wings. Okay, turn the piece of chicken over and, carefully now, cut through the breast bone. Trim the breastbone to look like a thin rod. Still with me? All you're left with is part of the breast bone, chicken meat and smooth chicken skin, still strongly attached. If you do it right you'll find it quite flexible – like a finger down to the second knuckle. Now, again using the craft knife loosen the skin around the edge of the 'butterfly' shape and remove some of the attendant meat from those parts. The rod has meat and skin attached. The artificial nail is then placed in position underneath the skin about half an inch in. The skin on one side of the butterfly wing is then stretched around the meat, any surplus is cut off. Exactly the same routine is carried out on the other side. What we have now is something that looks like a cigar. The skin at the nail boundary, on top, is then pressed down with the back of the craft knife, removing skin if necessary to make a neat join. The skin at the nail boundary underneath is also pushed down but not quite so far – look at my finger to see what I mean. It will now look like a finger. All we need do now is to tart it up. The skin will naturally be a greyish colour – that's the colour of the chicken. The nail is painted as normal. Some of the skin and meat, near the 'knuckle end', is dyed with a very light – and it has to be very light – blue food colouring to give an idea of bruising. Lightness of touch is important here. The finger is placed in a small plastic bag with a little blood added to it – pig's blood or my own if necessary. Some preserving fluid is added, like Milton, to keep the finger fresh for up to a week. However, it's likely to discolour too much after a couple of days. Now you have to trust me. I can do this. Look here's the finger you chucked away."

Brendan proceeded to "undo" the finger back to the butterfly stage, explaining what he would do at each stage. "I can make better than this. It'll be perfect when I do it for real. I am satisfied with the end result – it even puts me off and I know what's in it! Look, I'd guess that even if it was a very poor attempt at making a finger, Earl wouldn't question it. He'd think it was real, badly cut – even worse to a father. There's something inside all of us that would be appalled by such an object – bit like decapitation!"

"Okay, okay, you can make something that looks like a finger. It has some merit, I grant you that," said an increasingly interested Brian.

"You certainly come up with some schemes!"

Brendan tried to reassure him.

"Look what's the worst case scenario? Let's say he's an uncaring father – which is against all the evidence – and he doesn't cough up. He calls our bluff. The way I've planned it we can just walk away. We just walk away. It'll cost us two or three visits to London, a bit of stress, then I get back to my studies or on to another of my projects and you get back to plodding the streets of Keighley – apart from me and you nobody's any the wiser.

"The thing is we don't give him time to think, that's the trick in this case. He'll panic just enough to give us the money. By the time he realises what's happened we'll be over the hills and far away."

Brian thought for a few minutes, putting his palm towards Brendan meaning for him to keep quiet for a while. He got up and walked around. Finally, with a slight shake of his head, he agrees to a further meeting.

"Okay, we'll meet in Lund Park by the grandstand about 10 a.m. tomorrow."

"I'm not saying I'm in, I'm almost there but I'll think about it overnight. This is not the kinda thing you rush into. Plan A has gotta be foolproof or as near as dammit before I say aye. Let me have the finger, horrible little thing. Even now I think it's alive, I'll look at it."

The next day they met again. Brian unfolds an A4 piece of paper, with scribbled marks all over, front and back.

"Don't worry, some of this stuff is Mom's shopping list. I've got lots of questions. I threw the finger away. After a while I couldn't stand the smell."

"Yes, well I can deal with that. By the time I've finished with it, it'll be smelling of roses, well, not quite roses, well you know what I mean. It'll have no scent at all."

Brian starts with his questions.

"First, where does this Earl bloke get that kind of money in the space of half an hour? Even rich blokes have to ring up a banker – no?"

"That's the beauty of this, he always keeps at least fifty thousand in the safe in twenties. He was bragging about it. The night we went he had seventy-five thousand stashed away, he showed us all. All in twenties, looked like used notes too. We all handled it. You could tell he was serious. He was half wishing some burglar might try it."

"He's probably bragging. What if he's only got £10,000 in the safe. Is it worth doing for just that?"

"Well yes, agreed. We'll just have to accept that as a possibility. For myself, I was there, I really didn't think he was showing off, but yep that's a possibility."

"Just a minute. How much does that weigh? How much does fifty thousand quid weigh?"

"Good – thought you'd ask that. Well, these things are done in metric. A thousand in twenties weighs about fifty-five grams so fifty thou would weigh nearly three thousand grams or, to you, around six pounds – you're looking to carry three big bags of flour."

"Perhaps he loves the stuff so much that he won't sacrifice fifty thou for his daughter?"

"No way, he's very protective of his daughter, at his 'do' you could see that."

"What about his mental state. Perhaps the thought that his daughter might be kidnapped or her finger being chopped off might send him over the edge? Every bloke has a limit you know, what you're asking him to accept is something shocking. His wife's gone, all he has left is his daughter and she is threatened with kidnap and finger-chopping. He might have a breakdown or a stroke? Old Dorothy, that's the maid, would be on to the police sharp like. We'd have to scarper, which is okay but we don't get a cent if that happens. And also they'd be looking for us just as much as if we had the cash."

"From what I saw on the night, and I give you that I've only seen him for a three-hour period, my impression is that he wouldn't crumble under the pressure. Remember he's the head of a big organisation, he must be used to dealing with pressure all day long. Anyway, to relieve the pressure all he has to do is give us the money – a simple solution. This guy's not going to buckle, of course we have to believe that."

"Okay, some mundane questions. What if he's not there?"

"He's always there, on Saturdays, to him these are business hours. He randomly rings the managers of some of his branches. It keeps them on their toes. He'll be there. It's his modus operandi, it's what he's known for. He'll be there all right, him and his domestic, Dorothy."

"Run me through the plan again. As much detail as you can give me. We need to do a lot more background work."

"Yes of course. These are just the bare bones."

Brendan goes through the routine he was to use.

"Now, this Dorothy woman, what's she like?"

"I don't know much about her except they've been together quite a while, ever since Christine was a baby. She must be in her fifties at least. As far as I can gauge she's pretty ordinary, hard worker, doesn't get paid very much. I can't see her as a problem. She'll tow Chas Earl's line. When you first knock on the door with the stuff I'm gonna give you for Earl, tell her you're warning locals that there have been reports in the area of some shady characters around and can she get this stuff to Mr. Earl urgently. You'll need to wear your uniform which is bound to impress her. You're in a hurry and have to visit more addresses but to be sure that Mr. Earl gets the packages – that's the message we have to get across to Dorothy – a sense of urgency. This plan will fail if she doesn't perform, she has to be convinced that you're a policeman, somebody with authority with an important message for Mr. Earl, so important that it has to be delivered immediately."

"Well I'm not sure the softly, softly approach, the approach that expects Dorothy will act with urgency is one to guarantee success. I may have to wind it up a bit."

"What do you mean?" said Brendan.

"I mean I may have to put the frighteners on her. People of that age need a kick up the backside otherwise they go around in a namby-pamby way. They'll start up a conversation with you for God's sake. You can't let that happen!"

"I leave that to you. That's your problem. Remember though, not too harsh, she could be my Ma! Anyway I guess you've done this kind of thing before without drawing blood?"

"Once or twice. In interviews I usually play the hard cop. Okay, leave that with me.

"Now, what if the daughter turns up, or if she's there, then we're stymied."

"All we need is a fifty-minute window, less probably. I happen to know that on Saturday, exactly seven weeks from today, Christine will be on her way to Paris with her new boyfriend. You won't understand but it's a RAG 'do' – basically student's bunch together to try and raise money for charity."

"I know that for God's sake. They had that at Police Academy too you know."

"Anyway, they will be out of communication for at least six hours. The new boyfriend is the son of a viscount so Earl's given her special permission to get involved in the hope of kindling true love and move two or three rungs up the status ladder. These students all leave at 10 a.m. sharp. They have to hitch lifts and so on till they get to the 4 p.m. ferry at Dover. If she rings home she is likely to do it just before they get on the ferry. You will be long gone by then. They get a free ticket to Calais – an arrangement with the ferry people since it's for charity – and get to Paris as best they can. When they arrive in gay Paris they pick up a special rosette from the Union President, with the time of arrival. The winner is the couple taking the least time for the journey there. None of the couples can realistically arrive back before 6 p.m. 'cos the ferry back from Calais doesn't leave till Saturday at 9 p.m., so, you see, there's no chance of being 'disturbed' except, possibly, for a phone call. If I know Mr. Viscount he'll cheat, get a bed in London for the night, have his bit of fun with Christine, and then have one of the couples pick up the signed rosette on his behalf at Paris. He's got to have a rosette to show his future father-in-law that he was on the road and not in the bed overnight. He'll just have to avoid civilisation for a few hours. He or she wouldn't want to be in contact with 'daddy' in any case."

"So this is Plan A. What's Plan B?"

"There is no Plan B. We do this or nothing."

Chapter 31

RANSOM NOTES TO POUND NOTES

"Okay, I get the gist of the 'job'. You seem to know what you're doing. You obviously know you still have a great deal of research yet to be carried out. For what it's worth, assuming that what you've told me is true then it looks good. I think you have a chance of making a lot of money with little risk. So the important question, why do you want me? You could just about do it yourself."

"I need someone that will look like a copper, will act like a copper when required. I expect you to graft, to think of stuff that I haven't thought about. Somebody who'll watch my back. I need an airtight alibi to account for the time from nine in the morning to six in the afternoon, Saturday. Don't worry, you'll have plenty to do. I want you to deliver the ransom note, and to pick up the money. I want you as a policeman patrolling just outside Earl's house from 2.25 p.m., that's the time you deliver the note, to just after 3 p.m., where you collect the money just outside their front door. "You're right, as you know it's best to work alone, but some jobs are just too big. I need at least one other person, your name came top of the list. Actually there isn't a list, I've never worked with anybody before. That's why I want you. In any case you're almost family! If a question was asked I don't think you'd give me up. Just a gut feeling."

Brendan continued outlying the plan.

"I'll make the finger early on Thursday in my room. I shouldn't be disturbed, we'll all be in revision mode then. I will need to forensically clean my room afterwards. I want you to come down during the day on the Friday. I'll meet you at the station or possibly at your B&B and pass over the finger and the kidnap note. That Friday I'll play my fiddle in the bar for most of the night to give an ambience of normality – I don't want to be seen acting 'oddly' in any way. This is part of my alibi. On Saturday morning I'll be playing football for my college – an 'early' due to an important rugby match being played in the afternoon."

"Just a minute, that's the day of the Calcutta Cup, between Scotland and England," said Brian.

"I hate the game. But the rest of the office talk about nothing else."

"Back to my alibi. Even if I'm not picked – unlikely – I'll go along as a supporter. When I return I'll go off to King's – another part of the university – to join up with the large-ish crowd at the weekly relativity seminar."

"You say there's a lot of people there. What if no one remembers you?"

"Don't worry, they will. I'm going to engineer a situation that will stick in the memory. I'll ask a question so stupid that everyone will remember me.

"I suggest you take a fairly big suitcase, you know those ones with wheels. They're not too big and are easy to deal with if you've a lot of stuff to carry. Inside there you can keep your uniform, a change of clothing, a canvas bag for Earl to put the money in.

"Wear what you want on Friday. On Saturday, at about 1 p.m., you put on your uniform. Leave the B&B with the suitcase, the letter and the finger package. Get the Tube to Notting Hill Gate. Proceed to Earl's house. At the appropriate time, two twenty-five, or thereabouts, press the doorbell. Dorothy will answer. Give her the letter, the canvas bag and the finger package. 'Patrol' outside as a normal copper or whatever a 'normal' copper does. At exactly 3 o'clock you collect the canvas bag with the money. Put it into to your suitcase. Return to your B&B, or possibly head for King's Cross and home! We'll see closer to the day.

"If you can, choose a B&B that allows you to come and go without having to go through a foyer. If you do bump into someone just have a witty remark ready like 'I'm doing the matinees this week!' tut and roll your eyes, or 'what you have to do to get on stage nowadays!' tut and roll your eyes, then just walk past them, keep up your speed and don't engage in conversation. You'll need to book a B&B for two nights – not in your own name of course. When 3 o'clock comes round, give them a plus/minus 5 minutes to account for domestic blunders.

"If they don't follow the instructions leave the site and go back to your B&B. Better have leather gloves, we don't want to be leaving your fingerprints on stuff you may have to leave there. Pack everything into your suitcase and relax. Nobody will know who the hell you are. Go home on Sunday morning. We can sort out the details closer to the date.

"I want you to come down to London to recce the place, get a 'feel' for the area and to look for any problems that might arise.

"Now we come to a fairly important bit."

"It's all important," said Brian.

"Yes of course. The plan is to give them an envelope on which is printed:

"FOR CHAS EARL'S EYES ONLYPUT THIS LETTER INTO C. EARL'S HANDS URGENT: OPEN IMMEDIATELY.

THE TIME IS 2.25PM SATURDAY

"After pointing this out to Dorothy you give her the canvas bag and say 'DO THIS NOW'. Frighten her a tad with your voice so that she gets the message.

"The idea is to get Dorothy to respond immediately. We don't want her to simply put my stuff on a coffee table somewhere and leave it at that.

"Now look – I've concocted a ransom note."

Brendan points to material inside the envelope. Brian looks inside.

"That's a ransom note? I tell you now – and I haven't read a word of it – it's too bloody long."

"Okay, okay. I didn't think it was going to be perfect. I want you to look carefully at this stuff and tell me what needs changing or zapping. You must have dealt with some kidnap cases? What makes a good 'kidnap letter'? Now you sit here while I go for a tea. When you've done come over to the caff and I'll treat you to a full English."

Supplied with pen and paper, Brian takes the pages and gets down to work. After some forty minutes or so Brian takes his seat, a full English in front of him.

"Don't let the sausages put you off," smiles Brendan.

"Okay, first thing that strikes me is the length."

"Yeah you've said that."

"This is more the four-hour rant that Fidel Castro would give you. We want it more like the bloody Gettysburg Address, sharp and to the point. You've got to get rid of stuff and a lot of stuff at that. It's too friendly for a start, there's no 'menace' in it. You need to be a bit more threatening, I see what you're trying to do though. You're trying to get to his mind using a philosophical approach. You're trying to argue how reasonable our demands are. I'm not sure that'll work. If Earl reads all this blurb he will have calmed down and he may just decide to call our bluff. He might genuinely think it's part of this RAG thing. He has to read it and understand it and then weigh it up – is it a joke or is it serious. He's got to make a decision quickly. We've gotta give him time to think and not just bamboozle him with sentence after sentence.

"In short we've gotta tell him who we are, what we want and what we'll do if we don't get what we want.

"It's surely gotta fit on to a page – it's got to be clear and to the point. Get rid of the lines I've highlighted then let me see it again. But get rid of most of it, keep it short and sweet!"

Brendan goes home and edits the document. He returns within the hour.

"Good job it's nice and warm here – this could be a long process. I've had three more mugs of tea while you were away."

"Here you are. Comments please," said Brendan.

Brian examines the updated version, now reduced to just a single page.

"I've included two new versions."

McClusky examined both versions.

"Yes, that's better. More to the point and a lot less rambling. "There's still some stuff on there that could be left out. Why not let him just find the finger. Lead him to the belief that this 'finger' might be his daughter's."

"That's the second version."

"Yes I prefer version two."

"Leave it with me. I'll keep thinking about it. I've not dealt with that many kidnaps. It's not a common crime in the UK.

"Now we have to be careful. Don't phone me – ever. They are likely to suspect all students close to Christine, presumably that includes you."

"Yes it does, I'm on the RAG committee."

"They'll look at telephone records, no doubt. I'll back off seeing your Ma just in case they come to see you at your home. Tell her I've been seconded to help

Mr Earl,

THIS NOT A JOKE

DO AS WE ASK OR daughter will be took

At present she is ~~near~~ near Dover with Viscount son

Your house is watched

WE WANT £ 50,000

    put the money in Canvas bag

At exactly 3.00 pm today you will put the
bag with the money outside your front door

Then return, wait 30 mins ring   010 263 581 220
                                  for orders
We're not greedy. £50,000 is less than 5% of your yearly income

INSIDE ~~BAG~~ is A PORTION of a finGER

If needs be We can be ruthless

Mr Earl, we have no interest in you or
your DAUGHTER

    WE JUST WANT YOUR MONEY

put this note'm with the money

with an IRA threat in the Lancashire police force. That should do it for about eight weeks. Let's agree now about contacting each other. I'll get the number of a telephone box near here. If you need to contact me then phone me there every Wednesday and every Sunday at precisely 6 p.m. Two calls a week should be enough for the next month. After that we'll arrange more regular calls, perhaps once a day? If it's engaged then keep trying till I respond. You'll need to do the same for a London telephone box. Write to me with the number as soon as you get back." "I'll buy a new typewriter to get the note done. After we've completed the final version of the note we chuck the typewriter away." "Alternatively you could write it by hand using your left hand – might take some time but, probably worth it – yes by hand is better. Forget the typewriter. Do it a week in advance and then keep it safe. Use one of those new biros then chuck it away afterwards. As you say make sure your room is squeaky clean, we don't want any silly mistakes linking you to the job. "I'll come down next Friday and the Friday after that so, as you suggested, I get used to the place and to reserve a B&B."

"It might be sensible to get a B&B in Ealing Broadway – that's where I have my digs. By that time we should have the paperwork done. We should do a couple of dry runs a couple of weeks before we do it."

"Now, if we get it where do we keep the money?"

"If, I hear you say, if? I thought a safe deposit box, there are a couple of organisations in Bradford. If you get it in your name, you'll need a passport and a recent utility bill. For a year it'll cost about one hundred and fifty pounds. Once it's in we won't touch it for a year. Perhaps if you keep the key at work, presumably you have lockers? What do you think?"

"Sounds good, except for one thing."

"Yes?"

"I need a bigger share. I was thinking thirty–twenty. It's your idea I know but I've got a lot to lose and anyway, if my plans for the future work out your mum will be spending most of it."

"Remember Brian, this kind of thing can break up a team. When we settle this claim then that's it, no more coming back to the honey pot. When agreed you accept it in good faith, no jealousy. Agreed?"

"Agreed."

"I'll go halfway. I'll go with thirty-five–fifteen."

"Okay, thirty-five–fifteen it is."

"Good. I'm glad actually. You'll put more into it if you're getting more out. Okay, to be clear, thirty-five thousand pounds to me and fifteen thousand pounds to you. Shake?"

They shook hands.

"See you Friday – I'll look up the train times," said Brendan as they parted.

Friday came round. Brendan met Brian at King's Cross at 9.45 a.m. The train was on time.

"Let's do what we have to do first," said Brian.

"Okay. Here's the telephone number of the phone box I'll use. It's about six streets away from my digs in Sutherland Road, Ealing. I've been practising doing the note with a pen and my left hand. Tough going but I definitely will be able to do it. I'll try a complete one tonight and give it to you before you go back tomorrow."

"I'm not going back till Sunday. I think I need to spend time here – I'm concerned that this job is okay in your mind – you've been in London for about six months now, none of it is new to you. Me on the other hand, well, I hardly know the place. I need more time to get comfortable with it all."

"You're not having cold feet are you? This is going to be a doddle."

"No, I'm fine about going ahead. It scares me a bit 'cos we're playing for high stakes here. You have the confidence of a young bloke. I have experience, yes, but I only have the confidence of a fifty-five-year-old – which is not a great deal – I can tell you that. Never been that confident. I shouldn't be telling you this. You know a thousand things can go wrong."

"Sure, you're right to be scared. If you don't think I'm scared then you don't know me. Sometimes I'm scared shitless. But I know how to act, how to 'pretend' that I'm not scared or stressed. This job scares me. Course it does. I'm aware of the enormity of what we're trying to do here. This'll set us up for a very long time. I'm scared of Earl, He's got so much money he may take a perverse pleasure in spending a lot of it to tracking us down. The police don't scare me much, no insult intended, but they'll give up after a few months. You know that, particularly if there was no violence.

"But we know, you and I know, how to play this game. We practise, we analyse, we practise, we analyse, et cetera, et cetera, et cetera. We make sure we have all the best cards then, and only then, do we play them. If we get caught after that then, well, it wasn't meant to be. Now, enough of the bad vibes, shall we go with the attitude that the bottle's half full? We've got all day. Let's start this process now. I'll bet you'll feel a lot better come 9 p.m. Now, do you want to go on your own or do you want me with you?"

"I'll go on my own first. I'll get a rambler ticket and get off at Kensington High Street, then find Queen Elizabeth College and on to explore the area round Holland Park, Notting Hill and High Street Kensington. Let's agree a time to meet up again, say at 3 p.m. here at King's Cross?"

"Fine. I can do a bit of analysis myself. I'll look for B&Bs that might be suitable."

"Good idea. Don't forget – here's my telephone number in Keighley. It's about half a mile from my house. Should be far enough. Okay, see you at 3 p.m. I'll wait there till you turn up."

"Remember, bottle half full! And get a London Tube map. Bloody useful."

Brendan started back from Notting Hill to Ealing Broadway on the Central line. Luckily there was a Tourist Information Office at the Central line terminus, about seventy yards from the Tube entrance. They, helpfully, supplied an up-to-date list of hotels and B&Bs in the neighbourhood, together with number of beds and an estimate of present vacancies. With this information and his knowledge of the area he quickly made the rounds of suitable accommodation for Brian. He discounted the smaller ones – too intimate – a copper in their midst would spark too much interest. Others that he could see from the street, had an open foyer, open to all and sundry. He was sure Brian wouldn't like to walk in there in full uniform. Brendan homed in on five he thought were suitable – those of the right size, with many beds, good privacy.

He went in to all to ask about vacancies for the period they had in mind. The B&Bs all asked for a deposit of at least one night but there were many vacancies. Their advice was to book somewhere soon. It's the Calcutta Cup, the empty rooms will soon fill up. In return Brendan asked to see the rooms, how they were situated and the operation of the keys. He thought two of the B&Bs were suitable for Brian. He would let him choose which.

Brendan only just got back to King's Cross in time to meet up with Brian.

"I've got a couple of rooms for you to look at."

"Can we have a break first – I'm starving and believe it or not my legs hurt! Mr. Plod is not used to walking any more, give me my car any day of the week. I need something substantial to eat – I've been up since six you know."

"Yeah sorry, there should be something not far from the station, it's too expensive to eat in the booking area."

Brendan and Brian ordered food and ate to the sound of small talk for about half an hour.

"Okay I'm done," as Brian brought this little soirée to a close.

"Let's make progress," said Brendan.

"I've found two hotels. Either will be suitable. I don't know but it might be wise not to stay there until the day itself – they might ask too many questions."

"Yeah but I think one night would be okay. We've still got seven weeks to go. It would be nice to get a feel for the place."

"Mmm okay, your choice. "After today, by the way, we'd better not meet anywhere near Ealing or Notting Hill – too great a chance of coming across a fellow student. I suggest we meet somewhere in South London. I'll find somewhere tomorrow. Anyway, where did you go today?"

"I went to Earl's place – just had to have a look at it. It's in an odd spot, what with the college building to one side and a school to the other side. The frontage is set back from the road about twenty feet. They have plenty of space for 'UGE 1'. They have what looks like a garage with an automatic door. I'm half surprised they haven't been robbed.

"Now you may not like this but I knocked on the door. Well, actually I rang the bell."

"Why the hell did you do that?" said Brendan, shaking his head.

"I wish you hadn't done that. You don't know what kind of cameras and other stuff they might have."

"Look Brendan, what happens if we turn up on the day and I knock on the door and she doesn't let us in? We fail at the first hurdle. We've gotta make sure that Dorothy makes the judgement to open the door to us."

"So, what happened?"

"Not surprisingly they have an intercom system. Dorothy asked me what I wanted. I said I was looking for the Youth Hostel Association, the Tube map indicated that it was in Holland Park. I was hoping you would be able to help. Dorothy's response was 'Sorry

I can't help you.' And she shut the intercom system down immediately. She wasn't prepared to engage in conversation. They also have a camera – no doubt for Dorothy's benefit. That gives her some protection. Their door looked as if it is top of the range. I now see why you need a copper knocking on that door. There's probably an inner door as well – did you see one when you visited?"

"I can't remember seeing anything, but at the time I wasn't looking for anything. But look, we're not trying to break in, we want them to open doors, we're not going to break 'em down. Yes? Likelihood is, is that they'll open a door to a copper. Look, you knock on the door, as a policeman, and say that there's been an accident involving Christine, that'll open the door immediately."

"We shall see. This is a tricky one. We have no control over this part of the plan. We just have to hope that it works. I think you're right though, they will surely open the door to a copper."

"I don't like the word 'hope'," said Brendan.

"I had a look at the surroundings. Very smart, very classy. Didn't see any police which surprised me, I thought there might be one or two in a neighbourhood like this. The locals usually complain if there's no coppers on the ground. Have to be careful here – there might be coppers in plain clothes in cars. I'll go again tomorrow and see if I can spot one. I'll make sure I'm there at 3 p.m.

"I went into Holland Park. Lots of hippies around but lots of cover too. I'm anticipating here but if I have to scarper urgent like, then Holland Park might be the place to run to.

"Okay, I'll go back now, have another look around at the area between the college and Notting Hill and from the college to High Street Ken. I'll use one of those hotels you found in Ealing and then repeat the exercise from tomorrow till I get the train back. But remember to drop by so as I can pick up the ransom note to have a look at. Make sure you put it into my hand – no third party is to be used!"

Brendan turned up around ten and met with Brian. They walked into the local park not far from the B&B.

"Here's the ransom note, version two, done left-handed. I don't think it's too bad. I think it's clear."

"Make sure you handle the envelope by its edges or use gloves. Amazing what fingerprints they can lift these days and remember it's not just fingerprints, it's palm prints as well! When this is analysed they'll realise it's done by the 'wrong' hand. But that doesn't really matter they won't be able to see it's your handwriting. Do another one and keep it safe. Destroy all the others. Try and do it on a semi-hard card. Then, after you've done the letter, throw away the card, they might pick something off your desk surface you know an imprint of some kind, at your digs. "By the way young man, did you realise that bloody hotel is full of prostitutes? All hell would break out if they knew I was a policeman. Can you find me something 'clean' for next time?"

Brendan could see that Brian wasn't happy. Something was bugging him.

"Something's up. What is it?"

"A problem. I wasn't sure if I should tell you," said Brian.

"Yes, go on. You need to tell me stuff. Don't keep it to yourself. I need to know what you're doing too. I can't read your mind!" said Brendan.

"Well, yesterday I mentioned police on the ground, patrolling the area, the fact that there didn't seem to be any."

"Well you saw some, plain-clothes coppers?"

"Well that's what I thought at first, but they looked a bit rougher than plain-clothes guys and they were all male, usually if you're doing surveillance work you have at least one female. I sat in that area for an hour and a half. The 'car' drove past a few times. Couldn't see if they had a camera. Then just as I was about to go the car turns up again, further down the street. Two of them get out, they walked around the area, slowing down to tie a shoelace as they passed Earl's."

"So?"

"We might have a problem. I think we've got rivals. They were sizing up Earl's house. They're burglars for God's sake!"

"You think so?"

"I bloody know so."

"That's a bugger! What's to be done?" said Brendan.

"Nothing. Nothing changes – unless they do their job before we do ours. I could have a word. Put my authoritative voice on just tell them we got here first. Thing is I don't know that we did. We'll leave it, see how it develops. Okay with you?"

"On matters like this you're the boss though...get the number plate."

"Already have done."

"After we do our job we could, anonymously, give that number to the police – that would surely take the heat off us and on to them – unless it's stolen. "Can you find out when you get back to Keighley? This could give us an extra edge. This could be a real bonus. We get in before them, they take the blame, yes sireee. Home and dry."

Chapter 32

TWINKLE TWINKLE LITTLE CHARD?

On each visit to London, Brian became more and more confident about what was expected of him on the "job". He booked a room for Friday and Saturday for the ninth week of semester two. The booking was anonymous. It was fully paid for in cash. Throughout the next few weeks Brendan produced examples of "fingers". Brian was pleased and impressed with the quality of these gory objects. Another piece of good luck: the burglars' car wasn't stolen so, if needs be, the owners could be traced. A second piece of good luck – their tax disc was out of date – an anonymous call could tell the police that an untaxed car was continually parking on Holland Park Road. If the police have any nous they will put two and two together and arrest the innocent criminals – Bob's your uncle. Back in Yorkshire, Brian opened a safe deposit box agreement. The kidnap note had been completed sometime previously and the wording was adequate. Brian bought a strong suitcase with wheels to hold his police uniform, a strong canvas bag to hold the money, in twenties, about 6 lbs, which is about the weight of three big bags of flour. He tried it out numerous times to make sure it would be in good working order on the day. They were just about ready and ready to go before burglar bill gets there first. The week before the action they had a long telephone conversation.

"Hi Brian, how goes it?"

"Nervy but reasonably confident. Your half-glass-full 'thing' is more like a three-quarter-glass-full. It's definitely worth the risk and it's an opportunity that's unlikely to come again. However, I've been thinking. You know that bank of phone boxes just on the inside of Notting Hill Gate Tube, well get a couple of numbers, in fact get all those numbers, that you can ring on the Saturday afternoon, just in case there are last minute hitches. Let's say 2 p.m., you should be back from football then and well before you go off to that seminar thing. I don't want to be walking down to Earl's house with my dick hanging out, I want to be going down there with all guns blazing, with confidence that it's gonna be okay."

"What do you mean? It's all in hand."

"Look, I've been on this planet a good deal longer than you. 'Things' happen that you can't predict, I want a 'just in case' get out clause. I want to know what's happening just before I ring that doorbell. Just before I see Dorothy I want to know that everything is as it should be – get my drift?"

"Yeah. But honestly you've nothing to worry about. Well the only realistic worry now is the other gang – will they go or not? Apart from that we've looked at every aspect of this, we couldn't do much more in the way of planning. I've had enough with planning and analysis and practice runs. But okay, if it makes you feel better then we'll do that. At 2 p.m. I will ring one number from that bank of numbers. If it's engaged, as well it might be I go on to the next one and so on. I will give you any breaking news as the Americans would have it."

"That's it and if you don't ring one of those phones then the whole thing is off, agreed?"

"Look Brian, this isn't very bloody professional. For God's sake we've thought of everything, weeks ago."

"You might be bright but on this matter I beg to differ. We've only thought of those things that we thought about. We haven't thought of the other things, the things we haven't thought about. Get it! Mr. Random Event can easily put his finger in our pie. Now let's finish with this gobbledygook and just do as I ask. I'll be more comfortable, I'll be more relaxed which is likely to lead to a successful outcome."

"Okay, okay hold on to your horses. I want a happy crew so consider it done. Any other quibbles?"

"No."

On the final Friday everything was in hand, more or less. Brendan started making the finger on the Thursday just in case there were last minute hitches. Late Thursday afternoon he bought a prepared chicken, nice and small to give a nice petite "finger". All the other ingredients he had: craft knife, food dye, small plastic bags, small brown bag, false nails, nail varnish, small tube of black pudding. As well as these basic ingredients he had a large, sturdy brown paper bag. He told the landlady, Mrs. Woman, that he was feeling a little nauseous and he wouldn't be wanting supper. The attic room, often called the eyrie, had an excellent early warning system – the creaking stairs – should any callers present themselves at his door he could throw his eiderdown over the table to hide all his craftwork. As it happened he had no visitors that evening. He got down to work about 6 p.m. An excellent model of a girl's index finger was ready by 7.45 p.m. Brendan was pleased with his effort, though he had practised on many occasions and rarely had a failure. He had amended his method in just one regard. He couldn't easily get pig's blood and, for obvious reasons, was reluctant to use his own. Instead he substituted a small amount of black pudding mixed to a paste with a little water. It gives a very lifelike trickle of blood and light bruising.

The finger was placed in a small plastic bag together with a small amount of preserving fluid. The bag was closed with a shiny, metallic tag, making it almost airtight. It was then put into a small brown bag. The finger package was ready. This was placed by the open window to keep cool; weighted down at its edge to deter any scavenging crows from pushing their luck.

On past evidence the "condition" of the finger would keep for about three days as long as an airtight container was used for storage and the flies were kept away. He had to keep his window open at all times and he made sure the cleaner, who came on a weekly basis, didn't detect anything unusual. He kept all his ingredients and tools is a large metal tin. The rim, holding the lid, was layered with sellotape ensuring an airtight container. The tin and other artefacts connected with the "job" were kept in Brendan's lockable suitcase, shoved under the bed.

After the finger was complete, Brendan gathered together all the equipment he used together with chicken, knives, et cetera and put them into the sturdy brown bag. At this time all the students in the house were either watching TV in the communal room or were in their rooms revising. Brendan moved quietly downstairs and out of the house with the bag. He took the Central line into town getting off after just three stations. The Tube was still in its "overground" section. Brendan stood to one side and waited for the platform to clear. After two minutes the platform was empty. He quickly removed the chicken and threw it into dense shrubbery that adorned either side of the platforms. Within an hour a fox would be considering this his lucky day. That fox had had a few good days since this "project" had got under way. He then walked out of the station and proceeded to empty the remaining contents of the bag into metal refuse bins dotted around the street adjacent to the Tube. He returned to his digs, quietly, without being seen, and proceeded, with his facecloth and soap, to wipe down all surfaces, including windows and window panes that might have been contaminated with splashes of blood or pudding or slivers of chicken meat. Having a very small room helped considerably with the cleaning. However, the small sink was hardly adequate to the task. At the end it was surgically clean, perhaps over-clean. He proceeded to "dirty" it again by shaking his rug a few times to produce a fine dust. Now clean again with a plain cloth to give a used but clean set of surfaces (but not the cloth used in the first clean – that one would have to be chucked in case it contained contaminants from the first clean). He was happy that nothing could be detected to connect him with the crime. He also checked that all the paperwork relevant to the planning was also gone. He leafed through every book – only eight in his room – to check he hadn't left anything inside the pages.

After completing the deep-clean task he went down to report an improvement in his nauseous state and watched some TV before all the students retired to their rooms.

Brendan sat on the bentwood chair adjacent to the window, watching the planes coast down, in single file, on their approach to Heathrow. He'd not thought this before but the room was very much like the attic room he and Cormac shared in Bengal Street. He'd come a long way since those days. In the intervening years he had hardly seen Cormac, indeed any of his older brothers. He was tempted, for old times' sake, to pee out of the window, but thought better of it. As usual he used the sink instead.

He was feeling proud in what he'd achieved. This was his idea, to a large extent this was his analysis, his plan, his research.

He mused as to the outcome. Even if he is rumbled he could be pleased with his part, he'd tried his best.

As he lay down on his bed, weary and tired, a sparkle of light suddenly flicked passed his eyes. He only saw it once but it was enough to unsettle him sufficiently so that he started to seek it out. Somehow, he felt this was significant. He spent another half-hour seriously looking for the source of the twinkle. In vain. It was getting late so he had to abandon the search. Unbeknownst to him, the source of his discomfort lay stuck to a fibre near the top of the curtain. It was one of the thin metallic tags he'd used to tie up the plastic bag containing the chicken finger. This ghostly apparition might well come to haunt him.

Chapter 33

BRIEF ENCOUNTER

He tried to sleep, but failed. Even Brendan with his rock hard persona of "cool" couldn't sleep – there was just too much resting on the outcome. He got up at seven and went down to breakfast. All the talk was of the forthcoming rugby match between England and Scotland due to be played on Saturday. The students were regretting the fact that, with exams so close, they would have to miss this in favour of revision.

Brendan got ready to leave. He knew this was the start of a momentous journey in his life. Once again he was going to try the path less used:

...Two roads diverged in a wood and I
I took the one less traveled by
And that made all the difference

Old Robert Frost (Brendan thought of re-christening him as Robber Frost – that would be more appropriate in Brendan's case) was making another appearance in his life. Bloody Frost, he thought to himself. Couldn't he think of another poem less two-dimensional? Couldn't he have used the line "Seventeen roads diverged in a wood and I took one that seemed less traveled"? But no, Mr. Frost decided that the reader would only have two choices. Didn't Frost know that life isn't like that. Life is far more complicated, more probabilistic. To excuse Mr. Frost the ideas in quantum physics were yet to be explored. Oh well, back to reality.

Brendan, without the sparkle, left his digs at eight sharp. Brendan returned at eleven minutes passed eight. He'd forgotten the finger bag! Luckily the cleaner hadn't started on his room yet. He remembered, with nervous humour, the philosophy of one Brian McClusky, his partner in crime and the "things we haven't thought about!" Brendan left his digs for a second time at fourteen minutes past eight. At seventeen minutes past eight he returned for a second time. He had forgotten the brown bag, the receptacle of all the stuff he used in the deep-clean exercise.

This was becoming a joke, hardly professional. Perhaps he should have made a "list" of things to do before leaving the house? This time Brendan stayed in his room for a few minutes clearing his mind and checking that all incriminating material would be chucked. At thirty minutes past eight Brendan left for a final time on this day. He binned the brown bag on his entry into Ealing Broadway. At the suite of shops adjacent to the Tube station he purchased a bath towel and a small bar of soap. When he got to QE he took a long shower, taking particular care in washing his hair. He threw the towel and soap away, dressed, and made his way to King's Cross.

Brendan sat on the bench by platform four of King's Cross Station. He placed the brown bag with the finger by his right hand. McClusky's train was seventeen minutes late. McClusky sat adjacent to Brendan with his big case placed on the floor next to him on Brendan's right side. Brian deftly picked up the brown bag and carefully put it into his pocket.

"You've got the ransom note?" Brendan asked quietly.

"Check. And now I have the finger package. We're ready to go. Next time we get in touch is tomorrow, at exactly 2 p.m. yes?"

"Yes."

Brian stood, and as he was just about to leave there was a loud shout across the station.

"Brian, Brian my boy."

Brian looked up. He recognised the loud mouth to be Gordon Nesbit, actually Inspector Gordon Nesbit who shared an office with Brian, been friends for years and years.

Oh, shit, shit, shit, Brian thought to himself.

"Brian, Brian. What the hell are you doing here?" Gordon said, with genuine surprise.

"Never mind me – what are you doing here?" as they shook hands. Brian was desperately trying to think of something sensible to say. The best he could come up with was,

"I've come to rob a bank!" he said with a nervous laugh.

Brendan raised his eyebrows.

"Oh is that all. Me and the lads are off to the match – at Twickers – it's the England–Scotland match – for the Calcutta Cup."

"Oh is that the game I hate? And you're actually going to spend some money watching that shite?"

"I'm the only one on Her Majesty's Police Service – all the others are firemen or bin men, one or the other – I can't remember which! You can guess where they are."

"Give me three guesses, getting tanked, getting tanked, and getting tanked?"

"Right first time. We got the early train, thought we'd get a sup in before it gets crowded. We're off in a few minutes, to get our digs. Match is tomorrow, can't wait, we've got a couple of strip joints lined up for tonight. I only came out for a piss! Don't tell Masie, she thinks I'm on a conference."

"For Christ's sake Gordon, remember you're a senior copper. Don't do anything stupid, you'll lose your bloody pension!" said Brian, holier than thou. A fine example of a hypocrite.

"Oh for God's sake, you're not playing the Mother Teresa role again, lighten up Bri!"

Then the station pub doors open to around sixteen, fairly large, shouty blokes.

"Come on Gordon you twat, we're off." Exit the dancing swans from *Swan Lake*.

"Gotta go. See you Monday. What you doing again?"

"You mean apart from robbing a bank? Off to Kew."

"Cheers," and then Inspector Nesbit joined the dancers looking for the Metropolitan line.

Brian stopped and watched them exit the station – he returned to his seat next to Brendan.

"I guess you heard all that?"

"Every word. I liked the 'off to rob a bank quip', inspired."

There was a short silence.

"No I mean it, that's exactly the response an innocent man might use. Good job."

"Well?" said Brian.

"One of those things, bit unlucky," said Brendan, trying to play down the situation.

"This changes things."

"Why? How?" said Brendan expecting a "wobble" from Brian.

"Why? you say. Why. Well for the first time on this so-called job some policeman can place me near the scene of the crime. I'm feeling a bit exposed to say the least. They'll definitely get to you which means they might possibly get to me – they might just put one and one together, you know as coppers do, remember the fiddles? I knew it was you, felt it in my bones, couldn't prove it though. With this job, kidnap an' all, they'll try a bit harder.

"I know you can handle yourself, you're confident to the point of arrogance. But I'm a tad more fragile, most people are. You've never been in a police interview. I have and it's tough going. If it's in you they'll normally weed it out of you. I might not cope."

"Oh, don't be such a wuss. Look let's not go over the whole thing again," said an increasingly frustrated Brendan.

"I want to go over it again for God's sake. I'm that close to walking," he said, pushing his thumb and forefinger in Brendan's face.

"Look, they might put you near the scene –that's a very long shot indeed, but you're nowhere near the time at which the crime will occur. Now let's calm down, just calm down for a while. Take deep breaths. Look, instead of a one in ten thousand chance of being discovered it's now one in nine thousand – the odds are still overwhelmingly with us. We'd take those odds any day of the week. This is just a small blip in our proceedings. Our rivals will cop for it – you'll see – unfair on them but they were trying to burgle the place in any case. We're so close. It would be criminal to throw it away at this late stage. The police will pin it on them for sure – even though it's only circumstantial. They're not averse to inventing a couple of things."

Brian calmed down.

"*Carpe diem* young man, *carpe diem*. Seize the day. A horse, a horse, my kingdom for a horse, Onward through the valley of death, and dear friends unto the breach, once more unto the breach, all that guff. Where are your British balls? We'll fight them on the beaches…"

"Okay, okay. I'll have to think of a very reasonable reason for being here today and tomorrow as well. He's sure to ask me on Monday. I told him I'm going to Kew. But that could easily mean I'm going to queue for something."

Brendan thinks for a while.

"Okay, okay, try this. I'll get a train ticket back to Keighley this afternoon. It'll be franked, on the train as it speeds north in the usual way, so it'll be a record of your journey. The ticket will support the idea that you were back in Keighley on Friday afternoon. That way you don't have to worry about an excuse for being in London on Saturday, I can come back on the return journey – I've nothing else to do today anyway. Now all you gotta do is to find an innocuous reason for being in London on Friday from about 10 a.m. to 3 p.m. Perhaps you just fancied a day out to Kew gardens – you're a keen gardener. That might work, keep it simple. Ring your mum, so that there's a record of the call, keep her on the phone for about a minute – just talk rubbish. Just invent a reason for returning early, something as simple as 'you thought she was a bit down' so, as a loving son, you returned early, in fact almost as soon as you got here. Make the call now. They won't surely cross-examine your Mum? She must be close to eighty?"

Brian goes to one of the internal phone booths and calls his mother. He keeps her on the line speaking gibberish, speaking intermittingly as if there was a major problem with the line.

Brian returns to Brendan's side.

"Done. Now shall we get on with this?" said a much calmer Brian.

"Well, let's finish this bit. I'll go and get the ticket to Keighley. It leaves in about twenty minutes. We may as well stay here till it leaves. I'll be in contact tonight, usual phone just in case some other crisis arises. I'll get the franked ticket to you at your digs later today. It'll be touch-and-go as I said I'd play my fiddle in the common room tonight. So after I see you, I get my fiddle from the locker rooms then get back to the common room pronto! Aren't we having fun?"

Then, out of the blue, Brian gets philosophical and a tad sentimental.

"So, what the hell are you going to do with your life? Seems to me you don't know what you're doing. The university 'stuff', from what I know about it, from your Ma, seems to be going well – I hear you've won a few prizes from your school. This other string to your bow is, if you don't mind me saying, is stupid – for God's sake you know this game – you only have to make one mistake and it's behind bars for a few years – there are people in the clink that'll make mincemeat out of you – they're not civilised like me and you – you get my drift?"

"Well, thanks for that boost to my confidence. Yep, I've won prizes, two prizes, to be exact the maths prize and the physics prize, but they're sort of low grade prizes – the public outside, like you, think they must be great but believe me they don't mean very much – people think I'm super bright – nowhere near the truth. I struggle to understand a lot of mathematics – yeah I can follow all the stuff in lectures and it's nice that they've offered me a low-key tutorship. I'm nowhere near to understanding what I call real mathematics. I'll give you this, I'm bright enough to realise that I'm not bright enough to do real mathematics. Yes, if I stick it out for forty years I might, through shear good luck discover something of worth and that does give me a buzz – it's an encouragement to carry on. You may not believe this but I've been working on a specific problem since I was fifteen – before I started making violins. I don't tell anybody what the problem is 'cos I want the glory of solving it myself – it's a trivial sounding problem but it's proving difficult to sort out. In recent years, with what I've done at university, I have made one or two inroads into the problem but I'm finding the final bit difficult to get to grips with. And it's hard work, trying to sort a problem out. The awful thing is that I may never solve this problem – in forty years – or worse, someone may solve the problem before me. That would be heartbreaking! Not sure what I'd do if that happened.

"I get a lot of pleasure from dealing with a crime – I love the process, the planning and the execution – you'll know, you get a buzz of committing a crime that you make a lot of money out of and nobody knows it was you, bit like Clark Kent and Superman if you know what I mean.

"It's just like doing maths. I like to lock myself away in a semi-dark small room with an open fire, preferably in the winter time. Then I start to think about the crime – I start to write things down – everything to do with the crime. I highlight various parts as likely to be important. Then I construct a timeline of things I have to do to successfully carry out the crime. I often name the crime – this one is Gold Finger. I try and work out, as best I can, what are the chances, for each listed item, that that part would succeed. Obviously everything is subject to error and, worse still, to random effects – you see what just happened now.

"Now, to simplify matters, I want to carry out the crime without being caught, or preferably without any suspicion falling on me. In some cases it can't be helped – the violin caper is an example in hand. The way I set up the crime made it almost inevitable that suspicion would fall on me. You just made a guess that it was me – you didn't have any proof or, indeed, any grounds for suspecting me to be the thief.

"The Great Train Robbery is similar. The police didn't have any direct clues as to who was responsible, they simply wrote down a list of people who, given their past history, would be capable of carrying out such a crime, it took a great deal of organisation – these were the usual suspects. They arrested a few, those from the list they could find – started to question them and waited for one or two to crack. Within a relatively short period of time they knew who was responsible – all they had to do then was to find them! Now that's a different problem.

"Anyway I'm rambling on here – just take it for granted unless things change dramatically I intend to continue on this path. My major aim in any job I carry out is to avoid suspicion – I don't want to become one of the usual suspects.

"We don't know who the real clever criminals are – 'cos they never get caught or they are never suspects, let alone a prime suspect.

"So far most of what I've done in this area is simple stuff – stealing with a twist. Ever since I've been at university my interests are branching out. At the moment I'm working on a possible crime that strongly depends on me being able to speak Italian – well I don't speak Italian but I'm happy to learn – I'm a quick learner – I've allocated nine months to become proficient. The complete job will take about a year in the execution – if I decide to go ahead. That time doesn't worry me, it's very enjoyable, I kinda regret it when it's over. It's not a job I'll make a lot of money out of, but it's so enjoyable.

"I also have long-term ambitions to steal large amounts of money from people who have large amounts of money. For example, this Earl bloke is rich to the sum of sixty-three million pounds – can you take that in? Sixty-three million. Well young Brian we ought to have at least one per cent of that. Let's think futures. After this job I'm going to put my mind into extracting further wads of twenties from his back pocket.

"Don't get me wrong – I like the ordinary stuff – stealing from wall hanging safes and the like, but to make real money then we've got to move away from safes into Swiss Bank Boxes and the like."

"Well you certainly have enthusiasm! Not for me, it's a young man's game."

"I don't think so – you've just gotta think young. This thing we're involved with at the moment will bankroll future projects. You need money to make money – first law of thieving. That's my train. Better get off. See you later today."

Brendan left for the train singing "Goldfinger", feeling like Bond James Bond.

Chapter 34

INTO THE VALLEY OF DEATH RODE THE TWO

Friday night comes round. Brian has his franked ticket kept in the top pocket of his suit. It'll stay there until it's needed. Off he goes to his B&B. Brendan scuttles off to the QEC common room. The music had already started with a couple of excellent fiddle players, a flautist and an accordionist. He waved hello to as many as he could – to better strengthen his alibi.

Brendan played as best he could but the fiddle players were a level above his. He dropped out till that particular "set" had finished then made a point of saying:"Let's slow down a bit, my fingers are red raw!"

He started to play "Carrickfergus" – hopefully someone from the audience would take up the singing. He got through a couple of bars when two girls stood up to sing along. Brendan stopped and gave the nod that he would start again so as to give the singer a better "intro". The song was a famous Irish ballad but the singer was solid Glaswegian, Susan. A lovely singer, volunteered to "stand" up many times. She, obvious to everyone except Brendan, was sweet on him. She didn't push matters as Brendan had a very academic, very bright reputation which, in an odd sort of way, made him less of an attraction. Any woman "interested" in a relationship with Brendan would need to handle the situation with care. But she was attracted to his vulnerability.

Despite having even features he was a little short for the word "handsome" to be applied. None the less, many females found him sufficiently attractive to accept an invitation to the cinema or to a bar for the evening. His over-academic persona meant that a second visit to the cinema or bar was rarely warranted.

On this Friday evening, with the most momentous "job" about to go down, Brendan rejected all of Susan's obvious advances. His mind was elsewhere and would remain elsewhere for many weeks to come. He knows and Brian knows that the most difficult aspect is not so much the getting of the money, but in the keeping of the money and in the keeping them out of prison.

Brendan got back to Ealing very late. He crept into his room, slumped on the bed, and very tired after a very long day he slept for a short while. On waking after an hour he went through in his mind what was to be done later that day.

Brian had the ransom note and the finger. Brendan was to go to the common room at QEC to join with the other footballers. They were to make their own way to Petersham, South London, home of QEC's football field. Most would group together and catch a Green Line bus which would take them within two hundred yards of the ground. He smiled as he realised that the bus travelled by the outer wall of Kew Gardens!

He would get back about 1 p.m. He then had to wait till 2 p.m. before calling one of the numbers at the phone booths at Notting Hill Gate.

Meanwhile, in South London, Brian would get up and have breakfast. After breakfast he would don his uniform. He would put the ransom note, the finger and the canvas bag and his normal clothes into the wheeled suitcase. He would stay in his room till about 1 p.m., requesting no domestic help. Then he would leave the B&B without speaking to anyone. A "do not disturb" sign was posted outside his room. He would get a Tube or Tubes to Notting Hill Gate. There he would wait till 2 p.m. and expect a call from Brendan. If there were no further hitches, Brian would make his way to Earl's place and ring the bell at exactly 2.25 p.m.

Meanwhile, Brendan would get to Kings for the 3 p.m. relativity seminar.

Brian carried out his instructions in every detail except one. As he was travelling to Notting Hill Gate from his B&B, an English couple – clearly on their way to the England/Scotland match – requested he take their photo as a memento of the day. Brian responds positively to their request. He could see that they were on their honeymoon, as on the back of one of their England T-shirts was embroidered the word JUST, and on the other T-shirt the word MARRIED. He took two or three photos. Then they asked him if they could have a photo of MARRIED with Brian – as if Brian was arresting him, truncheon and all. Brian didn't see any problem with that, till later, so the photo was taken – a full mugshot wearing his uniform. This photo would place him near the scene of the crime, near the time of the crime. He decided not to tell Brendan – just yet. He'd blundered!

Meanwhile, Brendan has breakfast and engages in much small talk covering just one topic, the Calcutta Cup. He gathers together his football kit and makes his way to QEC. Brendan's task is, at this stage, a great deal easier. He got through the football game unscathed, another glorious nil-all draw. He showers quickly and makes it back on another Green Line bus to High Street Ken. He manages to get there for 1.55 p.m., just in time to ring the phone booths at Notting Hill. Within two rings Brian answers. It's all go.

It's Brendan's task now to complete his alibi by getting across town for the relativity seminar, due to start at 3 p.m. He manages to get there for 3 p.m. but no seminar. The main speaker, a Professor Roger Penrose, has cried off with a developing cold. (It was an unfriendly thought on Brendan's part that the cold might have been developing at Twickenham!) What to do?

He decided to go instead to Professor Hawking's room to ask a few questions. Brendan's colleagues have often said, despite his developing motor neurone disease, he was very approachable. Brendan was a little apprehensive but decided to go ahead. The porter directed him to his room, which was in another building quite a distance from the seminar block. Brendan had a couple of reasonable questions in the area of relativity, which Hawking might possibly be interested in. He also had a question on experimental mathematics which any ten-year-old might understand but Brendan could not prove – his Polygon Problem.

Gingerly he knocked on the door. Out came a nurse.

"Yes?"

Brendan is struck dumb.

"Yes, can I help you young man?"

"Sorry, forgotten what I was to say, sorry, emm. It'll come to me. Oh yes. Is it possible to see Professor Hawking? I was hoping to catch him at the seminar but as you will know, it's cancelled. I have a couple of questions. Any chance of speaking to him?"

"I'll ask. He's a bit tired though."

After some while the computer voice that was Stephen Hawking could be heard. "Yes, but only under the usual conditions," said the metallic voice box.

The nurse returned.

"Yes the Professor is happy to see you but we need your assistance first."

"Of course, I'd be delighted to help. Just point me in the right direction. I'm yer man."

The nurse ushered him into the room.

"Our usual motorised wheelchair is at the garage for repairs.

Now we need help to push this wheelchair. Okay?"

They pushed him out of the office and into a smaller room, some way down the corridor, on which was scribed the word "black hole". It was the men's lavatory!

Brendan and the nurse pushed the wheelchair to lie at right angles to the urinal. They then lifted Hawking, surprisingly heavy, up out of the chair, stood him on his feet and while still supporting him, unzipped him and pointed Percy to the porcelain. Brendan thought it might be regarded as rude if he asked for a glove. As the warm jet of yellow fluid made its way out of Hawking's Percy, a giggle of relief ran through his body. Thankfully, it was the nurse who volunteered to "shake" Mr. Percy on completion of the task. Another giggle of relief spread through Brendan's body, thankful that he was only called upon to help with number ones.

"It's a good job you're not married" said Brendan trying to lighten the slightly embarrassing episode.

The nurse responded immediately. "He is married, I ought to know. I'm his wife!"

A difficult moment for Brendan to deal with.

"Oops, my big mouth. I am so sorry. My stupid attempt at humour." Hawking was laughing – he didn't need a voice machine for that. His machine accent might be in American but he laughed in English.

There was no mention of this episode in the good hour that Brendan spent discussing his problems with the great man. Hawking's voice was difficult to follow but just about manageable. Hawking helped considerably with the first two questions on relativity but, refreshingly to Brendan, he didn't have a clue on the third question on geometry. Brendan clearly noted to the wife/nurse to look at the time and excused himself. His alibi was secure. How many other suspects could claim that at 3 p.m. on the Saturday of the England/Scotland game that he was taking Stephen Hawking to the toilet!

Across London a different drama is being acted out, close to its climax. The first phone booth at Notting Hill Gate rang at exactly 2 p.m. Brian answered.

"Any problems?" asked Brendan.

"No, no everything A-okay here."

"Okay here too. Let's get the show under way. Good luck – see you on the other side!"

"What do you mean, on the other side?" said Brian, somewhat tetchy.

"Nothing, it's just a turn of phrase for God's sake. It means see you when I do."

"Okay I'm off. Let's wish ourselves luck."

Brian makes his way down to Earl's house at a good pace. He has with him the trolley suitcase with the ransom note and the finger and the canvas bag. He puts down the suitcase and removes the canvas bag. The trolley suitcase is left just inside the road entrance by the Lamborghini. He makes sure not to touch it in case it had a car alarm. At exactly 2.25 p.m. Brian, canvas bag in hand, rings the bell.

His pulse is racing, his arms shaking, close to wetting himself. He is in two minds whether or not he should simply walk away now and forget the whole thing. He could just wait for Dorothy to answer, say "Sorry, wrong house" collect the bag and walk up the hill to Notting Hill Gate Tube. He can go back home to Keighley, and by that evening put his feet up over a blazing fire, and plan his retirement. It's perhaps Brendan's reaction, or his perceived reaction, that drives him on. "I'm not a wimp," he tells himself.

Within twenty seconds of sounding the bell the intercom wakes up.

"Yes, can I help you?"

"I need to speak to you about Christine. There's been an accident."

Brian hears the dull vibration of a motor opening an inner door of some kind. Then the main front door is unlocked. A heavyweight of a door edges open like a smaller version of a castle door. Within twenty seconds it is fully open.

There stands Dorothy.

Brian is transfixed. Of course he'd never seen her before. She is taller than he'd imagined. Grey hair. He couldn't focus on anything else. For some reason he looked down at her shoes, very plain, flat-soled, light brown.

He doesn't know what to say.

"Yes?" Dorothy asks.

Brian remains dumb.

"Yes, can I help you officer? What's happened to Christine?"

At last Brian attempts a few words, continuing to look down at her feet.

"Sorry, forgotten what I was to say, sorry, emm."

He slowly puts down the canvas bag and pulls himself together. Brian, bending forward, now looks her directly in the eye and holds Dorothy firmly by her arms. She moves back somewhat shocked.

Brian grows in confidence, realising this is now or never. Putting on a very strong, menacing voice he speaks directly into her face, his nose almost touching hers.

"Now listen to me lady." He shakes her slightly. Dorothy is scared.

"Are you listening?"

"Yes," she says, trembling.

"What do you want, what do you want? What's happened man, tell me what's happened?"

With one hand still being held, Brian removes the ransom note from the bag by its edges and puts it into her hand.

"Put this letter into his hands, directly into Chas Earl's hands. Then give him this small bag. Tell him it's a finger.

Do you understand?"

"Yes."

"It is extremely important. He must read it now. Do you understand?"

"Yes."

"Then give him this bag."

Finally he thrusts the large canvas bag into her hand and leaves. He looks back and says in a strong voice and pointing his finger at her,

 "I'm telling you lady, do as I say! It's to do with Christine."

For a moment Dorothy can't speak. Then, truly frightened, the poor lady wets herself and quickly goes inside, shouting,

"Mr. Earl, Mr. Earl. Please Chas. Please come here!"

Brian removes the suitcase and goes quietly and at a leisurely pace into Holland Park, which is almost deserted, it being a Saturday. Just a few kids kicking a ball. He slips into the rhododendron bushes, he removes his helmet and his jacket replacing them with a suit jacket. Back in civvy clothes he sits on a bench and waits till his watch indicates 2.58 p.m. He gets back to Earl's. He can see from the road that there is nothing on the front door. Brian waits two minutes to 3.02 p.m., then a further five minutes taking him to 3.07. Brian feels distinctly vulnerable now. He moves his position, thinking that the bag has been put out of sight. No bag to be found. He thinks Earl is not going to go with it. He waits a further two minutes to take him to 3.09 minutes. He awaits another three minutes. His watch is at 3.12 p.m. – seven minutes longer than was agreed between him and Brendan. He thinks the game is up. Perhaps he thought it was a RAG thing which he just ignored. Perhaps he couldn't read the ransom note? He was about to walk away when the door opens and the canvas bag is thrown to the ground. The door is hurriedly closed again.

Brian goes quickly to the door. He could see the bag was full of money. He calmly does up the zip, picks up the wheeled suitcase and goes back to Holland Park. The canvas bag, full of money, is transferred to the suitcase. He now makes his way quickly, but without running, to Notting Hill Gate, thence a Tube to King's Cross Station. He is there by 3.35 p.m. To his benefit the place is crowded with rugby fans. Within an hour he is on his way back to Yorkshire. All the time he clutches the suitcase to him. By the time he reaches Keighley it is dusk. He goes straight home and not even bothering to check on his mother he takes himself up to his bedroom. He ignores his mother's welcome.

"Hello, hello. Is that you Brian?"

Half believing that there has been some sort of double cross he counts the wads of money, returns the money to the canvas bag, then on to Bradford where all the money is placed in the safety deposit box, then he returns home.

The safety deposit key will be put into his police station locker first thing on Monday.

He calls in on his mother to check that she is fine. She is. At approximately 8.20 p.m. he pops into the police station just to show his face late Saturday evening. He says hello to a couple of friends – enquiring about the rugby match, grabs some papers from his desk and returns home. His task is complete.

Chapter 35

AFTERMATH

Brendan got back to his digs late Saturday afternoon. He fully expected to see a posse of police cars outside 12 Sutherland Road waiting for him to return. Nothing. He was almost disappointed. There would be no press conference in which he would deny his guilt.

He had no knowledge of how Brian had coped, whether it was a success or not. Did Brian pull out at the last minute, a case of kidnap interruptus? He wouldn't know for sure till Sunday when they had agreed to call each other at their usual phone boxes in Keighley and in Ealing. Brendan eagerly waited for the 6 o'clock news, nothing. As a member of RAG he thought it wise to go back to college and wait for returnees from the Paris jaunt. He got to Notting Hill Gate about 7.30 p.m. As he walked down the road he had walked down now for nearly a year he saw, in the distance, a police car outside the entrance to the Earl mansion. As much as possible he avoided eye contact with the single policeman standing guard. He saw all the lights in the house were on. He moved into the common room bar. There were five or six policemen milling around, talking to students.

Three or four couples had returned, the winning couple was celebrating in the bar. These were couples who had got to Paris in quick time but chose, at their own expense, to return by private helicopter. No sign of Mr. and Mrs. Viscount.

The place was pretty quiet, especially for a Saturday evening.

"What's up?" Brendan asked, not directing his question to anybody in particular.

"Catherine's gone missing. The police are trying to find her."

"Slow down, who's missing?"

"Catherine, you know, Catherine Earl, from the mansion."

"Oh, you mean Christine?"

"Yes, sorry, Christine."

"How do you mean she's gone missing? Aren't they supposed to be missing? They're not supposed to be back until tomorrow. We knew the rich buggers would be back today but aren't they supposed to be spending the night there on a wink, wink, nod, nod basis?"

"Well Earl wants her back pronto, apparently he thinks she's been kidnapped."

"What? What the Christ is going on here. What the hell's going on? She's just gone off with the viscount for a shag. Doesn't everybody know that?"

"Well everybody but for Earl himself. Apparently he's going hairless with worry. They found a finger in the post. And a ransom note. Actually, it doesn't look good. Doesn't look good at all."

"A finger, you mean a fish finger." Brendan was trying to look on the bright side.

"No I don't mean a bloody fish finger, I mean a fu##### finger, a severed finger, blood and all!"

Brendan thought he'd better move from questionable humorous remarks into a more serious mode.

"Now who told you that?"

"One of the coppers, the house is full of them. Apparently the woman, you know the maid, was involved and a bent copper."

Brendan began to realise that Brian must have pulled it off.

"Bloody hell, the maid? She must be pushing sixty, and a copper? Sounds like Bonnie and Clyde." Brendan found it difficult to avoid the odd "smart" remark.

"This is stupid. Look, where's Tristram?" Tristram and George were best mates.

"He's not here. He said he was going to come later. He left earlier this afternoon."

"But he knows where they're staying."

"He knows where Mr. and Mrs. Viscount are staying?"

"Yes, George had to tell someone in case of emergency."

"Are you sure? How do you know that?"

"Couple of weeks ago I overheard them talking, planning the whole thing. It was no secret."

A search party was organised. Tristram was found pretty quickly and ushered to the common room. The situation was explained to him. Tristram assessed the situation and decided, accompanied by two policemen, to cough up the information on the runaways.

The loving couple were holed up in a B&B near the Albert Hall. The police rushed to the premises and, after some embarrassing disturbances, located the not-so-very-happy couple. Within twenty minutes she was dressed and back in the arms of her father. With the so-called kidnapping solved, everyone was in a jolly mood.

The mood at the Earls' was more sombre. Earl had been well and truly kippered with a capital "Kip".

Earl, and to some extent the police, still thought, even after the daughter had been found safe and well, that this was some con trick carried out by a group of students. Soon the con would be admitted and the money returned. It was in the early hours of Sunday that Earl and the police accepted the so-called "civilised" kidnapping as genuine. He had really believed that object was his daughter's finger and he was at least fifty thousand down.

"You have to admit," said the inspector, "very clever, very clever indeed."

"I don't care how bloody clever they are I want them found, and if you don't do it then I will. I won't be dumped on. They won't know what's hit them."

The next morning Brendan phoned Brian.

"Well?" said Brendan.

"Well what?" said Brian feigning ignorance.

"Are you gonna tell me or not?"

"I got there for 2.30 p.m. as agreed. I did my bit with the threatening. I waited in the park till just before 3 p.m. I had to wait for another twelve minutes before they threw the canvas bag out!"

"Jeez, twelve minutes. That's cutting it fine. Well done you. You had some balls to stay there all that time. And, and?"

"The bag was stuffed with bits of paper all bearing the Queen's head and all had a number twenty on them."

"And, and?"

"My dear Brendan you will be happy to know that the bag contained £77,000. Let me say it again; the bag contained £77,000, which, if my arithmetic is right and using the same ratios as before, that's £53,900 for you and £23,100 pounds for me."

Brendan quickly did the calculation in his head.

"Your arithmetic has improved. Correct in every instance. Welcome to the upper middle class!"

"He must have put all the money from his safe into the bag. He was panicking. He didn't bother to count it! And it looks as if they are all used notes. This Earl bloke must be bloody thick. He also put the ransom note in the bag – another thing we don't have to worry about."

"Where are the little beauties now?"

"Safe in the canvas bag which is safe in the safety deposit box. We wait a year for that. We play this as a long-term project," said Brian.

"Too right. We're going to play it absolutely safe. Come hell or high water, we don't touch a penny for a year."

"Absolutely! I'll be up in a few days, Thursday, 3 p.m. We'll meet at the usual caff, but the heat may be on me so if I don't call you'll know why."

"See you then."

"Thanks Brendan. Thanks for including me."

"Now don't get all sentimental on me! You've done a great job."

"Anyway, what's happening down there?"

"Chaos down here. The police are completely disorganised. They don't know where to start. Just before I left they started taking names and addresses of students. They're going to get a list together, we'll all be contacted in the near future. They don't really think that there's been a crime! Good for us, all this chaos. We need to think about putting the other 'team' in the shit. If they get too close to us, or me, then that's what we'll have to do. We'll decide that when I come up, yep?"

Things were on the up. Brendan returned back to his digs. He threw himself on to the bed and, mentally exhausted, didn't wake up till it was dark. He woke and flicked the lights on. Bingo, another sparkle of light hit his eyes. This time he kept it in view. There it was, hanging by a thread, at the top of his curtains. It was the metallic twist he used to get an airtight closure for the finger. He then proceeded very carefully to look for any other such objects. None were found. This find didn't fill him with much confidence. How many other tiny little things might be hidden away in his room to connect him to the kidnap? It was his job to clean the room one more time. Of course it would be thorough. But it might well be the job of a forensic expert to clean the room also. They would be just as thorough, particularly if it was thought that Brendan was a strong suspect, and, as well as being thorough they would have special gizmos for dealing with tiny particles. So be it, he's done everything he can think of short of burning the house down.

"Mmm, there's a thought."

Two hundred miles away, Brian was in Keighley lying down on a sofa looking at the ceiling of his front room. His Mom was in the small chair asleep in front of the fire. He could see it needed a few repairs. But, try as he might, his mind would not focus on DIY but, instead, on a single photograph taken on a London Tube on its way to Notting Hill Gate by happy newly-weds. A photograph that could mean disaster for him and possibly for Brendan too.

Chapter 36

AN INSPECTOR CALLS, AGAIN

On Monday morning Brendan tries to act normal – after all he's got exams to prepare for. He gets into QEC at his usual time.

A letter sits waiting for him in his pigeonhole. He sees identical-looking letters parked in every other slot. He opens his letter:

Mr. Ryan,

Please attend for interview at Notting Hill police station between the hours of 10.35 a.m. and 1.35 p.m. on Tuesday, 3 June. If, for good reason, you cannot make that time please contact the duty Sergeant at Notting Hill Police station as soon as possible to arrange for another time.

Even though he was expecting this, still a shiver of nerves travelled down his spine. His external demeanour was confident, almost blasé about his situation. All the talk in lectures and in the refectory is on the kidnapping abbreviated to "napping" in reference to Chas Earl. What a plonker for falling to such a confidence trick. Rumours abound as to what has happened – from "the maid has been arrested" to "it was a robbery carried out by youth hostellers based in Holland Park", to "they've found the money in George's locker".

Brendan decided to keep his peace – best not to make out that he knows anything. He concentrated on his mathematics revision. Indeed his maths had occupied a back seat in the last two months. He was genuinely concerned that he might do very badly in the exam. At the same time he is desperate for information – what do the police know, if anything?

Brendan predicts that the whole interviewing business will run late so he decides that he will go around 10.15 a.m. and jump the queue.

Late on Monday the deputy RAG chair, Emily Pointer, organises a meeting of all RAG committee members.

Firstly, she informs the group that all the stragglers are back from Paris and all are accounted for. To much humour she reports that there have been no further kidnaps. George is still in custody. Apparently he attended the police station, together with his father, voluntarily. She reports that he is in good spirits and continues to strongly state that he had nothing to do with the so-called kidnapping. His father is confident that his solicitor will obtain George's release on police bail later today. Emily suggests that the group organise a card with all their signatures to show that George still has their full confidence in his innocence and they remain loyal. A card was organised and all their signatures appended. The meeting broke up after about an hour.

The next day, Tuesday, Brendan attends the police station for his interview.

"Eh up my friends, please don't stand!" says Brendan, jokingly, as he makes his way through the queue.

"I thought we'd left the headmaster's cane behind? Oops 'behind' is the wrong word. I hope you've all got thick fat arses." Then, addressing the group,

"Do you mind if I go in next? I've got stuff to do today."

There were no objections to his request. He quotes from a poem,

"Into the valley of death rode the one!"

Brendan, slightly nervous, knocks on the door of the interview room and pushes it open.

"Come in, yes, please come in. Do take a seat."

Brendan enters and takes a seat opposite an inspector and a police constable. To one side, on another desk, is a second constable operating a recording device. The desk is untidy with six or seven half-filled plastic cartons of tea and a couple of plates of half-eaten Rich Tea biscuits, overflowing ashtrays and a packet of cigarettes. The inspector and Brendan eye each other up. In the short staring game the inspector concedes first. He smiles.

"You beat me! That doesn't happen often. Hello. I'm Superintendent George Givens. On my left is Constable Jameson and taking notes is Constable Fairview. Just ignore them, it's really me and thee. First things first – cup of tea? And if you can just state your name."

"Hello. Em, no thanks and yes I'm Brendan Ryan. Hope you don't mind but I jumped the queue. They didn't mind. I'm reading mathematics – sounds like *University Challenge*!" Brendan starts to twiddle his eyebrow, a nervous tic recently acquired.

"Now, Brendan, you're not under caution, this is purely an informal chat so that we can get a more detailed picture of the situation at the college." He offers Brendan a cigarette. Brendan shakes his head and declines.

"Thanks but, em no, I never touch them and if I did you can bet that Capstan Full Strength would be bottom of the list – they're deadly!"

"Now I don't want you to feel nervous."

"I'm not nervous, I'm happy to help," says Brendan, calming down. He releases his eyebrow.

"This is but a small part of the ongoing investigation into the kidnapping. You'll have heard lots of stuff – most of it is just hearsay and conjecture. We have to speak to all of those that might, and I stress might, be involved."

"This is a bit scary." Brendan remarks. Then Brendan, trying to introduce a touch of humour, asks, in a southern American drawl,

"Should I have my lawyer present here boy?"

"Certainly, if you would like to have a solicitor represent you then I can call for one, but take it from me, we really don't need to go down that path. I am sure this will be a friendly conversation. I should say that, of course, you can leave at any time, absolutely. You will understand, more formal conversations may have to take place at a later date."

"No, no just joking. I've seen this situation in so many films – never thought it would happen to me, it's a tad surreal."

The inspector looks at his file.

"Oh, that Ryan," he murmurs to himself.

"First name Brendan. Age twenty-two, 'old' for a student?"

"Yeah, I was a late developer."

He looks at his notes again and putting on his glasses ponders over them for a minute or two.

The gap in the conversation gives Brendan time to observe the inspector more closely. Surely on the wrong side of fifty, a greying, full head of hair with circular indent around his head where his cap would fit. Wearing a wedding ring and two further rings on his right hand. He fails to hide a deeply wrinkled face suggesting much laughter in his life. He wears a plain suit. And his tie partially open in relaxed form with his top shirt button undone. Though not manicured his fingernails are clean and neatly presented. He presents a slightly bulbous nose concocted from two halves as if glued together. This leaves a distinct line down the middle from the tip to the bridge. This is a man who feels comfortable in his own skin.

He removes his glasses.

"I see you're Irish. Which bit?"

"All of me," jokes Brendan.

"Southern. I came here a long time ago – lost the accent. Am now a Yorkshire lad."

"Unusual – your education?"

"Yeah. Started off in an orphanage, well an Industrial school – bloody awful bugger of a place, like a prison – no lie. I was there for two and a half years. Progressed through the English school system up to a girls' grammar school, yes a girls' grammar. Well, on reflection, that was worse than the orphanage. Girls can be vicious at that age. Then a comprehensive for a year, then, eventually, after some time in a job, university."

The inspector returns his glasses and looks at his notes again.

"Oh, you're the genius are you? I've been looking forward to meeting you. I've been told to be wary of you," said the inspector.

"I'm not a genius though it may appear so amongst the students here but, you've talked to some of them, mostly thick as planks, from public schools, failed to get into Oxbridge and so ended up here. They are the only ones who can afford London prices. Okay, that's a tad unkind. They're not that thick, but they just don't care. I despise them, they've had opportunity after opportunity but wasted them.

"A hobby horse is it?"

"What?"

"Your dislike of the upper classes."

"Look, let's knock this genius thing on the head. I'm not a genius, far from it, but I guess I have a certain facility with maths. I can multiply quicker than most, that's about it – very popular darts player – just for the scoring! I can think deeper than most but I'm slow, really quite slow. See, I'm over-picky. Things have to be right, I hate to guess. I usually get things right in the end but mostly after a good period of time.

"People seem to think that if you pass an exam in maths then that's it forever more, you're a genius. I passed two A levels, good grades mind you, got a summer job at the university then my Ma thinks I'm a professor! I'm pretty poor at other stuff, like English, I couldn't tell you how to punctuate properly. Mind you, who the hell out there knows the difference between a colon and a semi-colon – and if they say they do then they're talking out of their arses! Joke, couldn't help it!"

"What joke?"

"Colon – arses. Get it?"

"Oh God," moaned the inspector, managing a smile.

Brendan continues.

"I shouldn't be here, I should have gone to Oxford but I made a mistake on my application form. Can you believe that? It's gonna affect my whole life. That shows how thick I am. Really – if I'm a genius then—" The inspector interrupts. "This is a ploy, isn't it? Are you playing a game? I remember this from my training in psychology. You've taken over this conversation. I'm the one supposed to talk, to ask the questions, you're supposed to be the one to answer them and to listen. You're trying to put me off my stride."

The inspector stands up to exercise his shoulders, putting his hands behind his neck and stretching, accompanied by an audible yawn.

"Excuse me. Been sat down all morning." He picks up a plastic box from the corner of the table. He walks around the table and sits on the desk immediately in front of Brendan. He removes the lid. Inside the box is what appears to be a severed finger.

"Are you responsible for this?"

"What do you mean responsible? No." Then, after a few seconds, "What is it?"

"What do you think it is?"

"Well, it looks like a girl's finger, with that varnished nail, a finger anyway, possibly belonging to a child. It stinks. Actually it doesn't look real. Oh, that's the finger from the kidnapping. Is it?"

"It's the preserving fluid. That's what's smelling. Sure you have nothing to do with it?"

"Positive. You're observing my reaction, aren't you? I have nothing to do with it, absolutely nothing. That's disgusting."

The inspector replaces the lid and returns to his seat.

"You're doing maths here. You must be pretty bright? Why are you reluctant to admit that you're a bit out of the ordinary? A number of your tutors think you're a genius. Shouldn't they ought to know?"

"Well, I guess I have my moments. But I'm not a bloody genius, for God's sake – how many times do I have to say it? However, I do have one claim to fame that I'm sort of proud of. Only happened last week!"

"And that is?"

"Wait for it, wait for it. It's a humdinger, hold on to your horses."

"Go on then, surprise me," said the inspector, impatiently.

"Drum roll please...

"I have taken Stephen Hawking to the toilet. That is, *the* Professor Stephen Hawking, to the toilet." The inspector turns to look at Constable Jameson, puckers his lips and nods.

"Well I'll be, there's a thing, Jameson." The constable presented a smile that knew it was going to develop into a snigger. It didn't as Jameson controlled himself.

"Glad you shared that with us. Now that is something to tell your grandchildren."

"Yes it certainly is," said Brendan.

"And who's this Stephen Hawking when he's at home?" asks the inspector, deflating Brendan.

"Oh dear, dearie, dearie me. You can't be serious? I'd better start at the beginning. This might take some time. I think I'll change my mind about that cup of tea!"

"Before you get started, what was it?" asks Inspector Givens.

"What was what?"

"Was it number ones or number twos?"

"Numero uno."

"What a relief that must have been. And look, of course we know who Stephen Hawking is. Look, I think we had a long enough chat. As interesting as your story is we've got loads of students still to interview. Now, can you account for your whereabouts last Saturday between the hours of 2 p.m. and 4 p.m.?"

"Yes, as I was saying, that's where I was – at Stephen Hawking's urinal! I got to King's in time for a 3 p.m. seminar, which was cancelled, the speaker was ill, and I left at about 4.15 p.m. I spent over an hour looking at relativity problems in Hawking's office. His wife will be able to corroborate that, she was there all the time."

The Inspector took a minute or so looking at the ceiling, deep in thought.

Chapter 37

THE NOTTING HILL THREE

"So, thank you for coming down Mr. Ryan. I hope we never see you again though, at this early stage in the investigation, you can never tell. Good luck with your studies." Brendan got up, gave the inspector a nod, waved a hand in his direction and left the room.

Brendan felt a little uneasy after the interview. He thought the inspector brought the interview to a close rather abruptly.

The local newspapers got hold of the story and ran with it on the front page on Tuesday and Wednesday. The broadsheets didn't rate the story much and could only accommodate a single column, hidden deep in the "human interest" sections.

On Thursday, Brendan calls McClusky, one of their regular calls, first making absolutely sure that he hadn't been followed.

"I was interviewed by the police last Tuesday. Nothing was said but I was left with a strong impression that I was a suspect."

"Well o'course you're a bloody suspect – you're an oddball and that will always attract the police, for a while anyway. Once they check your alibi – I'll guess you'll drop off their list of possible suspects."

"I don't know. Do you think we should put our rival team in the frame?"

"If you are feeling vulnerable then give it some thought. It's really your decision. It would certainly put the police off their stride – away from academic big-wigs and on to good old-fashioned criminals. Anyway, how would you do it, if you decided to go ahead? Have you given it any thought? Don't do anything stupid! We're in a good position and we don't want to spoil it."

"Well, if I do it, it'll have to be done soon, next couple of days. I'll just send a letter, anonymously of course, complaining about an unlicensed car continually parked in Holland Park Road. It's illegal and the 'resident' wants something done about it!"

On getting back to his digs that evening he concocted a letter which he would give to the police. He was careful not to leave any fingerprints on the envelope.

Dear Sir,

I wish to make a complaint. I live in the Notting Hill Gate area. There is a car, number A32 7BD, a black saloon, a big Volvo I think is continually parked near my house. The car is untaxed and they just park where they want. They have a disabled sticker but none of them look disabled to me!

I do not wish to say who I am, that is neither here nor there. The owners of the car are committing a crime. I am tired of paying my taxes when others driving fancy cars won't pay theirs.

Thank you

P.S. The last time I complained to the DVLA people with little effect, that is over four weeks ago. I have sent two other letters but they have had no effect.

Early next morning Brendan made his way to the Tube station with the "petite" typewriter under his arm. Unseen, he chucked the typewriter away. Then he made his way to Notting Hill Gate police station. For a couple of quid he persuaded a young lad playing in the street there to take the letter and give it to the sergeant in the police station.

"Do it right and there's another couple of quid for you."

Brendan watched him go in, throw the letter on the floor and then run out. The boy claimed his bonus and drifted away.

The duty sergeant picked up the letter, in a plain brown envelope, thinking it had fallen from his desk. He opened the letter and quickly scanned through it. He passed it on to Constable David Stirling.

"Dave, look at this will you?" Stirling spent three or four minutes reading the letter through a couple of times. The sergeant continued,

"Where she lives, isn't that near Earl's residence? Might be something to do with what's going on there. Get in touch with the DVLA will you. See what you can find out."

Within an hour the DVLA, on an enquiry from the police, came up trumps:

The vehicle, a black Volvo saloon is owned by an F. C. Parker, address 51 Victoria Road, North London NE12 D703. Only two years old. According to our records it is untaxed, and has been for some months. A reminder has been sent out. There doesn't appear to be an insurance policy on that car either."

Bingo. The name F. C. Parker (known as "Nosey" due to his Cyrano-de-Bergerac-level proboscis) was well known to the police in the Notting Hill area – for car crimes, robberies and the like. He was a petty criminal. He usually worked with two others.

Superintendent George Givens was informed. He quickly put two and two together. That same morning the instruction went out to arrest F. C. Parker and two of his sidekicks.

George Givens' initial enthusiasm waned somewhat. He chatted to the sergeant as they waited for "Nosey" Parker and his pals to arrive at the station.

"Kidnapping – that's not their game, that's a bit upmarket for them, but perhaps they were getting more ambitious – given that, they still haven't learnt their lesson – stupid to be driving around in their own car, and then some old biddy, presuming it was a woman wrote the letter, to spot them! It's gotta be a joke!"

By mid-afternoon everything was in place. Mr. Parker was the first of the three to come under Superintendent George Givens' scrutiny. The strategy was to get them talking before bringing the subject of abduction into play. The three would admit nothing. After many hours of questioning it was decided to frighten them by throwing an accusation of kidnapping at them. During the interviews their premises had been thoroughly searched, nothing incriminating was found.

"Look here Nosey, you know as well as I do that we're not here to talk about petty crimes. You've been naughty boys and you're going to pay dearly for it. Do you know what you're looking at for kidnapping? At least ten years, that's a long time in the scrubs, to a pretty boy like you, if you get my drift."

The word "kidnap" brought Nosey Parker to attention.

"Kidnapping, what bloody kidnapping? You know we're not in that game – you can't pin that on us! I've read the newspapers – nothing to do with us, absolutely nothing."

The two sidekicks felt more vulnerable, another hour of questioning broke their spirits.

"Look, the evidence against you is circumstantial but you've got history. We can pin this on you –no problem my friend. You were seen patrolling the area for God's sake. We don't need to see the money – this'll go through, no doubt. Now be sensible, admit your guilt and we'll try and get a more lenient sentence."

Nosey was the first to appreciate the seriousness of the situation they found themselves in. It was time to barter.

"Okay, okay. I admit that we were sizing up the job – but we never got anywhere with it. We decided it was too difficult without shooters and you know that we don't do that. In and out, that's what we were looking at, that's all it was going to be. In quick, frighten them a bit, then away. We haven't been there for over a week. On Saturday we were watching the rugby. No we can't provide an alibi, it was on the telly."

"I know this. There's a fourth member of your little team. He's gone off with all the money, hasn't he? He's a burly lad, acting like a policeman. We'll find him, then you're in deep doo-doo. There'll be no bargaining then, you'll get the full whack thrown at you."

"There's no bloody fourth man and we did no kidnapping. This isn't a thing about Russian spies. A fourth man, getting away with all the money – that's a bloody joke that is! I should know, I'm the man in this team. Is he going to turn up in Moscow is he?"

F. C. Parker refused to admit any connection to a kidnapping but his sidekicks couldn't spend any more time in prison. They knew nothing of a kidnapping but admitted to loitering with intent, a fairly minor crime – likelihood is they'd get a suspended. Nosey also admitted to the minor crime but admitted nothing else.

Brendan waited over two days for the news that kidnapping charges were to be put on three petty criminals from the Notting Hill area. A fourth man was sought and, so far, none of the money has been recovered. Dorothy was asked to produce a sketch of the man that confronted her. She couldn't remember much except for two characteristics,

"He was a tall man with jet black eyebrows." Luckily the sketch was only shown in London. Had it been shown nationwide then Inspector Gordon Nesbit might just have recognised the image to be Sergeant Brian McClusky. Furthermore, had the recently married couple travelling on the Tube to attend the Calcutta Cup rugby match lived in London then they too might well have recognised the helpful policeman as Sergeant Brian McClusky. Brian and Brendan were very lucky bunnies indeed.

Chapter 38

THE POLYGON PROBLEM, A PROBLEM NO MORE

The whole operation on the academic side was scaled down.

"Three local villains accused of Earl abduction. Fourth man sought,"

was the headline. By this time the press had moved on to other stories – to Brendan's relief all the excitement at QEC had died down. Brendan felt some sympathy for the villains he helped put away, but that's the law of the jungle. He noted mentally that he would, from his share, throw a few "bob" their way to ease the pain of prison when they get out.

So that was good news – all relayed to Brian McClusky.

"Yes the whole thing will die down – as soon as 'we' have a candidate for a crime, then that's it, we move on to the next crime. We can't afford to mess around, it's not like the TV. But listen, keep up thinking that they're following your every move. Continue to be ultra-careful – at least for the next six months. I'll do the same. Don't forget your own mantra, 'getting it is easy. Keeping it is the hard part'!"

Despite having credible candidates for the kidnapping, many of the police originally assigned to the Earl kidnapping still felt uneasy. It would take quite a while for their unease to dissipate. Out of all the interviews carried out by Superintendent George Givens it was Brendan's that stuck in the memory – not something that Brendan would have been happy to know. There was something wriggling at the back of George Givens' mind that would erupt from time to time. He thought,

Even savant autistics can be criminals. Brendan's exams came and went. He did quite badly, just scraping through to the second year. It was a tense six months but now he could relax. Or so he thought. Just three days after the start of the summer holidays he had the most atrocious news. Whilst he was flicking through the most recent issue of *American Mathematics Monthly* he came across an article written by a trio of researchers, two Americans and a Swede – all secondary school teachers in Utah State. They claimed to have solved the main part of the Polygon Problem. He flicked through the report. It looked authentic. It looked right.

He was sat alone in the QEC library, as usual going through research journals desperately trying to get up to speed with the latest research in mathematics. He was in shock, physically trembling, close to tears, his worst fear had occurred. All the time he had spent working on this project just to fall at the final hurdle. He had made tremendous progress in the last two years – all in vain. It was everything to be first, in this game you get nothing for being second. What was worse, the *American Mathematics Monthly* wasn't regarded as a prestigious journal, it normally reported on results obtained by "amateur" mathematicians. So that was it, that put Brendan in his place. Not only did he fail to solve the Polygon Problem, it was classed as being lower level mathematics not really worthy of serious consideration.

He spent the next few days going through their proof. He was half hoping to find an error. In fact, he found three errors in their work, but they were just minor. Essentially, their proof was okay. Using the theory of complex numbers he had also discovered a neater way to present the proof. Brendan would inform the trio of the errors he had found. The best he could do now was to send off a letter to the journal pointing out these minor errors and the complex number approach. If the editors thought it worthy of mention they would include his letter in next month's edition. So no Victoria Cross, just a mention in dispatches, that's all he had to look forward to.

So that was it. That's all he had, the possibility of a publication. This was the first time, as a man, he experienced a "black dog", a Churchillian-level depression.

He left London for home, back to his Ma and the lads. Even there he seemed to be losing control. McClusky had his feet well under the table. Brendan, now, was only second in command. He had a bit of money yes, but he had little happiness. He didn't know what to do. Struggle on with maths, or go down the criminal route full time.

Was he ready to call upon Robert Frost one more time?

A TOUCH OF FROST

The only poem Brendan knows. From time to time it has guided his actions: should he follow the accepted route or branch out to see where his future lies?

The Road Not Taken

Two roads diverged in a yellow wood,
And sorry I could not travel both
And be one traveler, long I stood
And looked down one as far as I could
To where it bent in the undergrowth;

Then took the other, as just as fair,
And having perhaps the better claim,
Because it was grassy and wanted wear;
Though as for that the passing there
Had worn them really about the same,

And both that morning equally lay
In leaves no step had trodden black.
Oh, I kept the first for another day!
Yet knowing how way leads on to way,
I doubted if I should ever come back.

I shall be telling this with a sigh
Somewhere ages and ages hence:
Two roads diverged in a wood, and I--
I took the one less traveled by,
And that has made all the difference.

Robert Frost (1916)

ND - #0210 - 270225 - C0 - 234/156/9 - PB - 9781780915470 - Gloss Lamination